DiAnn Mills delivers another pulse-pounding thriller you're going to love. *Lethal Standoff* combines gripping tension with a captivating mystery, skillfully woven by DiAnn's signature storytelling. She navigates the high-stakes world of hostage rescue, proving once again why she's a master of the genre.

JERRY B. JENKINS, author of the Left Behind series and The Chosen novels

In *Lethal Standoff*, DiAnn Mills works magic—weaving suspense and intrigue into a heart-pounding hostage thriller. Hostage negotiator Carrington Reed is a hero with heart who refuses to quit even when it means risking her own life for strangers. Don't miss this high-stakes gambit set in south Texas that will keep you flipping pages to the very end.

ANDREWS & WILSON, bestselling authors of *Dark Intercept*

Warning: do not start this book if you intend to put it down any time soon. This is a roller-coaster ride. A bullet-biter. A heart-thumper. This is DiAnn Mills at her best.

EVA MARIE EVERSON, bestselling author and CEO of Word Weavers International

Lethal Standoff has everything I look for in a great novel! Alongside a heartwarming romance, the plot and themes of this page-turner are pulled from current events and offer a hopeful, triumphant message for readers. Highly recommended.

DEBORAH RANEY, author of *Breath of Heaven* in the Camfield Legacy series

Mills delivers another action-packed novel that offers intrigue and an adventurous ride. . . . Well-developed characters, vivid imagery, and thorough research guide this story line every step of the way. Readers old and new will be left clutching the armrest as they quickly turn the pages racing to the end.

LIBRARY JOURNAL on *Concrete Evidence*

[In] the exciting latest from Mills . . . the confident plotting keeps the mysteries coming. [A] thrilling stand-alone.

DiAnn Mills took me on a wild ride with *Trace of Doubt*. . . . Filled with high stakes, high emotion, and high intrigue, *Trace of Doubt* will keep you guessing until the thrilling and satisfying conclusion.

DiAnn Mills never disappoints. . . . Put on a fresh pot of coffee before you start this one because you're not going to want to sleep until the suspense ride is over. You might want to grab a safety harness while you're at it—you're going to need it!

LETHAL STANDOFF

LETHAL
STANDOFF

DiANN MILLS

Tyndale House Publishers
Carol Stream, Illinois

Visit Tyndale online at tyndale.com.

Visit DiAnn Mills's website at diannmills.com.

Tyndale and Tyndale's quill logo are registered trademarks of Tyndale House Ministries.

Lethal Standoff

Designed by Dean Renninger

Published in association with The Steve Laube Agency, 24 W. Camelback Road A-635, Phoenix, AZ 85013.

For information about special discounts for bulk purchases, please contact Tyndale House Publishers at csresponse@tyndale.com, or call 1-855-277-9400.

Library of Congress Cataloging-in-Publication Data

A catalog record for this book is available from the Library of Congress.

ISBN 978-1-4964-8509-0 (HC)

ISBN 978-1-4964-8510-6 (SC)

Printed in the United States of America

30	29	28	27	26	25	24
7	6	5	4	3	2	1

This book is dedicated to my WOW group: Writers on Wednesday.

Dr. Deborah Maxey, Rhonda Dragomir,
Chris Manion, PeggySue Wells, and Candy Arrington.

I treasure our times together—the laughter, tears,
victories, and challenges. We are survivors.

ONE

SEPTEMBER

CARRINGTON

My role as a hostage negotiator often plunged me into the evil designs of the human mind. I embraced the responsibility and possible danger because it's my identity—a one-woman battlefront determined to free others from victimization.

The challenge excited me, but fear of failure stalked me, and respect for human life was my constant companion. Too often innocent lives depended on my ability to negotiate their safe release without anyone getting hurt. The demands, rewards, and sometimes the defeats with tragic outcomes kept me awake at night. How could I have done things differently? My apprenticeship began when I was eight years old, but thinking about those days didn't change the past. Right now, lives were in jeopardy. . . .

I'd driven ten minutes out from a critical situation on a Wednesday afternoon when my cell phone rang. My contact, a detective from the Houston Police Department, had spent several hours talking to an angry man who held his wife and son hostage.

"Carrington, we have the information you requested," Detective Aaron Peters said. "The man inside the home is the owner, Nick Henderson. Age thirty-five. Married to Christine. He's holding his wife and eight-year-old son at gunpoint. Yesterday, he was served divorce papers, and we believe this is in retaliation."

Hurt. Rejected. Probably a lit stick of dynamite. "You talked to him from the outside?"

"We've routed his calls through our mobile command center. I tried talking to him. Got nowhere. He hung up on me." Aaron blew out his frustration.

Domestic calls were the most dangerous, often violent, causing me to appreciate my Kevlar vest. I had a handgun in my purse, but I could count on one hand the times I'd pulled it. Never used it. "All right. I'm nearly there. SWAT in place?"

"Yes, two have clear shots. Not an action I want to take unless necessary."

"Me either. What are Henderson's demands?"

"Just to leave him alone or he'll pull the trigger on his family."

Cool, calm focus settled on me. My ability to mediate critical discussions depended on my wearing emotional blinders to the outside world. "When did the problem start?"

"The wife phoned 911 at 8:00 a.m. today. I don't know how long he was there before she reached out to us. We've been called here twice in the past month for domestic abuse."

I glanced at my watch, and it neared 4:00 p.m. "Have HPD negotiators been talking to him?"

"Yes. Henderson hung up on them too. He's drinking. Slurring his words. Seems to have trouble concentrating."

Alcohol could make him more volatile. Flashing lights appeared on the residential street ahead. "I'm parking now. Give me five minutes."

"I'm standing beside my car in front of the house."

"Aaron, do you have Henderson's work history?"

"Fired three months ago from Home Depot, where he held a management role. They walked him out of the store in front of his employees."

The man definitely had nothing to lose.

Phone in hand, I hurried from my parked truck and raced to where police cars barricaded the entrance to the street where Henderson held his family. A reporter blocked my way between vehicles. She rammed a mic in front of my face.

"Carrington Reed, do you think this standoff will have a peaceful resolution?"

My blood boiled. The last time I had verbally unleashed on her aggressive means to get the best story, she lied in her article about my concern for those in danger. I paused long enough to give her eye contact. "My goal is always a peaceful solution. Excuse me, I need to talk to HPD."

"Are the police advocating a violent takedown?"

"No." I sidestepped around her and ignored her shouts.

Aaron stood in front of the home and waved. He had the appearance of average—average height, weight, gray eyes, brown hair, and shoulder span—but nothing about his physical appearance showed his intense scrutiny of a crime scene. His rating as one of HPD's finest hit my respect button.

"Good to see you. I'd like the man's cell number," I said. "I assume my cell phone is routed through the command center too?"

"Sure thing." He gave me the information. "The wife's name is Christine, and the son's name is Rand."

I nodded my thanks and pressed in the digits. A man answered on the second ring.

"Nick, this is Carrington. I'm standing beside a police car outside your house, and I'd like to help you."

"I . . . leave me alone." He spoke fast and loudly. "I'm busy."

"What do you need?"

"You can get rid of all those cops. I can't breathe."

I expected a more belligerent response. "Nick, I can't do that. These officers are here to protect you in case someone tries to break into your home and hurt you."

"I'd kill my wife and kid first."

"Tell me why you feel that way."

"They deserve it for the way they've treated me." He stumbled over his words. "I'm a good husband and dad."

"I'm sure you're great at both. Tell me what's hurting you."

"Christine filed for divorce."

"I get it, Nick. I'd be mad too. How can I help?"

"Have her cancel the divorce proceedings." He swore. "Let me move back into my house. I make the payments, and I should be able to live here."

"I agree you have a right to be upset and have a say-so in your family's affairs. Are you saying if Christine agrees to drop the divorce, you'll let her and Rand go?"

I stared at the house while he delayed his answer. Blood raced through my veins. Plan B would be to dig deeper into his emotions.

"The divorce stuff is just part of it," Nick said.

"You're upset about the whole relationship thing."

"She talks to me like I'm scum. And in front of my son too." He sobbed, lowering his defenses.

"You'd like for her to agree to counseling?"

He slurped on some liquid and belched. "Add the nagging. She's on my case about drinking."

"Nick, I'm adding nagging to the list. Is there anything else? Tell me everything."

"Uh. Yeah. But if she agrees and I let 'em go, then she lies, I'll . . . I'll find 'em and kill 'em."

"Are you ready to release your family so we can work this out? I bet you'd like to get rid of these gawking people. Doing the right thing is the only way I can ask the police officers to leave and ensure you won't get hurt."

"Let me talk to her. I'll call you back."

"I'd rather wait on the line." I touched my chest and breathed.

He swore again. "Suit yourself." I heard him shout at his wife. She promised to meet his demands. "All right," he said to me. "You'll make Christine do the right thing?"

"I promise to talk to her and explain the seriousness of your demands. I'll do my best."

"She's stubborn."

"Nick, she'd be a fool not to hear me out. Let them go, and we'll find a peaceful solution."

I waited, my mouth dry, as though I stood next to Christine and her son inside the house. The door slowly opened. A woman limped out with her arm around a young boy. Blood stained her nose, mouth, and shirt. A dark-blue bruise marked her cheek. The boy seemed unhurt, but both trembled.

Officers escorted Christine and her son to a waiting ambulance. Before allowing a paramedic to treat her, she peered at me and burst into tears. "He's drunk and mean. Broke furniture."

I muted the mic on my phone and gave her my best reassuring smile. "I'm glad you and Rand are okay. Will he harm himself or open fire on officers?"

She glanced back at the brick-and-stone two-story home. "I don't know. He's really messed up. Drinks all the time and takes his misery out on us."

I understood Christine was wrestling with the idea of him pulling the trigger on himself. At one time she'd loved him, but people changed, and she'd seen the worst in her husband's behavior.

She swiped at her eyes. "He wasn't always violent. Losing his job for getting into a fight destroyed his pride."

"I'll do what I can."

The ambulance drove away, and I unmuted my phone before turning my attention back to Nick. "Are you ready to walk outside?"

"Will those cops shoot me?"

"Not if you first place your gun on the front stoop and keep your hands above your head."

"Then what?"

"These officers will escort you to a safe place where you'll find the help you need to feel better." I took a deep breath. "I'm on your side, Nick. I'd be angry and hurt if the ones I loved disrespected me."

The door opened, and a man dressed in jeans and a dirty white T-shirt stepped out. With one hand up, he laid his gun on the concrete before him and raised his other hand. Nick continued to walk toward the officers.

The first officer patted him down and cuffed him. My shoulders relaxed, but the adrenaline continued to flow. How good if all hostage situations ended without bloodshed. For a moment, a few that ended tragically scrolled across my mind. The outcomes all boiled down to choices.

I made my way to the cuffed man. "Nick, I'm Carrington."

"I didn't want to hurt them. Just—" He used a colorful phrase to describe his anger.

"You did great. I'm impressed with how you so unselfishly handled yourself." I added gentleness to my tone and gave him eye contact. I fought, as always, not to show a judgmental attitude or to condemn him. He needed counseling in whatever form the court system chose. The officers placed him in a cruiser and left the street. Other officers entered the home to assess any damage or evidence there. Two others talked with neighbors.

Aaron thanked me for the assist. I stayed awhile longer to debrief myself, to objectively process my communication with Nick.

I glanced around at the otherwise quiet community. The homes were less than ten years old, a striking subdivision hosting amenities for family life. Gated communities kept the unwanted people from the residents, but not today for Christine and Rand.

"Carrington."

At the sound of a man's voice, I turned to a familiar, tanned journalist who offered an engaging smile. "Hey, Levi. Good to see you."

He gave me a side hug. "You did an unbelievable job with the hostage situation."

"Thanks. Domestic situations can be a challenge." I paused. "Great article in last week's *Now America Reports*. Was that the conclusion to the series on Houston's flooding problems?"

"Yep. 'Water on the Rise.' No negotiation needed."

I bit back a grin. Levi Ehrlich didn't need to know his charms transported me to the moon and back. "Very funny. And well written."

"How about some coffee, conversation, and catch-up?"

"The last time we went for coffee, you tried to get an interview." I slid him a half smile. "Anything changed?"

Levi feigned a frown. "You *are* the most gorgeous negotiator on the planet."

"And you should get out more." I shook my head. "I have a ton of work. Next time?"

"I'll hold you to that." He studied me through dark-brown eyes, just a shade lighter than his hair. "You talked Henderson down when HPD got nowhere. What did you say to him?"

I started to walk away but hesitated. "I used the truth."

"How?"

"I told him I cared what happened to him."

"Seriously, I admire how you approach each case with respect for those involved."

His kind gaze held me captive. "Until next time, Levi." I walked down the street toward my truck.

Footsteps tapped against the pavement behind me. "How about dinner? You told me I should get out more."

I stopped and glanced over my shoulder. "I'll take a rain check."

"I have your number."

"No doubt." I bit back a grin.

TWO

Levi watched me drive away from the former hostage scene. I know because I saw him from my rearview mirror. What a handsome man—with a firm jaw and thick lashes some women paid a lot of money for. Not that I was looking. I couldn't resist a smile.

He'd done his homework and understood I rarely agreed to give interviews unless lives were at stake and public support raised the odds for a favorable outcome. The last time we talked, he had said he wouldn't give up. If I gave in to any journalist, Levi would be the one.

My thoughts rolled back to Christine Henderson and her frightened little boy. Tomorrow I'd check on the family. How could Christine forgive her husband, who supposedly loved her yet held her and their son at gunpoint? The stats showed so many abused women let their abusers back into their lives to repeat the same offense. How did those men convince the women that they'd changed? The same questions always nudged me. Why did people explode into violent actions? Were they wired from birth with a propensity to commit unthinkable crimes?

I arrived home to my private sanctuary—a one-story white-brick patio home in a gated community. My source of comfort and refuge. A silver-haired neighbor lady waved from a white wicker chair on her front porch, and I returned the gesture. I'd stop and chat, but I didn't know her name. Grandma would have lectured me on my bad manners. I'd look up my neighbor's information in the subdivision directory before dinner.

I slowly pulled into the garage and scanned the miniature red roses, yellow and purple fall mums, and shrubbery along the front of my home to ensure I hadn't neglected any of my "babies." Early morning, I'd examine each one. Grandma would have rolled over in her grave if I allowed a few weeds to infest nature's landscape. Flowers always invited distant memories of my parents, and I refused to let dirt and mildew suffocate my love for them. But I could argue that some weeds held more beauty than flowers. Like some people who might be considered unattractive, but their hearts were filled with love and compassion.

When the garage door closed, I laid my forehead on the steering wheel. Sometimes negotiations lasted for hours or days, and although this one took less than an hour to convince Nick Henderson to release his family, the adrenaline would stay in my body until I physically worked off the stress. I always had the same reaction no matter how long the process—worse when my efforts failed.

My phone alerted me to a text from HPD Detective Aaron Peters.

Well done today.

Thanks. I'll follow up with the Hendersons and keep you posted of any new developments.

My stomach growled. Actually, it snarled and roared. I'd skipped breakfast and lunch once again.

I pressed in the alarm code to enter my kitchen, and Arthur, my miniature schnauzer, greeted me at the door, his tail wagging in double time. He managed his usual gushing, then rushed to his empty water and food bowls.

"You are incredibly predictable." I laughed and patted his dark-gray furry head. His white beard, belly, and legs earned him the nickname of Old Man.

After filling one of his bowls with canned dog food and the other one with water, I swallowed a handful of vitamins and changed into workout shorts and a T-shirt. Back in the garage, in my therapy corner, I jumped on the treadmill and set the speed at nine. Exercise would rid my body of all the chemicals that fired into my brain, like lions, tigers, and angry bears were chasing me.

My mind replayed every moment of the case from the time I received the call. Personal debriefing hit the "I shoulda" and "why didn't I" worse than right after the police drove away with Nick Henderson in cuffs. An hour after the treadmill, I drank a quart of water before heading to the shower.

After writing up my report, I searched online to learn my neighbor's name—Stephanie Radison, sealing it in my memory. I bet she still sat on her front porch. I must say hello and stop isolating myself like a nineteenth-century spinster. Mrs. Radison might need someone to call in an emergency someday, and I'd not seen another person at her home. Truth was, I valued my privacy far too much to consider the whole neighborhood block-party thing.

"Be right back," I said to Arthur and ventured outside into the warm evening. The sky displayed ribbons of burnt orange, yellow, and gold. Great conversation opener.

Mrs. Radison appeared engrossed in a book, but she lifted her chin and offered a smile that displayed years of wisdom around her eyes. I walked to her front porch.

"How are you?" she said.

"Very well." I fudged the truth and hoped she couldn't read my tells. "Beautiful sunset."

"My Stan loved this time of day. He'd take pictures and compare the hues of color." Mrs. Radison sighed as though remembering. "He said no two sunsets were ever the same."

I admired the western sky. "I agree with him."

"We all have means of joy. Yours must be your little dog. What a cutie."

"Thanks. Arthur is very spoiled, and it's all my fault. I apologize for not introducing myself when I moved in nearly two years ago." I climbed the steps to her porch. "No excuse for my rudeness." I stuck out my hand, questioning if the woman feared germs. "Carrington Reed."

She extended arthritic fingers bulging at the joints. "Call me Stephanie."

"I'd like to give you my phone number in case you need me."

She held up her phone. "I'll type it in and send you a text. Then you'll have mine."

"Perfect." I gave her my number. "Thanks. Now we're friends."

"How very nice. Your mother raised you right."

"Yes, ma'am. She did her best." No point revealing my parents' deaths in a car accident when I was a little girl.

I bid her a good evening and made my way back home. Arthur wagged his tail for playtime while my tummy continued its protest. Inside the fridge, I wrapped my fingers around a bottle of raspberry vitamin water, retrieved last night's leftover pesto pasta for dinner, and heated it in the microwave.

My phone buzzed with a text. I picked it up and read a reminder for an ophthalmologist appointment in the morning. I despised any kind of medical checkup. Took valuable time. Spiked my otherwise low blood pressure. Put me in a sour mood. Brought up the terrifying past.

Recently, I'd noticed difficulty seeing from my right eye—a potential genetic problem. Prior to my parents' car accident, Dad faced a diagnosis of eye melanoma. Years later, when I lived with Grandma, she was confronted with the same diagnosis and quickly went blind. How could I manage life if I lost my sight?

THREE

LEVI

Curiosity consumed me about Carrington Reed. Despite her wary personality, she had chutzpah, as my dad would say. I'd seen her in action more than a half dozen times since her negotiation cases placed us in the same circles. My good luck, and that meant more than a potential interview with the best negotiator in the state of Texas. My opinion might be biased, but she had displayed outstanding wisdom in her six years with the private sector.

One report said she slept in a Kevlar vest. Considering a few shaky scenarios from her past and mine, that might not be a bad idea. This afternoon, she'd talked down a domestic hostage-taker in less than an hour's time. Not unheard of, but certainly an achievement. After watching her in action and considering my futile attempt to secure an interview, I understood her negotiator nickname—the Outlier. She indeed stood out from the rest, like with the case today. People were in danger, and she'd do everything within her means to keep them all safe.

I stopped my Tahoe at a traffic light, my mind still fixed on Carrington. She had a haunting beauty about her—light-olive skin, wide, earth-brown eyes, and long, thick, chestnut-colored hair that hung to her shoulders. We were both in our early thirties and still

12

single. An interview with her when no one else could pull information from her might put me in good standing with my boss. He hadn't been happy with me lately.

I snorted and hit Delete on my selfish thoughts. As much as I wanted to walk away, I supported an organization that helped those addicted to drugs and alcohol . . . a mirror of my past. My life's journey didn't involve pleasing everyone on the planet, only God.

I pulled into my condo parking spot, and the time caught my attention. I'd scheduled a DoorDash delivery from one of my favorite burger places, and the bag now awaited me. I'd grown accustomed to eating alone, but that didn't mean I liked it. At least I hadn't gotten to the point of talking to myself.

Inside my home, the normal quiet greeted me. I grabbed my food bag from the front door and set it on the counter. I placed my phone next to the bag and stared at it. I missed my sister and her dry wit. Although five years older with twin toddler girls and a little boy in first grade, we'd always been close. Until two years ago, when I converted to Messianic Judaism.

Once a month I tried contacting her or my parents. They never answered, but I left messages, always letting them know they were loved. Rosh Hashanah would be here soon, then Yom Kippur and Sukkot. Memories of younger days and observing religious celebrations knocked against my regrets, traditions that modeled the Jewish life, rich in history and embedded in what formed me into the man I was today.

Now my family and my old friends shunned me, the apostate. No Shabbat at my parents' home. No celebrations. I longed to see them and my sister, but I'd never regretted my faith in Yeshua. Sometimes I ached for the sound of my parents' voices and my sister's infectious laughter. But I daily renewed hope that one day we'd be reconciled. Yes, someday they'd dig me up from my symbolic Jewish grave and embrace me as family. Regrets? . . . no. Painful reminders? . . . yes.

Until then, the separation cut deep, like living in a dry riverbed. The rabbis and members of my Messianic church had embraced me from the moment I walked in their door. Many of them had been in my shoes and understood the consequences of my decision. I now shared the religious festivals with my new family and added the Christian ones.

Trying to do the right thing helped a man grow. My family's response to me in no way affected how God viewed me. I tapped the star beside my sister Deborah's name on my phone's Favorites list. The call briefly rang and went straight to voicemail. I left a message. At least she hadn't blocked me.

One way to find out. I called her using my Google number. The same thing happened. I tried texting, and it read *Undeliverable*. One last time, I pressed in *67 to mask my number. Deborah's phone rang as normal, but no one picked up. I tried the same methods with my parents and received the same results. While I wanted to believe they'd allowed their phone batteries to run down or anticipated my call was spam, they'd ordered me not to contact them.

Frustration rose. I understood their religious beliefs, and in their eyes, I'd betrayed them with my acceptance of Yeshua in the Messianic faith. To them, no emotion on the earth compared to the pain of betrayal. Oddly enough, we all felt it.

To temporarily alleviate my disappointment, I set the delivery bag in the fridge. My burger would have to wait. I changed clothes and made my way to the complex's workout room. There I took out my miserable feelings on lifting weights. Sweating and tears mixed a nasty brew—glad I was the only person there. After a shower, I reheated my burger and fries in the microwave—not a good mix either.

Get past it. Life wasn't about me, although sometimes I wished it leaned my way.

Munching on soggy, limp fries and washing them down with a watery Coke, I flipped open my laptop for the latest news, as if my phone hadn't bombarded me with plenty of tragedies and crises from all over the world. I scanned each one, and my mind examined the angles of writing pieces that featured a humanistic and truth-filled approach. Sometimes I requested a topic to cover, and my boss rarely refused me. Until recently. The publication, online and print, had been bought by a group who believed in expressing their agenda.

Not mine. I'd investigated other magazines, even freelance, although I fought another change and transition so soon after my family's rejection. Maybe a few months down the road I'd seriously look for another job.

As though my news editor had my thoughts on speed dial, my cell phone rang and listed his name on the screen.

I blew out a sigh, then answered. "Hey, Frank. Just got back from the hostage situation."

"Victims released unhurt?"

"Yes. A solid story."

He swore. "Too bad they weren't all killed. That would've been a great story for us."

I didn't respond.

"Levi, write it up and get it to me in an hour."

"What's the rush? Why not wait until the guy stands before a judge? I sent you a short piece and pics at the hostage site."

"We need to raise the ratings."

Frank must have gotten another rear chewing. "Our ratings have declined a little in the past year, but not as much as other publications."

"I'm not talking about other print, online, and video reporting. Nothing you've done lately has given us anything to brag about. Enough said. Do your job."

FOUR

CARRINGTON

The early morning jaunt to weed my flower beds accomplished zilch to refresh my attitude about the impending ophthalmologist appointment. Who was I fooling? When it came to anything about my eyes, hypochondria overtook me like quicksand. How long had my dad experienced vision problems before he sought a diagnosis? Or Grandma? So much I wanted to do with my life—career goals, meeting the right guy, family . . . even a white-picket-fence kind of home. None of my dreams were possible without eyesight. Without my vision, I'd be useless. My purpose in life gone.

I stood to stretch my back and admired a dew-kissed red rose. A squirrel scampered across the yard and up a tree with another one right behind. Clear blue sky—not just blue but azure. My reaction to this afternoon's appointment must be simply stress. What were the odds of eye melanoma being hereditary?

Not high but not impossible.

Dad and Grandma both had contracted it. Both were gone. Grandma said that Dad's vision problems were what caused the car accident that killed my parents. I, the survivor, knew the real story. The memory of Mom's and Dad's screams tormented me, still stalked me at night.

Arthur snuggled against my leg. Sweet dog. He knew exactly what I needed. If I admitted the truth, he was my therapy dog.

"Let's get you some breakfast," I said. He followed me through the garage, where I dumped a plastic trash bag of yard debris into the garbage can and made my way into the kitchen.

The urge to call Dixie, my dearest friend, nibbled at me. She knew me better than anyone, still I kept things locked away. I'd shared with her that my grandmother raised me. Good times, not the eye melanoma diagnosis that diminished her mental and physical health. I trusted Dixie and cared for her like a sister . . . yet getting too close to anyone sent me spiraling emotionally. Losing one more person might push me over a ledge.

While Arthur inhaled his morning meal, I ground beans for fresh coffee. Soon the hot brew fueled me for the day. I'd check on Christine Henderson, and if time allowed, I'd stop by the jail to visit her husband. By now he'd sobered and was either ready for whatever treatment cleaned up his act or his attitude measured hotter than a crackling bonfire. Contacting those involved in hostage situations didn't fall within my responsibilities, but the thought of walking away from hurting people made me feel like I'd abandoned them.

After showering and slipping into jeans and a green plaid shirt, I called Christine. "This is Carrington Reed. How are you and your son doing today?"

"Thank you for calling. We're doing well. Last night, Rand and I talked for a long time. We love Nick, but we can't trust him. If I thought he'd return to the man he used to be, I'd cancel the divorce proceedings. But we aren't convinced he'll agree to treatment or change his habits. Yesterday proved he could kill us."

"You and your son might need counseling."

"My mother said the same thing. She's on her way here for a few days. Probably afraid I'll let Nick back in once he's released."

"Would you?"

Christine inhaled deeply. "I want to say no, but Nick can be persuasive. Mom is adamant about me obtaining a restraining order. She also wants to pack us up and move us back to Dallas."

Wise mother. "I'm glad she's there for you."

"Mom and Dad have urged me to divorce Nick in the past, but that's hard when I love him. I admit his drinking and temper have gotten way out of hand." She sighed. "I'm rambling and taking up your time. Thank you again for your call."

"You're welcome. I'll check on Nick, but he won't know you and I have talked."

"Okay. Maybe you can convince him to get sober and rehabilitate."

I laid my phone on the kitchen table. I despised domestic abuse. Christine and her son would experience the same violence again unless her mother successfully moved them out of Houston. Even that didn't guarantee Christine would refuse to see Nick.

A call to Aaron laid out the truth. Nick had gone before a judge with a court-appointed attorney. He'd pleaded innocent, not behaved well, and refused visitors. Sentenced to jail for the next three days. That gave Christine's mother time to act. I requested that Nick know I'd called about him.

I blew out a frustrated breath. Nick had a beautiful family, but he appeared to prefer the mistress called alcohol. Arthur perked his ears as though he felt my agitation. I pulled him into my lap, nuzzling against his soft fur. "I can't fix the world. Why do I try?"

———

At the ophthalmologist's office, I waited for my eyes to dilate. My hands were like ice, and my stomach churned. Dr. Janet Leonard, a pleasant, dark-haired woman, asked if I'd noted any changes in my vision. After I explained Dad's and Grandmother's eye melanoma and my symptoms, she recorded my family history, symptoms, medicines, vitamins, and what I did for a living. She resorted to using my first name and a gentle tone from Negotiation 101 to help me relax. More like my internal alarm said someone poured gasoline around my house and lit a match.

"Any flashes or specks in your vision? Floaters?"

"No. Only the blurriness and some loss of peripheral vision on the right side."

Dr. Leonard peered at my eyes through a set of lenses—a routine examination. Then she reexamined the right eye extensively with a bright light mounted on her forehead. She typed into her computer and promised to discuss her findings when she finished. I stole a look at the screen, but the numbers and calculations meant nothing to me. My heart pounded in my ears.

She whirled her chair to face me, wearing a smile that didn't eliminate my anxiety. "When did the symptoms begin?"

"About six weeks ago."

"Is the problem continuous or occasional?"

"On occasion, when I'm tired."

"Carrington, I've detected enlarged blood vessels that could indicate a tumor inside your right eye. You have a nevus, an eye mole, that I recommend removing due to family history. I'm going to order imaging of the blood vessels in and around both eyes for a possible tumor."

"Will you have the nevus tested for cancer?"

"Yes."

"Did you see anything else suspicious?"

"Nothing caught my attention." She offered me another reassuring smile. "We'll find answers to your vision problem as quickly as possible."

"Is the imaging procedure done here?"

"Yes. I specialize in diseases of the eye, specifically melanoma. We can set up an appointment before you leave."

I had walked into a nightmare. "What is involved?"

"A dye is injected into your arm and travels to your eyes. Then a camera with special filters takes many pictures. I'm sure you have lots of questions and concerns, so let's find the answers to alleviate your fears. I have a brochure." She reached inside a drawer and handed me a pamphlet. "You can read this later after the eye drops wear off. Try to relax while I'm checking for the next available imaging and surgical appointments." Dr. Leonard opened another drawer for a pad of paper and pen. "I believe you can write down your questions while I'm gone. That might be easier than trying to read."

The pamphlet's two bolded words *eye melanoma* struck me like a death sentence. The contents of my stomach threatened to revolt. Did she have any idea the amount of information I'd researched and read and reread about my family's type of cancer? Years ago, I'd resolved never to give birth to a child who might inherit the condition.

She leaned in closer. "The testing does not mean you have the condition. First, we have a lot of ground to cover to rule out the possibilities. If the tumor is present, we'll handle it, and if it's melanoma, we have many options to treat the condition. Initially, the tumor appears small, and that's always good news."

I inwardly cringed. She must believe the worst. "My grandmother died when the cancer spread to her brain. My father died in a car accident soon after his diagnosis."

Dr. Leonard touched my arm. "You are not your grandmother or your father. If the problem is melanoma, we've detected it early and treatment can begin right away."

Or I could go blind and die.

FIVE

LEVI

After a fitful night of sleep and watching the sun rise, I decided avoiding a face-to-face with my parents made me look like a coward. Partially true, but shame enveloped me for disappointing them, like I'd been wrapped in a cocoon of pig slobber. Not kosher. The question plaguing me . . . was I ashamed of my belief in Yeshua or ashamed of my inability to talk to my parents about our problem?

Being ashamed of Yeshua meant when my time for this life ended, He'd not know me, and I'd endure eternity without Him.

Being ashamed of my reluctance to talk to my parents meant breaking the fifth commandment. Did I believe they were right to run me off?

Levi, who do you stand for? Me or your own self-preservation?

Truth always hit me as a voice in my head, a whisper like a faint breeze. The source of my faith told me who the voice belonged to, but it didn't stop the fear of insanity, like I was the only person in the universe who experienced divergent ideals—the world against myself. I hoped that wasn't the case for everyone. As a boy, I'd envisioned myself as a rebirth of the prophet Ezekiel or Daniel and destined to be a modern-day seer. Lofty aspirations for a boy whose voice hadn't changed or whose whiskers hadn't sprouted on his chin. As the years passed, I changed my perception of myself from a weird kid to an anomaly because I had more interest in the Torah, books, and writing than in sports. Not exactly a conversation I'd shared with another person. Doubtful I ever would.

Yesterday, when I had suspected Deborah and my parents had blocked my phone number, I told myself there was a way to find out. I walked onto the balcony of my condo overlooking the Galleria area, breathing in the fresh air and watching Houston slowly come to life. Birds called to each other before the honking of horns took precedence. I stared at the sky, begging for courage. Still took me two hours to grab my Tahoe keys.

I drove to the Meyerland area of Houston. On the way, I used Bluetooth to call a friend from church. "Hey, Caleb, do you have a minute?"

"Sure do. What do you need?"

I imagined him staring into the lens of his camera. Caleb lived and breathed photography, and we'd become solid friends. He saw things differently—no pun intended. "I'm on my way to talk to my parents. Could use a little prayer support."

"On it, brother. Not sure what your expectations might be, but God's there with you."

"Thanks."

"And Levi, call or text me later."

I agreed and drove closer to where I'd grown up. My parents, Joseph and Eva Ehrlich, lived in a predominantly Jewish area near their synagogue along with their many friends.

Their doctors lived and practiced in the area.

Their dentist lived and practiced within blocks.

Their retail stores owned by Jewish people were located close by.

Their favorite restaurants adhered to strict kosher guidelines according to Jewish law.

Their Jewish housekeeper lived within walking distance of my parents' home.

And the owners of their landscaping service and maintenance belonged to the same synagogue.

The familiar sights of tall palm trees and stately homes made me ache for the life once tied to home—acceptance and tradition. Tevye from *Fiddler on the Roof* didn't have much on me. Except I wasn't poor in the sense of money. What I craved was a full life and even seven daughters.

I hadn't been so bold to knock on Dad and Mom's door in the past since they emphatically told me never to come near them again. But the more I thought about their ultimatum, the more I used it as an excuse to avoid another confrontation. Loving Yeshua didn't mean my love for family should or had ended.

I parked at the curb in front of their red-brick two-story traditional home and turned off the engine. I prayed for the right words and their acceptance of my desire for reconciliation, despite all the signs pointing against it. Centuries of animosity rose against my best intentions, fueled by misunderstandings that only God could heal. I had no guts, and what I feared most moved me to press the engine button. It hummed like a sweet song, and I put my hand on the gear shift for Drive.

Talk to your father, Levi.

I pressed my head to the steering wheel, once again pushed the engine button to silence, and exited my Tahoe.

The sidewalk leading to my parents' door could have been ten miles. Every step echoed with the command to run. Ironic, me who'd chased down a story involving poaching through a pride of lions, ignored a rampant contagion in Africa to learn more about a virus that was killing thousands of people. I'd dodged Russian bullets in Ukraine so the world would know the truth about the Russian invasion. And now I trembled just to ring a doorbell.

The door slowly opened, and Dad stood in the entrance. I focused on the inside right doorpost at the mezuzah, a constant reminder of God's presence and His commandments.

"Shalom, Abba."

He stiffened, his face a mass of red. "You are not welcome here."

"I understand, and I'm not here to argue or cause trouble. I'm here out of respect for you and Ima. Can we talk outside?"

"Have you come to your senses?"

"In what way? My religious beliefs haven't changed."

"Neither has what you've done to our people."

He started to shut the door, but I stuck my foot on the threshold. "Abba, I'd like to be a part of your life even if we don't agree on faith matters."

"No." His jaw clenched. "You are dead to us."

"Abba, I love you, Ima, and Deborah. Nothing has changed there."

"You betrayed the foundation of our society, the Jewish people. You damaged the real religion."

"Adonai loves us unconditionally. Can't we have a relationship, be a *mischpacha*?"

"I no longer have a son."

I moved my foot and the door slammed.

SIX

CARRINGTON

I met Dixie for dinner at our favorite Greek restaurant. She chatted on about her role as a wife, mother to two young boys, and guidance counselor at an elementary school. We met in college as psychology majors. We loved people and were intrigued by their behavior, except she was best friends with all things breathing. Oh, I dreaded the results of the eye—

"Carrington, where are you?" Dixie rested her chin on her palm, her green eyes focusing on me.

I attempted to hide my preoccupation about the eye-imaging procedure . . . on Friday. "Thinking about how we're so opposite, and yet we're besties."

"There's more going on. You walk so close to the real you, then you step back and lock the door to your heart. On rare occasions, we make progress. I can feel it. But in the next instance, you slip into your own private world. It's dark there, friend. What are you afraid of?"

I moistened my lips. "It's personal. My business. Leave it alone." Immediately I regretted my tone. "I—"

She waved me away. "I get it. You are deep into one of your forbidden zones."

"I'm fine. Dix, if I could share, I would."

She offered a psychological "it's okay" smile. "Someday you'll learn to trust. If not with me, then someone else. I care for you, and I'm here when you're ready to talk. But I'll also tell you when your guarded ways are offensive. Like now." She leaned in. "I'm not the enemy."

I blinked back tears on the verge of spilling over my cheeks. "I'm sorry." We'd had this conversation in some form since college days. Dixie only wanted to help—except I wasn't ready to snap on the light to my inner fears. I might never be.

She lifted her chin. "Apology accepted. We're sister-friends, remember?"

"Thanks." I forced a smile. "Are you psychoanalyzing me? Because I know all the tricks." My spirit longed to be free of the burdens warring within me. "I'd unload, but it's stuff I can't talk about. I appreciate your putting up with my moodiness."

Dixie lifted her dainty little chin. "That settles it. I'm ordering baklava with extra honey. It won't solve your problem, but it will be sinfully sweet going down."

I laughed. "Incredibly decadent. One order with two forks or two orders?"

"What do you think?"

I pushed my problems aside and relaxed the best I could. With one bite of baklava left on my plate, a text sounded. I glanced at my phone—a contact from Customs and Border Protection. I quickly read.

Need your skills in a hostage situation. Expect a call from BP Agent Skip Reyes.

I acknowledged the text and studied Dixie. "I may need to leave. Depends on how quickly I receive a call."

"No problem. I hope it's an easy one." She paused. "But if you've been contacted, it must be serious."

My cell rang with an unfamiliar number. I took a deep breath. "Carrington Reed."

"This is Border Patrol Agent Skip Reyes. We have a hostage situation twenty miles west of Victoria and request your assistance."

"What can you tell me?"

"At around 1:00 p.m. this afternoon, a BP unit learned about a group of undocumented immigrants. We sent two agents to check them out. When our agents arrived, two men were herding more than a dozen men, women, and children into a delivery van. One man blew out our agent's front vehicle tires and barked orders at the other. They sped off, but not before the agents utilized a GPS tracker. We've located the van at a house where the men are holding the people at gunpoint."

My mind trailed back to other hostage situations. Desperate people who believed they'd chosen the only way for the world to hear their complaints and act on them. Raging tempers. And always the frightened person or persons at the murderous end of a gun.

"You're at the scene?"

"Yes, ma'am."

"What are the demands?"

"We don't know for sure. Our mobile command center has the two men's numbers, but they won't pick up. Neither have they called anyone."

I had my go bag in my truck. "It will take me three hours to get there. Do you have a helicopter?"

"Not here. Hold on while I talk to the commander."

"Agent Reyes, in the time it takes to authorize a helo, I'll be well on my way."

"Okay. I can fill you in more on the drive here."

"I'll head out immediately. If needed, I can talk to the captors while en route."

"Good to know. Thank you, Ms. Reed. Call me when you're on the road."

I dropped my phone into my shoulder bag. "Dix, I need a favor."

She grinned through a mouthful of baklava. "Let me guess. You've been called out and don't know when you'll be back?"

"You are so right. Arthur needs Aunt Dixie to walk him later."

"You got it. Want me to bring him home?"

My shoulders relaxed. "That would be amazing. You are the best sister-friend ever."

"My family and I love Arthur. Now I have a favor."

"Bring it on." But I already knew her request.

"Church with me on Sunday?"

"Sure. I'll flip for everyone's lunch since you're taking excellent care of Arthur." I'd postponed the God-thing for too many years, although He and I rarely talked, and it usually involved me ranting and Him quiet.

After running to the ladies' room, I gave Dixie a hug and left my woes behind. The tension in my neck and shoulders eased. Hostage negotiation wove meaning into my life, and for some peculiar reason, it wove compassion with adrenaline.

Once on the road, I returned the call to BP Agent Reyes. "I'm on my way. What's the status?"

"We've identified the two men, brothers—Will and Boyd Kendrix. I used a bullhorn to talk to forty-two-year-old Will, the oldest. He has a bullhorn too, and the van belongs to him."

"Why a bullhorn unless he planned to use it?"

"I know. Doesn't make sense. And he's not an auctioneer."

"Strange. I'm sorry," I said. "I interrupted you."

"No problem. Boyd is thirty-six, and I haven't spoken to him. Will's demands amount to law enforcement leaving him and his brother alone until they are ready to talk terms. Tells me our agents surprised them, and they're regrouping. Will wants no part of the BP or any law enforcement agency, making you a good fit. I told him a private negotiator would be here in a few hours. He shut down. Haven't heard a word since."

"That could mean he either will only negotiate with me, or he intends to do a lot of harm. Do you suspect any injuries among the hostages?"

He shook his head. "We don't believe anyone inside is hurt badly. The house is vacant, and Boyd Kendrix is listed as the owner."

"Do you have a definite number of people?"

"Thermal imaging shows seventeen, which includes the Kendrix brothers—fourteen adults and three children. I saw four women when the undocumented immigrants were loaded into the back of the van."

"How many BP agents are with you?"

"Counting me, ten."

"If Will refuses to talk to law enforcement, seeing me might push him over the edge."

"I'd rather think he and his brother would surrender instead of facing a firefight."

Hard to say because I'd witnessed both. "What else can you tell me about them?"

"We've learned more and assume they are retaliating for their father's recent death. Timothy Kendrix had a ranch near the border. A group of undocumented immigrants settled there, and he couldn't get them to leave. The father put his ranch up for sale, and then someone killed him. That happened seven days ago. Doubtful they're blaming the people held hostage, just all undocumented immigrants."

"The brothers want justice," I said. "If the death had occurred weeks ago, perhaps I could've persuaded them to give authorities time."

"Will is hot, irrational. As I said, haven't talked to Boyd." Agent Reyes sighed. "Just sent a pic of each brother to your phone. Will is the one without glasses."

"The hostages must be incredibly frightened." But who knew what made up the group. Some could be families looking for a new beginning. Some could be looking for a means to make money illegally. "Okay. If anything develops, please call me. We need to be armed with information."

"Yes, ma'am."

Agent Reyes didn't need to mention the dangers of negotiating at night in a rural area. The longer the brothers went without sleep, the more dangerous they became. More than likely, the two were using drugs to stay awake. Another concern focused on the women and children facing potential assault. Did they have food and water?

I put myself in the Kendrixes' shoes. Father murdered. No arrests. Wouldn't be the first time angry people chose the vigilante approach when they believed law enforcement weren't doing their job.

SEVEN

LEVI

I'd been asleep about fifteen minutes when my phone rang. Had been up on an overseas call since 4:00 a.m. this morning, and exhaustion had pelted me to get some sleep. I grabbed my device and saw Frank's name on the screen. At 10:00 p.m. he must have a story for me to cover. Shaking myself awake, I let my boss know I was listening.

"I have a lead for you," Frank said.

"Figured so. What and where?" I tossed back the blanket and sat erect. Flipping on the nightstand lamp, I grabbed pen and paper and clicked the pen to write. A long time ago, I learned to be ready at a moment's notice.

"Another hostage situation. Not an exclusive but not public yet. That's why I need you on-site ASAP. The location is west of Victoria. I'll send the address to your phone. I've pulled a few strings and granted you access. Just show your press ID card at the checkpoint."

"What's going on out there?" I moved into the bathroom and ran cold water to scrub the sleep off my face.

Frank relayed a kidnapping involving two Texan men holding several hostages at gunpoint in retaliation for their father's murder. "Slant the story to gain sympathy for the hostages. They're undocumented immigrants, not illegals. The publishers insist upon showing those people are being denied human rights."

"What if those held are part of a gang? Killers? Drug smugglers? Or the two men behind the guns are law enforcement needing backup to make an arrest?"

"Your story is the immigrants were denied access into Texas but found another way to enter the country. Tie that into two rednecks playing cowboy."

I put the phone on speaker and shrugged on a shirt. "Frank, you might be right in the whole assessment, but I've got to find out for myself."

"Your assessment is worthless. You've got to be on-site before other news media arrive. The important thing is the assignment might save your career."

"Save my career? How many awards has the publication earned because of me?"

"Levi, don't give me your—" The profanity continued. Nothing I hadn't heard before. "Forget your so-called principles. Show the perspective the publishers want for the readers."

"You mean the victim is always the one who shares their same political opinion?" I regretted the words the moment they left my mouth. "That was out of line. I'm aware your job and mine depend on meeting their criteria."

"Right. Levi, they are finished with your mouth. They've got to see you're with them 100 percent."

I reached for my jeans. "Respect for them direct depositing my pay is one thing. Dictating to me their personal preferences and verbiage in my articles won't happen."

"If your story doesn't raise our ratings, you're fired. It's out of my hands because I intend to keep my job. As much as I appreciate the status of our publication because of your coverage in the past, I have my loyalty, which happens to be who supports my livelihood. And you can be a pain with your truth banner."

I'd been expecting Frank's ultimatum, or rather the publishers' readiness to terminate my employment. I hadn't wanted to change jobs this soon, but I'd make the best of it. No reason to argue with Frank. If he rejected my coverage, then my plans stepped up a notch, including how to support the charity organization that had helped me put my life in order. My goal of working for *National Geographic* offered a lucrative position within the topics that appealed to me.

"I know where you're coming from." I reached for some socks. "Doesn't mean I agree or I'll comply."

Frank added a few more expletives. "You're a stubborn fool."

"Can't argue with that. Who gave you the tip?" I snatched my tennis shoes from my closet.

"Someone I trust."

Probably a paid insider at Border Patrol. Frank used to provide his sources before I became a mosquito to the new publishers. For sure, media coverage attracted more readers and viewers, and the more media, the more the hostage-takers would revel in the publicity for their own agenda. "What do the hostage-takers want?"

"Don't know. Doesn't matter. You have your assignment."

"Not without hearing the other side of the story."

"After what I've just told you?"

There were always two sides to every confrontation, and I'd show real people, real problems, and real emotions. My personal thoughts of right and wrong wouldn't be reflected in the article. The stories weren't mine but the readers', and I was motivated to take chances and risk my career for what I believed in—truth and balanced reporting, basic Journalism 101.

"Are the hostages men or women and children?"

"No idea. But women and kids jerk at readers' hearts. Reporters will be buzzing like flies. Get out there and cover the story. Lots of emotion to benefit us. Look, Levi, time's a-wasting. I expect a text in thirty minutes that you're well on the road."

"Who can I talk to for more info?"

"Me. I'll contact you with any updates. Remember, those are innocent people who were caught up in somebody's hostage-taking game."

"What else is going on there?"

"The BP has called in a private negotiator. And they're considering bringing in a Border Patrol Special Operations Group." Frank chuckled. "Sounds like more than they can handle."

"Is the negotiator currently at the site?"

"My source couldn't confirm it."

"A name?"

"You know her—Carrington Reed."

EIGHT

CARRINGTON

I'd avoided ruts and bumps on the dirt road leading to the hostage site, but I still hit a few and hoped that didn't mirror the negotiations ahead. The time neared 10:00 p.m. when I arrived at the hostage site. Two Border Patrol agents stopped me at a checkpoint, verified my ID before they allowed me to drive any farther. Once approved, I pulled onto a narrow back road. Gravel crunched beneath my truck's tires, and a chill of evil seemed to surround me. Not the first time I'd felt the viciousness of someone's actions, and the familiarity kept my senses on alert.

My vehicle's headlights illuminated the flat, remote area that held few trees. On the left, a dilapidated one-story house sat back on a rut-filled dirt-and-gravel driveway, approximately 150 feet long. Four BP vehicles lined the right side of the road close to the house like a barricade. Agents gathered at various points, and two ambulances sat ready behind the mobile command center. How many men were strategically hidden to minimize exposure? For sure the BP agents were using night-vision goggles.

I drove as close to the barricade as possible, parked on the right behind an SUV, and exited my truck.

A floodlight had been erected at the foot of the driveway leading to the house. I slipped on my Kevlar vest. Two agents approached carrying flashlights that bobbed with their every step. At least they didn't shine them in my eyes. One of them, of average height and weight, appeared in charge and young for a tough assignment. We shook hands.

"I'm Agent Skip Reyes. Glad you're here, Ms. Reed."

"Thank you, sir. I'm Carrington."

"Call me Skip." He raked his hand through nearly black hair. "It's been a tough afternoon."

"If the Kendrix brothers aren't communicating, the night will get a lot longer."

"Expected as much. This is my first hostage situation." From what I could see in the dim light, stress lines plowed across his forehead.

I longed to reassure him and all those involved that they could walk this path. Some might term the circumstances as hopeless, but I embraced my skills. No one wanted a role in a firefight that leaned toward a bad ending. "How long have you been with the BP?"

"Three years in another week."

A young agent caught in a mess that even a seasoned agent wouldn't want to encounter. "I'd like to tell you these issues get easier, but they don't. I promise to do all I can for a safe release of those people without anyone getting hurt."

"The boss said you're the best."

I met his gaze. "Doesn't mean I'm always successful. Dissipating conflict smacks against the hostage-taker's goals, and right now I have no idea what makes these brothers tick, and I won't until I talk to them."

I studied the small house, where emotionally charged hostages and kidnappers huddled with their own agenda. A faint light shone through a ragged curtained window out of possibly an empty room. "Does the MCC show anyone in the dimly lit room?"

"Empty. Weird. But the Kendrixes must have a reason."

"Let's move ahead on the negotiations. Where are we?"

Skip walked toward the crime scene, and I joined him. "Neither of the brothers has ever been arrested for us to predict behavior. They're known as hardworking ranchers. But they still aren't responding to our calls. We have two agents in place on the east and west sides of the house. I think having your conversation with the Kendrixes from a location separate from the mobile command center might relax them."

I nodded. "How close can I get?"

Skip pointed to a Jeep at the foot of the driveway. "That's my vehicle on the left, and the closest the brothers have permitted. The moment we advance from an area separate from the floodlight, shots are fired. Makes me think they have night-vision goggles too."

I mentally reviewed what I'd been told. "Although it doesn't sound like the two expected the BP to catch them nabbing those people, they are prepared for trouble."

"The BP tossed a wrench into their plan, but at least we haven't learned of a dead hostage."

"You said the property belongs to the younger brother," I said, depositing every word into my memory bank.

"Yes. Boyd Kendrix owns these eighty acres. Used to run cattle. No one lives in the house, according to land records. Will and Boyd's father owns or owned acreage thirty miles from here, and the two sons own ranches farther north from their father's property."

I had so many questions, but then I always did. "Since we talked earlier, do you think anyone's been hurt?"

"Hard to tell. My guess is some have been roughed up. A few blood spatters at the abduction site indicate so. We had an exchange of gunfire twenty minutes before you got here. Two agents tried to approach a side window, but the brothers opened fire before they could visually get a handle on what's going on."

"They mean business. You spoke with Will. Any signs of drugs, alcohol, or severe mental issues?"

"Not anything out of the ordinary. He spoke firmly, in control. We haven't heard from Boyd, but that doesn't mean he's not volatile."

I never knew what I'd walk into until I talked directly to the offenders and established a relationship. "The brothers believe they are justified, or they wouldn't be risking their lives. No one steps over the line without the conviction they are on the right side. That's what makes them dangerous."

"Are you thinking they originally intended to kill the hostages, then let someone find the bodies as a message to their agenda?" Skip said. "The investigators have nothing. And unless the Kendrixes have evidence proving one or more of the hostages killed their father, murdering those people is a stupid move."

I nodded. "I'm just glad the hostages are still alive. I'm ready for the brothers' phone numbers. Start with Will since you've already spoken with him. Negotiations are always easier when done in private, as long as he answers. My experience is the bullhorn often makes the offender increase their bravado or makes them angrier. I'll do my best to get one of them to agree to my call." We stopped walking, and I saved the digits into my phone with their names. "I'd like any other numbers, like a wife or girlfriend?"

"We have Will's wife's mobile."

"What has she said?"

"Haven't called her."

"Why?"

"Not sure it would help."

I swallowed my retort and saved her number. "All calls will be monitored through the MCC?"

"Yes. We'll stop there first so you can get acquainted with the men."

Inside the MCC unit, Skip introduced me to the commander, Miguel Lopez, who confirmed his support.

"Agent Lopez, I'd like to see the house's layout," I said. "From the size, I'm assuming it has two bedrooms."

The commander pulled up the small, single-story house on his computer. He pointed to the screen. "The hostages are being held in the front living area, but those lights are out."

I thanked him and joined Skip on the short walk to his Jeep. He reached into the rear passenger seat and handed me a bullhorn.

"Carrington, we need to get those people out of there. Won't be long before the area's flooded with media, and that will feed into the

Kendrixes' demands." Skip rubbed the back of his neck. "You've done these enough times to be telling me how it all could play out."

"I'll do all I can. Human behavior is unpredictable."

My first goal was to befriend the oldest brother. With a deep breath, I lifted the bullhorn to my lips. "Will, this is Carrington. I'm here to help you." His willingness to negotiate depended on how quickly he'd answer.

"You're not wearing a BP uniform," a male voice said over a bullhorn from inside the house. "Are you one of the agents or the person who's supposed to talk me down? 'Cause I'm not talking to a cop or a BP agent."

"I'm a private negotiator. I'd like to call you, hear your side of what's going on."

He huffed and swore. "I have plenty to say. What's your number? I'll call you."

Hurdle one. I gave him my number, and my phone rang. I brought up a mental image of Will from the pic Skip had sent to my phone—light-brown hair, gray-green eyes, scraggly beard. "Carrington here. Am I speaking to Will?"

"You bet."

"First, I'd like to make sure the people inside are okay."

"They're all right for now, unless I get tired of messing with you and pull the trigger."

"Do you need water or food?"

"Nope. My brother and I are good. These people aren't getting anything."

"I can arrange a delivery, so don't hesitate. What happened earlier today?"

He relayed the same story he'd given Skip. "Dad was sixty-five years old, fit, strong, a leader in the community. Now he's dead, and no one's doing a thing about it. We want the killer arrested."

"You sound angry, and I don't blame you a bit."

"I am." He swore again. "He was a good man. He raised my brother and me to respect others, and this is how they paid him back. Shot and killed right outside his truck on his own property."

"Definitely not what anyone wants for their father, and yes, something needs to be done." I purposely spoke slowly and quietly in hopes of calming him to listen to reason.

"The people squatting on his land killed him. I'm sure of it. He even dropped off food and water for them. Decent people respected Timothy Kendrix, and now he's cold in his grave."

"I'm very sorry for your loss. The community lost a fine man. Is your mother alive?"

"No, ma'am. She died years ago of a heart attack."

"Incredibly sad. It's just you and your brother?"

"Yep, me and Boyd."

"Married? Kids?"

"Boyd's engaged unless I talk him out of it. She's all right, but her mother is a—I'm married with two kids. They're great and my wife is too, but the responsibility can be hard."

"Responsibilities keep us busy and sometimes stressed, like the tragedy with your dad."

"Another reason why me and Boyd are here. Dad gave us 110 percent. We aim to do no less."

"My dad gave 110 percent in his career as a Houston police officer. He's why I chose to be a negotiator."

"Right. Making a hard stand for what's right has its risks, but now that it's done, we're not backing down. My family deserves a husband and dad who won't back down from a fight. I love 'em, and my actions prove it."

I didn't quite follow the logic, but that didn't matter. "Commendable, Will. Are you sure the killer is an undocumented immigrant? My sources say your dad's murder is still under investigation. I understand they have a team working 24-7 on the case."

"Who else would be on his property?"

"You have an excellent point. Did he have any enemies, anyone I could talk to or give their names to law enforcement?"

"No. I told the deputies all I know."

"I could do more for you and Boyd if you'd release those people inside."

Will snorted. "How so?"

"Your action would be a sign of good faith. Then you and I would have the opportunity to discuss the wrongs done to your father and seek a resolution."

"No way in—"

His swearing demonstrated his stubborn mindset. Nothing I hadn't heard many times before. "Will, I promise you justice. I just need a little help on your side. I need time to talk to those working the case, to gather evidence, interviews—"

"I'll make a deal with you. Give me the name of Dad's killer and evidence of his arrest by five in the morning, or I start shooting."

NINE

LEVI

At 12:30 a.m., the lack of traffic on Highway 59 south to Victoria cleared the road but not the heaviness of my conversation earlier with my abba. I tried to shake the rejection, telling myself nothing unexpected happened. But logic didn't stop the inner turmoil. Ironic how the truth was supposed to set us free, but the repercussions usually got me into a whirlwind of trouble. God cared . . . I was sure of it. I wish I had His insight into what lay ahead.

The closer I drove to the hostage scene, the more my determination increased to attempt talking to my parents again in a few months. The next time, I'd take on counseling beforehand and be armed with more than hurt feelings. One day I'd be reunited with my family, or I'd learn to live without them.

I'd forgotten to call Caleb last night. "Siri, send a text to Caleb. 'Meeting with my father went as expected. Bad. Thanks, bro. Sorry about the hour.'"

I shook my head at the brain cells I'd wasted on family issues out of my control. With an assignment to cover a controversial topic, I pushed my problems to a mental waiting room.

What were local and state news agencies claiming? I pressed my preset radio stations for fair reporting, but no one said a word about

41

a hostage situation. The Border Patrol could have avoided informing the media until they had a better handle on the crisis. Unfortunately, withholding news never lasted long. We reporter types were like bloodhounds. Frank had learned quickly from a source, and most likely that person informed other media too. For sure, the undocumented immigrant issue would garner a lot of coverage.

A critical situation must have occurred with multiple layers for the BP to call in a private negotiator. From my experience with her negotiation techniques, how would she approach the brothers?

More importantly, why had two men taken more than a dozen undocumented immigrants hostage? What did they hope to gain? The border dispute lit the fuses for many Americans. Who controlled the border—the US or whoever spoke the loudest? I refused to go there because I saw both sides. Good and bad people trekked here from all over the world—some intended to do harm and others to escape poverty or persecution. The immigration discussion needed more than my input to solve it.

I deliberated the problem west of Victoria and convinced myself the hostages couldn't be gang related, or they'd have overpowered the two men. Desperate people taking hostages never made sense to me. Often people were killed or severely traumatized . . . Atrocious crimes raised ratings and filled written, spoken, and visual communication with the means to frighten people.

Whatever I learned in the hours ahead, I'd sift through the facts to find the real story, even if what I discovered went against my beliefs and supported Frank and the publishers. Why had the brothers exchanged one crime for another?

Two Border Patrol agents stopped me at a checkpoint and blocked me from turning left onto the road leading to the crime scene. I rolled down my window to greet them.

"Sir," one agent said with a Hispanic accent, "this is an active shooter situation."

"I'm a reporter, Levi Ehrlich." I showed him my press ID card. "I've been granted access to the crime scene."

He examined my card and stepped away with his phone in hand.

In a few moments, he returned and gave permission for me to enter. "You will be given restrictions once you're closer to the crime scene."

"Yes, sir. Thank you."

I bounced over a pothole-infested road, parked my Tahoe behind a black extended-cab truck, and patted my jeans pocket for my phone. I typed faster with my thumbs and snapped better pics than with a ton of fancy gear. Besides, extra gear dragged me down . . . especially if I had to run, hence my tennis shoes. Experience was an amazing teacher.

I spoke an update into a voice message and sent it directly to Frank. The publication would be broadcast over the state and beyond.

I left my vehicle, and two agents approached me. Again I displayed my press card. One of them, a man in his late thirties from what I could tell in the shadows, maintained a stoic expression. He returned my card. "Mr. Ehrlich, we are in a dangerous hostage situation. For your safety, I need you to stay outside the perimeters or face arrest."

"Yes, sir, I understand. Can you tell me what's going on?"

The agent seemed uncertain how to proceed and repeated a fraction of what Frank had told me. "Thanks. I'll keep my distance. Anyone down?"

"We haven't been informed. Agents are unharmed."

I wouldn't get much information from Agents Stoic or Silent. They walked with me midway to the vehicle barricade where Carrington leaned against a Jeep, staring at the house, with her arms folded across her chest. She wore jeans, a long-sleeved shirt, and tennis shoes.

"Please wait here," an agent said.

"Sir, would you ask Ms. Reed if I can speak to her?"

The agent shook his head as though my question hit the ridiculous list, but he approached her. While they talked, she tossed her gaze my way. I waved and she returned the gesture. Expecting to be turned down, I prepared my persuasive attitude.

She walked with the agent back to me. I stuffed my hands in my pockets to keep from talking with them and irritating her.

"Levi, please, stay where you are."

"You know me. Have I ever stretched a story for public appeal or downgraded the humanitarian aspect of a crisis?"

She paused. "You've never disappointed me in reporting my negotiations. But an exclusive in the middle of a hostage situation is out of the question." She pointed to the dilapidated house. "My priority is the safety of those people inside and out. All of them. Including you."

"The innocent and the victims need a champion to defend them." I tipped a nod toward her. "That's you."

"I'm not a champion. I simply try to defuse the bomb."

I expected the humble yet resolute response from what I'd experienced with her. "I'm asking for an opportunity to walk the same path with integrity. To write a story that shows the truth about the current crisis, an opportunity to share both sides."

She focused my way, and even in the faint light, I sensed her eyes searching me for truth. "Are you flattering me for a story?"

"Not at all. But I might be grappling for the right words to defend truth and humanity."

She returned her attention to the house, as though bidding the men inside to free the hostages. "You don't need to prove a thing to me. Remember the robbery at the downtown Houston jewelry store?"

"Yes. It's where we met."

"Remember the woman who was shot escaping the store? I thought you were rushing in to snap a pic for an article. Instead, you hurried ahead of HPD, putting aside your own safety to help her."

"We witnessed the devastation of power fueled with anger and greed," I said. "You calmly convinced the robbers to surrender. I've watched you since then do what seems impossible."

"Can I trust you to maintain the path of integrity you just mentioned?"

"Without a doubt."

"You're the first reporter here, which means you have a contact."

"My boss does. Count on other media types showing up soon."

"With lots of agenda." Silence hung between us, while she seemed to deliberate her answer. High-pitched katydids and screeching cicadas filled the darkness with their mating calls while serenading the rest of us. "If I agree and see a hint of betrayal, I'll have you escorted outside of the barrier on your rear."

"I'd expect no less. A BP agent told me a little about what's going on. How many hostages?"

"Fifteen. Women and children too." Carrington's voice carried across the wind in a whisper.

"Innocent people always suffer the most. Evil is a relentless explosion." Sickening memories of the bloodshed I'd seen in Africa and Ukraine . . . No doubt she'd tasted enough violence to last a lifetime too.

"I could be here three days without a shower, and food would be cold takeout."

"I've gone ten days without a shower and survived on bugs and worms. If anyone can resolve the chaos peacefully, it's you."

Her tennis-shoed foot tapped the ground. "Don't put that kind of pressure on me." Her voice trembled a bit.

How many situations had she negotiated? She and I had been a part of seven, and her zeal and compassion had accompanied every one where I witnessed her sincerity. I'd experienced negotiators in the past, and they used similar tactics of persuasion. But mercy and warmth emanated from this woman, like empathy composed every cell.

I wanted—no, needed—to know more about Carrington Reed.

TEN

CARRINGTON

From the first time Levi had stepped into one of my hostage-negotiation cases and made known his chatty personality, I'd pegged him as an extrovert who'd adapted his personality according to the scenario. No doubt his experience proved more was said in silence and body language than in a page filled with words—a viewpoint I practiced and lived by, often as a mode of self-preservation.

Death came to those who attached themselves to me. I'd learned the hard way not to trust or care too much.

Although I hesitated to give Levi an opportunity to write a story about the current crisis, I was drawn to him, not just his reporting and writing but to him as a person. Not long after the jewelry store negotiation, he flew to Ukraine. While there, he appeared on Fox News during heavy bombing and reported on the strength of the Ukrainian people and their needs. Yet if I agreed to him joining me in the heat of danger, I took responsibility for his actions if he was hurt or if he did something stupid and paid for it with his life.

Something unexplainable nudged me closer to him. "I think honest coverage would benefit the public."

"Balanced and fair reporting." He nodded, still allowing me to process my thoughts—or rather my reservations.

"I'd like to see your releases before they're sent to publication. If you agree to my terms and wear a Kevlar vest, I'll allow you on this side of the barricade."

"I agree."

"Keep your distance from the driveway. Not a word to other media while here. Don't interrupt negotiations or speak when my attention is elsewhere. If I hold up my hand, that means silence. Sometimes I need to surround the problem mentally and stay there until a solution comes to mind. Veering from the process could be detrimental to those inside. Do I make sense?"

"Yes. Your energy is best focused on getting those people out of there and not on making idle conversation. I have a brief statement on my phone for your approval."

I read his reporting and had no problems with his portrayal of a tense and emotional situation.

"Thank you for the opportunity."

"You may choose to retract the gratitude later. Promise me you won't collaborate with any other reporters before or after I approve your articles. No photos, videos, or audio recordings unless I approve them. Those are my terms." I inhaled a cleansing breath. "While I can't enforce my guidelines—"

"Carrington, if you're attempting to discourage me, it's not happening. I respect your stand. I'll take pics, videos, and record conversations, but I'll not release them without your permission. You have my word."

"All right. This is a first for me." I waved at the BP agents at the barricade. "It's okay. I'm letting Mr. Ehrlich pass. I need a Kevlar for him."

"Yes, ma'am," an agent said.

Levi walked my way. "Thank you."

A text flew in from Skip. **Will's wife is on her way here. Call me.**

I held up my hand to stop Levi from continuing. "I need to make a call."

He stopped about fifteen feet back.

I got Skip on the line. "What do you have?"

"Will's wife, Felicia, was shocked about Will and Boyd. Since her father-in-law's death, her husband's not been himself, but she didn't anticipate this or Boyd's participation. She called Will's actions 'a steady gait of anger.'"

"How long will it take for her to get here?"

"I'd say nearly an hour. She's waiting for someone to stay with her kids."

"I'm contacting her now."

"Carrington, she's not doing well with this."

"Emotional? Irrational?"

"Add hysterical."

I pressed in Felicia Kendrix's number. She picked up on the first ring. "This is Carrington Reed, a negotiator at the site where Will and Boyd are holding undocumented immigrants as hostages. I'm working with Border Patrol to free these people."

"I . . . I want to help." Felicia's voice trembled. "I tried to listen to the news while driving, but I didn't know if reporters gave the right location. Why are they inside Boyd's vacant house?"

"I wish I had answers for you."

She broke into sobs. "Why have they done this? They'll be killed."

I needed to calm her over-the-top emotions before she spiraled into a mental breakdown. "Take a deep breath and slowly let it out."

The wailing continued. How could Felicia be an asset in her current state?

"Try again. You can't help Will or the hostages until you can think and talk clearly."

"I'm trying!"

I needed patience before Felicia had an accident. I pushed my voice into the zone of a late-night radio host. "Listen to me. Will loves you and your children. He told me so. If anyone can persuade him to release the hostages and surrender to the Border Patrol, it's you. But you must gain control of your emotions." I waited and played a mental game of "ten ways this waiting would make me a better person," a game my dad instilled in me years ago.

"Carrington, you'll never be successful in communicating with others until you learn how to manage your impatience."

"Daddy, I want to be a police officer like you. Teach me how to be patient."

Then he explained the Ten Ways game. After he and Mom were killed, I used his method to honor him and help me grow into a mature woman.

I was still a work in progress.

Felicia's voice broke my reverie. "I'm sorry. I need a few minutes to get myself together. I'll call you back."

Why couldn't people see that weakness was a threat to others?

Skip approached me. "A woman by the name of Charlotte Bolton called the BP office. My commander talked to her. Several years ago, she lived on a ranch near the Kendrix family and watched Will and Boyd grow up. According to her, she has information that might lead us to a resolution."

ELEVEN

Skip had given me Charlotte Bolton's phone number to clarify her statements about the Kendrix family. New information could open our minds to factors that might have led to Timothy's death. And possibly keep Will from shooting the first hostage. The time neared 3:00 a.m., but murder took precedence over sleep. Two hours until Will's deadline.

Levi jammed his left hand into his jeans pocket. "Anything you can tell me?"

I shook my head. "I need to make another call in private."

Levi took his cue and backed away while I pressed in Charlotte Bolton's number. She picked up on the first ring.

"This is Charlotte Bolton."

"My name is Carrington Reed, and I apologize for the hour. Earlier you spoke to the commander at Border Patrol about the Kendrix family. I'm a hostage negotiator at the crime scene where Will and Boyd are holding fifteen people hostage."

"Yes, ma'am, Commander Lopez told me you'd be in touch. I called when I heard the news on my scanner and couldn't sleep, worrying about those boys and what they'd done. I lived on a ranch bordering the Kendrix property for many years. Timothy's wife, Dorie, and I were friends, good friends. We shared our lives, motherhood, faith, everything sister-friends do. What I—"

A shot rang out over the night, followed by a woman's shrill scream. The sound indicated a firearm smaller than a rifle.

I inwardly moaned, a nightmare playing out. "I've got to call you back." I pressed in Will's number on my phone, while my foot tapped the earth. I checked to make sure Levi was compliant. He studied me and remained quiet.

I drew in a calming breath and waited for my opportunity to leave a message. "Will, I want to help you. The gunfire bothers me. Are you hurt? Please call me so we can work this out. I promise we'll find answers to your father's tragic death." I ended my message and pressed in Boyd's number, then repeated my request. Shaking my head in the shadows, I stared at the house. "Come on, guys, call me."

Moments passed. Agents scurried behind and beyond us, but my concentration stayed fixed on the house and any possible movement.

I grabbed the bullhorn from atop the Jeep's hood and lifted it to my lips. "Will, is everything okay inside? Do you need medical help?"

Only silence responded.

My phone buzzed—Felicia Kendrix. *Give me a few minutes.*

Skip appeared at my side. Before he spoke, I lifted my chin at Levi, who hadn't moved. My guess was he could hear Skip's and my conversation, even with my back to him. Would he disappoint me and write an article that increased ratings faster than the speed of lightning?

"What just happened, Skip? With the woman's scream, someone is hurt or worse."

He swore. "I just observed the thermal-imaging footage in real time. This looks more and more like we need to call SOG—US Border Patrol Special Operations Group. They'd force the Kendrix brothers out of there. In the meantime, I'm contacting the sheriff's department for backup."

"And then what?" I tamped down my anger. "The muscle and high-powered weaponry could push the brothers into behavior we'd regret. We already have the problem of satisfying them by 5:00 a.m." I glanced around. "The terrain is flat. No barn or other outbuildings. I know you have agents out there . . . I simply hate the potential for a bloodbath."

"Our men are trained. None of us wants to use deadly force to bring down the Kendrixes."

My phone buzzed again, and I peeked at the screen. "It's Felicia. I can't talk to her now."

"Want me to call her?"

I shook my head. "She'll want to know why I ended our conversation. I'll call her back in a few and prep her before she arrives. She was so upset when I talked to her that I asked her to pull herself together, then call me back. And now she's called twice and I haven't responded." I paused to focus. "Skip, we need a plan to convince the release of those people without any deaths. I've got to buy the hostages time. Neither man is answering his phone."

"I came here to get my thermal-imaging camera to show you what we saw inside the MCC." Skip reached into his Jeep and pulled out what looked like a portable Scion, a powerful device. He peered through the camera and handed it to me. "Looks like two small persons or children are down. Only one of the brothers is standing. Not sure what that means. See for yourself."

I looked and cringed. "I agree with you." I called out to Will on the bullhorn and asked him to call me. Then waited. "Skip, can you or the MCC help me with additional information?"

"I'll do my best." He yanked his phone from his pocket and nodded for me to begin.

"I'd like a full report on Timothy Kendrix—his friends, social life, potential enemies, his death, his reputation, the investigation. Everything you can give me. Did he hold any political offices, community work, church membership, or serve in the military? And dig deeper for information about Will and Boyd as brothers. I started a conversation with Charlotte Bolton, but that's when we heard the shot. I can only be in one place at a time."

"Ah—" Skip swore under his breath. "Never mind."

"You were about to say?"

He handed me a bottle of water. "Consider your requests done."

"Thanks." I took a sip and rolled my tight shoulder muscles. "I apologize for my impatience."

"It's okay. I'd be worse."

I smiled my appreciation. "Wish we had the status of those down." I stared at the house as though I could influence the brothers' minds to release those people inside. An idea crept into my thoughts. "Were the hostages' belongings confiscated when the Kendrixes abducted them?"

"What little they had was left behind, and I piled it all in the back of my Jeep. One of our dogs sniffed for drugs but he detected nothing. I patted down backpacks and bags for weapons. Nothing there either. At the time, my attention zeroed in on the hostages, and drugs and weapons were my only concern."

"Can you spare an agent to go through each one? Might be something there to help us."

"Sure. If any of the hostages are linked to the father's killing, we can use the info to negotiate." He wiped perspiration from his forehead. "The longer we stand here, the more tempers will fly from inside and out."

I peered up at the starless night. "I hate the darkness. Holds far too much evil."

I seldom prayed, but with the gunshot and the woman's scream, circumstances inside the house had taken a bad twist, and I needed supernatural help. How religious of me to call out to God only when desperate. The likelihood of someone hurt, and the victim being a small woman or child, soured my stomach. Only a coward bullied the weak.

Lights from the road pierced the darkness. The media had arrived. A helicopter hovered over the MCC. A distraction that could slow negotiations.

Will, call me, please.

TWELVE

My phone rang, and I immediately picked up. I closed my eyes to concentrate. "I'm here, Will."

"You haven't moved much since we last talked."

I shouldn't be so exposed even with Kevlar. "That's because you have 100 percent of my attention. You must have powerful binoculars."

"And a good rifle."

The shot in question sounded like a handgun. "I heard gunfire. Is anyone hurt?"

He snorted. "Maybe. Doesn't matter."

Skip walked away, no doubt to handle my requests and listen via the MCC. Levi stepped back a few more feet, giving me room to talk unhindered.

The pounding in my chest told me my instincts were right. Tempers inside had escalated. "What caused the gunfire?"

"I fired my gun to prove a point."

"Into the air or someone's body?"

"Nobody's dead if that's what you're asking."

Meaning at least one person was hurt. "Will, I need a show of good faith to keep law enforcement from yanking me out of here and taking aggressive action."

He laughed, a gritty sound. "You mean so they can break down the door and risk all these people getting killed?"

"I will do all I can to prevent loss of lives."

"How heroic."

"You and Boyd have clean records, and I'm willing to vouch for your cooperation in a court of law. All you need to do is toss out your weapons and exit the house with your hands behind your heads."

"You heard my demands." Will's voice took a higher pitch. "Nothing's changed."

"I'm working on those things for you. Can I talk to Boyd?"

"He's busy. I'm the man to talk to."

"Is he hurt?"

"He will be if he doesn't listen to reason."

"Are any of the hostages hurt?"

"None of your business."

The edge in his voice alarmed me. "Okay. Tell me about yourself." I wouldn't bring up Will's father, because the mention of his name might push Will further into his anger zone. "I know you're married with two children. What's your wife's name?"

"Felicia."

"Beautiful name. I think it means 'happy' in Spanish."

"I don't know, but she is beautiful. I married up."

A man who loved his wife. Would she be able to overcome her emotional status? "What do you like the most about Felicia?"

He drew in a breath, possibly taking a drag on a cigarette. "Understanding. Acceptance. Patience."

"Those qualities are hard to find. You're a lucky man."

"I am for sure. We have two great kids."

I'd found his tender spot. "Boys? Girls?"

"One of each. Jace is seventeen and Emma is thirteen. Smart too."

"You sound proud of your family."

"For sure. I bet you never thought the likes of me was good enough to get someone like her. Or have a family someone would be proud of."

Shouting erupted in Will's background. Voices in English and

Spanish tried to outshout each other. Not good when I hadn't gotten back to finding out who might be hurt. "What's—?"

The connection on my end dropped. And so did my stomach.

Until the argument broke out, the negotiations with Will seemed to move in a positive direction. Talking about his family appealed to his calmer side. The muffled voices had been unclear, diminishing my hope for a nonviolent solution.

Skip busied himself in the back of his Jeep, sorting through the hostages' belongings. He carried a tremendous amount of responsibility for his age and experience. Without a doubt, the other agents were watching to see how he handled the challenges of hostages in jeopardy.

I joined Skip. "I'm confident at least one person is hurt."

"We've got to get them out of there before Will does more damage." He blew out his exasperation. "You know that as well as I do."

Freeing the hostages might require extreme measures. But I hoped not.

"Carrington, I have a question," Levi said a few feet from me.

Would I regret my earlier decision to allow him access? But he'd shown politeness, and his voice had a way of soothing me, so I caved. "Go ahead. Make it fast."

"I'd like to talk to Will. Sometimes I'm able to get a different perspective. I could assure him that his concerns would be heard."

I'd never trusted anyone to help and possibly damage what I wanted to accomplish. Another reason I couldn't work with a law enforcement negotiator team. I had my own methods. "I can't risk his demands escalating."

I needed more information about all three Kendrix men to analyze what motivated Will and Boyd. Will refused me access to Boyd, and I questioned the reasoning. Maybe Boyd wanted to surrender but Will refused to discuss it.

"Carrington, I've found a few things." Skip handed me a tattered backpack. "Inside are a child's items. I'd say a boy—change of clothes, teddy bear, worn baseball." He drew in a ragged sigh and pointed to the various items. "There's a diabetic supply kit—syringes, needles, alcohol wipes, an ice pack, insulin, a glucose meter, test strips, lancets, a lancing device, and snacks."

I fought the urge to moan. "Will said the hostages didn't need food or water."

"Without food, the child's blood sugar can drop too low, resulting in a diabetic coma, brain swelling, and even death." He glanced at his watch. "Best I can figure, they've been held fourteen hours, and we have no idea when the child last ate or drank."

"Carrington." Levi's warm voice broke into my thoughts. "Would Will release the child for medical care? Or allow the child to eat so he doesn't die? Surely he'd want his own kids treated well in the same circumstances."

Levi stated exactly where my thoughts had trodden. I phoned Will and asked him to call me immediately. My stomach churned for the seemingly helpless situation. Inside the house, at least one parent struggled with not only the hostage crisis but a child who could die without food or insulin—a child tossed in the path of desperation and chaos. Even worse, the child could be alone with no one to look after him.

Levi stared at the house. Could he sense my preoccupation, or was he also gravely disturbed? He turned to me. "I despise people who pick on the weak to build their egos. Give the wrong person a gun, and trouble escalates."

I picked up the bullhorn. "Will, we have a problem. A child inside needs food. I think it's a boy. He needs medical attention. Would you call me so we can talk privately?"

Will responded without hesitation. "I see reporters out there. Let them hear what you have to say."

I relayed the findings, and the reporters got an earful. "Will, would you give the boy something to eat? Without food he could go into a coma and die. What if he were your son? He's innocent in your suspicions and shouldn't have to suffer. You are a good man, and I know you'll do the right thing."

"You want the boy, meet my demands. Yeah, there's a sick kid in here. He's crying and holding his gut. His mother got herself shot by not listening to me."

"How badly is she hurt?" Carrington's chest ached.

"Leg wound. No big thing. She'll live if she keeps quiet."

"Can any of the others help her?"

"They're tied up. Should have done that with her instead of letting her take care of the sick kid."

"I can bring food and insulin for him. Place it outside the door."

"One dead person for every step you take."

"Will, I know how proud you are of your family, and you wouldn't want anything to happen to them. That tells me you care about the mother and child and wouldn't want them to die either. Release them, and I'll speak in your defense. You have my word."

"Guess what? I don't care if they live or die. All of them. Deliver on what I've asked, and I'll let these people go."

"I can't give you much more time, Will. Do the right thing."

"We're done talking, missy."

Nausea assaulted me for the little boy and his mother. The dangerous trek here to the States could've been in hopes of finding medical help for her son.

Skip called my name. "Thermal imaging still shows only one man standing, and he's holding another person next to him. My agents aren't trained snipers to risk a shot. The Border Patrol Special Operations Group—SOG—will be here around five . . . the same time as Will's deadline."

"I'm counting on his wife to find the strength to help—convince them to surrender. Let's hope he cares more for Felicia and his family than his own demands. I'm calling her back now."

I walked away with the phone to my ear.

THIRTEEN

Like before, Felicia picked up on the first ring, and I jumped into my agenda. "I'm sorry for not responding to your calls. I had an emergency and couldn't pick up."

"I understand. Is . . . is the situation any better?" A more controlled voice met me, and my own misgivings lessened. "I'll do all I can to persuade Will. He's been so distant, angry since Timothy's murder."

"Have you talked to him since yesterday afternoon, before the confrontation with Border Patrol?"

"He called yesterday, told me he loved me and the kids." Felicia gasped and swallowed what sounded like a sob. "Said he decided to seek justice for his dad's death. I asked him what he planned, and he said it didn't matter. He said I shouldn't worry. I've tried calling him three other times, but he didn't pick up. Then once more on the drive here."

"What about your children? Are they aware?"

"I told the kids their dad and Uncle Boyd had taken desperate action because of their grandpa's death, and they were in trouble with the Border Patrol. I also gave them permission to stay home from school. I hope the weekend settles down before they endure the cruel things kids might say. Who knows what the media will report?"

"I remember school days and the damage words can inflict. Do you work outside the home?"

"I'm a bank teller. I woke my boss to let her know I wouldn't be in today or tomorrow. How can I help? You said an emergency had happened?"

"A boy inside the house is sick. Will refused to let him or his mother leave for medical attention. I offered to bring meds and food, but he rejected that idea too."

"How can I convince him to release those people?" Her voice broke.

My idea of Felicia helping to rectify the dismal situation might worsen the crisis.

"I can do this." She inhaled sharply. "There's more to Will's behavior than grief. He's carrying a huge burden of inadequacy, scars buried so deep that he doesn't recognize them."

"Issues related to his father's death and the hostages?"

"Not exactly."

"Once you have tonight behind you, those issues can be addressed. With your job at the bank, I imagine you've had training in dealing with volatile people. Will is your concern. Not an irate customer. Right now, I need you to concentrate on your upcoming conversation with him. When you can speak to him, pretend the two of you are alone. Share those things that are special to you, and do not condemn or criticize. No matter what he says, avoid the words *should*, *need*, *must*, or anything that could be translated as negative to him. Also avoid the word *you* in an accusatory manner and replace any urge to use *but* with *and*. Felicia, simply be your loving, compassionate, and empathetic self. Use the words *that's right* freely, agreeing to whatever is upsetting him. He can't hear blame from you. He must feel in control."

"Some of what you've said has been part of my bank training. The goal is to calm him down. I'll remember what you've said. I simply want him to release those people."

"I caution you, if you ask him to say yes to anything, you risk him losing control. Doing the right thing must come from his perspective.

If Will and Boyd maintain their current position, they stand a good chance of getting killed. Other innocents could be hurt too. Border Patrol has requested help from their special team of trained snipers. They will be here around 5:00 a.m. Once you're on-site, you'll see county deputies. How long before you arrive?"

"Fifteen minutes or so." She sobbed. "I don't want to lose him. He's a wonderful husband and father."

"I understand. You love him and want the best for him. I believe he'll listen to you." I paused for my words to sink in.

"I will do all I can." She sucked in a breath and apologized. "What else can you tell me?"

"Will answered his phone most times when I called. He has binoculars, and he'll see you due to a floodlight near the driveway. Hopefully he'll pick up. We'll start there. If you don't receive a response, we have a bullhorn and so does he."

"I asked him why he bought that thing, and he said it was impulse. Now I know better."

"I'm impressed that you can move from your emotions and be clearheaded and ready for the next steps. That is exactly what we need. Remind Will of special memories. Think back to when you were first married, when your children were born, vacations, any of the times that would touch his longing for better times." I kept my tone low. She provided a key to unlock Will's mental instability. "I have confidence in you. Once you arrive, we'll move fast to get you fitted with a Kevlar vest and then you can have your conversation with him."

"Why the vest?"

"Protocol. The mobile command center will be listening to all calls."

"Okay. Great, my son is calling again. He wants to be there, talk to his dad. I refused. If . . . if the worst happens, I don't want Jace to see it."

"You're a wise and courageous woman. I'll see you very soon. In the meantime, call me if you need to talk. If I fail to pick up, understand I'm busy with negotiations."

Felicia had not only her husband's vengeful choices to deal with but two teenagers, who undoubtedly were worried about their parents. If those kids became orphans, how would I ever explain to them what happened? Sure, I could recommend the best counseling, but acceptance of a loss didn't compensate for a parent. I should know.

FOURTEEN

LEVI

Carrington returned from briefing Will's wife about the situation. "She'll be here in roughly fifteen minutes," she said. "Will believes he has power over us, and for the moment he does. The man's angry and a manipulator of people and circumstances. Yet he does have a weak spot—his family."

Not good. My concern for the hostages took on a new level of fear. The boy's mother's wound needed attention. She could bleed out, and if the boy didn't get food, he'd face a coma or even death. An average person could live up to three days without insulin, but did those stats apply to a child? And how could they be sure when the child had eaten or when his mother had last administered the treatment?

"Can I use Felicia's willingness to talk to her husband as a media update?" I said.

"Wait until she arrives and begins the dialogue. If Will finds out she's coming, he might feel betrayed."

Headlights and voices on my left indicated additional law enforcement and reporters were on the scene. The road to the right swung to a single lane of dirt and a dead end to pasture. Those entering the crime scene had one way in or out.

"Victoria County deputies are in place." Skip watched them pull onto the road. "I need to reach out for an update on SOG and brief the deputies. Keep in contact, and I'll do the same." He chin-pointed to the arriving vehicles. "Media's filling up the road too. Looks like at least two are TV vans."

"No more reporters," Carrington said. "Wish I could confiscate their cameras and video equipment. Please, keep them beyond the barricade."

"Yes, ma'am. Are you still okay with Ehrlich here?"

"Yes, he's good for now."

I reached out to shake Skip's hand. "Levi."

"I'm Skip."

Carrington blew out a breath. "I should have introduced both of you. My apologies."

"No problem. We have other fish to fry here." Skip returned the gesture with good eye contact and a firm shake before he walked toward the barricade.

"There's a Jewish proverb that fits," I said. "'Do not withhold good from those who deserve it, when it is in your power to act.'"

"Wise, Levi. Thanks."

I silently pleaded for guidance and a whole lot of wisdom. "There are two sides to every story, and we're defined by the choices we make. The people who crossed the border. The brothers avenging their father's death. The mother or parents worried about their sick child. They all have reasons motivating them into action, and those are more important than anything else going on."

She peered at me in her peculiar way that made me feel like I was splayed out on a slide under a microscope. I wanted to say more, but my talkative nature sometimes made others uncomfortable.

She brushed her chestnut-colored hair back behind her ears. "You're a good friend, Levi. I hope I don't live to regret my transparency with you or the outcome of the negotiations. Seems like I'm wading in murky waters."

"You have nothing to fear from me. I despise injustice as much as you do. You've got this."

"You have more confidence in me than I have in myself." She

glanced at the time on her phone. "I need the BP to move faster before SOG arrives. The info I requested from Skip is critical to figuring out what happened to Timothy Kendrix, the brothers' father, but I'm afraid it doesn't matter at this point." Her shoulders lifted and fell. "Never mind me. I'm a bit anxious."

"Waiting is the hardest when lives are at stake."

"Waiting is my Achilles' heel. I keep telling myself to focus on the now and not to fixate on what might happen."

I moved closer to her, our shoulders nearly touching while we leaned back against Skip's Jeep. I longed to put my arm around her waist. Another time. Another place.

Shouts from behind us demanded we answer questions. Neither of us acknowledged the reporters. "I detest all the media showing up like flies on manure." She tossed me a sad smile. "Nothing personal. We all have jobs to do."

"The difference is in how we do it."

"True. My problem is, without more detailed background, I can't get inside Will's mind. Without empathy for Will himself, I won't get anywhere. Then we contend with a serious problem before sunrise."

"Wish I could be more help, other than a sounding board and pray."

"I'm not on God's welcome list, but I've been asking for a little help." She drew in a labored breath. "If not for the sick child, Will and Boyd might try to use the media to garner sympathy. If those brothers look like victims, they still might succeed."

My cell pinged. Frank. I answered out of respect.

"Levi, I'm here at the site, but I can't get through the barricade. Looks like you have an exclusive. Makes for front-page news. I brought a camera guy." He sounded like a kid with a new bike.

"Ms. Reed is approving every word."

She pointed to the MCC and disappeared.

"Forget that. We need the ratings. A live reporting gets the ball rolling. We want an interview with the Reed woman ASAP."

"Not happening. I've sent timely updates." Call it fed up or righteous indignation, but my mouth hit fourth gear. "I gave my word, and I'm not backing down."

"I see you up there. Turn around and look." I glanced behind me. The balding man, tall and thin, stood with the phone at his ear. "When do we listen to what someone wants?"

"I told you I gave my word. I can't invite any media inside the barricade unless she agrees. The camera guy can shoot his footage from back there. His zoom works just fine."

"Your sarcasm has reached its limit. Video coverage will put us at the top and ensure we have the best exclusive."

"No, Frank."

"I also need live interviews with the negotiator, Border Patrol agents, family of the hostage takers, family of the hostages, and any other key figures. Even the men holding the hostages. Get over here. You're wasting time."

I pocketed my phone and walked to Frank, where three BP agents kept the crowd behind an erected barrier of men, crime-scene tape, and vehicles. Reporters and news anchors rushed forward, calling out my name and firing questions. Cameras flashed and videos rolled, but I focused on Frank. No matter what I said to the media, they'd demand more. Or twist my words.

The camera stayed on me. Great. A live feed. My normally composed temper rose a notch.

"Tell these uniforms that it's okay to let us inside. Why are you dragging your feet?"

"If I let you through, we have no story."

"I need an interview with the Reed woman." Frank scanned the area. "Where is she?"

"Taking care of responsibilities."

"She's in the house negotiating the hostage release?"

I said nothing.

"When can I talk to her?"

"I'm not sure."

Frank pointed behind me. "There she is leaving the command center. Call her over here."

Carrington wasn't a dog that I could whistle at, and she'd come running. "I'll tell her you'd like an interview."

"Either persuade the woman to allow me and the camera guy inside the barricade or you're fired."

I inhaled to gain control. "Suit yourself, Frank. Freelance looks real good right now."

"One last chance or I ruin your career."

I sensed more than one camera aimed at Carrington and me. I made my way back to Skip's Jeep and faced her. "I apologize for the heckler. He wants an interview."

"Not happening. Is he a reporter?"

"My boss." I huffed. "Ex-boss since he just fired me."

"How did you manage to lose your job when I agreed to give you an up-front and personal story?"

Telling her the truth made me look like a schoolboy vying for the teacher's favor. "Differences of opinion. No worries. My gain." I'd figure out how to continue giving to help other people who struggled with drug and alcohol addiction.

She laid her phone on the Jeep's hood. Her impassive expression led me to think her mind had waded deeper into the murky waters she'd mentioned earlier. Not sure I could keep my composure in her shoes.

"Are you okay?" I said.

"Just processing. Will is watching us through binoculars." She turned to me. "No indication if he reads lips but be careful."

FIFTEEN

CARRINGTON

Before Felicia arrived, I needed to call Charlotte Bolton back. The poor woman wasn't getting much sleep tonight—or rather, this morning. Pressing in her number, I stepped a few feet away from Levi for privacy.

"Mrs. Bolton, this is Carrington Reed. I'm sorry for the delay in getting back to you."

"You have your hands full. I'll continue with my story about Dorie and me. One morning I surprised her with a jar of homemade prickly pear jelly and a loaf of homemade bread. Dorie answered the door with a black eye and broken nose. Ah, she was a mess. The boys should have been in school, but I heard the TV going. She stood in the doorway, and we talked. Will and Boyd got curious and wanted to see who was there. Will had bruises on his face and arms, and I asked Dorie what happened. She said they'd fallen chasin' chickens. They'd got loose and needed to be put up so the coyotes wouldn't eat 'em. Trust me, I knew Timothy had beaten his wife and oldest son. Nobody gets hurt chasin' chickens till they're black and blue. I wanted to take a switch to him."

Mrs. Bolton blew out her exasperation, but the gesture might have been for my benefit. "Some folks thought he hung the moon, but that day I saw the devil in him. I confronted Dorie about what I was sure he'd done, and she broke down with the truth. She begged me not to tell anyone. Said she and Will would suffer for it. I kept my word until now, and she's been gone a long time."

How had Boyd escaped the beatings? "Was that the only time you knew about Timothy abusing his family?"

"Mercy, no. After the first time, Dorie opened up more about his temper. He'd destroy things. Hit her and Will usually where nobody could see. I told her to leave him, but he'd threatened to find and kill her if she did. Tell you what, whoever blew a hole through Timothy Kendrix did the world a favor. Dorie died of a heart attack, and she's in heaven. But I think she lost the desire to live, especially after the boys were old enough to leave home. Not sure why she stayed."

"Why did he favor Boyd?"

"I always thought it was because he looked more like Timothy. Boyd made good grades and excelled in sports."

"Do you have any idea who had motive to shoot him?" A twinge of suspicion caused me to question her involvement. She'd called the BP office . . . to help or cast any doubt from herself?

"Not my way to accuse anyone. I'm in assisted living, so don't go thinkin' I pulled the trigger. Dorie wanted to, and who would have blamed her? Back then, Timothy liked the ladies from south of the border. Mistreated them too. Dorie said at least when he was out with one of them, he wasn't botherin' her. Ma'am, I have no idea who killed him. No one in particular. I'm just repeatin' what I heard and saw."

"Thank you, Mrs. Bolton. Is there anyone I can talk to who might have additional information about the Kendrix family?"

"Let me think . . . Far-fetched, but you might see if any of the boys' teachers are still alive. They don't keep records that far back. Dorie said the middle school principal came to see her and Timothy about the belt marks on Will's back. The PE teacher saw and reported it. Timothy told the principal that Will had slipped on some rocks while playin' and cut himself. I don't think either of those boys would have told their friends about their dad for fear of what might happen at home. The few people who befriended Dorie are gone now or have dementia."

"I'll look into what you've told me. Thank you for calling in your information. If you think of anything more, would you please contact me or the Border Patrol office?"

"I sure will. Hate to see those boys in trouble, and I sure don't understand why they care if that scrum of a man is gone."

I thanked her again and stared at my phone. The conversation with the Kendrixes' neighbor stunned me, and I thought I'd numbed myself to surprises. My mind seemed to explode with the discrepancies of Will and Boyd's reason to abduct the hostages and Mrs. Bolton's words. Had one of those brothers killed their dad and blamed the undocumented immigrants? Was money involved? If Timothy still abused women prior to his death, one of them or a family member could have decided to seek revenge. Had Mrs. Bolton told me everything?

Did Timothy truly have an abusive side? Had the worry about my eyesight shattered my reasoning?

When I had time, I'd check out her accusations. The MCC had it all recorded for them to analyze. I'd prefer to keep the information to myself for now and not share it with Levi. He'd heard far more than I ever permitted.

Getting answers before 5:00 a.m. slipped into an impossibility, but Skip might be able to speed up the negotiations. I pressed in his number.

"Hey, Skip. I know you're dealing with this crowd and searching for solutions, but do you have time to check on a few more things?" When he agreed, I gave him my list.

"I can pass your requests to the MCC. The info you requested won't be available for a few more hours. I heard the conversation with Charlotte Bolton from there."

"If she's telling the truth, and I have no reason to doubt her, Timothy Kendrix might have had more than one person who wanted him dead. Confirmation on her claims would help. I want to think about it more, perhaps listen to the MCC's recording."

Skip cleared his throat. "I have a notepad in front of me. Regarding her suggestion to contact the schools, they aren't required to keep records that far back. Slim chance that any of the boys' teachers are still around, but I could check."

I smiled sadly. "Locating anyone who knew them could take days. I wonder if the principal of the middle school is still alive or if he has family in the area. Hmm. Google might have answers to those questions. What about hospitals?"

"Highly unlikely we'd learn anything before sunrise."

"True. I need to use every tactic I can think of to delay Will's actions. Could we ask if any of the doctors, nurses, or staff are still around who might remember Will, Boyd, or their mother?"

"I'll have someone check with one of our directors. Anything else?"

"One more thing. Has the sheriff's department investigated Timothy's financials? What about his will? I really appreciate your help, Skip, and for keeping the media back. You are doing an outstanding job with crowd control and working toward a peaceful end."

He hesitated. "Thanks. As soon as I have the answers to your requests, I'll pass them on. For the record, the media's not happy. Gotta go."

I held my phone and mentally walked through my tactics. Would Will pick up on a call after he said he was finished? I tried his cell. As expected, it went to voicemail. "Will, I've learned critical information. It has an impact on solving your father's death. Would you call me? I need your help. We don't want all these people to hear our conversation over the bullhorn."

Another waiting game. But instead of concentrating on my normal overcoming method, I waved at Levi to approach me. He smiled and I shivered. Not sure why his presence offered an eerie comfort. I'd always liked and admired him, but having him this close caused my secret longing for a relationship to wade into deeper waters. Who'd want a woman going blind? How could I master tells without my vision?

"Did the neighbor woman give you helpful info?" he said.

"Oh, yes. My mind's whirling with the best way to proceed." I reflected on part of the conversation with Mrs. Bolton. "Will claimed his father left food and water for the undocumented immigrants, but the image Mrs. Bolton gave me was quite the contrary."

"You deal with people's behavior, earning their trust and helping them make good decisions. But murder is a beast because it's seldom simple. You do all that's humanly possible to prevent the bear from charging." No flattery infused his voice or existed in his body language.

"I long for Will to talk to me. I sense a motive here that we haven't detected."

Levi stood beside me. No conversation. He had somehow sensed my turmoil and given me silent support . . . just as he'd done right from the start. I needed to find a few flaws in him. After this was over. Nobody was that perfect.

I picked up the bullhorn. "Will, listen to your voicemail and call me. I have new information and need you to confirm it. I'm your friend, but I'm being pressured by the BP and county sheriff's department. Please respond."

Levi lifted his face to the dark sky, his eyes closed. He was praying.

SIXTEEN

Memories and techniques used in other negotiations scrolled through my mind. All were different. All were the same.

Perspiration dotted my forehead, although the early morning humid temps settled in the low seventies. My typical overheated reaction to worrying about the safety of those held against their will while I searched for a solution. I craved composure and attempted to toss my mounting concerns aside. My purpose in life simmered through me—to help others see that loss of control and vengeance only made matters worse. Taking lives to satisfy an emotional madness never worked, but too often those wielding a weapon were beyond convincing.

Getting inside Will's head was key to finding out what set the stage for his behavior. Had Mrs. Bolton lied? Why would she? A personal vendetta? Her words and Will's drastic steps to avenge a supposedly cruel father confused me. Unless he possessed a deep-rooted desire to please his father at all costs. Was the hostage situation Will's misguided attempt to somehow gain approval from his father? For that matter, did Will have an alibi for the time of his father's death? Did Boyd?

My phone rang, and Will's name hit the screen, but I didn't motion Levi away. He'd hear the one-sided conversation and might offer insight. If the conversation edged toward confidentiality, I'd gesture for him to step back. I desperately needed this attempt to persuade Will before 5:00 a.m. crested the horizon.

"I'm here," Will said. "This had better be good. I'm losing patience."

His high-pitched voice neared manic, a mental lack of control. "Will, first of all how are you and Boyd?"

"My little brother is a wuss."

"What's wrong?"

"I got it handled."

Dare I hope Boyd wanted out? I feigned a yawn. "I'm having a hard time staying awake. What about you?"

"I'd share my pills, but I don't want to run out."

His response confirmed the Kendrixes' level of advance planning. But not what he'd taken. "How is the injured mother and sick boy?"

He swore. "Both are still alive. Of course, what happens to them is up to you and the law enforcement storming the area like I'm a fugitive. Stupid when I'm helping you in a murder case."

I heard *I* and not *we*. I'd pray, but no deity had answered my prayers when my loved ones stared down death, and I couldn't expect preferential treatment from a God who might not be there. "I'd like to bring the boy food and insulin, plus a first-aid kit for his mother. You and I will talk about how best to resolve the problems. Doesn't change your demand for justice, only provides medical care for two suffering people."

"Nope. They should have thought about the risks before they crossed into Texas."

"Will, I know you're blaming all undocumented immigrants for your father's death."

"You bet I am. If they hadn't been allowed into our country, my father would still be alive."

"One person pulled the trigger, not a whole culture. Not innocent people or a child. Law enforcement is working hard to gather evidence and make an arrest."

"About time." Will snorted. "I asked them to find the killer, not strut their stuff in front of me."

I looked for a different approach. "You and Boyd want justice for his unsolved murder. I can't blame you. But information has come to my attention that bothers me, and I'm sure you'll know if it's true or false."

"What is it?"

"A person claimed your father beat your mother, Boyd, and you. And he was unfaithful."

"Who told you those lies?" His low voice seeped anger. "I'll kill the person for dishonoring him."

"I'm not at liberty to provide a name or names. I thought your answer might help find his killer."

"Who's trying to destroy my father's reputation? Boyd's girlfriend? That crazy old woman Mrs. Bolton?"

"Will, it's confidential."

"I'll find out. Or I'll strangle it out of you."

"Why are you threatening me? I'm the one who doesn't want to see you or the others hurt." From years of experience, I'd learned to put aside any apprehension for my personal safety during negotiations. A Kevlar vest boosted my courage unless the shooter aimed for my head. "I'm not the enemy. What's going on that you don't want to tell me?"

"I never asked for your help. I don't need you."

"Do you understand the outcome if I walk away?"

"Yep. I'll either have the killer or I'll eliminate these hostages."

"I'd rather talk through your concerns and come to an agreement. Abandoning you to the Border Patrol and county deputies has serious implications."

"You have my terms."

"Are you ready to sacrifice your life and possibly your brother's? I don't want that for either of you. Think about your family and the legacy you want to leave your wife and children. You claim law enforcement is doing nothing, but you haven't given the authorities time to conduct a thorough investigation."

"I demand justice!"

"Will, are you afraid of what they might uncover? The family abuse? The other things your father did and thought no one knew?" I took a deep breath to let my words sink in. "Family secrets are the hardest to resolve."

From the corner of my eye, I thought I saw movement on the right side of the house, but my peripheral vision was questionable, especially in the darkness. A man stepped into my full vision with his hands up. Could he be Boyd? I concentrated on the dialogue with Will.

The man moved toward the blockade. "I'm Boyd Kendrix." His voice rose above the night sounds. "I'm unarmed and coming in. I was tricked into what has happened by my brother's craziness, and he held me at gunpoint too. I haven't shot or hurt anyone."

I'd keep Will talking until his brother made it to safety. "Tell me about the last time you and your dad were together."

Boyd, hurry before it's too late. I glanced around at the MCC. Skip rushed my way.

Will cursed. "What is Boyd doing out there? I'll show him what happens to a coward and a traitor."

I heard a crash as though he'd tossed his phone. Would Will shoot his own—?

Rifle fire rang out. Boyd fell face down.

SEVENTEEN

LEVI

Carrington tensed with the gunfire. "No," she whispered. "Please, no."

Another shot rang out and zoomed past her head. I grabbed her shoulders and pushed her to the ground out of the line of fire. Law enforcement fired back. The threat of the hostages being hit in the crossfire shook me.

"Are you hurt?" I said.

"No. What about Boyd?"

A quick look at the man's still body about seventy feet away shoved adrenaline into my system. "Stay put. I'll get him to safety."

"Levi—"

I ignored her protests and bent low to rush toward him past the floodlight into the enveloping shadows of the landscape. I prayed the man still breathed life and I could help him to safety. Shots whistled dangerously close, but I couldn't dwell on them. A strange sense of empowerment swept through me, more than my body infusing energy into my muscles. I'd felt the hyperfocused sensation before in similar situations, as though I wore blinders to the world around me. I wasn't invincible, and I had no illusions about life and death—with a few scars to prove it.

I raced closer to Boyd, and the surreal stayed strong with a purpose beyond my comprehension. Shots continued to ring out. Dropping beside the injured man, I spoke Boyd's name. He moaned. An increasing dark liquid pooled on the back of his left side where the bullet had entered. He'd die without immediate medical attention.

"I'm getting you to an ambulance."

"No . . . use. He's a . . . good shot."

"Stay with me, Boyd."

"I . . . can't."

But God was more powerful than a crazed man. "You're hurt bad, and I've been right where you are. You don't want to move or have anyone touch you. But you can survive and live. Don't even think otherwise."

Two BP agents hunched around us. I hadn't heard or seen them approach.

"Hey, buddy." I recognized Skip's voice. "We have an ambulance ready." He glanced up at me. "You and I can carry him while my partner here covers us."

"Let's do it." He hesitated and I captured his attention. "What's the problem? Boyd is hurt badly and needs medical attention."

"Your arm?"

I startled and whirled both ways to find out what Skip was talking about. Sure enough, I'd been hit in the left upper arm. Hadn't even felt it. Still didn't. Must just be a surface wound. "I'm good. Time's wasting."

We positioned our arms around each side of Boyd's waist, me using my right arm. We lifted and half dragged his body toward the awaiting paramedics. That's when I felt the sting in my arm, like a swarm of bees had attacked me at the same time. I blinked and kept my side of Boyd steady. I never thought the short distance could seem like such a long mile. I blinked back dizziness and sucked in air.

Help us, Lord. Help Boyd.

Once beyond the barricade, paramedics took over Boyd's care. One took his vitals while another applied a bandage and started an IV. Boyd slipped into unconsciousness. A third paramedic kept the engine running in the ambulance. In one smooth movement, the paramedics placed Boyd on a gurney, and the vehicle left with flashing lights and screaming sirens. He hadn't regained consciousness.

A female paramedic from the second ambulance, a younger woman who enjoyed eye makeup, asked to look at my arm. "We should get you to the hospital."

"No way. Pour some hydrogen peroxide on it and slap on a Band-Aid." I had a personal stake in those people inside the house—the diabetic boy, his mother, and the others.

Skip chuckled. "Such a hero. I've read your articles and viewed your interviews. You've survived a few scary scenarios. The BP needs to recruit you."

"No, thanks. I don't like guns."

"That's an understatement. From the looks of your arm, they don't like you either."

The paramedic went to work. "It's a little deep, but the bullet exited."

I winced. Her digging hit my pain threshold. "Just patch me up. I'm all right."

"You need stitches and an antibiotic. When was your last tetanus shot?"

"I get them on a regular basis."

She laughed and gave her attention to Skip. "Make sure he sees the ER when this ordeal is over."

"Yes, ma'am."

Carrington made her way over from the MCC. She rubbed her arms. "You crazy fool. You could have been killed."

"Amazing what a man will do for a story." I drew in a breath to mask the pain. "Oh, I bet you saw my irresistible charm. I'm alive and well, in the good hands of a lovely, capable paramedic."

"You talk a lot when you're hurt?" Carrington said.

"My nature. I'll make sure to mention your compassion in my story."

"Wrong. Going after Boyd had nothing to do with your assignment or shoving me out of harm's way or impressing me. It's who you are." She offered a faint smile. "Thanks, I owe you."

Strange how a man could endure an open wound and feel strangely whole because of a woman's smile. "You're welcome. And yes, I have a reputation for being a crazy fool."

She crossed her arms over her chest and blinked.

When the hostage situation ended, I'd do my best to convince her to give me another chance. "Hey, anyone else hurt?"

"We don't know about the hostages, but law enforcement are unharmed."

"Have you heard from Will?"

"Nothing." Her haunting eyes penetrated me. "I won't give up."

"The hostages—"

"They are more in danger than before." She peered around me. "Are you Felicia Kendrix?"

I turned as a petite woman with long, dark hair and eyes approached with an agent.

"I am. I heard shots. Will shot this man?"

Carrington drew in a breath. "Three people—a woman inside the house, Boyd, and Mr. Ehrlich here, who risked his life to get Boyd to safety."

Felicia covered her mouth and nearly fell if not for the agent supporting her. "I saw the ambulance speed away, so that must have been Boyd. What hospital?"

"DeTar in Victoria."

"I should have gotten here sooner. How badly is he hurt?"

Carrington shook her head. "The mobile command center will receive any updates from the first responders. I'll give those to you as soon as we hear."

Felicia gave me her attention. "Sir, I'm so sorry."

"The paramedic is doing a great job."

Will's wife, short-haired and slender, sobbed softly. "Please, get me ready to talk to Will before anyone else is hurt."

EIGHTEEN

CARRINGTON

I led Felicia to the MCC for a Kevlar vest fitting. She trembled and more than once gasped for air. Her gaze captured mine.

"Thank you for coming and for your willingness to help your husband and the hostages," I said. "I don't want anyone else hurt. We simply want the nightmare to end."

Felicia studied me. "I've been to this house a few times. Never thought it would be a crime scene. Boyd wanted to renovate it for renters." She expelled a sigh filled with agony.

"And you fully understand the risks?"

Felicia nodded.

"At any time you feel uncomfortable, return to safety."

"You're recommending I don't walk up to the house?"

"Felicia, he shot his brother with the intent to kill. Boyd may die."

She took a few deep breaths, no doubt to ward off the panic. "Do I even know my husband?" Her lips quivered, and she rubbed her forehead, but otherwise she appeared okay.

I would not desert her, Will, the boy with diabetes, his mother, or any of the other hostages. Their welfare seared my commitment to them as though their cries for help were branded on my soul. Perhaps I should be the one knocking on the door for Will.

"I believe love rules our actions, and love rules who we are," I said. "We don't want Will to know we're monitoring the conversation. If he asks, please tell him you're unsure."

"Lie? I can't break his trust."

I couldn't blame her, considering Will's emotional stress. "I appreciate your respect for him. Let's hope he doesn't pose the question." I stared at the house. Every moment sped toward his mandated deadline.

Together we walked to where Levi stood by the Jeep. "Levi, would you mind moving back several feet? Felicia is calling Will, and I'll be in the mobile command center."

He lifted his chin and smiled—one filled with reassurance. Whatever confusing attraction I felt for him needed to take a hike. I had no time for emotional indulgences. The only rush I needed was a clear head and stamina to work successfully through this negotiation.

I wanted to give Felicia a hug, but with Will watching, he might think we'd coerced her into talking to him. Which in essence we had, but no point tossing reality into the mix of his unpredictability.

Felicia pulled her phone from her jeans pocket and walked about fifteen feet up the light-filled driveway.

Please, Will, don't shoot Felicia.

I made my way to the MCC. There I'd listen in with Commander Lopez and Skip. No conversation in a negotiation ever went to waste. Facts were drawn. Behavior understood. And mistakes used as teaching moments for those longing to learn new techniques.

Inside the center, I picked up headphones and adjusted them. Skip stood to give me his chair, but I shook my head. Too antsy to sit, and I needed to hear every word. Will's voice sounded in my ear.

"I saw you with the negotiator woman. Nothing's going to change my mind. Go home, Felicia. The kids need you." Will's tone displayed gentleness. A good beginning.

"They're fine. My place is with you."

"No. Never has been. You're too good for the likes of me. Like Dad always said . . . I'm a coward."

"You're my hero."

"Has the news broadcasted what I've done?"

"Reports are conflicting. I ignored them."

"Why are you here?"

"Because I love you." Felicia drew in a sob. "And to ask you how I can help you through this. Border Patrol and the sheriff's department are upset about the hostages."

"I can't release them until they show me proof of an arrest for Dad's murder."

"Why?" She kept her voice soft. "You hated him, and you're such a good man. Explain it to me, Will. I don't understand. He treated you and your mother horribly. Beat you. Left scars. Now you're finally free of him." She drew in an unsteady breath. "I don't mean to sound callous. I'm simply confused, and you've always explained things to me."

"He got away with lots of crimes, but his troubled ways didn't make it right for someone to kill him."

"You're right, Will. Absolutely right. I beg you to let those working the investigation do their jobs. They need more time to gather evidence and talk to people. We could help them."

"Whose side are you on?" Will's words grew louder.

"Yours, always yours. My concern is, how long will the law enforcement assigned to this hold out before they take drastic action?"

"I have life insurance. After all these years, don't you get me at all?" He spit out his words.

"I want to. I'm trying to."

"This goes deeper than you realize. More than I've ever told you."

"Tell me now. No one has ever listened to you like me."

"What if you disrespect me for what I have to say?"

"Never."

"I'm not sure. It's impossible."

"Don't make your children orphans and me a widow. We need you. Love you."

"Some things a man must do for himself. For the record, Boyd had no clue what I planned. I needed help and used him . . . my own brother. Is he alive?"

"As far as I know. If I walk up this driveway to the house, would you let me take the sick boy and his injured mother for medical help?"

"No way. If I shot my brother, why would I release those two? Or not pull the trigger on you?"

"Because you're a good man. You care about others, not like your father. You. Aren't. Timothy Kendrix."

"How do you know?"

"I've seen your heart." She took a step forward. "Once there with you, I need your strength to help me through every day." Felicia's voice never wavered from a soft pleading.

I closed my eyes while she fought for her family.

"Take one more step, and I'll pull the trigger on another hostage. A body for each step. I won't shoot you, but I have no problem killing these people."

"Then what do I tell Jace and Emma?"

"Make up a good story."

"You love your children. You have always been here for our family. You've shown us a man who loves unconditionally."

"I have nothing to lose, Felicia. The sleepless nights and memories won't give me peace."

"All right. Whatever you choose to do, remember I love you. I'm staying on-site until you release those people. I know you will do the right thing. I believe in you."

"Those illegals robbed me of the right to kill that animal. My right!"

My stomach flipped! Now I understood his retribution. The rage mounting in him all these years from his father's abuse and betrayal had shoved Will into an emotional state where he'd be difficult to reach. He needed professional help, and those hostages needed to be free of his madness.

Felicia placed her phone at her side and stared at the house. Firm. Resolute. She blew him a kiss. I had underestimated an incredibly courageous woman.

How could I talk Will down when uncontrollable anger had driven him to madness? I had an idea how to show Will my sincerity.

NINETEEN

My dad used to describe intuition as an unexplainable gut feeling, a reason for action that had no logic or conscious thought. He claimed intuition saved lives and solved crimes. When I was a child, I didn't understand what Dad meant, but later I became involved in learning how and why people responded to life's ups and downs. Behavior intrigued me, and the science led me to develop negotiating skills. My dad had used intuition to save lives and solve crimes. Together we'd have been a formidable team . . . if he'd lived.

Will's unpredictable behavior and mental instability had more twists and turns than hairpin curves on a mountain road.

Tears flowed down Felicia's cheeks. "He is in God's hands."

"You did a wonderful job. You can be very proud of yourself. Will could think about your conversation and change his mind."

Felicia shook her head. "Never thought he'd threaten to kill others if I tried to help injured people. He has never raised his voice at me or the kids. He doesn't drink, smoke, swear, or chase women. What happened to him? Has his father's abuse taken over his mental state?" She paused. "When this is over, I'll tell you what I know about Timothy Kendrix."

"Abuse paves the way for victims to show unpredictable behavior."

She stiffened as though dispelling reality. "You work with people who say and do strange things. Why do you think Will took those hostages?"

I ached for the hurting woman. "Without counseling him, I can only offer possibilities. Perhaps Timothy had a sense of power or control over him, even in death. Will indicated Timothy was respected in the community, but I haven't spoken with anyone who verified it."

"Timothy bragged about doing things for the community, but I never saw any evidence." Contempt laced her words. She focused on the road lined with cars and flashing lights—trained men and women with weapons, while others fought with words. "Timothy damaged Will in a way I don't think I can fix. A part of him is unreachable. I'm not ready to leave here in an ambulance. Neither am I ready to bury my husband. I did my best to help him and those poor people trapped inside. I need to let Lyndie, Boyd's fiancée, know about the shooting." Felicia walked into the shadows behind me.

I took a glimpse of the time—4:20 a.m.

TWENTY

LEVI

I turned my attention to the dirt driveway and house. How many victims and offenders had Carrington lost? From what I'd witnessed and knew from our brief conversations tonight, I sensed she hit bottom when negotiations turned into a tragedy. And that very thing was about to happen.

Carrington stood beside me at the Jeep.

"How are you holding up?" I said.

"I must be tired, or why else would I be sharing case information with a reporter?"

Ah, a bit of humor. "I'm the good guy."

"I believe you are, Levi. I appreciate all you've done tonight." She massaged her neck muscles. "A peaceful solution won't happen with SOG."

"If it's any consolation, I'm praying for that too."

"You mentioned prayer before. You're Christian or Jewish?"

"Messianic Jew."

"I see."

"Are you a believer?" When she glanced away, uneasiness settled between us. "I've posed an awkward question. My apologies."

"I've asked plenty of uncomfortable questions in my lifetime. As a child and a teen, I attended church, but I have no idea if God even exists. I've seen too much evil from those who are supposedly made in God's image."

"People choose their behavior. It's their right."

"True. I've prayed a few times in my life. Even about the current situation. As a teen, I asked God to show Himself so I could understand the whole faith thing. Nothing then and nothing now resulted from prayer."

"The thing is, God can't be explained. He must be experienced."

"Which requires faith, and I don't have that. Not so sure I want it."

I looked into the quiet, starlit night. Here I stood with a beautiful woman at a hostage site where peoples' lives were at stake, talking about God. Thinking about spiritual matters and asking for wisdom and guidance flowed into my life, but discussing them with Carrington made me feel like I was peddling a cure-all. Looked like my faith had a long way to go.

"I apologize for talking about spiritual things in the middle of negotiations," I said.

"It's all right. Strangely enough, I hope someone inside that house is praying for God to intervene." A few awkward moments passed until she picked up the conversation again. "Even if SOG is the only way to end this, I can't drive home without offering some assistance to those who need it. A good ten minutes have passed without a sound from inside the house. How long does Will intend to hold out?"

"Another reason why regardless of the outcome, Felicia and her family will need counseling."

"Right. And the resources are out there." She sighed. "How do you take notes?"

Good, a change of topic. "I use my phone to record or type."

"If it's hacked you have the Cloud?"

"Yes. And I have lots of security extras. When I finish covering a story, I transfer the info to my laptop and delete what's been on the phone."

"Makes sense."

"Are any of the media people here your friends?" she said.

"If I confide in them about what's going on here, I'll only have friends until tonight is over." I chuckled to break the despairing tension around us. "We aren't all bloodthirsty parasites sniffing out the worst to write a news piece. Many of us fight for accuracy and to eliminate fake news."

"You're rooted in ensuring that others have access to both sides of a story. The truth and how actions affect others."

"Like you, Carrington. We are passionate about attempting the impossible and willing to die for what we believe in."

She moistened her lips. "Who are you, Levi Ehrlich?"

"I could ask the same of you. We seem to have known each other a lifetime instead of snippets of danger and a conversation over dinner."

"Definitely awkward when . . ." She looked at the ground and her cheeks flushed pink.

Carrington felt the chemistry too. The woman had captured me, created a longing to pursue a relationship. She scared me, and I'm sure I shook her too. Now to see which one of us ran in the opposite direction first.

While Carrington appeared deep in thought, I typed into my phone additional hostage-negotiation info with my thoughts in quotation marks. Will's reason for holding the hostages made sense to only him, considering his father's cruelty. Boyd had escaped the insanity and his brother's betrayal. I'd taken a few pics with my phone of the surroundings and the house holding the hostages, but no identifying faces to exploit those involved. I'd share them with Carrington for her approval. My typing continued.

Hecklers called my name. Not worth my time to respond. A few would stab me in the back for a story. A few were friends, good friends. Later I'd explain how I'd given my word to Carrington. A quick visual showed the road had exploded with more law enforcement and media vehicles. Lights flashed, and the area lit up like an arena. A female reporter conducted a live accounting. Normally I'd be in the thick of digging for a solid story, listening, and forming my angle. According to a news bulletin on my phone, the crisis had gone national. How would Will respond to the attention? My guess, in his state of mind, he'd increase his demands.

Felicia walked to us from the shadows, and we greeted her. "I'm having a hard time focusing on where Will's choices are taking him."

Carrington wrapped her arm around the petite woman's waist. "Our emotions are the most difficult to understand. I'll do all I can to make sure he's treated fairly."

Felicia glanced at me, a twinge of alarm on her face.

I should have stepped back so they could speak privately. "Your words go no farther than me."

She nodded and turned to Carrington. "I'd like to talk to Agent Reyes. Will you go with me?"

The two women disappeared. SOG's expected arrival would hit the radar any minute. They were Border Patrol's SWAT team, trained and tactically equipped to aid law enforcement in volatile situations.

TWENTY-ONE

Everyone involved tonight had seized desperation in various stages of stress . . . from the hostages longing for rescue to the media craving the best story. I'd seen the worst and best of mankind, and given the right circumstances, we all could lie, plead, placate, manipulate, and however else we chose for our benefit. Truth reigned king. Always.

A notion punched me hard, and I studied the house. The events of the evening spread across my mind. Where had such a crazy idea come from? I huffed. The same place as my other wild antics. My overprotective gene had kicked in for those in danger, and I refused to stand by and watch with a helpless mentality.

I grasped the bullhorn from the hood of Skip's Jeep and the backpack containing the child's snacks and meds. I brought the bullhorn to my mouth and moved up the driveway—the forbidden zone. "Will, this is Levi. I'm unarmed. I want to talk—help you find peaceful means to solving your dad's death."

"Are you a negotiator?"

I hadn't expected him to respond. "No. I'm a man who looks for truth and lets the world hear about it."

"You're gonna get yourself killed. I've pulled the trigger more than once tonight."

I lifted my bandaged arm and winced. "I've met your rifle." I moved along the dirt and gravel driveway.

A crack of rifle fire and a whistle flew over my head. "That's a warning. Next one meets flesh. Like your arm."

"Levi."

Carrington's voice blared, but I wore blinders until I talked to Will. Hurried footsteps sounded closer. In the next moment, Carrington walked alongside me.

"You're assuming a role that's mine," she whispered and grabbed the bullhorn. "Will, we're both coming. I believe we can find a satisfactory solution." She laid the bullhorn on the ground, removed her Kevlar, and tossed her Glock. "Looks like he'll need to shoot both of us."

Although not surprised by her actions, frustration doused me at Carrington deliberately putting herself in danger. "Are we fools together?" I said.

"Depends if we have a plan."

"You're the negotiator."

"You claim to have the God-thing."

"I do. But God knows you're trained. I'm not. Note, Will hasn't said a word or fired another shot."

"He wants a way out or we'd be dead," Carrington said. "Are you sure you want to continue? I expect SOG at any moment."

"Yes, without a doubt."

We walked to the front door in sad need of paint. No hint of sunrise, so we entered darkness in every respect. She squared her shoulders and knocked.

"Door's open," Will said.

I turned the knob and stepped in first. The house smelled of unwashed bodies and fear. Quiet sobbing came from the left.

"Welcome to your death sentence." Will kicked the door shut behind us and jabbed a rifle into my chest.

I glanced at the rifle barrel aimed at my heart and the angry man above it, meeting the hooded eyes of Will Kendrix.

"The lady's a negotiator," Will said. "But why are you here? Trying to prove you're a hero?"

"Not at all. I see a man who's about to throw away his life when his wife and kids care about him. If my dad had been killed, I'd do everything I could for justice."

Will humphed. "You wanting to join me and fight the system?"

"No. Just toss back and forth ideas. Who knows? Between the three of us, we might figure out who's responsible for your dad's death. For sure the investigation will find the guilty person. Your input is an asset."

"I'm doing my part right now." He pushed me back against the wall with the rifle barrel.

Looked like I'd successfully irritated him.

"Will," Carrington said, "put the gun down. Let's talk about how to resolve the problems without anyone else getting hurt. It's clear the system has disappointed you."

He swore. "It has. More than once. When my family needed intervention, rescuing from an abusive man, we chose to keep our mouths shut. Boyd and I feared what might happen to Mom. As a kid, I didn't want to live. But who'd take care of Mom and Boyd? Life moved on, and now I live with the past, like a coward who could have prevented so much harm. I didn't even say anything as an adult."

"You kept your family from him."

"I could have done better. I still hear his voice or Mom cry. Felicia said I should be glad he's gone."

"She wants the best for you."

Will slowly lowered the rifle. "Even in death, he cheated me out of what was rightfully mine."

"How?" she said. "Inheritance? Because there are legal means to help if there's problems with the will."

Carrington's easy, relaxed tone would calm the devil. I admired, respected the woman who put others ahead of herself.

"Not money. Cheated me out of revenge. He told me once after a beating that I didn't have the guts to fight back."

"What did you say?"

"I said one day I'd kill him, and he said I didn't have the guts to do it."

"I'd be angry too. Unfair. Cruel. How old were you?"

"Twelve." He sneered. "Then I lie to my brother about what we were doing and shoot him when he wants out. Threaten my wife. Bully these illegals. I'm no better than my dad."

Carrington continued. "So not true. You are a wonderful man who loves and cares for his family. Right now, the hurt and pain have you overwhelmed. I promise to make sure you are treated fairly. Do you want the standoff to end?"

"Yes," Will whispered. "Tired of being angry. Hearing the voices accusing me of not manning up."

"You are a man of integrity, and I never doubted it. Are you ready to give me the rifle and handgun?"

TWENTY-TWO

CARRINGTON

I'd made the right choice to confront Will. In a matter of seconds, I'd have his weapons, and the chaos would end. The sick and wounded would receive medical care, and the other hostages would find freedom from fear of death.

"I'm proud of you." I reached out to take the rifle. "I promise to get you out of here safely. Felicia is waiting."

Will set his jaw and raised the barrel. "I've changed my mind. Nothing to live for. What I know will go to my grave. None of my family is guilty of this mess."

"Don't give up," I said.

"Too late. You and all the others here will taste my bullets." His finger rested on the trigger.

What had happened?

Levi bolted from my right, grabbed the rifle, and shoved the barrel up. He tackled Will to the floor. The dark struggle left me helpless. Will had the advantage in size, and Levi struggled with a wounded arm.

Rifle fire exploded.

Women screamed.

Levi and Will wrestled for the rifle. I wanted to help, but how when the fighting men were barely visible?

"Stay back," Levi managed, as though reading my mind.

I moved to where I saw the others huddled together. Prayer hadn't helped in the past, but Levi had risked his life for me. Will said something, but I couldn't make it out. Then something again.

"*Dios ayúdanos*," a man said.

Yes, God help us.

Will pushed to his feet. Rifle fire burst again.

"Levi!"

The wrestling stopped. I held my breath.

"Carrington, Will shot himself," Levi whispered through a moan.

The door burst open, and SOG agents poured into the small room. Flashlights switched on.

Will lay in a pool of blood pouring from his neck. His eyes vacant. Gone.

I knelt by Levi, blood seeping from his bandaged wound and spatters on his shirt and jeans.

I blinked back the tears, not sure if they were for Levi, Will, or all the others hurt during the tragedy. "Thank you." I touched Levi's cheek. "You are a brave man."

His brown eyes bored into mine. "The boy and his mother."

I nodded and hurried to where the SOG team had cut the zip ties binding the wrists of the men and women. In a flurry of Spanish, the team confirmed the hostages were safe. One of the male hostages hurried to the wounded woman and comforted the boy. "*Mi hijo*," he said. The man's son.

Three paramedics rushed in. One bent to the boy, who appeared unconscious. I smelled antiseptic alcohol and watched the man inject lifesaving glucagon from what looked like an EpiPen. A second paramedic examined the woman, who'd been shot, and flipped open a first aid kit. A tiny woman with huge dark eyes reached out for the man who held the boy and sobbed. A third paramedic checked for Will's pulse, then examined Levi and ordered he be transported to the hospital. The same paramedic returned to Will, pulled a sheet over him, and spoke into his wrist. "A man is dead. Injuries incompatible with life."

The paramedic's words confirmed what we all knew. My gaze swept to Levi lying on the floor. "What can I do for you?"

"Nothing. I'm sorry the situation turned out badly."

"You were nearly killed in the process. Twice."

He closed his eyes. "We did what we thought was best."

I swiped beneath an eye. "I'll see about Felicia. She must be frantic."

"She'll need you."

"Your arm needs more than a Band-Aid, Levi."

"I'll take the ER trip and get it stitched up."

"Good." I took one last look at the tragedies. Had Boyd survived? I longed to give Felicia positive news amid her grief. At least Jace and Emma hadn't been here. "I'll look in on you at the hospital."

"I'm fine. In excellent hands."

Outside hints of dawn lifted over the horizon in vibrant shades of gold and orange. More ambulances had arrived. I picked up my Glock and Kevlar vest. At the end of the driveway, Felicia raced toward me.

Help me.

Did God hear? Did He ever?

Felicia fell into my arms, sobbing. "He's gone, isn't he?"

"Yes. I'm sorry."

She attempted to break free, but I held her tightly. "There's nothing you can do, Felicia. Remember Will as happy and at peace."

"Who shot him?"

How did I tell a woman her husband lost the desire to live?

"Tell me! Was it you?"

"He pulled the trigger on himself. Levi tried to stop him."

A flood of torment seemed to engulf her. "Please tell me he's not dead. His rifle went with him everywhere except to bed. And he used it to kill himself. What do I tell Jace and Emma?"

"Tell them their father loved them."

Felicia's second-guessing conversations and actions with Will reminded me of every critical debriefing I'd been a part of. "You are a courageous woman. You can walk the road ahead and survive, and I will be with you when you tell your children."

She trembled in my arms.

"Take a deep breath. Then slowly let it out." When Felicia exhaled, I encouraged her to repeat the breathing.

"Thank you. I . . . I kept ignoring the probable ending to what he started. He'd gone so deep into the hurtful parts of his mind until the pain took over. My Will is free of nightmares and the accusations. Jace said earlier that Grandpa pushed his dad to the dark side."

"Your children were aware of Timothy's abuse?"

"Only Jace. I told him about six months ago. He'd overheard Timothy cursing Will and didn't understand why his dad said nothing."

"What about your parents? Are they local to help you through the hours and days ahead?"

Felicia nodded. "Yes. My father especially is very supportive."

"Would you like me to call them?"

She stepped back and moistened her lips. "I'll do it. They're waiting to hear. Mom and Dad will be with me when I tell the kids. But thank you for your kindness. Once I tell my parents about Will's past, many of their questions about our relationship will be answered."

"Take it slow."

"And it matters little who killed Timothy now."

"Justice needs to be served, Felicia. The investigation will expose the truth."

She touched her chest. "I have details for you about Timothy, but my family comes first."

Behind me, the paramedics shut the door to the ambulance. It sounded like gunfire, and we both shuddered. Felicia and I moved to the side of the driveway so the ambulance could pass.

"Before talking to my parents and children, shouldn't I drive to the county medical examiner's office?"

"It's not necessary for you to be there. Will's been identified."

"Being there is my way of honoring him." Panic rose in Felicia's voice.

"You're in no shape to be behind the wheel." A text alerted me from Skip. **BP has requested a rush on Will's autopsy.** I took Felicia's hand. "I'm driving you. It's settled."

"Isn't your place with the woman and her son who need medical attention? Boyd is there too, unless he had to be life-flighted to Houston."

I didn't understand her line of thought, but she carried a huge load. "You are my priority."

"What about your friend Levi? Is he all right?"

"He's okay. The ambulance is taking him for stitches."

Felicia took another deep breath. "I've never been to the medical examiner's office. Not sure what I'm supposed to do."

"I have, and I'll be right by your side. How about I drive your car, and I'll arrange for someone to bring my truck to the hospital."

Tears rested on her eyelashes. "I appreciate you so much."

My concerns never had a cutoff when people and tough emotions dragged them into despair. Not until they found help.

The upcoming sunrise brought a reminder that I was supposed to have the procedure done today on my eyes. I'd reschedule and endure the dread of going blind awhile longer.

TWENTY-THREE

LEVI

I'd been lucky when I considered Will had pushed to his feet and aimed the rifle at me, then himself.

The tragic ending of a tragic situation. His final words echoed in my mind. Later, without the agony in my arm, I'd think about what he meant.

I gave Skip the keys to my Tahoe and rode in an ambulance to the DeTar Hospital in Victoria. The sound of sirens, the jerky movement, and the rough journey told me the emergency vehicle was in a hurry. Not sure why unless they were keeping up with the other ambulances. Will had done a number on me in the struggle, and at one point, he'd dug his fingers into the wound in my upper left arm. Right now, I felt like he'd lit a match to my flesh.

I formed words in my mind to battle the pain. I prayed for the right way to tell Will, Boyd, and the hostages' story and honor all of them. All were victims. All suffered. No winners. Who was to blame? Timothy Kendrix? Why had the elder Kendrix chosen to treat his family and some women shamefully? A supposedly respected man in the community's eyes but with a dose of venom in his blood. Had he been abused as a child? Had a mental imbalance? I'd research what I could about him and take notes as soon as a doc stitched me up.

I wanted the reader to experience the entire picture and form their own opinions about the Kendrix disaster. I hoped they would apply what occurred here in the community to their lives and fight domestic violence.

My phone buzzed with a text, but I had an IV in my good arm. I turned to the paramedic. "Would you get my phone? It's in my right front jeans pocket." When she agreed, I continued. "Please read the message and tell me who it's from."

The woman, the same paramedic who had bandaged me before, gave me a smile and retrieved my phone. Her extended eyelashes touched her thick brows. A rather strange cosmetic additive for a paramedic. The throbbing in my arm contributed to my rambling thoughts.

"It's from Carrington and says, 'I gave a statement to BP. They'll get yours later. Driving Felicia to medical examiner's office. Catch up at the hospital later.'"

I closed my eyes to reach for strength. "Let her know I'm the last of her worries. Tell her shalom." Once the paramedic finished typing, she sent it to Carrington. I thanked her.

"Is shalom a greeting, or does it mean peace? I've heard both," she said.

"Shalom means more than hello, good-bye, or peace, but for the recipient to receive wholeness, and for God to offer all His blessings upon the person."

"I'm sure she'll appreciate it. Are you Jewish?"

"Messianic." Odd how my chest hammered with all the chemicals pumping fight-or-flight extras into my system, but I hurt like I'd been stoned. Similar, I guess. "Would you keep my phone until we get to the hospital in case someone else contacts me?"

"Absolutely. I suggest resting. You've been through quite an ordeal."

"Not any more than the others." A stab of fire tore through my shoulder. My eyes flew open, and I cringed. "Do you know the status of Boyd Kendrix?"

"We were told he's in surgery. Keep your eyes closed, Mr. Ehrlich. Think rest."

"I'm not so old that I'm a 'Mr.'" My attempt at humor sounded like I could have been her grandfather.

She giggled. "Yes, sir."

As always when I needed closure on circumstances out of my control, I thought back through the night's events and my responses. Could I have better chosen my words to Will? If I'd gotten to Boyd sooner, would he be in better shape now? At the house with Will, could I have foreseen his suicide and attempted to shove the rifle barrel toward the ceiling? All my alternatives risked lives. Horrific scenes from the past lived with me. Innocent victims, too many women and children, who stood in the wrong place and lost their lives. I'd seen atrocities in Ukraine, Sudan's civil war, and other areas of Africa. Even in my own country. I despised them all, but this morning, Will brought suffering to the forefront of why I communicated through words that every human deserved dignity and value. The tragedy that had destroyed a family was one more unforgettable memory. God must believe I could handle the terrifying.

My phone buzzed again, and I opened my eyes to meet the paramedic's gaze. She checked my phone. "From Frank. He says, 'I hear the hostage-taker is dead. Happened before the big guns broke in. Saw you left in an ambulance. Are you alive? Did you get the story?'"

"Would you like for me to type a message?" the paramedic said.

"Not needed." Frank had fired me. He'd made the decision, and I intended to find a publisher who valued humanity.

TWENTY-FOUR

CARRINGTON

Felicia and I sat in the waiting room while the medical examiner performed Will's autopsy. Still not sure why she wanted to be here, maybe to process her family's past and future. On the way there, she'd talked to her kids. Lots of tears and brokenness. Felicia's parents were with them, and that provided time for her to work through the grief.

"Would you like to talk?" I said. "Sometimes verbally expressing our hurt and anger to a safe person helps."

"No. Not yet." She swung a look of misery my way and made it worse with a poor smile.

I took her hand, offering silent support.

"You're right," she said. "I want to tell you about Timothy." She squeezed my hand as though I might let her go. "He had a nasty tongue, and my timid self veered away from him. Will never let me or the kids spend any time alone with Timothy. Nothing suited the man or was done to his satisfaction. I have no idea who the person might have been who talked to you. Ah, maybe the neighbor woman who became a good friend to Dorie. But yes, Timothy had an abusive streak. I couldn't believe it at first, then Will told me horrible stories." She gulped for her next breath, and I believed she hadn't revealed the story to anyone in the past.

"I thought my love for him would heal his emotional scars, but I was wrong. He loves Boyd, and he shot him. That's outrageous."

I strained forward. "I've never been a wife or mother, but I've experienced the pain of seeing others suffer and feeling helpless."

"You are so compassionate, Carrington. The more time that passed, the more traumatic Will's hurt and anguish became. When the three Kendrix men were together, an awkwardness existed thick enough to cut with a knife. Everything was superficial. Why didn't I insist we move away?"

"What did Will and Boyd say when their father criticized them?"

"Nothing, as though they reverted to little boys."

I formed a mental image of an older man belittling his grown sons. "Why did Will and Boyd let him continue the verbal abuse? Why choose to live in the area? Why have anything to do with a man who abused them, especially after their mother died?" I stopped myself. "I'm sorry. No reason for me to fire questions at you."

Felicia drew in a sob. "Timothy accumulated a lot of wealth, and no one else stood to inherit it." She paused. "Maybe they believed they were entitled to their share, and if they left the area, he'd leave it to someone else. Timothy's attorney has been on vacation, so there hasn't been a reading of the will." She stiffened. "Timothy did a good job of convincing them they were worthless. Sometimes I think Will and Boyd believed him."

"I think you're on to something about Timothy convincing both men they were worthless. The mind can play horrible games on us. They might have been convinced they deserved whatever happened to them in their younger days and even now."

"Boyd escaped the physical abuse." Felicia shrugged. "Timothy favored the youngest. No idea why."

"Do you think either of the brothers were capable of killing their father?"

She drew in a sharp breath. "No . . . maybe."

"Was Timothy verbally abusive to you?"

"Yes, and to Jace and Emma too. He claimed Jace couldn't be a Kendrix because he didn't work hard with his back and hands. And he said Emma must have a learning disability because she's quiet. Other things too. He said I played the role of a good wife while I cheated on Will with the men who came into the bank."

I hid my indignation. "What was Will's response?"

"One word, 'Enough' or Timothy would take care of his ranch by himself. For some reason, that shut him up. Timothy had rheumatoid arthritis, and paying for additional workhands meant dipping into his pocket. Will said Timothy was so tight with his money that spending it made him crazy."

I tucked Timothy's money practices into the back of my mind. "Did Timothy ever try to force himself on you?"

"No. Will would have killed him, I'm sure."

"What can you tell me about Boyd?"

"Much quieter than Will. He's engaged to a nice young woman from Victoria, and I have no idea if she is aware of the abuse. I've never heard Boyd speak a word against Timothy. Once when Will and I were at Boyd's place, I saw a prescription on the counter. Will picked it up, read the name, and teased him about not manning up. Told him to toss out the meds, or—never mind. That wasn't nice. The pills were antidepressants." She touched her mouth. "Don't repeat that. None of my business."

The ME returned, a craggy-looking man. I took Felicia's damp hand into mine.

"Mrs. Kendrix, we've completed your husband's autopsy. He died of a gunshot wound to the neck. Blood tests will reveal any drugs, alcohol, or abnormalities. That will take a day or two. In his youth, he broke his right arm twice."

"Thank . . . thank you," she said. "You'll contact me?"

"My report will go to Border Patrol. You'll need to ask them for the blood results."

We left the ME's office, and I drove Felicia to the hospital. I suggested she eat or drink something, but she refused, remained quiet, ignored texts and phone calls. I'd seen shock enough times to recognize her pale skin and rapid breathing pushed her there. I again reached for her hand across the seat. Her clammy skin and blue fingertips told me trauma had seized her. As soon as we arrived at the hospital, I'd inform medical personnel that she needed an exam.

People grieved in various ways, and the process involved emotional turbulence that didn't follow a pattern. Those who chose to work through the sorrow instead of ignoring it were the healthiest. But the series of steps to endure inner angst threatened the sanity of the strongest of people.

"Felicia, I encourage you to accept all your feelings. No matter what they are, own them."

She turned to me, her first reaction since leaving the ME office. "I'm sure you've been through deaths before."

I missed my parents still. "Yes. I'm here for you as a friend. In addition to recommending you and your family seek professional counseling, I have resources to help all of you walk through the tragedy. A suggestion is looking into psychological autopsy."

"What is that?"

"A means of gathering info from all of those who've been around Will, both past and present, to determine if his suicide could have been prevented. Not just family and close friends, but the Border Patrol agents who worked the scene over the past several hours. Even me. It's a means of addressing a crippling situation and understanding why things happened."

She slowly turned to me. "What if a tendency to suicide is hereditary? Then Jace and Emma might lean toward the same thing."

A tendency to suicide did follow family genealogy unless there was treatment. "Your children haven't been exposed to an abusive father. Will loved them and expressed his love for all of you. Jace's, Emma's, and your confusion will be in finding answers to his final decisions. Professionals can help provide an explanation."

"But what if they can't?"

"Then you'll be given tools to accept Will's choices. And to forgive. Family treatment is essential, and I suggest beginning immediately."

Felicia leaned back against the headrest. "I need to be aware of my children's needs. My little family is broken, and no Humpty Dumpty therapy will bring Will back. I keep thinking I should have done something or used different words to stop him." She gasped. "Guilt has me dreading each minute and the horror of moving ahead without Will. The scars on his back told the story of Timothy's habitual beatings. I've kissed those scars, but my love failed to heal his mind."

"You did your best."

"Wish I could believe you."

"In time you will. Have your children ever questioned their father's scars?"

"Jace did as a little boy. Will told him he'd been hiking in the Colorado Rockies and fell. After that, Will kept a shirt on all the time."

"What was the explanation for not allowing any of you to be alone with Timothy?"

"Another lie for our children. Will claimed Timothy had received threats on his life, and he wanted to keep us safe. I hated the evil man for what he'd done and being around him even with Will made me angry. When Will got the call about Timothy's death, I was glad. Sounds terrible. But it's true."

"Your feelings are normal. The man had repeatedly hurt your husband. And what you felt was relief, not gladness." My words emerged from my wheelhouse, but I wasn't the one going through the abandonment.

"With Timothy gone, we finally had a chance as a family. Now, who plays the role of father when Jace graduates from high school? Emma enters high school? Proms, college, careers, weddings, and one day when they have families of their own? Why wasn't Will stronger? Why didn't he love us enough to seek help?"

Felicia had hit an anger spot, and I let her rave about what Will would miss until blaming him moved her to tears.

She buried her face in her hands. "I'm sorry. You shouldn't have to hear my worries when you've been so patient." She paused. "My children will never hear from me about Will feeling cheated that someone else killed their grandfather."

I'd be on the lookout to ensure Levi's article didn't include Will's claim. "Go ahead and scream, shout, cry, or whatever you feel like doing. I've lost loved ones through tragic means too. The pain doesn't last forever, but at times it feels like it." I let my words settle. "No one's asking you to stop being human. Do you have a pastor to call?"

"No, but my parents belong to a church. I suppose I could contact their pastor."

"Good idea. He may be available for counseling too."

"Will wasn't the churchgoing type. He refused to believe in a heavenly Father who cared for His children. But Mom and Dad would appreciate me asking their pastor to conduct the service."

I let Felicia continue to talk. Her emotions zigzagged in so many directions. Only by releasing them could she survive the distress ahead. "Where are you meeting your parents?"

"They'll be at the hospital and have Jace and Emma with them. Boyd was special to Mom and Dad too. In fact, Dad's best friend's daughter is Boyd's fiancée." She paused. "Perhaps I should text Dad and ask if his pastor can join us at the hospital."

"That's a step in the right direction."

Her fingers failed to pick up her phone. "Will is gone forever," she whispered. "He's never coming back. Never. All our plans lay in blood . . ."

Before I could stop her from slipping mentally, my phone rang. "Hey, Skip. I'm on my way to the hospital with Felicia."

"Boyd is still in surgery."

I heard the trepidation in his voice. "How bad?"

"Doubtful he'll survive. Agents and deputies are here to offer support to the family."

I glanced at Felicia. "Boyd's in surgery." She stared out the windshield silently.

"Felicia, did you hear me?"

Again nothing. I touched her arm. Damp coldness. She'd slipped into shock.

———

I parked in front of DeTar Hospital ER and hurried inside for help. Two nurses and a doctor rushed to Felicia's aid with a gurney and rolled her away for treatment while I provided information to a receptionist. From my previous experiences, I assumed she'd receive oxygen and an IV until the doctor evaluated her level of shock.

With the receptionist's help, I located the surgical floor and waiting room where two Victoria police officers checked the IDs of anyone seeking information about Boyd's condition. Their diligence disallowed media access. A small group gathered, including two teens, an older couple, Border Patrol agents, and Victoria County deputies. In a corner chair, Levi sat with a bandaged arm. His pale features and the deep lines around his eyes told me he should be in bed, but he typed into his phone.

I approached Levi and smiled. I inwardly shuddered at the blood covering the front of him. Some of it came from Will. "Do you want me to look at anything?"

I quickly scanned the article on his phone and gave him permission to send. Nothing there to discredit the family, only the emotional aftermath of all those involved. "Where is this going since your boss dismissed you?"

"Nice way to say I'm fired. I've been sending the updates to a connection with Fox."

"Just curious. I'll be with you in a few minutes."

He set his jaw. "I'm not leaving until I find out if Boyd's pulled through."

"I figured as much." I lightly touched his uninjured arm and moved to the two teens. "Are you Jace and Emma Kendrix?"

"Yes, ma'am." Jace had his father's slim build, light-brown hair, and gray-green eyes. He pointed to the dark-haired, petite girl who resembled her mother with large brown-black eyes. "This is my sister, Emma."

"I'm Carrington Reed, the negotiator who handled the hostage situation with your father. I drove your mother here. She's in the ER."

"Why?" Jace's eyes widened. "Has she been hurt?"

"She'll be all right. The doctor is examining her for potential shock—"

"No." Emma sobbed.

The older man placed his arm around the girl's shoulders. "Hey. Your mama is one strong lady."

I took a step toward them. "I assure you, your mother is receiving the best possible care."

"Miss Reed," the older man said, "I'm Felicia's father, Howard Westfield." He pointed to the woman beside him. "And this is Felicia's mother, Zora."

I glanced at the white-crowned older woman who nodded slightly but said nothing.

Mr. Westfield breathed deeply. "Thank you for telling us about our daughter and taking care of her."

"No problem, sir."

"Border Patrol Agent Reyes told us how you tried so hard to convince Will to surrender. Thank you."

"I'm sorry about what happened." I didn't want to upset Jace and Emma with insensitive wording.

"We are too." Howard's deep-blue eyes studied me. "The kids need their mom right now, and I know she needs them."

"Healing begins when a family is ready to help each other," I said.

Howard nodded at Jace. "Son, take your sister and grandma to the ER. I'm right behind you."

When the three disappeared down the hall to the elevator, Howard turned to me and ran his fingers through thick silver hair. "I understand you and the man with the shoulder injury risked your lives to stop Will from doing more damage. I've thanked Levi, and now I'm thanking you. I have no idea why Will did such a crazy stunt or went off the deep end. I heard a lot of rumors about how Timothy Kendrix ruled the roost, but I'd never seen questionable behavior from Will or Boyd. The brothers were hardworking men. What were Will's words in the house?"

"I'm sorry. I need to clear everything with the Border Patrol and the sheriff's department first."

"Of course. Anger sure causes strange behavior." He pressed his lips together.

"And leaves us wondering why."

"Will's behavior makes no sense. I have no idea who that Will Kendrix is. Certainly not the man I consented to marry my daughter or called my son. Trust me, I'd do anything to protect Felicia and my grandkids. Guess we never really know what's going on in a person's head."

"That's true, sir. He did tell me of his love for Felicia and his children."

"Those feelings weren't enough to stop him from pulling the trigger to take his life. I'm not sure how my daughter and grandkids will manage. I'm here to help. Zora has a few health issues, but she's loving."

Poor man. "On the way to the hospital, when Felicia was coherent, she wanted to see if you'd contact your pastor for the funeral service."

"Yes. I'll call right away."

"I suggested the pastor might be available for counseling. I have other resources to recommend, and I hope I'm not overstepping."

He offered a smile that resonated with sadness. "Not at all. Maybe the horror of what went down will encourage her and the kids to attend church. God is who will get them through the nightmare. Right now, the priority is Boyd pulling through from the surgery. Then I want answers to Will's actions. Makes me wonder if Felicia kept things to herself."

Howard Westfield would learn the truth about Will's demons soon enough.

TWENTY-FIVE

LEVI

I always learned more about Carrington by watching than anything someone might say or do. Compassion and sincerity emanated from her without my hearing a single word of the conversations she had with others in the room. She moved gracefully from Will and Felicia's children to the grandparents and on to others. I'd never heard of a negotiator who followed up with family and law enforcement after living through trauma. Undoubtedly she'd check in with the boy and his mother who'd been admitted to the hospital. My thoughts had traveled there too and to the welfare of the other hostages.

Carrington embodied integrity. I no longer wanted to write a story about her but a biography. From what I'd seen of far too many people—including myself—we had much to learn from her giving nature. Although she kept me at a distance, she'd set off my attraction meter, and I couldn't imagine a single flaw.

I chuckled. I'd clearly become crazy over a woman I'd admired for so long.

Skip walked my way and sat beside me. Weariness stamped lines across his forehead. He handed me the keys to my Tahoe. "Would you like an agent to drive you back to Houston?"

"Not sure how I'd bring him back."

"A second agent would follow."

"I appreciate the offer, but I'm not ready to leave the hospital. Like you, I'm waiting to hear about Boyd."

"He's been in surgery for over five hours."

"I'm patched up, but who's taking care of you?"

Skip paused before answering. "My wife is home waiting for me once I'm finished and debriefed." He glanced at the BP agents standing in the hall where the surgeon should appear. "Glad this is over. Don't care to repeat any of it."

"You did an excellent job managing the crisis and the people."

He shrugged. "*Excellent* means no bodies to bury and no one in the hospital."

"You covered all the bases, and I've experienced hostage cases all over the world."

"Nothing helps how I feel at the moment." Skip moistened his lips. "The sheriff's department will continue the investigation alongside Border Patrol."

"The suicide?"

"Not much to do there. I'm referring to Timothy Kendrix's murder. Evidence must be uncovered to find out who pulled the trigger." He took a sip of water from a paper cup. "What happened inside the house? Consider this your debriefing." He pulled his phone from his pant pocket and hit Record.

I told him what occurred moment by moment. "Will and I were wrestling for the rifle, and I was losing. He grabbed the barrel out of my hands, and I gave in to dying. But he stood and stuck it under his chin, then pulled the trigger before I could stop him."

"Did he say anything?"

"Said he had no choice." I should tell Skip the rest of it. "He asked me to protect his family. Odd for a man to say to a stranger."

"Dying words don't always make sense. You're a good man, and Will recognized it." Skip shook my hand. "Thank you for all you've done. The offer's open to give you a ride home. Just text or call. In the meantime, get some rest."

"You too."

The Border Patrol offered counseling for job-related stress, and I hoped he and others who dealt with the hostage situation took advantage of it. Skip joined his men. We all felt like Skip—overwhelmed with too many emotions.

———

Carrington made her way through the small crowd to me, taking the chair Skip had vacated. She reminded me of a mother hen looking after her charges, but I wouldn't share that comparison. Not exactly the best line to impress a woman.

"Where to now?" I said.

"I'd like to run five miles. But I have other miles to go before then. Surely the doctor will have a positive update on Boyd soon. I'm told the hostages are being taken care of by a local church. I want to check on them. Also the little boy with diabetes and his mother, then back to Felicia."

"Can I tag along?"

"Are you up to it? Looks to me like you should be in bed." Her incredible brown eyes seemed to peer into my very being.

"When was the last time *you* slept? Besides, sitting here makes me crazy, and our adrenaline hasn't slowed either of us down."

"We're a lot alike. I'll let Skip know our plans so he can text me with any word about Boyd."

A man in scrubs appeared in the hallway and caught our attention. "Is there a member of Boyd Kendrix's family here?" His demeanor gave no indication of Boyd's condition.

Carrington and I were near enough to hear the conversation. I prayed the man had survived surgery.

A young, auburn-haired woman stepped forward. "Boyd has no immediate family. I'm Lyndie Moore, his fiancée." She held up her left hand to display an engagement ring.

"I'm Dr. Sanchez, the surgeon." His soft voice was to disarm

Lyndie's fears, but I feared the worst. "Mr. Kendrix made it through the removal of the bullet. A centimeter closer to his heart, and he wouldn't have survived. We're doing all we can, but right now we wait, which can be several more hours."

Lyndie gripped her hands in a prayerful position. "He's alive. Thank you. Can I see him?"

"Not at this point. He's lost a lot of blood and is in critical condition. I wish I had better news."

Her lips quivered. "When do you expect to see improvement?"

"That's difficult to say. Every patient is different."

"What do you mean? Is he breathing on his own?"

The doctor studied Lyndie. "Miss Moore, he is on life support."

"How long?"

"For as long as it takes." His response wove honesty together with sympathy. "Boyd has survived the odds. That's optimistic. I'd say he has someone worth fighting for." He gestured around the room. "Looks like you have a good support group here. I'll keep you updated." He disappeared down the hall with Lyndie's attention focused on his back.

"I need to talk to her," Carrington said. "She's shaking. Alone. Frightened."

A middle-aged woman, with chin-length white hair, walked Lyndie back to the seating area.

I watched the two women for a moment. "She looks to be in good hands."

"Possibly her mother or an aunt. I'm ready to find out the status of the little boy and his mother."

I struggled to stand, and once on my feet, I moved to the hallway with Carrington. Once alone, she took a deep breath.

"Levi, I don't have an explanation, but more is going on with the Kendrix family than what we've seen."

My gut told me the same thing. "Two men are dead, and a third struggles to hold on to life. We both understand the authorities won't keep the case open for very long."

"My apprehension is still working overtime, and it has nothing to do with logic."

I'd vowed to learn the truth when called to the hostage site, and nothing had changed. The outcome of the past several hours prodded me to keep digging for truth.

TWENTY-SIX

Outside the surgical floor elevators, Carrington and I met with reporters. They blocked the elevator doors, and each sounded their agenda. Cameras clicked, videos rolled, and microphones were shoved under our chins. Faulting their enthusiasm meant belittling myself, but their persistence annoyed me. The slants varied from reporter to reporter, publication to publication. I refused to sensationalize the victim list. Gutter journalism had never been my style.

Frank stood among the reporters, and I renewed my vow not to get into an argument. "Best not to say a word," I whispered.

"My thoughts exactly."

Hecklers outshouted each other—

"How are the hostages?"

"Levi, who's releasing your coverage?"

"Ms. Reed, we need a statement on what happened at the hostage site."

"Miss Reed, what did Will Kendrix say before he died?"

"Ms. Reed, what is the condition of Boyd Kendrix?"

"Why has Levi Ehrlich been granted an exclusive?"

"Mr. Ehrlich, what happened at the end of the negotiations?"

"Mr. Ehrlich, did you shoot Will Kendrix?"

"Miss Reed, Mr. Ehrlich, why are you working with Border Patrol and Victoria County Sheriff's Department? What are you hiding? What can you tell us?"

I'd enjoyed myself more listening to my *bubbe*, my grandmother, carry on about my sister being the smarter of the two of us.

Carrington had been on the opposing side of media many times, but I was venturing out of my comfort zone. I managed to press the down arrow on the elevator, but when it opened, four reporters piled in with us. While she and I ignored the bombardment of questions and interview requests, we kept our gazes glued to the elevator door.

Carrington whirled around and faced the media, and I imitated her stance. "Ladies and gentlemen, neither Mr. Ehrlich nor I have a statement for you."

"Why?" Frank's familiar voice rose. "People care about the welfare of the hostages."

"I suggest you talk to Border Patrol and the county sheriff's office for their statements," she said.

"Levi, hey bro, how's the arm?" Frank said.

I didn't bother to respond. *Bro?*

"Wanna go for a drink like in the old days?" Frank chuckled.

So not funny, but he'd not hear it from me.

We walked to the reception desk, where Carrington wrote on a slip of paper and slid it to the young woman behind the desk. **Where are the wounded mother and the undocumented boy being treated for diabetes?**

The nurse read the note, wrote her response, and handed Carrington the slip of paper. She allowed me to read it—the boy and his mother were in a room together in the ER. Neither of us had received an update on them, and I questioned if that was a positive or a negative. Another death added more fuel to the hostage situation explosion.

Carrington approached the security guard, and he escorted us to the ER without the media. A quote came to mind, and I chuckled despite the circumstances.

"What's so funny?" she said.

"Laughing at myself. G. Gordon Liddy said, 'The press is like the peculiar uncle you keep in the attic—just one of those unfortunate things.'"

She smiled, and the stress faded from her lovely features.

A nurse in the ER directed us to the treatment room for Rosa Cedilla and her son, Lupe.

Inside a curtained area, a man I assumed was Rosa's husband and Lupe's father stood over the bed and held her hand. The boy slept in a brown vinyl chair, and a white blanket covered his small frame. The man nodded at us.

"How is she?" Carrington said in Spanish, which I understood.

He returned his gaze to the tiny woman. "The doctor removed the bullet. My wife has lost too much blood. She sleeps now so her body can heal."

"I'm sorry, señor. My name is Carrington Reed, and this is Levi Ehrlich. How is the boy?"

"My son will be okay. He's tired." He reached out and shook Carrington's hand and mine. "I'm Agustín Cedilla." He pointed to my bandaged arm. "You are a brave man. Both you and the señorita. *Gracias.*"

I acknowledged his thanks. "Would you like for me to find a *padre* to pray with you?"

"Sí, I'd like that very much."

I phoned the hospital chaplain from the room phone, and a priest assured me he would be there within minutes. "Agustín, Senorita Carrington and I are trying to figure out what happened when the two men took you hostage. Can you tell us what you remember?"

"We were walking in a field when a van stopped on the road beside us. Two men jumped out. One man, the one who is dead, had a rifle and ordered us to get inside and leave our belongings there. The other man seemed angry, but the first one shouted back. Then Border Patrol showed up. The man with the rifle fired. One of his shots flattened the tire of the Border Patrol car." Agustín adjusted a sheet around his wife's neck.

"We were driven to the house. There, the boss man pointed his rifle at the unarmed man and said something. The unarmed man tied our wrists with zip ties, while the other man held his rifle on us. My son needed food and diabetic supplies, but they were left behind in his backpack. Rosa panicked and tried to make the boss man understand our son needed medicine. But the man shot her. The unarmed man shouted again. I thought he'd be shot too. We heard voices over the bullhorn, but none of us understood what was said. The boss man grabbed the other man by the jacket. That's all I can tell you. And it's what I told the Border Patrol men too."

"The men believed undocumented immigrants killed their father," Carrington said. "The unarmed man wanted no part of the kidnapping."

Agustín stiffened. "And they blamed us? None of us had any weapons."

Carrington spoke with gentleness. "We know you aren't guilty of their father's death. Sometimes people who are angry behave erratically, without logic."

The man sighed. "Others suffer."

"You have been through a horrible ordeal. I'm glad your family is receiving good medical care, and I wish you well. *Gracias* for talking to us."

The priest entered the room, and he spoke to Agustín in Spanish. I gave Agustín my card before we said our goodbyes and left.

Tears crested Carrington's eyes, and she hastily blinked them away.

"Hey, you've done a rock-star job with every person you've encountered," I said. "You've impacted my life for good, and I'll never forget it."

"My grandmother used to say tragedies make us stronger and better people. She believed in God, like you. Honestly, I feel like a weak, miserable failure. People dead. People hurting."

"What more can be done but show kindness?" I said.

"We've already seen the power of anger in the wrong people. Where are the answers, Levi? Certainly not with a deity who allows the innocent to bleed and die." She dug her fingers into her palm.

Stating we lived in a sin-infested world would invite her emotions to escalate, so I said nothing. An all-powerful God did care, but doubts where the innocent became victims always tossed stones at my faith.

We checked in with Felicia in another part of the ER. In a curtained examining area, she lay with an IV carrying healing fluids into her body. She thanked Carrington and me for checking on her. Jace and Emma huddled around the bed. Howard and his wife introduced a man in his thirties as the Westfields' pastor. Carrington modeled composure and control, successfully hiding her disappointment in herself and God. We left shortly afterward to allow the family privacy.

In the ER waiting room, Carrington phoned the church caring for the hostages. They'd been fed and would spend the night there before the BP handled the crisis.

Once more we rode the elevator up to check on Boyd.

No updates.

In the surgical waiting room, we slumped into chairs and slept. I needed to tell Carrington Will's final words, but not with so many people around. Hours later, Boyd still hadn't regained consciousness.

TWENTY-SEVEN

Day three since the hostage situation, and Boyd hadn't opened his eyes. Until he wakened, no one had answers to the motive pressing against so many minds. I'd driven back from Victoria yesterday afternoon, and Levi drove himself home, but he should have allowed Skip to arrange his transportation.

I sipped my morning coffee while Arthur enjoyed his breakfast. My thoughts stayed fixed on Will's suicide. Why had he destroyed himself when he had reasons to live? A family who loved him must now tackle the devastation of his actions. Will said he'd been cheated out of killing his own father. I shuddered at the thought, especially when I remembered my father's caring for me.

I placed myself in Will's shoes. All his life, he'd been treated shamefully and hidden the abuse. Timothy should have been a role model. Instead he betrayed his wife and sons.

Who had killed the older Kendrix? Someone had pulled the trigger and walked free.

The unsolved murder stole my waking and sleeping hours— needled me, as my grandmother used to say. While I had no tolerance for taking a human life—even the likes of Timothy Kendrix— I believed laws were in place to protect others. Justice needed to be consistent. I'd promised Will that justice would reign, and although I knew little about accessing evidence to find a criminal, I intended to keep my word. Timothy's murderer had caused a series of tragedies, and my probing tendency refused to let it go.

I picked up my phone, which served more like an appendage, and searched the Internet for updates. Nothing grasped my attention. Without evidence or Boyd's testimony, the story would grow stale . . . and another bigger event would take its place.

Dixie had texted from work, and I responded with a huge thanks for taking care of Arthur. I'd missed church with her yesterday, but I assured her I'd be there next Sunday.

Felicia and I texted often, but she didn't mention the investigation. Neither did I. Bringing it up seemed inappropriate since she blamed Timothy for Will's death. She also blamed Timothy for Will shooting Boyd. What a dysfunctional nightmare. Felicia and her kids had begun the counseling process with a recommendation from her parents' pastor, a psychiatrist who specialized in trauma and family issues. He or she could prescribe an antidepressant if the doctor believed Felicia or one of the kids needed additional help. Will's blood analysis showed signs of drugs and alcohol, and I sensed even deeper regret from the family.

Dread dug its claws into the day. I'd rescheduled the eye procedure for later today. I should be glad to have a diagnosis, to get it behind me, but not knowing seemed better than confirmation of my fears. Or rather it compounded the stress.

My doorbell rang. Who at 8:00 a.m. wanted to socialize? With my fingers wrapped around a hot cup of freshly brewed coffee, I headed to the door with Arthur padding behind me. A quick whiff of me after an extensive workout would chase away any sales types. A glance out the window showed Levi's silver Tahoe in my driveway.

I opened the door and met his irresistible smile, reminding me of a little boy's innocent charm. "Good morning. You're up early."

"I had a Zoom job interview with the East Coast. Thought I'd see if you'd like breakfast."

"Got a restaurant in mind? 'Cause I'm not in the mood to cook."

"Kenny & Ziggy's."

I pretended to think about it, although I welcomed his company more than the tasty food from the Jewish delicatessen. "I need a shower."

"Time is my new best friend while I'm in between jobs. I can keep your dog company."

I picked up Arthur and introduced him to Levi. "Not much of a watchdog, but he's great company."

"We'll get along fine."

"You're on." I stepped aside to let Levi inside. "How is your arm?"

He glanced at the bandage and sling. "Getting better."

I looked down at my lovable dog. "Arthur, you have a playdate."

Levi winked at me. "I've been called a lot of things, but a playdate isn't one of them."

Admitting the man had tossed out a net that might capture my every dream went against my personality . . . Never thought I'd meet someone who'd give me space and caring at the same time. Yet every time we'd met over the years of running in the same circles, he'd never pushed himself on me.

"Coffee is ready," I said. "Help yourself. A mug's in the cabinet above the Nespresso machine, and creamer's in the fridge. Later I want to hear about your job interview."

"Thanks. I could use a listening ear."

"With me, you get an opinion, solicited or not."

He laughed, and I enjoyed the sound of it. I refused to even think the word *future*. But I had dreamed about his kiss and secretly wanted it to happen. I walked down the hall and remembered the fear-claws of the afternoon appointment. Spending time with Levi would serve as a nice distraction, and I appreciated every minute. He and I acted like we were old friends. Sort of in a professional way. Odd because we knew so little about each other. No wonder our relationship scared me.

After taking a hot shower and dressing, I joined Levi in the kitchen. Arthur sat in his lap, snuggled against Levi's chest.

"Arthur's playdate reporting in," he said. "He's been outside to tend to business, and someone left a message on your phone." Levi gave her the once-over and his eyes lit up. "You clean up good."

How jeans, a T-shirt, sparse makeup, and a ponytail translated into good were beyond me. "You'd make a great negotiator."

"Don't think so. I ask too many questions."

"Questions are okay. Depends on how they are phrased."

He placed Arthur on the floor and stood. "Do you need to return the call before we leave?"

"I'm hungry. I'll return the call on the way." I bent to Arthur and held his head with both hands. Staring into his big brown eyes, I gave him the smile meant only for my sweet pet. "I'm coming back. Take a nap. Food and water are in your bowl." I grabbed my purse and phone. "One minute." I swallowed my assortment of supplements and followed Levi.

Outside Stephanie Radison sat on her front porch. I waved and so did she. I assumed she'd ask about Levi the next time we chatted. In a strange way, I wanted to report a promising relationship.

Once inside the Tahoe, I checked my phone. "It's Skip." I pressed the redial.

He answered. "Hi, Carrington, thanks for getting back to me. Do you have a minute to talk?"

"No problem. I'm with Levi. If his hearing a one-sided conversation is a problem, let me know."

"That's fine. Remember when you asked me for info about the Kendrix men? Do you still want it?"

"Yes. I'm still processing what went wrong in the negotiations."

"Nothing on your end, in my opinion. I'll e-mail the background checks later. What I'm about to say will hit the news today. We have a new development on the Timothy Kendrix murder. Sheriff Corbin Macmire confirmed the bullets that killed Timothy, wounded Boyd, and Will used to commit suicide came from the same rifle."

TWENTY-EIGHT

My blood turned to ice. Had I heard wrong? "I'm not sure what to say, except the evidence must be wrong. It's . . . it's impossible. Are you sure the bullets came from the same rifle?"

"Yes. Sheriff Macmire is sending a detective to question Felicia, but I'm trying to get there first. Will's fingerprints are the only ones on the rifle. We both know others could have been wiped off," Skip said. "I've developed a rapport with the family, and I'd rather share the findings than have strangers shake her and the kids up."

"Maybe her parents could meet you there," I said. "To soften the blow."

"I left a message with Howard. But he hasn't returned my call."

"That means Will could have killed his dad. But that seems ludicrous." I blinked to focus while I wanted to deny Skip's words. "Would Will have taken hostages to cover his own crime, wounded others, and then committed suicide?" I whirled to Levi, who hadn't backed the Tahoe onto the street. He'd grasped enough of the conversation to give me his full attention. "When Will said he blamed the undocumented immigrants for his father's death, we saw the reason for his irrational behavior. But if he committed the crime, why did Will tell Felicia whoever killed his father had robbed him of pulling the trigger?" I paused. "I know you're wrestling with what we've just learned too. Any secondary prints on the rifle?"

"Nothing discernable. He must have suffered from more mental problems than anyone thought. Sheriff Macmire scheduled a press conference at noon to give the department's conclusions. I'm supposed to be there."

"But Boyd hasn't given his side of the story."

"Tell me about it."

"I should be with you, but I'd never make it in time. Skip, behavior follows belief. Will must have been suffering mentally for years. Possibly Boyd too." Why hadn't I remotely considered the severity of the mental illness? Wasn't that my background, my training?

"Doubtful Will masterminded nabbing those hostages by himself. But who? He claimed he lied to Boyd. This is complicated, and right now I don't know who is telling the truth."

"An elaborate design gone wrong?"

"Not sure what I'm going to say to Felicia," Skip said. "Except I don't want her kids to hear the news from a stranger."

"I'm glad you're reaching out. I agree Jace and Emma's mother should be the one to tell them, but who knows how she'll handle the news? All I can say is tell the truth, slowly, and maintain eye contact. The family is in counseling, so you could suggest she contact the pastor who's working with them." I rubbed my arms. "This doesn't mean for certain that Will killed his father."

"I know. But something's not right, Carrington. While the sheriff's office will want to close the case, I'm questioning the well of dysfunction in the Kendrix family and if other crimes have been covered up." He sighed. "It's not my job to investigate them. Neither can I get involved any more than I already have, but I'm committed to those hours we worked with Will to surrender. Hey, I'm at the Kendrix place now. I'll let her know you and I talked, and I'll check back once I'm finished here." Skip ended the conversation, and I relayed the update to Levi.

"Not what I expected," he said. "Reality is never comfortable. Can't imagine how Felicia will feel."

"Abandoned, I think. I've tried to put the crimes out of my mind, but it's impossible. I should have read more into my time with Will. You have the journalistic background. What are your thoughts?"

Levi backed into the street, quiet as though deliberating. "Will's final words refuse to leave me alone. Something else was going on. Anyway, he said he had no choice and begged me to protect his family. I told Skip at the hospital."

"There's more, more than what you told Skip."

"You're good at tells." Levi tossed me a slight smile. "At the time I thought Will's statements were from a deranged man. Even so, he said evil stalked his family, and no one could be trusted."

"Do you plan to tell Skip the rest of it?"

"I should, but something keeps holding me back. I've got to see this through—for Will and his family."

"I feel the same way," I said. "Nothing logical about it at all."

"Do you want breakfast, or do I drive us to Victoria?"

I had no problem rescheduling the testing for my eyes again, but I didn't want to overwhelm Felicia when a professional had her and the kids in counseling. "I think we should wait to hear from Skip or Felicia."

"Okay. The sooner Boyd is awake, the sooner we can all have answers."

"Maybe he'll give the reason he was the favored son."

He shrugged. "Where were Will and Boyd when their dad was killed?"

"I imagine the detective requested Will's and Boyd's alibis. Hold on a moment while I check online." A few moments later, I reported my findings. "Will claimed he was repairing a tractor, and Boyd was buying feed. A worker at the feedstore backed him up, which means Will had no alibi."

"With the new evidence, the detectives will reexamine their statements. Had someone framed Will for Timothy's murder. But who? And why?"

My mind settled into suspicious mode. "Levi, what about Felicia? She hated Timothy and loved Will."

"I thought about her too. She watched her husband struggle with unresolved issues for a lot of years. Maybe she had her fill? Decided to end the problem and free her husband from the nightmares? Then again, she would have been at work during the shooting. Right?"

I scanned the Internet. "Yes."

Levi muttered an unrecognizable phrase.

"What did you say?"

"Whoever is guilty is crazy to think he or she can get away with murder."

"Criminals always believe their actions are right."

"Makes for a good story. Who else had access to Will's rifle?"

"Felicia claimed Will always had it with him." I pondered what little I knew. "That eliminates anyone breaking into their home to steal it." I studied Levi. "Were we duped by Will's behavior? What is the truth?"

"I've always prided myself in being a decent judge of character," Levi said. "And I believed Will was a victim. If he's proven guilty, I've been knocked down a peg. Another thought is Lyndie Moore, Boyd's fiancée. She might not be as passive as Felicia. If Boyd had told her about his father's abuse, she could have chosen a way to ensure he didn't interfere in their marriage. If we suspect her, the investigators had to be a step ahead of us." Levi tapped the steering wheel. "I'm not using my head. Will owned the weapon."

"Neither of us like being lied to. I've only seen Lyndie at the hospital and talked to her briefly. She was upset. Then her mother arrived and calmed her by explaining Boyd's condition and the time needed for his improvement." I sifted through my recollections. "Who else had motive to kill Timothy? Lyndie's mother? Howard or Zora Westfield? The women he'd abused or one of their family members? I can't seem to let it go."

"Carrington, from what I've seen with your interactions with others, you want to help them make sense of their lives and find a reason to live. The mess with the Kendrix family will take time for the detectives to sort out."

"You're right. I negotiate, not solve the world's problems. The Kendrix case is out of my wheelhouse, more your mindset."

"I chase down stories, not solve crimes. Do you pour yourself into every case?"

"I care and make recommendations, but I haven't had a situation as complex or as challenging."

"Not sure how you keep your mind in gear."

"Or you." I forced a smile. "I had a professor who said hostage negotiation is like being stranded in a leaking lifeboat—until the hole is plugged, all will drown."

"Lot of wisdom there. Would you check for a media update?"

I pulled up the info on my phone. The headlines from Levi's former employer ground at my nerves.

"You moaned," he said. "Give it to me straight."

I frowned at what Frank had written. "'Journalist Levi Ehrlich resigned from *Now America Reports* after witnessing a hostage situation with negotiator Carrington Reed. While Ehrlich was trying to help Boyd Kendrix escape from his older brother, Ehrlich received a bullet wound. Boyd Kendrix was shot and is currently in critical condition at DeTar Hospital in Victoria, Texas.

"'Reed and Ehrlich entered the house where Will Kendrix held fifteen undocumented immigrants, one a boy suffering from diabetes and his mother, who'd been shot. Neither Reed nor Ehrlich would comment on what happened inside the house moments before Kendrix was killed. Did Kendrix take his own life as Reed and Ehrlich reported, or did Reed or Ehrlich kill him? This morning, authorities announced evidence that indicates Will Kendrix murdered his father less than two weeks ago. What really went on inside that house? Why aren't Reed and Ehrlich making a statement? Why are they working with Border Patrol and Victoria County Sheriff's Department?'"

"I'm not surprised," Levi said. "Frank wanted to raise ratings, and today's update accomplished it. He's looking for me to refute his article or come crawling to him. What he's reported makes you and me look like we're killers and hiding critical information. My releases on what was going on didn't reach his ratings. Hmm. I'll add a boost to mine."

"There's nothing for us to do, is there? In your career, have you turned a wrongly reported segment to the truth?"

"No. Readers like the bizarre. I'll continue to add my findings, but when this is over, I'll cover the entire situation. I'd like to believe my reputation would garner readers."

"What if the truth is bizarre?" I said.

"Wouldn't be the first time."

TWENTY-NINE

LEVI

Kenny & Ziggy's restaurant usually had a long wait, but we'd timed our arrival just right. I plastered on a smile and pretended Frank's account of the hostage negotiation hadn't caused a reaction in me. But I lied to myself. I felt like someone had taken a knife to my insides and the innocents involved. I focused on getting the Kendrix issues off Carrington's mind. I ordered my favorite stuffed French toast, and she opted for a veggie scramble. I picked up on her preoccupation and assumed it centered on the last few days.

"Do you travel much with your job?" I said to break the silence.

"Looks like we're avoiding the wild animals chasing us."

"Exactly."

"Okay. I need think-time too." Those mysterious brown eyes met mine. "At times. I've been contracted as far as California to Vermont."

I took a sip of coffee—a brew I never grew tired of. "Are your parents in the Houston area?"

"No, they were killed in a car accident when I was a child, then my grandmother took me in. She died right after my high school graduation."

"I'm sorry. Any other family?"

She took a sip of her coffee. "Just Arthur."

"Boyfriend?"

She laughed lightly. "Just Arthur."

Good news. "Does that mean I have a chance?"

"Friendship has always worked for us. You mentioned an early morning job interview. How did it go?"

"The interview was with *National Geographic* and went well. Their interests and priorities mirror mine. Wildlife. Oceanography. Documentaries featuring a humane approach on all levels. I'll see if they request another interview."

"From what I've seen of your work, it sounds like a good fit." She shook her head. "Your accomplishments and awards make my head spin. Have you considered freelancing?"

I chuckled. Would *National Geographic* cross me off their list if they contacted Frank about my job performance? "Certainly. Beginning with the Kendrix story. Fox picked it up immediately."

"No reconciliation with your former boss?"

"I've closed the door and tossed the key. My relationship with the publisher's new owners hasn't gone well for a while." I started to say God stepped in when I wasn't getting His message, but I believed my faith discussion with Carrington needed to emerge gradually, not forcefully.

Our food arrived, and my stomach growled. I bowed my head and prayed, still unsure about faith with her. When I lifted my eyes, she did too. We talked throughout the meal about safe things like the Astros, great food, and hobbies. Arthur and gardening made her top list of fun. Mine settled on reading and photography. Our two in-common hobbies were the Dallas Cowboys and hiking.

"Do your parents live in Houston?" she said.

"Yes, the Meyerland area."

"I've always heard Jewish families are close knit."

"Not mine." How did I feel about getting into the thick of a personal topic? I laid my fork beside my plate. "I grew up in an Orthodox Jewish family. My Messianic conversion went against everything they believe in. They held a funeral for me. Their response should give you a clue to our relationship."

She tilted her head. "Is it because they don't believe Jesus came to earth over two thousand years ago?"

"You're talking about two separate issues. Belief in Jesus or Messianic." When she frowned indicating more confusion, I continued. "If I'd converted to Christianity and joined any of the many denominations, then I'd have chosen a new religion. They'd have been upset but not like now. Messianic Judaism is viewed as a betrayal of all the Jewish people believe in. Those who have died because of Judaism would have seemingly died for nothing. To them, the Messiah hasn't arrived yet."

"The Jews have been persecuted for hundreds, thousands of years."

"Right. My paternal great-grandparents died at Auschwitz. My actions damaged what my family refers to as the Real Religion."

"I had no idea. Do all practicing Jews follow the same thought?"

"Depends, but definitely the Orthodox."

"I'm sorry."

I sensed she meant it. "Thanks. I learned what faith meant."

"Why did you convert? Or is that too personal?"

"My Jewish faith was more of my identity than what I believed." I hesitated to say more. I wanted Carrington as more than a friend and didn't want to run her off. "Are you sure you want to hear my story?"

"I do. Transparency is a part of getting to know each other better."

I inhaled deeply and exhaled a prayer. "The uncertainty about faith and where I fit caused an affair with drugs and alcohol."

"But why go down a dead-end street and destroy your body and mind?"

She hadn't asked how I'd kicked the demons, but why I slipped into addictive behavior in the first place. "Good question. Felt empty. No purpose. Rebelled against my family and chose an escape."

"How'd that work out for you?"

I grinned at her candid question. "The escape worked until it didn't."

"Overdosed and had a miraculous come-to-Jesus experience?" She held up her palm. "I apologize. I'm serious, not ridiculing you or your religion. What determined your decision to leave the drugs behind?"

"My father suggested I read the Jewish Scriptures, the Tanakh. I had nothing to lose, so I did. Sometimes I was drunk or high when I read it. Without telling my parents or sister, I also read the New Testament and compared it to the writings of the Old Testament. That sobered me up, so to speak. What I found surprised me. Had the Messiah already come in the form of Jesus? The more I researched, the more I believed He did. I counseled with a rabbi at a Messianic synagogue church and converted. With my acceptance of Jesus, I gave up the substance abuse. Still active in AA." I'd said enough unless Carrington asked more questions.

She took a long sip of her coffee. "Did the Messianic rabbi warn you about the sacrifices ahead?"

"I already knew, but the shunning didn't sink in until I experienced it."

"Any regrets?"

"None. My former disgusting self—physically, mentally, and spiritually—had smacked into disaster. No denying I miss my family and the many times we were together. I hope one day they change their minds."

"I hope so too. I see the longing in your eyes."

I grinned. "Thanks. Miss Reed, again you have pulled confidential matters from a man's soul."

"Are you offended? That wasn't my intent."

"I'm fine. Unless I've made a tactical error, my story's safe with you."

"Very much so. Have you made new friends?"

"Oh yes. Like a new family. Some of us are in the same boat."

"A lifeboat?"

I gave her a thumbs-up.

"By the way, thanks."

"For what?"

"Sweeping me away in your silver Tahoe when my mind overflowed with concern about the Kendrixes. The diversion relaxed me so I can later return to the problem with a clear head. If Felicia needs to talk or cry or shout, I'm her gal."

"But you pulled stuff out of me, not the other way around. Who do you talk to when you're troubled?" I glimpsed a flicker of panic, then she quickly calmed her features. "My guess is you value your privacy. Or is that too personal?" I posed the same question she'd spoken minutes before.

"I have Arthur." A spark of humor glinted in her eyes. "He's a grand listener and always believes I'm right." She hesitated. "I have a dear friend from college who's like a sister."

For certain, Carrington Reed had experienced tragedies of her own and built a wall to protect herself. The beauty before me with unforgettable eyes moved me to think about a future with someone other than myself.

THIRTY

CARRINGTON

Levi lingered over the bakery display, studying every tasty item after devouring his huge mound of decadent French toast. He reminded me of a little boy. He turned to me when I least expected it. The man looked way too good in jeans, and his shoulders spread across his knit shirt. Not over-the-top muscular, just tempting.

Too bad a relationship other than friendship would never happen.

With his bulging bag of pastries, he returned to our table. "Were you checking me out?"

"What?"

"I felt your eyes drilling through me. You think I'm a good catch, the man of your dreams."

I propped my hand in my chin. "Think again, hotshot. I wasn't checking you out. Period. I had my eye on a slice of carrot cake."

His eyes crinkled with laughter. "Right, Carrington. You can't schmooze your way out of it. You're blushing."

I laughed. "You wish."

For a moment, I let my mind drift to a place where dreams never failed, flowers never faded, and where people didn't die or go blind.

My phone buzzed with a message, and I pulled it from my shoulder bag. "Rats," I said.

"From Skip?"

"No, and he should have called by now. Sorry for my outburst. A medical procedure scheduled for later today has been moved up. I need to get home." I caught myself. "A simple thing."

"Are you all right?"

"Sure." But I couldn't give him eye contact.

"Is anyone going with you?"

"I'm fine." I replaced my phone and gave him a counterfeit smile. "Are you ready?"

"Let's roll."

But I wasn't ready for the medical procedure ahead.

Back at my little house, I searched for Skip's e-mail. Not here yet. I glanced at the clock. My upcoming ophthalmologist appointment crept closer. What was worse, putting off the inevitable or getting it over with?

I despised public transportation. If I didn't have my own car or trust the person behind the wheel, I stayed behind. Thanks to the text message I received from Dr. Leonard's office while at breakfast, she not only escalated my surgical procedure but also insisted I have someone provide transportation. Dependency wasn't in my vocabulary. My obsession with driving stemmed from my parents' accident and Grandma's bizarre driving habits, but this afternoon I had no choice but to use an Uber.

Whoa. I hadn't flinched when Levi drove today. And he would have driven me to the appointment, waited, and driven me home. The thought terrified me. I took care of others, like he said. Not the other way around.

Later I'd analyze the potential of us when I had my own life physically, psychologically, and spiritually on the right path. Levi had the faith I'd seen in Dixie, the trust in God I'd experienced in my grandmother before blindness created an inextinguishable anger. Although I questioned an afterlife, the idea of heaven appealed to my whimsical self when death knocked at my door. Especially today when I feared a cancer diagnosis.

My Uber arrived precisely on time. After grabbing my shoulder bag, I glanced down at Arthur. "I want to see you when I get back." He offered pleading brown eyes to take him with me. All I could do was plant a kiss on his soft, furry head.

In the car, I tried not to think about the appointment, but dread held me in its snare. A negotiator prided herself on eye contact and reading body language. How could I handle people feeling sorry for me? I'd need education in another field suitable for the blind. But what? Nothing else interested me.

My phone rang—Skip.

"What's going on?" I said.

"Have you heard from Felicia?"

"Not today."

"Did she mention going somewhere to regroup after Will's suicide?"

"No. Why?"

"She and the kids are not at home."

My stomach churned. "Have you checked with Howard and Zora Westfield?"

"Her parents have either lied or haven't see any of them. Felicia hasn't contacted her employer or notified the school about her kids' absence."

Felicia appeared more responsible than a woman who'd disappear without telling anyone. "She's under a counselor's care. I don't remember hearing a name, but her parents or their pastor would know."

"Tried that angle too. Felicia and the kids had an appointment yesterday. No-show. She also had a time scheduled with the funeral home and pastor yesterday. No-shows there too. The third time she's refused to make arrangements for Will's burial."

"Money might be a problem."

"I thought of the money issue. Will's life insurance policy is under two years old, which means it might not pay in a suicide. Which brings me to another topic. The sheriff's office issued a BOLO when her parents voiced concern about another possible suicide."

"I hope not. Would she convince the kids to do the same? Skip, she wasn't doing well, but I didn't detect that depth of mental anguish in her. Maybe she simply needed time to regroup."

"Whatever her reason for disappearing, my hands are tied to help her if she's skipped town."

"Have you learned any new developments?"

"A few questions hit me when I read the backgrounds." He swore, and I'd not heard cursing from him before. "Once I'm back in the office and think through the evidence and what we experienced, I'll e-mail you."

"Could Felicia have learned about the matching bullets? Maybe she needed time to figure out how to tell the kids?"

"Unless the news wasn't a surprise. Would she and Will have agreed to cover up Timothy's murder?"

"Really doubtful with the display of behavior we saw at the crime scene," I said. "Has she withdrawn any money or used an ATM?"

"Not to my knowledge. The sheriff's office is working with our detectives to bring the case to a close." He sighed. "You became her friend, and I thought she might have made contact. Sorry to bother you."

"Wait. Will you call me if you hear anything?"

"Sure. My wife told me I'd gotten too involved, and she's right. I let myself get too close during the hostage situation."

"Compassion isn't a bad trait. Just shows you're human, and caring means finding justice for the victim."

I held my phone and stared out the rear passenger window of the Uber, silently willing Felicia to call me or Skip to let me know Felicia and the kids had been found safe.

Soon I'd be at the ophthalmologist's office. Levi deserved a text, and I wearily typed in a message.

Skip called. Felicia and kids are not at home.

Missing? Took off to avoid repercussions?

Don't know.

Not another suicide.

Others are thinking the same thing. BOLO out.

Leads?

No. Skip said he'd keep me updated. The Uber driver pulled into the clinic parking lot. **I'm at my procedure. I'll contact you later.**

I dropped my phone into my shoulder bag and momentarily closed my eyes, emotionally debilitated.

What motivated Felicia to leave the area and not tell anyone where she was going? Was she afraid for herself and her children? Why? Did she know a different story that led up to Timothy's murder? Could she not venture into the future?

I shivered at the thought of a mass suicide. I'd walked a fire-laden path with Will, and death didn't have a reversal switch. I begged whoever was in control of the universe to keep Felicia and her children from harm.

My mind trailed to other scenarios. Hiding out only worked for so long unless she had a plan. Then it hit me. What if Felicia, Jace, and Emma had been kidnapped? What if they'd been killed?

THIRTY-ONE

LEVI

I paced the floor of my condo like a caged cat Monday afternoon after driving Carrington back to her home from breakfast. I'm sure doubts about Felicia ran as strong through Carrington as they did with me. Had we been used? Had Felicia chosen to hide with her kids? Or worse?

Fear of Felicia taking the lives of Jace, Emma, and herself soured my stomach. I'm sure Carrington, like me, had experienced suicides long before Will's. But the mind's rationale when faced with no way out went beyond my comprehension.

I peered down at my laptop, at the notes, jumbled reflections, and bits of dialogue. My story wasn't coming together. The releases I'd done during the negotiation had been easy, but I wanted a piece that inspired readers to look around them, to view life as a community of people helping people. Not a sappy piece with a Christian flag waving in the breeze but a documentary-type format. Felicia's viewpoint to show the empathetic side of a woman who loved her husband but couldn't get through to him was my primary focus. Chances were, Boyd would have much to contribute. But with Felicia missing and all that entailed, I questioned if anything she'd said had been fact.

I could speculate until this time tomorrow, but without facts, my writing fell into the pits of sensationalism. Rather dramatic, but the truth. I hated watching some of my colleagues fall prey to the ratings quest. I refused to go that route. Initially the hostage scene focused on Will and Boyd taking a desperate stand to speed up an investigation. Then the story morphed to Will's struggle with abuse, then he chose the unthinkable. What other damage had his deranged mind caused?

Phone calls, e-mails, and texts from all over the state and country requested my story or an interview. I had my sights on Fox, but until key players revealed the story behind the story, my writing had come to a halt.

I read the two-by-two card taped to the top of my laptop screen, a quote from Isabel Allende. "From journalism I learned to write under pressure, to work with deadlines, to have limited space and time, to conduct an interview, to find information, to research, and above all, to use language as efficiently as possible and to remember always that there is a reader out there."

Standing from the kitchen table that doubled as my desk, I walked outside onto my balcony looking for insight. I plucked a yellow leaf from a vine that screamed for water, reminding me of the withered clues somewhere in my mind indicating what I'd missed with Will and Felicia. Some reports on the story claimed Will resembled a rabid animal, biting poison into those who tried to help him. I agreed his actions were inexcusable, but he wasn't rabid. Some reports focused on the undocumented-immigrant situation, stating the people pouring into our country needed more protection when crossing the border. The media and our country were split on the acceptance of undocumented immigrants. Like many articles, each took a spark of truth and zoomed it into an agenda.

I chilled in the eighty-degree weather. Neither the wind, with a mind of its own, nor the sounds of nature whispered answers. What had we missed? Carrington and I had watched and experienced the disaster unfolding, and Skip scrambled for answers too. An entire family subjected to vile behavior and the agony of emotional trauma.

None of us foresaw the surge of violent actions. Unless someone unraveled the crimes and found a missing woman with her children, the Kendrixes' tragedy twisted into an open case with no resolution.

I peered into the branches of an oak tree. A crow shrieked at me and spread its wings.

My phone rang, and I recognized my sister's number. Snatching it up, I answered with expectations of a positive restoration of our relationship. "Hey, Sis."

"I'm not your sister."

"Pardon me, I forgot about my burial service. You called me, so what can I do for you?"

"Someone broke into our synagogue. Several items were stolen but with minimal damage done." She stopped. "Never mind. Thought you might be called to the story, but we prefer you stay away."

Images of the synagogue, its beauty and reverence swept through me. Treasured and sacred memories. "I don't work for the same publisher anymore."

"I see. Guess it's a good thing. Dad's at the scene with the rabbi, and you'd upset him."

"You called to make sure I didn't show up at the synagogue for fear of upsetting Dad?"

"Yes. He has enough problems without your interference. We don't want you near him."

"Who is 'we'?"

"All of us who care about Abba and Ima."

"Listen carefully to what I'm about to say, Deborah. I have no plans of disrupting our parents or you by arriving on a scene without an invitation."

"Showing up where you're not wanted never stopped you before." Deborah's cool tone distanced the sister I remembered.

"I'll make an exception."

"Another thing, don't send any of us cards anymore. You're wasting money. As soon as we see who they're from, we toss them in the trash. Under no circumstances do we want any calls or contact. Is that understood?"

I shouldn't be surprised. Still, anger—more like hurt and abandonment—raised my blood pressure. "Any other ultimatums?"

"I'm trying to protect my family and parents from harm."

"They are my family too. Our parents, Deborah. Not—"

She hung up on me.

THIRTY-TWO

CARRINGTON

Waiting for doctors gave me a headache. Another reason I avoided them. To me, they watched the time until they were officially late, then made an entrance with canned pleasantries. I rubbed the chill bumps on my arms and frowned at the stark white walls and straight wooden chairs. Used to be doctor offices had magazines and a little color. Made me wonder if the staff had poured antiseptic over everything.

Goodness, a bad mood had smacked me in the face. Dr. Leonard had devoted her life to caring for her patients. She answered questions and offered her text and e-mail info to those who needed her. Had she ever caused another patient to wait an extra five minutes?

Patience, Carrington.

I silenced my phone and checked for updates.

The door opened, and Dr. Leonard stood with a clipboard. "Carrington Reed?"

I stood as though my name had been drawn for the guillotine. "Yes, I'm ready."

We walked together down a hallway. A large painting of a field of Texas bluebonnets and Indian paintbrush offered color. Except we were at the beginning of fall, and those depicted spring.

Dr. Leonard gestured for me to enter an examining room. "First, I'll do an eye ultrasound. I'll use a handheld wand to produce high-frequency sound waves. Afterward, I'll conduct an angiogram by injecting a colored dye into a vein that travels up to your eyes. A camera will take pictures of the eye and the tumor. I'll also image other areas of the eye. Finally, I'd like to biopsy the nevus. It's not a requirement or absolutely necessary for a diagnosis, but I prefer to have all the testing completed. Are you okay with the added testing?"

"Yes. Do whatever is necessary. When will you have the results?"

"Anywhere from two to five days. Often sooner. When the lab sends the diagnosis, I'll call you."

Over an hour later, the receptionist handed me my paperwork. She insisted I wear sunglasses and use my phone's Uber app to arrange a pickup. In my blurry-eyed state, I couldn't have driven myself home from the appointment. Toss mental overload into the mix, and my stress rang the tilt bell.

On the Uber ride home, my phone notified me of three texts but reading any messages was out of the question, and I couldn't translate them to audio until I reached home. Curiosity stormed me to hear the texts now.

In the privacy of my own home and through courtesy of Siri, I managed to listen to text messages.

One from Levi. "Checking in to see how you are. I'm free if you need company."

I audibly returned his text. "Thanks for checking on me. I'm fine. About to crawl into bed."

Text number two came from Skip. "No updates on Felicia and the kids' whereabouts. I still suspect foul play. Sheriff Corbin Macmire suspects the same, as bad as it sounds. Text or call if she contacts you."

Again I audibly recorded my response. "Nothing from Felicia on my end. Thanks for keeping me posted."

Text number three came from Levi's former boss, Frank. No last name. "Carrington Reed, this is Frank. You probably saw me during the hostage ordeal. I represent *Now America Reports*. You're the type of person we want to highlight for our viewers and listeners. We'd like to offer you the opportunity to appear on our live TV show, which translates into radio, podcast, and print. Kindly let me know your availability. My offer is a lucrative one for you."

No point in responding to the man.

After fumbling to take care of Arthur and inserting prescription drops into my eyes, I flipped back the blankets on my bed and slid onto the cool sheets. Arthur crawled up beside me. Sweet dog. Perfect friend, and I needed one. My stomach roiled in fear of the test results, while the nightmare of cancer and blindness repeatedly marched across my mind. The whole ordeal over the past few days had reality stamped on it.

My failed negotiations with Will had caused him to take his life. Where were Felicia, Jace, and Emma?

Two hours later, my phone buzzed with a call. I struggled to find it on my nightstand, knocked it on the wooden floor, and finally was able to hold it to my ear.

"Carrington, Skip here. Wanted you to know Boyd has regained consciousness. Apparently he's coherent and lucid. I'm on my way to the hospital now. I didn't plan to wade through these waters any longer, but I have a boatload of questions, beginning with if he knew Will killed their father."

"Please call later," I said.

"Are you all right? You sound—"

"Sick?"

"Yes."

I inwardly groaned. "A migraine has me in bed." One more time, I lied.

"Sorry."

"Commonplace. Have you heard anything from Felicia?"

"Not yet. Take care and get some rest."

I laid my phone on my nightstand. Thank goodness for Siri's ability to call Levi. I placed my audible request.

"Yes, Carrington, are you feeling okay?"

"I'm fine. Skip's on his way to the hospital. Boyd's awake."

"How about a road trip?" he said.

"I can't today. Possibly tomorrow. But go ahead if you need to see Boyd."

"I'll wait. We don't want to get in the way of investigators. Been there, and it doesn't make for a good relationship with law enforcement."

"Okay," I said. "I'll text to confirm in the morning. But I should be fine."

"Did your medical procedure go as anticipated?"

No, but I'd not tell him that. "Yes. No big thing."

Levi touched my protected emotions where I thought I'd erected a barrier. I liked him . . . too much. He stood for life and people like no man I'd ever met. His faith intrigued me, a trait I wished I could emulate.

I rolled over and instantly jumped on board another nightmare train. This time, I stood in front of a full-length mirror with a long, trailing white wedding gown. I carried white roses with baby's breath. Around my neck were Grandmother's pearls, the same ones she'd worn on her wedding day, and my mother had worn on the day she married my dad. An organ played the "Bridal Chorus." Today was a dream come true. I would marry, and happiness filled me. The door opened and Dad towered in the doorway, just like I remembered, except he wore a patch on one eye, smiled, and reached for my hand.

"Carrington, you look lovely." He kissed my cheek. "I'm so sorry, baby, but I have bad news. Levi talked to Dr. Leonard and learned you're going blind with eye melanoma and cancelled the wedding."

THIRTY-THREE

LEVI

The evening wore on, and the conversation with Deborah continued to shake me more than I wanted to admit. My parents and faith instilled that caring for and respecting family were essential to worship. God instituted family from the time of creation. Yet my family chose to bury me.

Love hurt—physically, mentally, and yes, spiritually. Words and actions since my acceptance of Jesus showed me what believers endured in countries that persecuted Christians.

I needed to talk to someone who shared empathy for what I felt. Caleb, my buddy from church who had met with similar family problems when he converted to Messianic Judaism, now stood on the other side of survivor mode. Except his family hadn't shunned him, just let him know of their disappointment. I pressed in his number.

"Hey, Levi. I was about to call you. What's up in your world?"

The sound of his voice grounded me. "Everything and nothing."

"Start with the everything because with you, nothing is ordinary."

I chuckled. "You're the photographer who sees the believable and unbelievable."

"Ah, but you see the stories."

I laughed. So freeing. "I'm working on an article about a hostage negotiation."

"The one with the undocumented immigrants and the man who committed suicide?"

"Yes. Digging up facts to bring it all together."

"Your publisher should give you a raise."

"Not exactly. He fired me, so I have a freelance article."

"Ouch. Sorry. I knew you two didn't see eye to eye."

"I'm okay. I think my old boss did me a favor. Anyway, I caught up with a woman I've known for a while."

"Whoa. That's a first since I've known you. When do I get to meet her?"

"As soon as I convince her of my irresistible qualities."

Caleb roared. "Hold on while I lift my boots out of the . . . mire. Wait. Whoa, we're in Texas. It ain't mire but manure."

When we stopped laughing, I opened the door to what happened when I visited my parents and up to receiving Deborah's call. "Thanks for listening. There's nothing either of us can do but pray."

"The best thing we can do. I'm not saying the relationship with your family will ever get better, but I can assure you God cares."

"Appreciate the reminder. Is Shabbat dinner at your place on Friday?"

"You got it. See you then?"

"I plan to unless I'm in Victoria. I missed last Shabbat, and I like the idea of getting together with everyone."

"Text me when you know for sure. Levi, I have a question for you."

"Go for it."

"Where do you want to go with your life? I know, God's path. But I'm referring to your life goal. The reason I ask is, sometimes I think you're lost in transit."

Smart man. "I think you already know, but I want my relationship restored with my family. I want the right woman in my life. And I want to write articles that show truth and humanity while planting seeds for God."

"Okay, bro. I thought it best for you to voice those things with the changes in your life."

"Thanks."

I typed in *Carrington Reed* on Google. She had a website containing her negotiation services, contact info, a tab on various ways people could protect themselves and their property, and emergency guidelines complete with a list of resources. Her bio tab showed a recent photo and media information. Referrals upon request. Carrington's website displayed the private person I'd come to admire. She valued others above herself.

I spent the next hour attempting to find background on her, but all I managed was the city she lived in, where she'd obtained her master's in psychology, and her brief work history for Houston Police Department before forming a private negotiation business. The rest reported on her work with various businesses and private individuals. Nothing about her family.

"Who are you, Carrington Reed? Have you always been a loner?"

THIRTY-FOUR

CARRINGTON

Dr. Leonard called at 8:00 the following morning to check on me.

"I'm doing great." As if I'd say otherwise.

"Take Tylenol if needed and continue with the eye drops. I know you don't have family, but is there a friend you can talk to until we have the test results?"

"Yes." Contacting Dixie about my eye procedure soared outside my comfort zone. Lie number two in a matter of fifteen seconds.

"Good. I've put a rush on the testing, so I'll contact you with the results no later than Friday. We can discuss treatment then and set a follow-up appointment."

"Sounds like you're convinced it's eye melanoma."

"Not at all. We'll find what is causing your eye discomfort and vision discrepancies. In the meantime, wear sunglasses and rest."

"I will and thank you for calling."

I glanced around my bedroom. My eyes blurred, but I could make out the vivid shades of my favorite color—blue. The faint light peeking through the slats on the window blinds irritated my eyes. I forced myself to get out of bed and find my sunglasses on the nightstand. I fussed over Arthur and let him out. While he chased a bird, I admired the morning sunlight through oak tree branches, as though promising a good day.

Levi said he'd call about a drive to Victoria. With Boyd awake, I wanted to talk to Levi—as a friend. How Will had tricked him into abducting those people stayed on my mental front burner. My obsession with the welfare of the Kendrix family seemed over the top, but finishing strong meant more to me than anyone could imagine.

Had I convinced myself either blindness or cancer marked my future? What happened to optimism and hope? As a child and young teen, I believed God could and would heal. Then my faith took a dive into shallow waters, and my dreams drowned with the loss. God chose to leave me alone in a cold world to tackle the injustices and tragedies for myself. Like every challenge in my life, I'd walk through this fire alone too.

I texted Levi to see if he wanted to drive us to Victoria. With his bandaged arm, I had no idea how he felt.

Levi messaged me back. **I can be there in an hour.**

I tapped back an okay sign. I'd wear sunglasses and if anyone asked, I had a reaction to the eye drops from yesterday's eye exam. Not far from the truth. I increased the font in my e-mail and saw Skip had sent an attachment. I assumed the document contained the backgrounds I'd requested. It took several moments, but I finally initiated the text-to-voice software on my e-mail program. Levi and I could listen to the message on the way to Victoria.

Getting my mind off myself and focused on those in worse shape zapped my feel-sorry syndrome. For now. I sent a text to Dixie and asked if she'd look in on Arthur this evening. I told my sweet dog that I'd be back later to tuck him into his bed.

Levi rang the doorbell, and my pulse sped. How could I fall in love—was that what I felt?—with a man I barely knew when a death sentence hovered over me? What virus had infected this logical, in control, independent woman? I reached deep for my negotiation persona and opened the door. The mere glimpse of him sent my heart racing.

"Mind if I say hello to Arthur before we leave?" Levi said.

Since my loving dog rubbed against my pant leg, I picked him up and invited Levi inside. He reached for Arthur like a long-lost friend. I laughed.

"Make sure he doesn't think I've arrived for another playdate. I wouldn't want to disappoint him." Levi winked at me. "Are the sunglasses to hide from the paparazzi?"

"I had an ophthalmologist appointment yesterday, and I'm allergic to the drops used for dilation. I look like a drug addict."

"Can't have that. Was that before or after your medical procedure?"

"Part of it." I avoided his scrutiny. "Do you want a cup of coffee for the road? Won't take five minutes to brew a pot."

Levi lifted a brow. "I'm one step ahead of you. I drove through Starbucks on my way here, and fresh coffee is awaiting you in the cupholders."

No wonder he held my emotions in the palm of his hand. "Thank you. You're so sweet."

He set Arthur on the floor. "I've been called a lot of things but sweet isn't one of them."

I inwardly laughed at the thought of telling him I called Arthur *sweet*. Instead, I motioned Levi outside and locked the door behind us. The perfect medicine for whatever plagued my body—and my splintered past—stood before me.

Rush-hour traffic had thinned, which would shorten our two-and-a-half-hour drive to Victoria. The coffee perked me up, and I desperately needed the caffeine boost.

"Do you mind if I call Skip?" I said. "I haven't heard from him. He left me a doc to view, and we can listen to it on our way."

"Sounds good. I thought he'd call or text you as soon as he left Boyd."

"Me too. Maybe he's been called in to work." The idea of Boyd not making it bothered me. I suspected the worst. The call to Skip went straight to voicemail, and I left a message.

"He might be out in the field," Levi said.

"True. But my anxious thoughts fear he's in trouble."

"We'll be there soon. What about checking on Boyd at the hospital?"

"Good idea." I soon had the receptionist on the phone. "My name is Carrington Reed. I'm checking on a patient by the name of Boyd Kendrix."

"I'll put you through to the nurses' station on his floor. They can give you the patient's status," a woman said. "Hold on, please."

I waited . . . my dreaded pastime.

"Ms. Reed," a female nurse said. "Boyd Kendrix is under a doctor's care."

I repeated her words for Levi's benefit. "I thought he wakened yesterday?"

"Yes. Are you family?"

"No, a friend."

"I can't tell you any more about his condition other than he underwent surgery last evening."

"Thank you, and I understand." With the phone in my hand, I stared blankly at the highway ahead.

"We'll find out more once we're at the hospital." Levi's gentle tone broke through my rampant thoughts. "And why you haven't heard from Skip."

"I'll call the BP office and ask for him." I fought my vision to look up the number and pressed it in. "Is Skip Reyes available?"

"Ma'am, he's unavailable. Would you like to leave a message?"

"Yes, please. Ask him to call Carrington Reed."

"Oh, hold on a moment. Agent Reyes left a message for you."

"Would you read it?" I put my phone on speaker for Levi to hear.

"'Carrington, an emergency has me in the field. I talked to Boyd. Interesting conversation. He'll give you the same info.'"

I thanked the agent. "When do you expect to hear from Agent Reyes?"

"No idea, ma'am. Influx of problems have our agents busy."

I dropped my phone into my shoulder bag right next to my Glock. Could the Kendrix family, what was left of them, endure anything else? "Before the day is over, I want to visit Will and Felicia's home and Timothy's. I don't care how late we get back to Houston."

THIRTY-FIVE

Skip claimed an emergency regarding the Kendrix case? What had attacked the family now? Had something happened to Felicia and her children? I rubbed my palms on my jeans.

"Levi, I don't want to think Felicia and the kids' bodies have been found."

He reached across the console and took my hand. "You're freezing."

"It's my body's reaction to stress."

"Want me to pull over and wrap my arms around you?" His voice held no hint of teasing, but a dear man who put others first.

"I'll be fine. Hearing bad news often paralyzes me until I can focus."

"For the sake of others, we need an armor of optimism. Skip and the other agents might have found evidence to close the case permanently."

"I hope so." I imagined Levi praying. In critical times, I wanted a God who listened to those facing horrendous situations. "But since Skip isn't supposed to be investigating it, has he accidentally stumbled onto critical information?"

"I have a contact who works for HPD," he said.

"So do I." I hesitated. "Let me call mine, and if he can't help us, you can contact yours. Time for me to cash in on a few favors." When he nodded, I asked Siri to call Detective Aaron Peters. He answered on the first ring.

"Carrington, what's up?"

"Can you tell me if the Border Patrol has found the bodies of Felicia, Jace, or Emma Kendrix?"

"Are you investigating the Kendrix crimes?" Aaron said.

"That's the job description for the Border Patrol investigators and the county sheriff detectives."

He chuckled, a deep-throated sound that brought his robust personality to life. "Far be it for Carrington Reed to revert to unorthodox behavior."

"I promised Will Kendrix justice. Something is missing with those crimes."

"He committed multiple crimes before killing himself. Now his widow has disappeared with her kids. You're right. There's more going on than meets the eye. But you're not law enforcement, and the Kendrix clan has trouble stamped on their fingerprints."

"If you'll check for me, I'll hold."

"Why does helping you always cost me?" He snorted.

"Because you always owe me favors."

"Right you are. Hold on while I press a few keys."

I glanced at Levi, and he smiled. Why hadn't I seen the dimple on his left cheek before? Must be the angle of his smile. He still held my hand. I eased it back in case he accused me of a silly attraction like at Kenny and Ziggy's. If not for all the tragedies, I'd be—

"A body's been found on Timothy Kendrix's ranch," Aaron said. "It's a man. Hispanic. No ID. My guess an undocumented immigrant."

"How did he die?" My insides spun like a windmill.

"Bullet to the head. According to my findings, he is the third body discovered on the property. The other two men were shot at close range."

"I hadn't heard about those," I said.

"BP's been keeping the murders quiet. They suspect the cartel."

"Makes sense. If those poor people don't have the money to cross the border, then the cartel funds them and demands they move drugs."

"Try negotiating that mess," Aaron said.

"Seems odd the bodies were found on Timothy Kendrix's land, and the ranch doesn't border Mexico."

"Yep, odd, but those involved in the investigation will get to the bottom of it. Back to your original question. The people you're concerned about are still missing."

"Thanks, Aaron. Have you heard if the cartel is involved in the Kendrix deaths?"

"Border Patrol and Victoria County Sheriff's Department believe the killings on Timothy's property are connected. His ranch sprawls out over several hundred acres of desolate land, perfect for those gaining access farther inland. I'd tell you if there was any indication."

"Okay. I appreciate you."

"The next time I might not be so accommodating. Seriously, I can't stop you from looking into the matter, but be careful. If you get in the cartel's way, they will make an example out of you . . . like your headless body swinging from a power line."

THIRTY-SIX

LEVI

I doubted if we'd learn about Skip's field work or the conversation with Boyd anytime soon. Critical condition sounded like a complication from the previous surgery—and the prognosis shook me to the core.

"I'm worried Lyndie will lose Boyd." Carrington waved away any comments from me. "I know worrying solves nothing, but my mind still goes there."

"We'll find out what's happening once we're in Victoria. I admit I'm a hunting dog in pursuit of a story, especially ones where my compassion's invested. Part of me wants to be with Skip and the agents, and the other part tells me to be at the hospital waiting to hear about Boyd."

"Me too. Will and Boyd were victims of family violence, and those left behind have more questions than we do. When we have the facts and I can lay out the progression of behavior, then professionals in similar fields will have the knowledge to help others." She rolled her shoulders. "I sound like I'm quoting a textbook when I'm really thinking aloud."

"Fine by me. The tragedy needs answers. Carrington, you're the one to help the countless people caught up in domestic violence situations."

"We are," she said.

"We're a good team."

She laughed. "I'm a horrible partner. Picky about everything and bossy."

"Anything else? I want to be prepared." How would she feel if I told her I was serious about us?

"Spend time with me, and you'll find out." She glanced at the phone in her hand. Her fingers trembled. "Ready to listen to the Kendrixes' backgrounds?"

"Probably several times until I have them memorized. You haven't read or listened to them yet?"

"No. It'll be new to me, too." She laid her phone on the dash, and we listened, stopping after hearing each section. It began with a rundown on Timothy Kendrix.

"So Timothy spent two years in the Army." I reiterated more for my sake than Carrington's. "Worked his ranch from the time he received an honorable discharge until his death. Nothing's out of the ordinary with his financials. Bank account is good but not what I expected. No church membership."

She pressed the button to continue listening. A few moments into the reading, she hit Pause. "Oh, my goodness. Charges were filed three times against him for aggravated assault and attempted rape. All by different women with Hispanic names, and each time the charges were dropped."

Carrington peered out the windshield at the road, still wearing her sunglasses. "Levi," she said barely above a whisper, "I can't confirm this, but remember Mrs. Bolton, the woman who used to be the Kendrixes' neighbor? She claimed Timothy chased Hispanic women. Her words, not mine, but I'm sure you get the picture. I should call her. Is there more about Timothy than she originally revealed?"

"Do you suppose he tried to push himself on Felicia?" I said. "She's an attractive Hispanic woman."

"I asked and she said no, although he sounds like a predator."

"Yeah, it's sensitive. If the women who filed charges are undocumented immigrants, I assume they dropped the charges for fear of being deported," I said. "Or feared for their lives. Makes me question who else Timothy bullied for his power-filled empire." I shook my head. "I don't think I'll ever figure out the Kendrix men."

"Timothy seems to have fed his ego by manipulating people," she said. "From the marriage records, Dorie was ten years younger. He probably hid his ruthless personality until after they were married. By then, he'd have convinced her she couldn't survive without him, and his sons were too young to understand their home life needed changes. By the time they realized the dysfunction, what kept them close to their dad?"

"The family needed an overhaul before it got to the breaking point," I said. "I'd like to see Timothy's phone records, but it might take a bit of arm twisting to get our hands on them."

Carrington tapped her finger on her lips. "I can retrieve them."

"Legally?"

"I have security clearance to some things. I don't use the source much, only when necessary."

"Dark web?"

"Do I look like a dark web kinda gal?"

Gorgeous. Brilliant. "In short, yes. Willing to share what you find?"

"I might be persuaded." She smiled and stole my breath. "I'll see what I can do now, but I'd guess I won't have them until we're back from Victoria. If we're still awake."

"There's always tomorrow."

We listened to the backgrounds on Will and Boyd. Solid. Two men who worked hard and kept their noses out of trouble. Until recently.

"Have you got any information on Timothy's will?" I said. "I realize it might still be in probate, but I wondered if Felicia had mentioned it."

"She said Timothy's attorney has been on vacation. I checked and it's too soon for the will to be posted in public records." She paused. "The investigators surely looked into the will's contents for motive. Did Timothy despise his sons and leave them nothing? Definite grounds for murder." She shrugged. "Another task for us when we get back to Houston."

"Do you still have Mrs. Bolton's number?"

"What do you think?" She asked Siri to call the woman. A younger woman's voice picked up over the speaker.

"Is Mrs. Bolton available? This is Carrington Reed."

"I'm a hospice nurse. I'm sorry, but Mrs. Bolton has taken a bad turn. Her son is with her."

"Is she dying?"

"Yes, ma'am."

"How long does she have?" Carrington said.

"Hours."

"Please give my condolences to the family. I had no idea she'd been ill."

"Mrs. Bolton has been ill and in a memory-care facility for the past four years."

THIRTY-SEVEN

The waiting room on Boyd's floor held familiar faces who looked paler and more worn than in the previous depressing wait. Lyndie Moore and her mother sat in the corner, flanked on each side by Howard and Zora Westfield.

Howard lifted weary eyes to us with a tight-lipped smile. His shoulders slumped . . . and rightly so. "Appreciate you two driving here." He nodded at my arm. "Are you healing okay?"

"Yes, sir. How is Boyd?"

"Still critical," Howard said. "Dr. Sanchez gave an update about an hour ago."

"We were on our way here when we learned Boyd had been rushed back into surgery last night." I pulled a chair in front of the group, rather clumsily with one arm, and pointed for Carrington to take it. She frowned and grabbed a chair for me. I'd have teased her if not for the grim circumstances.

Carrington gave the four her attention. "How are you holding up?"

Howard wrapped his arms across his trim chest. "Zora and I are all right. Not so sure about Lyndie and Patti."

"Having my mom and other good people here helps the unbearable waiting, the not knowing." Lyndie had her auburn-colored hair pulled back into a ponytail, making her look much younger . . . and too pale.

"I'm so sorry," Carrington said. "We both are. Skip called yesterday to say Boyd had awakened. This new development shocked us. What happened?"

Lyndie moistened her lips. "He regained consciousness. He was very weak but coherent. Boyd held my hand and told me he loved me. He asked if Skip Reyes was available, so I called him. Agent Reyes immediately came to the hospital. They talked privately." She gripped her hands into a tight fist. "I have no idea what they talked about."

My mind charged into research mode. Why Skip? Why talk privately? Carrington stared at me with a slight frown. The same questions plagued her too. We waited for Lyndie while she dabbed at her nose.

"After Agent Reyes left, I went back into his room. Boyd started mumbling. He jerked and went into a seizure. I screamed for help. Nurses hurried in, ordered me out of the room. Doctors arrived, and within a few minutes, they rushed him back into surgery. According to Dr. Sanchez, the original surgery to remove the bullet caused an infection and stress on his heart."

"How hard for you to endure the emotional roller coaster." Carrington's voice softened to a whisper.

A white-haired woman who resembled Lyndie with the same hazel eyes introduced herself. "I should have gone into the room with her." She took her daughter's hand. "I could have helped or read the signs earlier."

"Are you an RN?" I said.

"Not at all. But I pay attention to details. Boyd should have been life-flighted to the Texas Medical Center in Houston."

"Mom, stop going over and over it," Lyndie said. "It's my fault. I wanted to be alone with him."

Lyndie's drawn features showed her misery. Every crisis I'd covered left people wishing they'd done things differently. Best to get their minds off themselves. "Can we get any of you something to eat or drink?"

"I've had so much coffee that my stomach's burning." Lyndie rubbed her palms on her jean thighs.

"How about some soup, bread, or ginger ale to settle your stomach?" Patti said. "I'm sure the cafeteria has chicken noodle."

"Your suggestion sounds good to us, too," Howard said. "We'll get it and stretch our legs a bit."

"Make it four orders of soup and bread, but I want coffee with cream." Patti reached for her purse, but Howard refused. He and Zora disappeared to the elevators.

"You are the woman who led the hostage negotiations, and you're the journalist?" Patti's eyes narrowed.

Carrington nodded. "Levi and I were there the entire time. It's important for us to support you and the family."

"I'm sure somewhere Felicia is pleased."

Lyndie gasped. "Mom, what a horrible thing to say. No one knows where she and the kids are or if they're alive."

"I'm saying she can't lift her head with all the humiliation. Will's a killer, and she's the pitiful, unsuspecting wife. Imagine putting your kids through that kind of trauma. They are better off far away from here. Or dead, like the media suspects. I mean, how could she expect them to return to school?"

"Mom, please." Lyndie's frantic tone brought the attention of a couple on the opposite side of the room.

Patti rolled her eyes like a sixteen-year-old. "You need to get away from Victoria. All I see is misery ahead. Planning for a wedding should be the most exciting time of your life, and instead your fiancé's life is hanging by a thread. I wanted so much more for you than this . . . this disgrace of taking on a crime-infected family. I'll move with you. That way we can support each other."

"I have no plans to leave Boyd, my home, or my business. Dad said he'd help with whatever we needed for the wedding. But help from either of you isn't necessary."

"Your father has a habit of saying one thing and doing another. His home and girlfriends have his priorities."

Poor Lyndie had a drama queen for a mother. "When's the wedding?" I said to Lyndie.

"Valentine's Day."

"What a perfect date," Carrington said.

Lyndie smiled. Between us, we might defuse the caustic mother.

"Be prepared to change it," Patti said. "Reality is, he could take nine months to a year to recover. I refuse to have you supporting a man who might not live and—I forgot! Boyd might face jail time if he can't prove his innocence in Will's fiasco. Why would anyone believe he didn't help Will rustle up those illegals? The wedding will not happen with my money financing it."

Lyndie arched her shoulders. "Mother, be quiet. I've heard enough. Boyd and I are paying for our wedding. It's our lives, not yours. Will exonerated Boyd of all wrongdoing. You've made a grandiose statement about your involvement when all you've done is criticize and complain."

"You ungrateful, poor excuse for a daughter. You even chose Felicia to help pick out your wedding dress. I shudder to think about the design. I won't lie to you—take a word of advice from your mother. No man is worth your reputation or your hard-earned money."

Why couldn't Patti give it a rest?

"Mother, I've bent over backward to please and look out for you." Lyndie's cell phone buzzed with a text. "It's Howard. They are on their way back with our food."

Patti glared at her daughter. "I'm not finished with our conversation. I'm looking out for your own good. Mark my words, Felicia will milk her missing game for all it's worth. Once the poor, poor widow has gained nationwide attention, she'll return home. The drama will begin again."

"Enough, Mother!"

Patti pointed a finger at Carrington, then me. "The Kendrix family's problems are none of your business. You, Mr. Reporter, are working on dollar signs for a story, and you, Miss Negotiator, wearing sunglasses, must think there's money in it for you too."

Lyndie slowly stood. "Carrington, Levi, I apologize for my mother's sarcasm and rudeness. She is leaving."

"People will find out soon enough that you're no saint." Patti huffed. "The only reason you're sticking here is for the dollars beside Boyd's name. You plan to drain him dry."

Lyndie's eyes widened. "How can you say such things? I'm in this with Boyd for better or worse. I don't care about money. I care about the man."

"You're not serious?"

"Very much so. You have destroyed what fragile relationship we might have had. I'm not making any more excuses. Leave and don't ever return. I'm finished with you."

THIRTY-EIGHT

CARRINGTON

Patti Moore had my vote for most disagreeable woman of the year. A few other descriptions fit her, but my grandmother would rise from her grave and wash my mouth out with soap if I used them. The woman needed to be on medication, or her mouth taped shut. She stretched my patience and negotiation skills beyond textbook-approved responses.

The Westfields returned with a meal for Patti, and Lyndie explained her mother had to leave unexpectedly. "I'll pay for my mother's meal."

"No way." Levi whipped out his wallet. "I'm buying the soup and bread and the coffee. Besides, I am one hungry man."

Did he always know the right thing to say or do? I needed to find a few faults before Prince Charming swept my emotions to the point of no return.

Poor Aaron, I was about to cash in another favor. I excused myself to call him. I wanted some background on Patti. If he refused, I'd ask Levi to use his resources or I'd dig into secure sites, when my vision cleared. Then it hit me. Felicia had said her dad's best friend was Boyd's fiancée's father. . . Patti's ex-husband. What a spiderweb of relationships.

Aaron answered on the second ring, and I gave him Patti Moore's name for a background check. "Carrington, really? Twice in one day?"

"I think having Patti's information is important. Besides, you're the best."

"Flattery? You must be desperate. What has she done for you to need her background?"

"She's Boyd's fiancée's mother."

"And?" Aaron had his own interrogation tactics.

"Not a pleasant woman."

"Plenty of those out there. What else?"

"Not a Kendrix fan."

Aaron drew out a heavy breath—all for my benefit. "Give me a little while and I'll text it to you. I have some work on my desk that has priority. Heed my warning, Carrington. Be careful. You've been caught in the line of fire too many times for me to sit by and watch it happen again."

"Yes, sir."

"Don't be giving me lip service."

"I won't break the law or wade into danger. I know my boundaries."

"Write that on the back of your hand."

"It's tattooed."

"You heard me. Danger growls at your heels like a mad dog."

⸻

I walked back to Lyndie, the Westfields, and Levi. Dr. Sanchez, the surgeon who'd removed Boyd's bullet, approached them and they stood. I hurried with a mix of fear and a smattering of optimism.

"How is he?" Lyndie's lips quivered. "Can I see him?"

"Not yet, but soon. Perhaps in an hour or so. He is still critical, Miss Moore." Dr. Sanchez punctuated each word. "The good news is his vitals are improving. He's strong and a tremendous fighter."

"That *is* good news," she said. "Thank you."

Howard wrapped an arm around Lyndie's waist. "Told you he'd pull through the surgeries. We'll keep praying for a full recovery."

"I'm encouraged with his latest vitals," Dr. Sanchez said. "I'll inform the nurses' station to give you timely reports. If he continues to progress, he'll be removed from the critical list." He pointed to the soup. "Glad you're eating. I don't want another patient."

After he left, we sank into the chairs to wait. I focused on how I'd be a more caring person by waiting with them to hear about Boyd. Levi and I had decided not to mention Felicia unless someone else chose to talk about her. But asking tempted me. Conversation swung like a pendulum from the weather to Lyndie's business to the wedding.

Howard took Zora's tanned hand. "My dear wife needs a nap. If y'all don't mind, I'm taking her home. I'll check back later, and I've asked our pastor to stop by here. If you get an update from Boyd or hear from Felicia, please text me."

What a kind and caring man. The Westfields didn't need any more bad news. *Felicia, where are you?*

THIRTY-NINE

LEVI

I longed to be out researching, looking for Felicia and her kids, driving across Timothy's ranch—anything but coughing up conversation topics with Lyndie Moore. I had an antsy streak, and it pulled at its leash.

Carrington moved from facing Lyndie to easing down beside her. "We all want answers here, and we share concerns about the Kendrix family and those who care about them."

"Finding Felicia would be a relief to all of us."

"If you don't mind sharing, what has Boyd told you about Timothy and Will?"

Lyndie stared beyond Carrington and me, beyond time. "I guess it doesn't matter, and I'll tell Boyd later about our talk. He said Timothy had been abusive, physically and verbally, to their mother and Will. At times Timothy verbally tore into Boyd. I'd always heard rumors about a disagreeable side of the man, but I'd only talked to him a few times over the phone. Boyd intended to break all contact once we were married due to Timothy's temperament and how he'd treated his mother and Will. Timothy claimed I wasn't fit. Not sure why and Boyd never asked, and trust me, I wanted to know. I planned to talk to Felicia about it before Timothy was killed."

Lyndie wrung her hands. "Boyd is my life, my reason for breathing. If I believed for one instant that he'd inherited any of Timothy's disgusting traits, I would not be in a relationship with him."

"What kind of rumors did you hear about Timothy?"

"Conflicting. He and Mom had a relationship at one time." Lyndie shook her head. "In my opinion, they deserved each other. Boyd said his dad hung on to money like a kid with candy, but his ranch was worth a couple of million dollars. The brothers stood to inherit enough to keep them both in solid financial shape. I have nothing to verify what I've heard, but another rumor is Timothy contributed to politicians who promised him favors." Lyndie paused. "Strike that. Gossip only gets people into trouble."

"Of course," Carrington said. "What about Will?"

"He acted friendly around me, but we never shared a private conversation. Felicia immediately included me in things going on with her and Will. When Boyd and I got engaged, she helped me select a wedding dress and directed me to a few event centers for the reception. I like her very much. She and Will do, or rather did, a good job parenting Jace and Emma. I grew up with Mother shoving her agenda at Dad and me until Dad gave up. Anyway, Felicia's kids are polite and make good grades. Jace plays football, and I've gone to games with Boyd. Emma is quiet and enjoys piano. She's quite good."

Lyndie stood and paced. "I'm talking too much. Just scattered watching the clock until I have a few minutes with Boyd. Maybe he'll open his eyes again and talk."

"You're doing great, Lyndie." I imitated the mannerisms I'd heard from Carrington. "I have a question about the brothers."

Lyndie returned to her chair. "Levi, for you I'd do about anything. I'll never forget how you risked your life for Boyd and Will."

But my efforts hadn't worked out well. "Were the brothers close?"

She leaned back against the chair. "They were best friends. Talked every day. Spent time together helping each other out on their ranches. Took time off to hunt and fish." She swiped at a tear. "I don't know why Will shot him."

"Did Timothy have a will?"

"Boyd said so, but I didn't ask about the contents. Who else would Timothy leave his estate to but his sons?"

"You're right. Neither Will nor Boyd would want to risk losing an inheritance. I'm sure the brothers providing for their families seemed like a way to make up for what they missed growing up."

Lyndie nodded. "I wanted to move as far away as possible, but Boyd believed we could build a good home here. Not construct a physical home but establish a satisfying and meaningful relationship to raise our family." She glanced at the clock on the wall. "Six more minutes."

Carrington studied Lyndie, no doubt picking and choosing her words. "How long can you keep up this pace at the hospital?"

"Until he's stable."

"When was the last time you slept?"

She pointed to a blanket on the back of her chair. "I can't miss my hourly time with him. In between visits, I run home for a shower. There'll be plenty of time to sleep when Boyd's well."

"I could make a restaurant run later," I said. "Hospital food gets old."

Lyndie gave me a thin-lipped smile. "I'll stick to what is served in the cafeteria. If Boyd needs me, I want to be here. I appreciate the offer, though. Maybe another time. My thoughts aren't on food."

Skip walked into the waiting room and greeted the three of us. Lines around his eyes showed he hadn't slept much. He'd aged in a week's time under the stress. Once he learned Boyd hadn't spoken since his second surgery, he glanced around the empty room. "I'd like to discuss what Boyd said to me."

Lyndie stood. "I'll have to hear about it later. Right now, I'm going to see him."

Skip watched her leave and took a chair. "Talking to you two is better, since the three of us are not supposed to be investigating this mess." His gaze darted between Carrington and me. "Strike that. I'll run by Sheriff Macmire's office once I leave here and relay the same thing. I suggest keeping the info to yourself until I talk to him. Then I'm heading home and sleeping. So here goes. When I talked to

Boyd, he was clearheaded. He said Will had more on his mind than their dad's murder, and he'd learned something about their dad that he couldn't ignore. He believed their dad was rear-deep in a human-trafficking ring and Will wanted to pick up a group of undocumented immigrants who were in danger. Boyd wanted to call Border Patrol, but Will insisted there wasn't time. Once they located those people, Will crossed the line of sanity. Boyd refused to go along with abducting them at gunpoint, but Will turned his rifle on him."

Skip shook his head. "I didn't tell Boyd that Will's rifle had shot their dad. He'd find out soon enough."

When Carrington didn't add anything to the conversation, I chose to reveal what we'd heard from Felicia and Lyndie. "In short, both women were told Timothy abused his family."

"Confirming the call I received from Charlotte Bolton," Skip said. "Evidence shows Will shot his dad, but I don't think Boyd suspected it or he'd have told me."

"Why are you staying on top of the case?" I said.

Skip appeared to ponder the question. "I'm eligible for an entry-level investigator position at the CBP. Before it had a chance to go through, Timothy Kendrix was killed. While I'm behind the scenes with this, I feel it's what I'm supposed to do. I don't like the idea of Timothy Kendrix running a human-trafficking operation on my watch. If he was, then I'll find the evidence."

"You might lose your dream job," I said.

"Doesn't matter. I'm in."

FORTY

CARRINGTON

The Westfields' pastor stopped by, and after a few cordial words, I turned to Levi, who must have been reading my mind.

"Ready to take a drive?" he said.

What an amazing smile. "Great idea."

We bid the pastor and Skip a good afternoon and took the elevator to the lobby en route to the parking lot.

In the Tahoe, my phone alerted me to an audio text from Aaron. I filled Levi in on my earlier call to him. "He must have received background on Patti Moore. The way she spoke to Lyndie left me questioning her personal agenda."

"She is one difficult woman. Bring it on."

I allowed Aaron's rich voice to sound through Levi's speakers. "Carrington, Patti Moore owns an accounting firm. Two years ago, she announced her intentions to run for Congress in her district. A huge sum of money showed up in her account, and she claimed not to know how it got there or from whom. Inquiries followed. She pulled out of the race."

I stopped the recording. "There's our answer. It's certainly not against the law to be ambitious or obnoxious. Makes me wonder who made the hefty deposit."

"My mind goes straight to someone who wanted to destroy her or gain a political favor," Levi said. "Both are speculation."

"I question if the run for office occurred before or after Patti and Timothy were no longer an item." I swung my gaze to Levi.

"We're on the same wavelength."

Levi drove his Tahoe by flat ranch land dotted with cattle and horses to Will and Felicia's home. A black, newer-model Ford truck was parked in front of a modest one-story brick home. A border collie barked and wagged its tail. Oh, I wished my vision would take a giant leap to clear.

"Somebody must be feeding the dog," Levi parked in front of the home and pointed to fresh tire tracks. "For that matter, who's taking care of the cattle and horses?" He squinted. "I see goats too."

"The Westfields? But that would indicate Howard's been in contact with Felicia. Unless he's simply managing things for her out of concern. I'm sure that's it." I glanced around at the barn and two outbuildings, one a chicken house. Modest, like the home, but neat and clean. Cattle and horses grazed in the distance. At least from what I could tell with my distorted vision. Quiet. Peaceful.

"Ready to knock on the door?" he said.

I opened the passenger-side door as my answer. Levi bent to snap pics of the tire tracks. The border collie trotted around to my side, and I patted her head. No doubt the beautiful animal smelled Arthur on me. "She is definitely not a watchdog."

Levi stood in front of his Tahoe and scanned the house. "Do you think Felicia and the kids are here, just lying low?"

"I wish. But then I'd have to curb my tongue because I'd let her have it for scaring everyone."

We walked to the front door. Levi pressed the doorbell. Twice more. He knocked. No response. "Let's try the back door."

At the rear of the home, a sixteen-by-twenty covered patio with a picnic table, chairs, and an outdoor grill showed family life. Levi knocked on the door while I felt the grill.

"It's cool." I lifted the lid. "Hasn't been used lately."

He peered into the back windows. Nothing. Deserted. "Doesn't eliminate them as hiding until we leave." He turned the doorknob, and it opened. "Makes me wonder if they left in such a hurry that someone forgot to lock the door."

"Strange. Law enforcement must not have tried to gain entrance."

"Or they searched and left the house like they found it." He stepped inside.

"You're trespassing."

"Right. You coming in?"

Against my better judgment, I followed him.

"Felicia, are you here?" Levi called while walking through the kitchen, living area, and on to the bedrooms.

The home felt welcoming, homey, with a southwest ranch décor in turquoise and red. I stopped at the master bedroom. The same western furnishings. The bed hadn't been made, so I took a look in the master bathroom. Using a hand towel to avoid leaving fingerprints, I checked in the drawers. No toothbrush, toothpaste, facial creams, or makeup.

"Levi, I think I'm onto something." He joined me. "Felicia planned this trip." I explained my reasoning.

He took another towel. "I'm checking for luggage."

I did the same in the master bedroom.

No luggage.

"A kidnapper wouldn't have allowed them to pack," I said.

"Right. At least there's comfort in believing they're alive."

"Would the BP or sheriff's department have kept that info to themselves?"

Levi inhaled and slowly exhaled. "Why? Unless they found something that indicated where they'd gone." He shook his head. "We aren't in any position to relay our findings."

We left the house, chose not to lock the back door, and walked to the barn. Levi noted the horses inside had fresh hay. "We could hang around to see who's feeding the animals."

"I didn't bring a tent."

He chuckled.

We checked for trash, but nothing offered a clue.

Levi and I slowly made our way back to his vehicle. Our attention darted in all directions. The distant cooing of doves and an occasional bawling cow were the only sounds.

"Timothy's ranch is about thirty minutes or so from here," Levi said. "Shall we see if anyone's out there?"

"Skip and his buds might run us off."

"They weren't here. Besides, wouldn't be the first time I've been chased away from a story. Or stuck in jail for not minding my own business."

Not sure why being with Levi lightened my mood, but I liked it.

On the drive to Timothy's ranch, I checked on Boyd. His vitals had steadily improved. Good news for a change.

The elder Kendrix's ranch was a showcase. A sprawling two-story farmhouse and massive barns. No dog trotting around. But herds of cattle and horses grazed on the surrounding pastureland.

Levi's gaze spanned the grounds. "No way Timothy worked the ranch by himself."

"Even the fields look manicured. So where are the workers?"

"A hired man would have sussed out Timothy's nefarious behavior. Maybe more than the BP or county sheriff's department have uncovered."

"It still doesn't eliminate Will's guilt," I said. "But maybe more was going on leading up to the shooting. What if the bullets that killed the three men found on Timothy's ranch matched the rifling patterns in Will's rifle? Then what?"

"I'm sure Sheriff Macmire will ask Boyd about those bodies."

Hired workers, friend or foe, might be in the barns watching us. Curiosity had the best of me, and I approached the largest building. A dog barked inside the one nearest us. The closer Levi and I walked, the louder and more vicious the barking.

He grabbed a wooden pole leaning against the barn door and turned to me. "How—?"

FORTY-ONE

LEVI

An arrow pierced Carrington's left side, and the blood flow soaked her shirt.

She gasped and fell against me.

I helped her to the ground on her stomach. The arrow had sunk deep into her flesh.

She moaned. "Pull it out. Please."

I jerked off my shirt to stanch the blood pooling around the arrow. Caution set in.

Another arrow whizzed past, grazing the top of my shoulder on the same arm where Will had done damage. I leaned over Carrington's body, protecting her and maybe myself too.

"Do you see anyone?" she said through a ragged breath.

I lifted my head slightly. "No. Maybe behind a shed to the right of my Tahoe. But someone views us as a threat." I calculated—about sixty feet to my vehicle.

"I know it's not smart, but please pull it out."

"Listen to me. The barb on that arrow is like a fishhook, and we don't know what internal organs are in its way. I'm not causing you to bleed out."

She let out a groan.

The dog inside the barn scratched to get out.

Another arrow flew over my head. The archer wasn't giving up. "Hey, we're leaving!" No response but I didn't expect one. I took a quick glimpse of her white face and closed eyes. "I'm going to carry you to the Tahoe. Put you in the backseat and we're out of here."

"Okay," she whispered. "I'm sorry."

"Nothing to be sorry for." I prayed for my own speed and for poorly aimed arrows. Tucking my shirt around her wound, I prayed for divine strength and a miracle to get us out of there alive.

I scooped her up, and fire lit my injured arm while I ran in a zigzag pattern. The dog continued to fight the door. Bending low, I hurried closer to my Tahoe.

An arrow soared over my head on the right.

Vicious barking alerted me that the dog had escaped the barn and raced my way. Looking back risked dropping Carrington. The growling moved closer.

My vehicle loomed ahead of me. I'd endure the dog attack, but I had to get Carrington to safety. At the rear passenger side, I swung open the door and felt the dog sink its teeth into my lower leg. I shook my leg to rid myself of the animal while positioning her on the seat.

Swinging around, I kicked the huge, snarling shepherd, using more strength than I imagined. The few seconds of time allowed me to open my door, but the dog managed to take a chunk out of my ankle.

Bringing my Tahoe to life, I raced off Timothy Kendrix's property with the killer dog and unseen archer behind us.

"Carrington, talk to me."

"Hurts."

"I know. I'm sorry. Racing to the hospital."

"Thanks." Barely a whisper met my ears.

"Stay awake. It won't be long."

"The dog . . . loose."

"I'm good." I called the hospital and explained Carrington's arrow wound. The ER assured me there'd be no delay in treating her.

Between the bullet wound, the arrow that nicked my shoulder, and two vicious dog bites, I fought to keep from passing out or throwing up.

Lord, Carrington and I need a little help.

FORTY-TWO

CARRINGTON

From Levi's strained voice, he must have been hurt badly. He wanted me to stay awake, and I vowed to honor his request. Still, I faded in and out. Oh, how I wanted to yank out the arrow. Pain and I were acquainted but not friends. My hearing resembled a tunnel, my vision blurred, and nothing chased away the lit fire in my flesh.

Levi rolled the Tahoe to a stop. "We're at the hospital. Hold on, Carrington."

Too weak to respond, I resolved to thank him later. The rear seat doors at my feet and head opened, and the voices of strangers assured me of their caring. They were gentle, but I failed to stop the screams. They lifted me onto a gurney and wheeled me inside glass doors. Somewhere in the journey, I slipped into comfortable unconsciousness.

I startled and smelled antiseptic. Forcing my eyes open, I noted a blinding light and medical people hovering above me. Someone had removed my sunglasses. I craved the strength to speak. "How is Levi?"

"He's receiving medical attention for his injuries," a woman said, her voice gentle.

I gave myself permission to allow blackness to take over, but my body neglected to obey. Over the next several minutes, I screamed and attempted to endure excruciating pain. I worried about Levi and if his body could handle much more abuse.

A man said, "Surgery," and I welcomed the anesthetic.

———

My eyes fluttered open and for now, nothing hurt and my vision had improved. A lamplight gave the room a warm glow, rather comforting instead of stark white. Levi sat on a brown vinyl sofa smiling at me. Looked like his arm and shoulder were wrapped in another bandage.

"Hey," he said. "You scared me."

I swallowed hard while a dull throb in my side reminded me of the arrow. "I think I'll live. Am I okay?"

"The arrow's gone. It nicked the side of your stomach, and the surgeon repaired the damage."

I forced my eyes to stay open. "What about you?"

"I'm good."

"Levi?"

"An arrow skimmed my left shoulder and required a few stitches. According to the surgeon, the archer used a carbon arrow, which means it was shot from a compound bow, a popular choice for target archery and hunters. The dog managed a mouthful of my leg, and that took a few more stitches. But only two stitches to my ankle, where the dog nipped me again."

Horror raced through me. "Your left arm again? And the dog? I'm really sorry. What can I do?"

"Kiss me and I'd feel amazing."

Tempting but I moaned instead. "Then I'd have to move. Please tell me the doctor doesn't want to keep me overnight."

"All right. I won't."

I wanted to be needy, complain, but I remembered his sacrifice. "Thank you for saving my life. I should have asked how you were doing the moment I opened my eyes."

"You asked about me plenty of times in the Tahoe and when we got to the hospital."

"Glad to hear my subconscious is in the right place." I paused. "You're such a good man, a true hero."

"Your IV has taken over your good sense."

"Doubtful."

"Have we been found out?"

"Not yet. I did some googling and learned Sheriff Macmire and Boyd are friends."

I took a deep breath, wanting to summon a nurse for pain meds. "Did you make a hotel reservation?"

He nodded.

The doctor walked in with the typical keeping-you-overnight-for-observation speech.

Then I learned Levi's hotel was the sofa in my hospital room.

Shortly after 8:00 p.m., Howard and Zora stopped by my room. They were a kind couple, and Zora brought me a piece of homemade carrot cake. Her smile lit up my room, and I saw Felicia in her. Levi must have told her I had a weakness for it. Felicia needed to contact them . . . if possible.

Medical personnel had moved Boyd to a private room. No longer critical but serious. His improved condition proved benevolence had risen to the surface today. My mind had cleared enough to talk about who'd targeted us with a bow and arrow. I glanced at Levi stretched out on the sofa, softly snoring. I'd let him sleep. Sweet man. He'd shown me repeatedly his kind spirit, not only for me but for others. How could his family have turned him out like an unwanted animal?

Arthur. He must wonder what happened to me. I spoke an audio text to Dixie. Told her I was stuck out of town. Would she look in on my dog? She responded immediately with a smiley face emoji.

I closed my eyes but sensed someone had entered the room. They flew open to show a blurred Skip standing in the doorway. His frown dropped to his boots. Another man stood next to him. It didn't take a PhD to figure out the red-haired, thin-framed man worked for the county sheriff's department.

Skip rubbed the back of his neck, a gesture I'd seen when confusion worked its way through him. "First of all, how are you feeling?"

"Like someone shot an arrow into my side."

"Glad to hear you still have spunk." His gaze settled on Levi who must have heard Skip talking because he opened his eyes. "He doesn't look much better than you do."

The sheriff laid his phone on the bed table. "I'm Sheriff Macmire. I'd like to hear why you were on Timothy Kendrix's ranch and who attacked you. Miss Reed, you can go first. I'm recording our conversation for accuracy."

I wanted to demand he leave. So much for my own negotiation skills. I pressed the nurse's button, and a female voice responded.

"Yes, Ms. Reed?"

"I'm in quite a bit of pain."

"I'll check your charts. Someone will be right there."

I thanked the woman and gave the sheriff my attention. More like I glared at him like he had horns. "We were curious about Timothy's property and drove there to see if anyone might offer information."

"Information about what?"

"Why?"

"Ms. Reed, you're in pain and I regret the questioning. But I can't find who attacked you and Levi unless you cooperate."

I moistened my lips. How many times had I talked to belligerent people, and now I made them look like saints?

A nurse arrived to give me a few moments to regroup. She placed pain meds directly into my IV. At least I had the courtesy to thank her.

"Sheriff, I promised Will Kendrix justice, and too many findings make little sense."

"You're a hostage negotiator, not law enforcement."

"I'm a compassionate human who refuses to back down from her word. Levi and I found the Kendrix ranch deserted except for a successful archer and a dog that broke out of the barn and took two bites out of Levi's leg."

"Was anything said?"

"I have no idea."

"Sheriff," Levi said. "I called out, but no one responded."

Sheriff Macmire nodded and turned his attention back to me.

"Levi carried me to his vehicle, put me in the back seat, and we left the ranch."

"Do either of you have any idea who might have attacked you?"

"Someone who had a problem with us on the ranch." I held up my hand attached to the IV. "My apologies for the obvious."

"What did you expect to find on the property?"

"At least one hired hand," I said. "The place is immaculate, which means Timothy had help." I peered into the sheriff's eyes. "Whoever worked there still does and undoubtedly knew the owner's personality and habits."

"Will Kendrix shot and killed his father. Case closed."

"What about the three bodies found on separate occasions on the property?"

The sheriff frowned as though I wasn't supposed to have that info. "Isolated. The deaths were related but not to the Kendrix case."

"Really?" I wanted to say I'd heard more, so much more. "Have Felicia and her children been located, or has anyone heard from them?"

"No, ma'am."

"Levi," Skip said. "Why were you two at Will and Felicia's place before the assault?"

Levi flinched, revealing his pain, and forced himself to sit. He held his injured arm. Why hadn't I asked the nurse to give him something? And how did Skip know we'd been to Will and Felicia's ranch?

"Is the house under surveillance?" Levi said.

Sheriff Macmire chuckled. "What do you think? We saw you two. We saw it all. Shame we didn't have a team at Timothy's. Go ahead with your answer."

"I thought Felicia and the kids might be there keeping a low profile." Levi shared some of what he and I had observed, leaving out what looked like a planned getaway.

"Howard's been feeding the animals," Skip said.

The sheriff picked up his phone but didn't appear to end the recording. "Both of you listen up. Whatever your reasons for keeping your noses in the Kendrixes' crimes, consider the matter closed. You could have been killed today, which tells me my job isn't over." He paused, no doubt for effect. "But it's my job, not yours. Stay away from the Kendrix properties. Any so-called private investigation will be viewed as obstruction of justice."

FORTY-THREE

Levi and I entered Boyd's hospital room late on Wednesday afternoon to the hum of his life-monitoring machines. After two life-threatening surgeries, no one needed to say Boyd would be recuperating for several days. Lyndie held his hand.

"Thanks for coming . . . to my rescue," Boyd whispered, as though it hurt to talk. He had darker hair and Will's gray-green eyes.

"No need, but you're welcome."

"Lyndie . . . filled me in on what you and Ms. Reed . . . have been through." He took a breath that caused him to wince. "You tried hard with Will. He just sank into a deep well. I know Skip gave you and Levi the rundown . . . on what happened."

"Yes, he did. I wish I'd done more, and I'm Carrington. You have a beautiful fiancée who loves you and is cheering you on."

He nodded. "She's the reason I fought death's call."

Lyndie dabbed at her nose.

"Have you heard anything from Felicia?" Boyd said.

"Not yet. Do you have any idea where she is?"

Boyd closed his eyes. "None. Will promised to tell me . . . what he'd found out about Dad. But the happenings escalated before we talked. If I could add any facts to Corbin Macmire's investigation . . .

I would. I've told the truth. And I understand the former hostages have backed me up."

"Cooperation goes a long way," I said. "Right now, you need rest."

"We're heading back to Houston," Levi said. "We'll be checking back with you. See how you're doing and if we can help."

Boyd closed his eyes, obviously exhausted. We bid Lyndie good-bye and left the hospital.

In the Tahoe, Levi studied me. "I keep forgetting to tell you that it's good to see your gorgeous brown eyes again."

"You are so good for my ego."

His stomach growled. "Want to stop for dinner?"

"I'm hungry, but home is more important."

"How about I schedule a food delivery about the time we arrive at your place?"

If the odds weren't against us for ever having a meaningful relationship, Levi held all the signs of a keeper. "You are so sensitive to other people's needs. I appreciate all you've done for me and others since we've met. The hospital sofa looked like it was stuffed with rocks."

"I never noticed." He swung me a weary smile. "I had a beautiful woman in the same room with me."

"You're one lucky man."

He picked up on my sarcasm. "If it happens again, it'll cost you."

"Let's hope it doesn't."

"Yeah." He sobered. "How about Greek food?"

"Perfect, and my favorite. I would love an orzo chicken salad, fresh hot pita bread, and lots of humus with olive oil."

"I have an app for a great restaurant."

If only he had an app to cure eye melanoma. He'd call it "God."

"Settled." He phoned in an order to a popular Greek restaurant and set up delivery.

My side hurt where the arrow had pierced me. I had pain meds, but I didn't want to sleep, and I put them off as long as possible. Now to keep my mind off myself. "If given a list of those who might've used the bow and arrow on us, whose name would be there?"

"Good question. Timothy's ghost is at the top. My list is filled with probabilities, like a friend of Timothy's or Will's who'd stoop to anything to keep details private. Or Felicia for a variety of reasons . . . protecting her children for starters. Some families have principles or traditions that must be preserved at all costs."

He must be thinking about his family's treatment of him. "Do you think Timothy might have been in cahoots with the cartel?"

"Because of what Will told Boyd? And the three dead bodies?" Levi stared out at the highway. "I'm not discounting a connection. There's nothing impossible in our unauthorized investigation."

"You've been tossed in jail for snooping—"

"Researching. It's called researching. And yes."

Viewing Timothy's cell phone records once we were home targeted my thoughts. My blurred vision had cleared some, but the semi-handicap still prevented me from reading the tiny security code assigned to me. I didn't own a pair of readers, a purchase that would soon be made. I studied Levi. Dare I trust him? I must have confidence in his driving because not once in our time together had I questioned it.

"Do you have a photographic memory?" I said.

He laughed. "I wish. Why?"

"My access to secure sites requires entering a series of numbers and symbols. If the sheriff's department received Timothy's cell phone records, then we could access it. The thing is, the password on my security card is super small, and I can't read it until my eyesight clears."

"You and eye dilation don't mix well. But in answer to your question—have I let you down yet?"

Not exactly dilation but a surgical procedure. "No, you've been a superhero. Amazing. Thoughtful. Protective. I can't imagine you ever disappointing me."

He grinned my way. "It will happen—we're human. But thanks for the vote of confidence." He sobered. "Carrington, you can trust me."

Levi had nearly sacrificed his life for Boyd and gone beyond sanity to save me. Dad had told me once that when we risk our lives to protect others, expect the opposition to draw blood. And the enemy had succeeded. *Dad, if you were here, you'd show me what I should do about Levi, my eyes, and what I've missed with the Kendrix family.*

Had my illusions yanked me out of reality?

FORTY-FOUR

LEVI

The drive back to Houston sent my thoughts into a quicksand of doubt. Now might not be the best time to tell Carrington about my growing feelings, but each time I saw her, I feared it might be my last. I'd had a few romantic relationships, and I'd been hurt far too many times. The last woman nearly sent me to a counselor's chair. When she broke off our engagement, I swore never to chance feeling that pain again unless God put the right woman in my path.

Maybe God had. Carrington touched me in a way that flew between unimaginable and unexplainable.

Her guarded emotions and how she sometimes withdrew into herself told me she either didn't share my feelings or the world had hit her with a devastating blow. Neither scenario sounded good. But if God was in—

"We're both quiet," she said. "Are you hurting?"

"A little, but I'm okay."

"Do you want to change off driving?"

I tossed her my best don't-think-so look. "I have a better idea. Ready to tell me about your preoccupation?"

She smiled faintly. "You pick up on my moods far too easily. Right now, my concern is Felicia. Why she disappeared, and why she hasn't contacted her parents. What other forces are vying for her attention? Did she need time alone with her children to figure out a path forward? And those are my positive thoughts."

"She'll be bombarded with questions when she returns. Media will be all over it. I'd like to see a stronger woman who can make solid decisions and stick with them. Right now, she's disappointed those of us who were rooting for her. We both thought the worst of her and feared for her life." I palmed the steering wheel. "I hope she and the kids are alive. Jury's out on all of it."

"Her parents must be devastated. When I first talked to her, I thought the conversation between Will and her was headed for disaster. But she rose as courageous and let me coach her. She listened to everything I said. But her latest actions confuse me." Carrington sighed deeply. "I'm trying not to think about more deaths. Especially given there's not been any electronic activity picked up that would suggest her whereabouts." She tilted her head. "Like a planned suicide."

"Should we have told Skip and Sheriff Macmire our thoughts?"

She offered a closed-lip smile. "Seems unlikely for them not to draw the same conclusion."

I needed to voice my thoughts about Carrington, about us. I craved guts to move forward, but it battled with the agony in my arm.

God, I don't want to make another mistake. Zip my mouth if I'm out of line.

I reached across the seat and took her hand. "I need to talk about something, not the Kendrixes. Your mind is spinning. I can feel it humming through your fingers, but I don't want to intrude where I don't belong."

She stared at my hand around hers. "I'm tired and analyzing a complicated situation. You're preoccupied too. We're a fine pair. What's on your mind?"

If not for my pounding heart, I'd have laughed at her turning the tables on my question. "My guess is you've already figured it out. I . . . I want you to know how I feel about you. More than a friendship, and I know we're not strangers. But I want to know your favorite color, your dreams for the future. What you were like as a little girl. I have no idea your middle name."

"Yana. My mother's name. She was Bulgarian. Yours?"

"Benjamin, after my grandfather on my dad's side."

Carrington swallowed hard. "I enjoy your company very much, but we're not a good fit."

"My faith?"

She shook her head. "I admire your commitment to God and the stand you've taken with your family. The step you took with your faith has changed your life, and I believe for the better."

"Then what doesn't work for you? My charm and irresistible charisma?"

She rolled her eyes. "Neither of those. It's me, not you. Not sure how to put my issues into words."

I wanted to say something witty, considering her negotiation skills. But her lack of emotion told me she carried an emotional load of boulders. "Whatever it is, I'm listening."

Carrington stared out the passenger window at the approaching sunset closing around us like a shroud. "I'm under a doctor's care for potential eye melanoma. That was Monday's medical procedure. I'll have the final diagnosis by the end of the week. I could go blind in my right eye or die of cancer." She paused. "If I'd seen Boyd emerge from the side of the house sooner, he might not be in the hospital now."

The weight of fear settled on slumped shoulders. "That wasn't your fault. Delete that from your brain cells. None of us are guaranteed tomorrow. You are doing what the doctor's recommending, right?"

She nodded. "I'm not ignoring any of it." She peered at me. "Why would I want to subject you to the stress and potential sorrow of the unknown?"

"Sounds like every moment since we've met, and I mean the years of danger-filled scenarios."

"Levi, I'm serious."

I squeezed her hand. "I'd rather walk an uncertain path with you than go another day without you."

Carrington startled. "You sound poetic . . . and delusional."

"Those are the words of a man falling in love. *Ahavah* in Hebrew. Not a word I toss around. I see the same thing in your eyes." She paled. Had I touched the truth? "Are you feeling more than friendship too?"

"Levi, didn't you hear me? I could go blind or die!"

"You haven't answered my question, or have you?"

"There's more," she said. "Remember I said my family was gone? My dad . . ." She told me her family's story—the medical issues and the tragedies. "Now do you see why a relationship between us won't work?"

"What are you not telling me about the accident?"

"Not sure I can. No one's ever asked me that before."

"Maybe it's because I care and see a burden you shouldn't have to carry alone."

"Who would you tell?"

"Your story is not for me to tell, only to listen."

She gripped my hand and peered out the passenger window. "You scare me, Levi Benjamin Ehrlich," she whispered.

"We're on equal ground there."

"The accident with my parents? The crash was my fault." She turned to me with sorrowful brown pools. "I'd asked Dad if I could wear his sunglasses, and he gave them to me. The clouds gave way to bright sunshine, and he wanted them back. As a spoiled eight-year-old, I said no. He scolded me and reached around to get them. That's when he took his eyes off the road and didn't see the car coming at us."

"Again, that was not your fault. You were a little girl. How could your dad have avoided a head-on collision even with sunglasses?"

A soft sob met my ears. In the corner of my deepest caring reserved for Carrington, I gave her secret to God. "Nothing has changed for me. We have a powerful God."

Carrington stiffened. "Where was God when my parents were killed? When my grandmother received her diagnosis and gave up on life? The people who died needlessly during my failed negotiations?

When we faced bullets and arrows? Boyd? What about the deaths you've seen? Where was God then, Levi?"

Her reluctance to trust God fell into place. I prayed for wisdom. "If I had the right answer, I'd shout it to the world. All I know with certainty is God is real, and His ways are beyond our understanding. He took your family and others from us, and the loss makes no sense. But I will pray for your physical and mental healing every day. God does hear. He cares. The one thing I feel in my bones is His love."

"I want to believe you. But I don't. Can't."

"Developing faith takes time."

Silence seemed deafening between us, and I put an invisible clamp on my mouth.

"Levi," she said after several minutes, "I have a friend who is Christian. Her faith has been challenged many times, but she always relies on God."

"Is she happy?"

"More like joyful. She bubbles from the inside out. Dixie is an elementary school counselor and is married with two sons. She's forever inviting me to church. I've gone a few times, but my mind wanders. Or I allow it to take off at breakneck speed to avoid dealing with God."

"Want to try my church?"

"I need to think about it. What time is your Sunday service?"

"Messianic Jews worship on Saturday. Services are at ten o'clock."

She tilted her head. "I should have made the connection. Maybe I'll try your church when I can move around without cringing."

"Thanks. For the record, what I've said about my feelings is real."

She smiled. "For the record, I've already researched you. I saw a few stints in jail for not listening to law enforcement, but I've never found a woman mentioned."

"I was right! You were checking me out at Kenny & Ziggy's."

"Sir, my thoughts at a public restaurant are private, under lock and key."

She hid her emotions with humor, and I tucked away one more of her traits. "Finding out info on you is hard. If I wanted to hire a private negotiator, your credentials are all laid out online. Nothing personal, though. Just the facts. No background info other than when and where you received your degrees."

"I value my privacy," she said.

I'd prodded her enough. "We're more comfortable attempting to figure out the Kendrixes. We believe Felicia is covering up information, possibly a secret. Will went to his death with it, and Boyd might never figure it out."

"Which brings me to a question," she said. "Why are you sticking with me through their life-threatening situation?"

"I vowed when Boyd was shot to see this to the end. When he lay sprawled on the ground after taking a bullet and Felicia tried to talk Will down, I resolved the family needed more than a Band-Aid. Another reason is, just before Will pulled the trigger on himself, he whispered a few words I'll never forget. He said, 'Please keep my family safe.' I don't understand why I was supposed to take on the role, but I'm not backing off until someone figures it all out. Looks like Howard and Zora are doing their best, and they're worn out. Friends, their pastor, and organizations are in place to encourage too. I'm there until I'm not wanted or needed. And you?"

"Two men are dead in a strange set of circumstances. Three other men are dead on Timothy's property. People are missing. Like I told Sheriff Macmire, I promised Will I'd find justice. Truth and reality always seem more convoluted than fiction, and I never walk away from a crisis without closure."

FORTY-FIVE

CARRINGTON

Deep shades of navy blue had settled in the night sky when we arrived at my home. I did my best to shove aside what I'd told Levi about the car accident, and yet for some strange reason, I believed I'd made the right decision to tell him. Could it be my heart had taken the plunge?

Weariness stole my energy, but discovering the contents of Timothy's cell phone records nudged me to stay awake. Granted, the investigators working the murder case had reviewed the calls, but I had to see for myself.

Levi parked his Tahoe in my driveway. "Shall we head back to Victoria on Saturday? I'll drive. We can attend my synagogue the following week."

"I'd like that very much. I want to check on Boyd again, and maybe Felicia will surface. I'll fill up your gas tank. Buy our meals."

"No, thanks. I'm as curious as you are. Is eight too early?"

"I'll be ready."

The Greek food leaned against my front door in a generously sized bag. The aromatic flavors—an enticing blend of basil, thyme, garlic, and onion—tugged at my hungry stomach. Levi let Arthur out and filled his bowl with water and dog food while I set the table. Between

Levi's one-handed operation and my throbbing side, we were rather pathetic looking.

"Did I hear you say we were pathetic looking?" he said.

"I thought it." I laughed. "Guess I said it too."

He pointed to his bandaged arm and shoulder, then to mock my bandaged side. His incredible smile made me weak-kneed. I wish he hadn't told me about his growing feelings . . . or did I? The caring in his eyes told me his words were true, but I didn't have the courage to confess my tender spot for him.

After dinner, Levi helped me clear the table with comments about the arm-cripple hero and the aching-side heroine. I positioned my laptop, rather clumsily, on the kitchen table and tried to read the small print on a card containing my secure passwords. Useless.

He stood behind me, his warm breath against my neck. Tingling. How could I concentrate with such a distraction?

I pulled up the website and handed him the code card. "Would you read this to me?" I sounded like a helpless female.

As he read the numbers and symbols, I entered them. His breath continued to heat up my senses. I shivered, and I wasn't stressed. Concentration came at a premium.

"You have all you need?" he said.

What a loaded question. I turned to thank him, and his lips met mine. Warm. Firm but not demanding. I didn't want the moment to end, but it did.

"I meant to thank you for helping me," I said.

"You did. Care to try one more time in case I forget?"

I shook my head, but my lips curved upward. "Maybe later."

"You drive a hard bargain."

"And you're a little crazy."

I pointed to a chair beside me. "Sit, so we can get through our investigating."

"Is that what you tell Arthur?"

"Only those people who are crazy."

He closed his eyes. "I love the way you say I'm crazy." He shook his head. "But let's see who Timothy had been talking to."

The cell phone report gave the prior six months of incoming and outgoing calls. I zoomed in so I could read the numbers. "Those two belong to Will and Boyd." I gave Levi my phone. "Would you check to see if Howard and Zora Westfield or Lyndie Moore's numbers match any of the records? I'll call them out from my laptop."

Levi took a few minutes to see if there were any similarities. "Lyndie's number is there, and she told us she'd talked to him. I should have asked why. Two numbers are unaccounted for. He frequently called and took calls from those." He studied the screen. "I wonder who and why."

"Two numbers seem odd."

"My mind goes to illegal activities or women. Makes me wonder if any are burner phones. If so, keeping his calls private makes sense."

"Others might have motive to kill Timothy, but how would they have gotten their hands on Will's gun?"

"The killer is either Will, who displayed mental imbalance, or someone he trusted with his rifle," Levi said.

"I'll be the first to admit my brain is numbed by meds. And I took a pain pill during dinner. There's something we're missing, something that ties all our findings together."

"I'm right there with you, Carrington. I've seen bizarre things . . . Men who shoved their wives and children in front of flying bullets. Suicide bombers. Boy soldiers who laughed at the sight of bloody carnage. Children promised candy to run a lit stick of dynamite into a crowd of people."

"We've both seen the innocent suffer because of someone's evil." My mind drifted to the hostages who'd been denied food and water. "Would you check to see if the Victoria County Sheriff's Department has made an official ruling or held a press conference on Timothy's murder? I'm looking for an update." I turned my laptop his way.

Levi navigated to an update. "Boyd has been exonerated of any wrongdoing. Additional evidence shows Will Kendrix suffered critical mental issues." Levi touched my hand. "The case is closed, like Sheriff Macmire told us. There's more info in a video if you want to hear it."

"Yes, please." I squinted to see Sheriff Macmire and made out a few details. He reminded me of my eccentric eleventh grade chemistry teacher with wiry red hair and a fencepost-thin frame. My chemistry teacher was so brilliant that we students thought he had extra brain cells. I hope Sheriff Macmire held the same qualities. I listened to the video relay info we already knew.

"At 1:00 p.m. today, Lyndie Moore, Boyd Kendrix's fiancée, gave her statement to Sheriff Macmire. Timothy Kendrix offered twenty thousand dollars to Miss Moore if she cancelled the wedding. When she refused, he threatened to destroy her business." Levi shrugged. "I saw on the Victoria website that she owns a women's boutique."

I let Lyndie's words settle into my mind. "With Timothy dead, her testimony can't be verified."

"True. But why would she lie? What did she have to gain? Many will believe her because of all the stories circulating. I guarantee you the media will show Timothy and Will in the worst way. Like father, like son. It's already started. Maybe we're the ones playing devil's advocate, and Will and Timothy were rotten all the way through."

"It takes a lot to prove me wrong, especially when it comes to a person's character," I said. "But I could have made a terrible mistake. I might have ignored evil in Will and wanted only to see the good in him. Like a blind woman." Why had I used the word *blind*?

"If so, I'm guilty with you. Having Felicia here to answer questions would go a long way toward finding the truth."

"I'm not sure she could handle the media or questions. If she's still alive."

FORTY-SIX

LEVI

My cell phone buzzed with a call. I checked the screen—Frank. I started to let it go to voicemail, but I had a check coming.

"That's my ex-boss," I said to Carrington.

"Might be good news."

I shrugged and pressed Speaker. "Yes, Frank."

"Are you doing all right?" Almost sounded like he cared. Maybe he had a new approach to bringing me back on. "I saw you and Carrington Reed were hit by arrows on Timothy Kendrix's ranch."

"Yes. We're working on the healing part. What do you need?"

"I received a call from a man looking for you. Thick Spanish accent. Burner phone. When I told him you no longer worked here, he said he had a message for you."

"You have it?"

"Yeah, but it's not one you want to hear. He said for you and the Reed woman to stay away from the Kendrix bunch, or the next arrow would find its mark in your heart."

"Did he say anything else?"

"No. Refused to give me a name. I stalled him by asking if he wanted to make a statement. No dice. Although the number didn't appear on my phone, I went online and got it from my call log."

"Can I have it?"

"I've thought about contacting you ever since the guy called this morning. We have our differences, but I don't want to be the cause of you or anyone else getting killed. So here's the number . . . Probably hard to trace."

I jotted it down. "Thanks. Appreciate it."

The call ended, and a thought struck me. I pulled up the tab on Carrington's laptop containing Timothy's cell phone records. "The smoke continues to rise."

"Why? Is there a match?"

"Yes. It matches the most used of the two unknown numbers."

FORTY-SEVEN

CARRINGTON

The doorbell rang on Thursday morning at six thirty, waking me in a foul mood. I hurt at my incision, and my head beat like a thousand war drums.

The doorbell rang again. Couldn't be Levi because when he struggled to move last night, I gave him the sofa for the night. Maybe Mrs. Radison, but I'd never seen her out early.

Then it hit me. Dixie. She must have stopped by to check on Arthur, and I hadn't told her I was home. To make matters worse, Levi's vehicle was parked in my driveway. I slowly swung my legs over the side of the bed and moaned like an old woman. At the rate I was moving, she'd let herself inside with her key before I hobbled to the door.

Voices caught my attention, and I moaned again but not because of pain. Those voices belonged to Dixie and Levi, complete with introductions. I opened my bedroom door a crack.

"What happened to you?" Dixie said to Levi.

"I met the wrong end of a gun and an arrow."

"With Carrington?"

"Ah, yes. You haven't talked to her?"

"She texted me and asked if I'd look in on Arthur."

Don't tell her about my injury. She'd worry like an old mother hen. Worse yet, she'd ask questions. "Hi, Dixie. I'll be right there." I feigned a perky personality. Snatching my robe from my bed, I limped down the hall to the kitchen.

Dixie held Arthur in her arms. Her eyes widened when she saw me, and she put my sweet dog on the floor. "You look like warmed-over crisis. What can I do to help?"

"I'm good."

"Why are you limping? And you're pale as a sheet." When I hesitated, she continued. "Do I need to check the latest news, or are you going to tell me?"

Not sure if Levi and I had made the news, but did I want to chance it? "I had surgery to remove the damage caused by an arrow."

She raised her hands. "What? What were you two doing? Playing on the wrong side of an archery field? Taking down an army of professional archers?"

"Don't you have a whole school of kids who need you?" I said.

Dixie anchored her hands on her hips, a mom stance I hadn't had the opportunity to master. "From the looks of you two, no worries about a romantic interlude last night."

Levi grinned at me, standing on bare feet and leaning against the kitchen counter. "Go ahead, Carrington, you're the negotiator. I'm just the bodyguard."

"Lousy bodyguard." Dixie wagged her finger. "I've heard better tales from eight-year-olds. Whatever you two have been doing backfired. Tell me, great concealers, what gives?"

I quickly concocted a partially true story. "We were driving across a ranch that didn't have private-property signs posted. We decided to take a walk, and someone took offense."

"Totally unlikely. Is that someone in jail?"

"No." Levi picked up the conversation. "No way to ID them."

"You're not driving back there today, are you?" Dixie said.

"No," I said.

"Glad you've found a little sense." Dixie took a peek at her watch. "I'll check in with you later." She turned to Levi. "Good to meet you. I've read some of your articles. Impressive."

He thanked her. The man looked far too good with his tousled brown hair and his even darker brown eyes. Dixie would most assuredly ask me about him later.

"Thanks for stopping by and looking after Arthur. Sorry I forgot to let you know I was back home."

"Carrington, I will find out all the trouble you've gotten into. You can't skirt around the truth with me. I have negotiation skills too."

After Dixie left, I released a huge sigh. "I'm going back to bed, and I suggest you do the same. Later, with more sleep, we'll discuss our next steps with the mess we're in." I turned to limp back to my room.

"Dixie doesn't know about your eyes, does she?"

Without facing him, I shook my head. "She'd worry. Do we tell Sheriff Macmire about the threat shared with Frank?"

"Not sure. Could have been a hoax."

"Hoaxes don't shoot arrows."

He chuckled. "If I'm not here when you wake up, then I'm at home."

"For the record," I said, a common phrase since yesterday, "we're pathetic."

FORTY-EIGHT

LEVI

I couldn't sleep in my condo for thinking about Carrington. She'd done her best to sound perky, but I heard the hint of fear in her voice. The decision to keep the diagnosis from her best friend showed the private world of Carrington Reed. After googling what a diagnosis of eye melanoma included, I believed her ophthalmologist had found the issue early on. To be sure I'd interpreted the condition correctly, I called a friend who specialized in eye diseases. He explained in detail what Carrington potentially faced, and I didn't lose my optimism. For certain, I'd not tell her what I learned.

I stood and a bolt of pain caused me to wince, but I refused to flip the lid on the ibuprofen. I'd rather hero it out and toughen up. The prescribed painkillers had been donated back to the local pharmacy, too much of a reminder of my drug-filled days. Seeking more info on Timothy Kendrix—his habits, friends, and how he spent his time—could unlock the truth to the secretive family.

An online search on who Timothy supported showed a surprising report. He'd been suspected of contributing to a local woman's campaign for Congress in the amount of fifty thousand dollars. I chuckled when I saw Patti Moore's name. She'd supported tax breaks for farmers and ranchers. Violations occurred when Patti attempted to cover up the fifty-thousand-dollar donation to her campaign. That was the end of that political venture. Someone accused Timothy, and an investigation ensued. He was exonerated of any wrongdoing, and Patti withdrew from the campaign.

Did she keep the money? I dug deeper and found a pic of Timothy and Patti having dinner together before she backed out of the race. That supported Lyndie's statement. They'd posed for the picture cozy-like. A puzzle piece slipped into place. Patti had reason to despise Timothy.

At the hospital, when Patti stated her dislike for the crime-burdened family, she hadn't mentioned Timothy. Her animosity and disapproval of Lyndie marrying Boyd might have more to do with Timothy than I originally thought. But Patti hadn't indicated her ex and Timothy were best friends. Oh yes, lots more was going on in rural Victoria. Will pulled the trigger, but he'd been one of many who despised Timothy.

I checked with another media site to see if Patti still wooed the public for a potential congressional run. The man in office had supported programs and platforms that went against the grain of the Victorian community. She made personal appearances, building up her stand.

Carrington and I needed to stay away from Victoria to recuperate. I'd look at the whole picture of what we'd experienced and offer a few options for moving forward in a behind-the-scenes investigation. Sheriff Macmire had thanked us for our commitment to the Kendrix family but assured us that his department would complete the paperwork for the investigation.

I didn't appreciate the threat to leave Felicia and her family alone, but threats were a part of my job, and over the years I'd received more than I wanted to count. I wanted closure for Felicia and her kids. I wanted them found safe, to obtain peace, and have their fears eradicated. But Carrington, Skip, and I had been told "Hands off."

I grabbed a notepad and scribbled my thoughts about Timothy. When finished, I'd e-mail them to Carrington.

Will killed Timothy. Lots of reasons there.

Boyd wanted no part of his dad or to subject his future wife to his abuse.

Felicia had seen Will's emotional trauma. Had she lied?

Lyndie knew a fraction of what Timothy had done to Boyd. Maybe more if she had told the truth about Timothy's attempt to buy her off. That appeared to be the case for everyone they'd talked to.

I had no doubt Patti Moore blamed Timothy for ruining her campaign.

What about the women Timothy had abused and those who wanted revenge?

For sure Timothy had a buddy out there. Carrington and I carried arrow wounds to prove it.

FORTY-NINE

CARRINGTON

I slept all day Thursday and didn't accomplish a thing. Sometime during my sleeping hours, Levi went home. We never talked. Yes, we were pathetic. Dixie called and I tried to reassure her that I just needed rest. She must have stopped by to tend to Arthur after school, but I neither saw nor heard her, only the note that said she hoped I was feeling better. She wrote a PS that once I recovered, I would be thoroughly interrogated.

Today I'd receive my test results.

Today I'd learn if I had eye melanoma, aka eye cancer.

I'd rather wrestle with another arrow and Timothy Kendrix's dog.

The clock said 8:00 a.m., and I desperately needed to take some semblance of a bath that didn't interfere with my stitches. Been there before with spit baths, and I never felt really clean. I'd manage—this trouper always did. An hour later I drank coffee, nibbled on toast and almond butter, popped three Tylenol, and flipped on my laptop. So glad my eyesight had cleared.

My laptop alerted me to over 400 e-mails. Luckily 355 hit trash and junk. Levi's hit one of the good ones.

Carrington, does anyone ever call you Carri? Anyway, checking in to see how you're feeling. Today you're supposed to receive your test results, and I'm praying. I'd like to spend the day with you, be there when you get the doctor's call.

We could pick up our conversation about the Kendrix situation. Lots to figure out from our end. Respond, call, or text. I'm here.

I took a few notes today about Timothy and attached them to this e-mail.

Levi

I stared at his e-mail. Me, the independent one who had a stubborn streak, battled my urge to type three letters: *Y E S*. I'd done quite well alone for thirteen years. My mission of helping others make impactful decisions for the good of others had filled my significance-and-security tank. I missed the relationship part, but two out of three wasn't bad.

Inviting Levi to spend the day with me meant inviting a spark to burst into a flame, and my damaged emotions forbade it. Fear paralyzed me, and if my rejection of Levi Ehrlich placed me on the coward list, then so be it. Control best described me, and with him, I slipped to powerless.

I typed a reply to his e-mail.

Hi Levi

No one has ever called me Carri. Neither my parents nor my grandmother. Makes me sound too docile and prissy. ☺

I hope you're resting up and letting your body heal. I'm feeling better. Slept all day yesterday. Thanks for checking.

I appreciate your offer to be with me while I wait for the test results. Arthur would welcome another playdate, but we're fine. I've handled good and not-so-good news before. Paperwork is awaiting my touch, and I plan to sleep more. Oh, thanks for the attachment. Haven't had a chance to open it yet.

Not sure if we should call Sheriff Macmire or Skip about our threat. My concern is they'd order us to stay in Houston with their own threat of cuffs.

I'll call later.

Carrington

———

Two hours and twelve minutes later, my phone rang. Dr. Janet Leonard. With my fears rising hot into my face, I answered.

"Carrington, Dr. Leonard here, calling about your test results."

"You have them all?"

"Yes. Are you in a position to discuss the findings?"

That sounded like gloom. "Sure. I'm listening, and I have pad and paper before me."

"The testing shows a small melanoma. There are two ways we can approach the diagnosis. Plan A is to simply watch the melanoma. It may never progress any more than it has currently."

"And plan B?"

"I can order additional tests to determine if the melanoma has metastasized to other parts of your body."

A sickening lump rose in my throat. "What kind of tests?"

"Blood work to measure liver function. Chest X-ray. A CT scan of your entire body. An MRI scan. An abdominal ultrasound and a PET scan. If any of these show the cancer has spread, then radiation and/or laser therapy can be done."

"Dr. Leonard, what would you do in my shoes?" My voice quivered, and I couldn't help it.

"Keeping an eye on the small melanoma is the easiest. But with your family history, peace of mind could be your preference."

I already knew my answer. "I'd like to be certain. Is it possible to schedule the tests on the same day?"

"No, but they can be accomplished over a three- to four-day period. I'll give you the hospital's outpatient number and let you arrange convenient times. I'm assuming you'd want to get started right away."

"I have stitches resulting from an accident, so I imagine positioning myself for some of the scans might be painful. Plus I need an okay from the doctor to drive." I took the medical testing numbers and thanked her.

After the call, I pressed Levi's name to text him. I'd make it brief.

Received my test results. Small eye melanoma. Although I could monitor it, I'll do a battery of tests to be sure.

Within seconds he typed back. Not bad news at all. Is Dixie aware?

She has enough to worry about. No one is to have the info. Private.

Ok. Do you want company?

No. Swamped with paperwork. Not sure I want to tell anyone about the threat either. I'm itching to go to Victoria in the morning.

Me too.

I'm set for 8. Is that ok?

Perfect.

Truth was, I wanted Levi at my front door now. Impossible. I couldn't get past reality—I still had an eye-melanoma diagnosis.

FIFTY

On the Saturday morning drive to Victoria, I intentionally chose silence between Levi and me. He filled me with confidence in one breath and frustrated my rock-hard independence in the next. I liked him and yet wished I despised him. He'd crept into my life with his easy mannerisms and faith, then attempted to interfere with who I am—a negotiator . . . a negotiator possibly going blind. He didn't deserve a life sentence with the likes of me. Neither did I relish the idea of pity. He periodically tossed me a smile or said something witty. I laughed when I wanted to cry.

Get the lights back on in your head, Carrington.

Our conversation broadened to what he'd learned about Patti Moore and her association with Timothy Kendrix. All business. The mask I wore all my life to avoid emotional turmoil threatened to slip, but the problems with the Kendrix family weren't about me.

"I think we should review what we've learned," I said. "Then what has us puzzled."

"Don't shut me out, Carrington."

"What do you mean?"

He blew out obvious frustration at my deflection. "Okay, I'll play. In chronological order?"

"Yes." I pulled my device from my purse. "First, Timothy Kendrix is murdered. Will takes hostages to force law enforcement to find their dad's killer and forces Boyd to help. We learn Timothy didn't win any awards for father of the year. Will shoots Boyd. Felicia is unable to talk down her husband. You and I try to reason with him, and Will turns the rifle on himself. Hostages receive medical care." I glanced over my notes, thankful I could see again.

"We meet members of Felicia and Will's family and Lyndie Moore. Skip informs us that Will's rifle killed Timothy and was also used to shoot Boyd and you. Felicia and her kids are missing. Three dead bodies were discovered on Timothy's ranch. We've heard implications that Timothy might be involved in human trafficking with undocumented immigrants. On a second trip to Victoria, we meet Patti Moore. Then you and I do a little detective work and end up with arrow wounds. What happened next?"

"Back at your house, we looked at Timothy's cell phone records. Two numbers were used frequently but unaccounted for. I talk to Frank, and someone left us a threatening call from one of those unaccounted-for phone numbers."

I nodded. "Patti attempted to run for Congress, but Timothy or someone made a sizable, illegal contribution to her campaign, resulting in her withdrawing her candidacy." I looked over what I'd typed and forwarded the contents to Levi. "We have a running list of those who wanted Timothy dead."

"I'm thinking. Who had the most to lose or gain in his death?"

"Will and Boyd—if they knew the details of the will and it was to their advantage."

Levi frowned at me. "I've searched my brain for what's hidden on Timothy's ranch that impacted someone's future. Nothing makes sense, so I only have speculation."

I tapped my cheek as though willing answers to march into my brain. "Patti Moore? She might have been pro-Kendrix during her initial campaign for Congress. Then the illegal contribution changed her political aspirations. Although Timothy was exonerated, he could have set out to damage her name. Could be motive for murder."

"She left the hospital before we drove to Timothy's property. Makes me wonder if she has an archery background," he said.

"Or she hired someone, like the man with the Hispanic accent. Or she has voice-altering software. Levi, I'm a lousy investigator. Because if all those people have motive to see Timothy dead and Will killed him, then who tried to kill us? And what happened to Felicia, Jace, and Emma?"

Levi and I walked into the DeTar Hospital on Saturday morning not expecting to see Felicia in the lobby with her son and daughter. They huddled together near the elevators, but the up arrow failed to glow red. The closer the distance between us, the more I saw a woman beaten by life who hadn't combed her hair or changed from her rumpled clothes. Jace and Emma showed droopy eyelids, but they wore fresh clothes. Obviously their time away from Victoria wasn't at a resort.

I hugged Felicia, although I wanted to shake her, and greeted Jace and Emma. Jace, taller than his dad, held such an incredible resemblance that it seemed eerie, especially the shape of his body and gray-green eyes. He slid his arm around his mother's waist. Emma avoided eye contact, but her pain was evident in her drawn and pale features.

Levi embraced Felicia and shook the kids' hands. At least the media hadn't located her yet, or the hospital reception area would be a zoo.

"Glad you're safe," I said.

She stared at Levi and me. "You're both hurt. Again. What's going on?"

Levi forced a chuckle. "We got in the way of a few arrows."

Her eyes widened. "I'm so sorry. Where were you?"

"On Timothy's ranch. Know any archery experts?"

She covered her mouth, then spoke. "Timothy, Will, and Boyd."

I watched Felicia for tells. I shouldn't be so suspecting, but too much had happened for me to trust every word and gesture. An involuntary muscle twitched beneath her eye.

Felicia continued. "I'm sure Mom and Dad are upstairs. I've been working up the courage to see them and Lyndie."

"They don't know you're here?" I said.

"No. I was afraid one question would lead to another. Seeing you sort of pushed me into getting it over with."

I nudged gentleness into my tone. "Your parents love you and have been deeply concerned."

"I know." She glanced at Jace, who still held her in a protective stance. "They deserve an explanation. Lyndie and I are friends. It's her mother who can be intolerable. If Patti is there, I'll ask to speak to Mom and Dad privately."

I doubted if Lyndie's mom sat with them after the previous blowup, but mother and daughter could have reconciled. "We can visit them together."

"Thanks." Relief eased the tension around her eyes.

The five of us rode the elevator to Boyd's floor. The only ones in the seating area were the Westfields and Lyndie.

The moment Howard and Zora saw their daughter, relief crested their faces. They stood, and Felicia rushed into their arms. Levi and I kept our distance.

"I'm sorry," Felicia said. "I'm ready to explain what happened." She pulled away and embraced Lyndie. "How is Boyd?"

"He's very weak, but he's opened his eyes. Speaking exhausts him. He squeezes my hand to acknowledge something I've said."

Felicia swiped at her eyes. "How often can you see him?"

"Ten minutes on the hour." Lyndie wrung her hands and plopped down on a chair.

"Felicia," Howard said, "Sheriff Macmire asked me to contact him the moment you arrived."

She swallowed hard. "Yes. I need to tell him the same story that I'm about to share with you."

Howard pulled his phone from his jeans pocket and pressed in a number. "Sheriff, this is Howard Westfield. Felicia and the kids are here at the hospital." He paused. "Yes, sir. I promise you, she won't leave." He raised a brow at his daughter. "No one is hurt." Howard slipped his phone back into his pocket. "He'll be here in about thirty minutes."

"Thanks, Dad. When I talk to Sheriff Macmire, I'd like for you, Mom, and Lyndie to join me." Her shoulders lifted and fell. "I don't want to repeat what I have to say more than necessary." She turned to me. "Carrington, you tried so desperately hard to save Will, and I'll forever be grateful. Levi, your sacrifice is sainthood. Before Sheriff Macmire gets here, can I have a word with you two in private?"

FIFTY-ONE

Before we left the waiting room, Felicia requested Jace and Emma stay with their grandparents.

"Mom, I'll come with you," Jace said.

"I'm fine." Felicia kissed his cheek. "I'll be right back."

In a private corner of the cafeteria, we eased onto chairs with hot cups of coffee. When Felicia stared into her cup and the awkwardness grew, I opened the conversation.

"You look so tired. The last few days must have been horrible. I'm not overreacting by saying we feared the worst. Where were you?"

She lifted her blotchy, tearstained face. "A campsite near Laredo. I rented a cabin."

I touched her hand across the table. "Why didn't you tell anyone where you were going?"

Felicia looked around to ensure no one could overhear them. "Promise me you and Levi will keep the information to yourself until I talk to Sheriff Macmire. What I'm about to say could put others in danger."

"Yes, of course."

"You have my word too." Levi's kind words caused Felicia's drawn features to relax slightly. "Nothing you say will go any further than here."

"You can trust both of us," I said.

"I do. You and Levi are a good team. How long have you two been together?"

Felicia assumed Levi and I were an item. Rather humorous . . . in a weird way. Yet her words slammed into my attraction to Levi.

I had no time to identify or label my crazy emotional reaction to a man who had grown into one I could trust. I plastered a smile on my face. "Levi and I are friends who believe in the value of every human."

"We're outliers," he said. "Neither one of us is afraid to step outside of our comfort zone to stand up for what is right. We thrive on being different. We're peculiar people and proud of it."

My heart thudded against my chest, almost hurting. How did he comprehend those things about me so quickly? And accurately? "Right. Just like you took a walk on a dangerous path to help Will and the hostages. Not everyone would take such a daring chance."

Felicia rubbed her temples. "No, I'm not like either of you. I'm scared on a lot of different levels. My mama's heart aches for Jace and Emma. My nurturing instinct aches for the man I couldn't convince to do the right thing. My compassion aches for those who were held like caged animals. I've frightened my parents, and my kids are confused. I'm numb."

Felicia closed her eyes. Was she lying? Or afraid?

"Before I left Victoria," she continued, "a man called me, spoke in a Hispanic accent. He claimed to have seen who had killed Timothy and said I wouldn't like what he planned to tell the sheriff's department. He wanted fifty thousand dollars to keep his mouth shut. I refused. Told him to go to . . . never mind where. He said I had information that I'd better keep to myself, or he'd destroy my children and parents." She paused.

Fifty thousand dollars, the same amount deposited into Patti's campaign fund. "How horrible. Did he say anything else?" I said.

"He gave me three days to come up with the money, which has come and gone. I was afraid and in panic mode. After he hung up, I woke the kids, told them we were in danger, and we packed and left the ranch. I forbade them to ask questions. Believe me, I did what I thought was best at the time."

"You ran," I said. "The man could have been watching your home and followed you. It gives me chills to think what might have happened to all of you." Felicia might have held back from the truth, but that didn't stop my caring.

"The thought of others fearing for our safety didn't occur to me then. My worries were about getting as far away as possible. Will and I had a hidden safe in our bedroom with emergency money, so I could support us for a while. Jace and I destroyed our phones at home, and I drove to a campsite that a woman at the bank and her husband frequented."

"And you didn't tell your kids anything?"

"Jace woke me on Thursday morning. He wanted to go home. I shared with him about the blackmail, and he said hiding made us cowards. That wasn't how we should honor his dad, and he asked me how long we could hide out. Answers failed me. I was paralyzed by fear and told him so. Jace accused me of being no better than the one who'd killed his grandpa. Jace said I was stronger than I thought, and he'd stand with me." Felicia blinked back tears.

"Jace helped me understand that no matter what the man claimed to have seen, we'd go to Sheriff Macmire's office before paying him. I listened and drove home. I couldn't bring myself to call Mom and Dad about the threat. Selfish as it sounds, I needed to clear my head and figure out how to get over losing Will and raise our children. My parents, Lyndie, and Emma will learn the truth when I give my story to Sheriff Macmire." She clenched her fists. "I hoped Boyd would have recovered by now."

Levi leaned in. "He woke up for a little while and asked to talk to Border Patrol Agent Skip Reyes."

"Skip, Sheriff Corbin Macmire, and Boyd went to school together."

Now I understood more why Boyd wanted to speak to Skip when he wakened the first time.

Levi continued. "Infection set into Boyd's first surgery site, and he slipped back into unconsciousness. Skip is currently working in the field. I assume Skip relayed Boyd's conversation to Sheriff Macmire, but I can't confirm it. Do you have any idea who called and threatened you?"

"No. The voice sounded muffled, had a thick accent."

"Be sure to tell the sheriff everything," Levi said. "Did the blackmailer give you a drop point?"

Felicia shook her head. "He said he'd call back. But he must have been looking for a handout. The media claims Will killed his dad. The blackmailer having some kind of hidden information is impossible." Tears rolled down her cheeks.

Levi lifted his chin for me to take over the conversation.

"Have you talked to your counselor?" I said.

"No point. I lost my job, which means my health insurance runs out at the end of thirty days. Will's life insurance won't pay with his suicide, and I need to take care of funeral expenses. There's a savings account for Jace's and Emma's college, but I hate the thought of using it for the funeral. I'm assuming Will has an inheritance from Timothy, but who knows how long probate will take?"

"Perhaps your boss would reconsider?"

"Jace said the same thing. For my children's sake, I'll ask for another chance." Felicia shook her head. "My son has been a rock. Whatever I need, he does it. I understand he's grieving, but his overprotectiveness might be his way of working through his dad's death. I'm still the parent though." She paused. "Another weakness for me to work on."

"How's Emma?"

"She's taken to not talking or eating. I understand because she was a daddy's girl. Emma should be the one under the care of a counselor, which means I must find a job. If I asked my dad, he'd pay for family sessions, but they're on a fixed income. I can't accept money from them."

"Have you filed for Social Security for Emma and Jace?"

"Not yet. I dread sitting in the office waiting for my turn. But I need to make it happen."

"I despise waiting too," I said. "What about taking a book to read?"

"Concentrating is hard right now, but I appreciate the suggestion."

"Do you have any other resources?"

"Jace asked about selling off some of the cattle. That seems like the proper thing to do."

"I know you see a bleak future, but it's amazing how often in life things turn around so quickly. And you are so strong and smart, you'll work through this."

"I'm trying. I'm having problems thinking clearly. Lack of a job, health insurance, and instability fogs my mind. I refuse to saddle Dad with any more problems than he already has dealing with Mom's illness and Will's death."

"I admire your consideration in not burdening your parents." I started to mention that her counselor or attorney could offer wise advice, but that highlighted her money issues. "Do you trust me to find local legal, financial, and employment sources? Those that are affordable? We could explore job opportunities if need be and how to move ahead with your life."

"Why even consider such a thing with all my dysfunctions? Am I such a pitiful, needy mess?"

"You are nothing of the sort. You're a woman reaching out to a friend, one to walk a rocky path with you. Before you know it, you'll learn to navigate on your own. Simply stated, tools are available to train your mind and emotions for a better tomorrow. Organizations and churches are equipped to help you, like your parents' pastor. I hope one day you'll be able to help someone who is struggling from your experience of learning to live victoriously."

"Who is your friend when life's pieces don't fit?"

How many times had I been asked that question? Not even Dixie knew my inner turmoil. Levi . . . "I have dependable relationships."

"Have you been through a death and struggled with unanswered questions?"

I nodded. "My parents were killed in a car accident when I was a child. My grandmother took over parenting, then she passed too. Like you, I have experienced seemingly insurmountable despair."

Felicia's eyes watered. "How did you survive?"

"Through listening and reading lots of wisdom." What a lie, but the conversation focused on Felicia's good mental health, not mine.

"You've been kind and caring since we met."

I took her hand. "Many good therapists do pro bono work. It's their own standard of care."

"I'm a little afraid of it all. But for me to be a strong mother, I have to step into my role with confidence. And believe the trauma will all work out." She squared her shoulders. "After I give the sheriff my statement, I'll talk to the kids, let them know I'm taking positive steps to be a better mother and take care of our family."

I must help this desperate woman. With the confirmation of eye melanoma, the Kendrix case might very well be my last negotiation.

FIFTY-TWO

LEVI

I sat with Carrington in the downstairs visitor area while Felicia, Jace, Emma, Howard, Zora, and Lyndie met with Sheriff Macmire. Carrington typed furiously into her phone. She'd been avoiding me since the diagnosis, and while I understood she didn't want to saddle me with her health problems, it hurt. I wanted to be there for her, but now wasn't the time to bring the matter up. I let the past days scroll through my mind since the original hostage situation, reviewing conversations and unexplained behavior. Carrington had spent more time with Will and Felicia than I had.

At least Patti Moore didn't sit there tossing kindling into the fire of emotions. I disliked a whole lot about Patti Moore, which left shadows of doubt about Lyndie. *God, forgive me for judging a daughter's character by her mother's.*

Minutes ticked by. Had the group slipped out a back exit to the sheriff's office? Curiosity often got me into trouble, but I'd really like to be a fly on the wall of that discussion. I glanced at Carrington. "You're shaking. Has Felicia's story upset you that much?"

"I care about her, but I picked up a few tells."

"Me too. She's afraid."

"Lying gives her momentary control. Wish she'd unload with it all and let us help her."

Sounded like how I felt about Carrington. "Your compassionate streak has a habit of getting you into trouble. Curiosity meets compassion. Both demand closure."

She smiled at my wordplay. "I've contacted a few resources to pass on to Felicia." She laid her phone on her lap. "I'm sorry. I haven't even asked about your job search."

"Another interview with *National Geographic* on Wednesday." I wish I had more time to pray more about the possible job. I wanted it if God had purposed it for me. "The opportunity fits my personality."

"I want the best for you too."

Before I could respond with more than a thank-you, the sheriff and the family returned. The Kendrixes and Lyndie shared reddened eyes.

"Carrington, Levi, we need to talk." Sheriff Macmire's face showed no emotion.

We stood and followed the tall sheriff into the hallway. I licked my lips to keep from asking the what-now? question.

"I have Felicia's statement." He hit the high points enough for me to hear she'd revealed the same to Carrington and me. "Any idea who threatened her?"

Odd for him to ask when Carrington and I were ordered not to get involved. "No." I wrestled with telling him about the similar message that we'd received. But we'd decided to wait.

Carrington studied Corbin. "What does Zora Westfield have to say?"

"You're fishing without bait on that one. Zora's a quiet woman who observes before speaking. If she says much at all. I wonder about her state of mind. But trust me, she has thoughts about Felicia's father-in-law. I can tell by the ice in her eyes at the mention of Timothy's name."

Carrington cleared her throat. "Levi, why not tell Sheriff Macmire about Frank's call?"

Not sure what that accomplished when we withheld other info, but I shared that we'd been threatened too. He frowned and stared at us like we were complicit in an atrocious crime. "You two are rear-deep in manure." He swore. "And the pile keeps growing. Why haven't you told me about this guy?"

"We assumed the man is using burner phones, but my old boss found a number in his online call log. It matches one of the two unknown numbers on Timothy Kendrix's cell phone records. Wish Felicia hadn't destroyed her SIM card. Might have learned more about the caller or—"

"How did you get Timothy's phone records?" The sheriff's tone hit somewhere between flat and angry.

"I have connections," Carrington said.

"I'm sure you do. Is Skip privy to what you've told me?"

"Felicia might have told him about her call, but it sounds like she panicked and ran. Sir, have you asked him?"

"Cut the *sir* stuff. It's Corbin." He glanced into the waiting room at the group we'd left behind. "I'll talk to Skip and the BP investigators today. I might as well fill you in, but you didn't hear it from me without my permission."

"We understand," I said, and Carrington echoed my response.

"I talked to the fella who is taking care of Timothy Kendrix's place until arrangements can be made with Boyd. He's not Hispanic."

Anyone could fake an accent with a little practice or use software. I bit my tongue to keep from asking for a name and who was paying him since Timothy's death, or if he used a bow and arrow. I'd find out from Boyd or Felicia.

"He claims Timothy dabbled in more than one illegal venture. The three bodies found on the ranch might be connected to some of the crimes but not Timothy's death."

"Do you believe him?" I said.

"Just relayin' what the man said."

"Why are you telling us about it now?"

"Because if you two survive, you might lead the sheriff's department and Border Patrol to who is behind it all. Stands to reason you are closer to the truth than we are, even if you're not smart enough to figure it out."

"If we're stupid enough to put ourselves out there for target practice, then you'll take advantage of what we learn?" I said.

Corbin grinned. "You got it. I could throw both of you in jail for obstructing justice, but what good does that serve? You'd be released in a few days, or the killer could post bail and follow through with his threats."

Or hers, which was where my thoughts had wandered. Corbin had just given us a glimpse of his personality, and the sarcasm shoved him off the train of a stereotypical county sheriff.

Corbin continued. "Felicia told me all of what apparently transpired leading up to her camping trip, but who knows if there's more."

"Have you questioned Patti Moore?" I said.

"Yep. Right from the start. She and Timothy were an item until the money debacle."

"We read about Patti's attempt to run for Congress and what happened," I said. "We figured Timothy sabotaged her campaign."

"She claimed so, but she lacked proof. The two were seen everywhere together. For a while she lived on the ranch with him."

"Talks of marriage?"

"She wore a big hunker of a diamond. Doubt she returned it."

"If documents or cash were hidden on the ranch, would she have known?" I said.

"Timothy didn't trust anyone. If Patti wanted a slice of the pie, she'd have searched when he wasn't around." A nurse walked by, and Corbin paused until she left the hallway. "Patti had an alibi when Timothy was shot. Her receptionist backed it up. Even if she didn't, the evidence proves Will killed him."

"Patti left the hospital before Carrington and I took our drive. Is archery on her résumé?"

Corbin squinted and held up a finger. "I'll find out. Before we go any further, we suspect Timothy's involvement with trafficking undocumented illegals for the cartel."

I refused to tell him we'd heard the same thing. "I take it proof is like spitting in the wind."

He nodded. "If so, you two are in more danger than you realize. I suggest you choose. Continue your behind-the-scenes snooping in the name of helping Felicia and her family and keep me informed, or head back to Houston and stay there."

"I'm in," Carrington said.

I chuckled. "Me too."

"If I find out you're keeping anything from me, I'm tossing you in jail. Understand?" We nodded and Corbin laughed. "You two are either the bravest fools I've ever seen or undercover cops."

Brave fools fit, but I wouldn't admit it.

FIFTY-THREE

CARRINGTON

After speaking to us, Sheriff Macmire left the hospital to meet with Skip. No doubt he'd be given the same instructions as we had.

Levi and I chatted a few minutes before we joined the group. In truth, I wanted to leave soon for home.

Lyndie slipped in to see Boyd, and Howard took Felicia and the kids to the cafeteria. I sat beside Zora. The poor woman looked exhausted, and I imagined she'd not rested since the ordeal began.

"Do you ever voice your opinion?" I said.

"Sometimes." She smiled with a lift of her chin. "Depends on who I'm talking to. You're a good person to care about Felicia. Regrets matter, you know."

"Thank you." My thoughts immediately transported back to Dad and Mom's accident. I couldn't go there. "What do you mean about regrets matter?"

"You'll figure it out. Are you a believer?" Zora said.

"Depends on who I'm talking to. Levi is. He's a proponent for truth."

She smiled. "The bottom line is truth and love go hand in hand. You can't have one without the other. Because Jesus is both truth and love."

Was I about to get a sermon? "Does Felicia follow those principles too?"

"Depends on who she's talking to. She claims God isn't looking out for her, but that doesn't stop Him from having a purpose for her. She'll figure it out."

I laughed. "Do you know why you believe?"

"Do you know why you don't?"

I no longer cornered the market on answering a question with a question. "Life and regrets."

She took my hand, and I felt the calluses and viewed the blue-veined, parchment-thin skin. Wisdom. Like Grandmother.

"Listen carefully." Her dark eyes probed me. "You never know what you believe until it's time to believe. Then you'll know Who truth is."

"We're a pair, Mrs. Westfield."

"I think we want the world to be safe from evil."

"What is evil to you?" I said.

"The absence of all things God."

"Unfortunately, I see that in Felicia's life."

"She must learn to forgive Will, and forgiveness costs. She must release her pride and redirect her anger. Lord knows I've been tested with it all. Forgiveness requires rage against evil. Until she lifts her fists against the evil that she's lived with all these years, she'll never survive. Jace will end up raising himself and Emma."

Zora's words struck my sympathy chord. Felicia deserved love and understanding, not a sound shaking to gain control of her life. If He was Zora's God, I wanted no part of Him.

"Miss Reed, who haven't you forgiven?"

"What?"

Zora shook her head. "You're angry and hurting. I can feel it. To you, regrets matter more than life."

For a woman who supposedly observed others and spoke very little, she'd given me an earful. But the whole family grieved, suffered for the unexplainable chaos erupting around them.

Zora blew her nose on a less-than-clean tissue. "I should apologize for my bluntness. I never wanted Felicia to marry Will, but she was determined. I loved him as a son, and I saw the good, but he'd been damaged. Yes, that's the word I kept searching for. Timothy Kendrix damaged Will with his inhumane treatment. Charlotte Bolton, God bless her soul. She's the one to talk to."

"Why?"

"She and Timothy's wife, Dorie, were best friends. Charlotte belonged to our church, so she came to us years ago about the abuse. Howard and I tried to get Dorie to take those boys and get out of there. Dorie claimed she had nowhere to go. So scared. Now she lives with Jesus."

The cafeteria group returned, and Zora resumed her quiet mode.

Levi gave me his I'm-ready-to-go look, and we announced our departure.

Felicia turned to Jace and Emma. "We're ready to leave too. For now, let's go to Granddad and Grandma's. I need to tell you a few things, changes on my part to be a better mother."

"What about the counseling stuff?" Jace said.

Felicia lifted her shoulders, as though she needed courage. "I spoke to the pastor after we finished talking to Sheriff Macmire. He will handle individual and family counseling. If he sees we need more than his skills, he'll make recommendations. His desk is clear to help us."

"Is he just a pastor, or does he have any creds in counseling?"

"He has a master's in theology and psychology," Felicia said. "I believe the spiritual influence is good for all of us. We'll talk about how I'd like us to approach faith later on."

"Maybe," Jace said. "We never bothered with the God-thing before. How would Dad feel about it?"

Felicia's chin quivered. "I'm moving forward in what I feel is right for our family. We'll make many decisions together, but on some things, I call the shots."

"Felicia." Howard Westfield clung to his daughter. "We need to arrange funeral services as soon as possible. You and the kids need closure and—"

"Dad, we'll have the services day after tomorrow. I scheduled it with your pastor. A small ceremony at the funeral home with a closed casket."

Jace agreed, taking over the role of man of the house. "If we bury Dad on Monday, does that mean we go back to school on Tuesday?"

"Are you ready?" Felicia swung her attention to Emma and back to Jace. "We can do homeschool if you'd like. Online makes sense."

"I think doing normal things is good for us." Jace set his jaw. "It'll be hard but putting it off means facing the other kids will be worse."

Emma shook her head and crossed her arms over her chest. "Not me. I'm never going back. I hate school."

"We'll work it out, Emma," Howard said. "Homeschooling is an option."

Howard walked us to the elevator. "Miss Reed, I saw you talking to my Zora. She's a dear lady. Dementia has taken over her mind. Some days she makes sense, and other days she doesn't know me."

FIFTY-FOUR

LEVI

Carrington searched for information on her phone about Zora Westfield. I'd watched them together at the hospital, but I had no idea of their conversation. Strange since the sheriff claimed the woman seldom spoke, then Howard said Zora suffered from dementia. Now I understood his concern for her.

"Are you ready to hear about my conversation with Zora?" Carrington said. "I just learned a few interesting facts about her."

"Bring it on. She seemed talkative with you. Not like I expected."

"Zora earned her master's in psychology at Berkley. After she returned home, she and Howard married, and she took a job as an elementary and middle school counselor. Stayed in that position until she retired at age fifty-five." Carrington paused. "I confirmed she worked at the same elementary and middle school as Will and Boyd."

My mind whipped into full speed ahead. "What did she say to you about the boys?"

"Zora suggested I talk to Charlotte Bolton, but she's passed." Carrington shared with me how the Westfields did their best to get Dorie to leave Timothy, and Zora's disapproval of Felicia marrying Will.

"*Damaged* is a good description for Will," I said. "The Westfields invested time and energy to help Dorie, but it did little good. Do you believe Zora was lucid when you talked to her?"

"I have no idea. According to Charlotte Bolton's obituary, her son and two grandchildren are listed as immediate family members. Looks like the kids she counseled were her extended family. She has a brother in New Jersey. Learned he's in hospice care for stage 4 cancer. Not a door I want to go through."

I waded into deeper waters. "Are you okay? You seem distant. Need to talk?"

She offered a forced smile. "I'll be fine. Please don't tell anyone about my eye melanoma."

"Told you before, you can trust me."

Carrington sighed deeply. "I've been thinking. Remember what you said about us . . . the start of a relationship? Remove any notion about it. Once we're finished sorting through the Kendrix family, I'll go my way and you can go yours."

"Why?"

"No future in it. Like swimming in quicksand." She stared at the road ahead. "I apologize for not telling you this sooner, but I have no feelings for you."

After returning to Carrington's home, I asked if I could join her on a walk with Arthur.

"Why?"

I wanted to know why she'd tossed me to the curb, but what I said was, "I have a few thoughts about Felicia and her kids to run by you."

"Wait outside while I get him." Her stiff form exited my Tahoe and made her way to the front door.

I found it difficult to believe she had no feelings for me, and the walk might encourage her to open up. Maybe I wanted a relationship with her so badly that I'd pushed her. Maybe my need for a family had poured into an overpowering desire for closeness with her. Or maybe I wanted to take care of her. Or I was falling in love with her, and I'd fight for her. When she returned with Arthur, I'd stay off the topic and just be her friend.

Carrington returned, and we walked around the park near her home.

"Have you wondered how Jace handled responsibility before his dad's death?" I said.

"Are you thinking he's taken on too much and Felicia won't follow through on her parental commitments?"

"Jace, as head of the household. It seems odd a junior in high school who is sports minded and extroverted would step into a demanding role that would pull him away from his friends."

"He's just lost his dad." Carrington stopped on the sidewalk. "Felicia told me earlier that he's taken the initiative to help her with the budget and generally run the house and the ranch. In my opinion, school and activities will need to slip in here and there."

"Has she mentioned his level of responsibility before?"

"When I drove her from the county medical examiner's office, she said Jace would have a difficult time with his dad's death. He wasn't one to step up to the plate. He struggled to do chores, but he enjoyed spending time with Will. Love for his mom and honoring his dad's name could mean a change of focus."

"And Emma is the introverted one," I said.

"According to Felicia, she's moody and quiet. Could be her age. Why ask about the kids?"

"I think it's worth researching, especially Jace. What's motivating him to take over his dad's role? I'd like to talk to him, get his feelings on what's going on with his family. If he's levelheaded, then he's been thinking about the future."

Carrington stomped down the sidewalk. "Those kids have been through a lot without being interrogated. No, I can't go along with questioning either of them."

I thought back to Carrington losing her parents and then her grandmother. Would she have survived better with another person to talk to? "I disagree. I'm sure the pastor doing the counseling will dive into those issues, but I want to know where those kids were when Timothy was killed."

"You mean if they saw their dad pull the trigger? Heard an argument?" She stopped. "How dare you consider subjecting them to such an ordeal as though they were criminals. They are children. They need their mother whole and mentally healthy to get through the trauma. They deserve a future free of pain. Leave me alone, Levi, starting now. Thanks for your friendship, but I'm better off without you."

"Really?" My face flamed. "You're running from your past and projecting your experiences onto Jace and Emma. Sure, I'll leave you alone." I held back a huge dump of sarcasm. "If you want to talk to me, you'll need to make the call."

"Trust me, I won't. I am better alone, and you just proved it."

FIFTY-FIVE

CARRINGTON

I rolled over to look at the clock for the umpteenth time—1:46 a.m. My mind slammed against the dreadful things I'd said to Levi. I'd lashed out at him without cause, a response to emotional triggers. The tells were there—the anxiety of what Jace and Emma faced now and in the future mingled with flashbacks of the crash's moment of impact, taking my parents and abandoning me. Moments of depression, Grandma's diagnosis, and the burst of anger I directed at Levi late yesterday afternoon. They all tumbleweeded through my thoughts with no signs of stopping.

I couldn't recall ever losing control like that before. I must have reached my limit. What if Levi thought I always reacted irrationally? I'd slammed the door on a man I cared about and feared at the same time. Was I so pitifully damaged—using Zora's words—that I'd never recover from life's regrets? If the situation were a part of Dixie's life or even a stranger's, I'd be their cheerleader, encouraging them as I'd done so many times.

Physician, heal thyself ranked impossible.

Staring at the ceiling, memories of the times Levi and I had shared together soothed me. He *was* a good man, a man who'd been hit hard by his family. A man who had confessed to caring for me.

I needed the courage to apologize. What if the eye melanoma turned out to be no big deal? Was that what it took for me to try again with Levi? Did I have the courage to apologize for what I'd done wrong today? Very wrong.

I grasped my phone from the nightstand and held it to my chest. Three huge breaths later, I pressed in his number. He picked up on the first ring.

"Carrington, are you okay?"

At the sound of his voice, I burst into tears. I seldom cried. It was a waste of time and energy and solved nothing. "I'm so sorry for what I said to you."

"You were upset and concerned about Felicia and the kids."

"Please, Levi, don't make excuses for me. I sensed my triggers and failed to stop my reactions. You were right. Jace and Emma losing their father was too close to my own experience. The pain is still there, always there, and I've built this stone wall to protect it."

The phone stayed silent, and I pushed ahead.

"Zora wears the same perfume as my grandmother. No excuse for my actions. My fault, and I'm so sorry. I do value our friendship, and I don't want it to end. Unless you do."

"The idea of walking away is furthest from my thoughts."

"Just friendship for now, okay? Too many things are vying for my attention. I really like you, the way you put others before yourself. You refused to let me run over you, but—"

"You're scared to death. Carrington, I am too. I'm afraid I'm not good enough for you, that you'd grow bored with me."

"That's a crazy thought, Levi. What about spending your life with a blind woman or worse? You are the most entertaining, wisest man I've ever met."

"I've never been described like that before, right along with sweet and playdate. But seriously, nothing in life is guaranteed. We'd walk the road together whether the challenge is me or you. Think about the odds of two unlikely people finding a lasting relationship."

"We are different, and yet passion for helping others makes us alike."

He chuckled. "And our passion for each other."

Could I raise the courageous flag? "Can we take it slow?"

"Of course. Gives me more time to spend with you."

"So, you forgive me?"

"I did the moment the words were spoken. I prayed you'd contact me."

"Thank you." Zora's words of faith, truth, and forgiveness replayed. Had she spoken to me out of the well of dementia or her convictions? "I don't deserve you."

"Keep talking. You're better than a bag of candy for my ego."

I heard the smile in his words and giggled in the darkness. "You answered on the first ring. Were you expecting a call from someone? I don't want to interfere."

"I couldn't sleep."

"Me either. Would you like me to go with you when you talk to Jace and Emma?" I said.

"Definitely. I'd rather we do it together. Ms. Compassion and Mr. Curiosity team up to help bring peace to the Kendrix family."

"Two weeks ago, I'd never heard of them. Now they are all I can think about."

"Neither of us want them to walk through the pain of loss with no support."

His words convicted me of how quickly I'd grown to care for Levi. He saw through me and refused to run. I hated my role as a coward.

FIFTY-SIX

LEVI

If the situation permitted after Will's funeral, Carrington and I would talk to Jace. Felicia or the kid might refuse, and if so, I understood. Carrington and I were outsiders. My journalistic and her negotiation backgrounds lent themselves to distrust.

I drove us to Victoria, and we discussed Corbin Macmire's request to share information. "Timothy must have been part of an illegal trafficking operation for Corbin to consider we might have information, like more deaths than the three we know about."

"We could search online to find out."

"I already did and found nothing," I said. "Are you having second thoughts about upsetting the cartel?"

"No. I'm good." She laughed. "Facing the cartel can't be worse than cancer. I think we should monitor who attends Will's funeral service. We both know the person who attacked us may be there."

"Be really helpful if the person brought their bow and arrow."

"We haven't been lucky yet, and I doubt it will happen today." She paused. "Who do you have the least respect for?"

An unusual way to phrase who I suspected of targeting us with a compound bow. "No one. Everyone. I hesitate to toss out a name."

"Neither of us care for Patti Moore," Carrington said. "Corbin said she had an alibi, but she has a hateful streak."

"Today could provide a few answers."

"Hope so," she said. "Time is precious when I could be called anytime for negotiation."

"I have a job interview on Wednesday, and if that falls flat, I'll try plan B."

"What's that?"

I raised an eyebrow. "A private negotiator?"

We laughed until tears rolled down her face.

"Carrington, do you mind leading the discussion with Jace? I don't want to say something that causes him to shut down."

"Of course. You'll be with me, right?"

"Yes."

She rubbed her palms together. "I spoke to Dixie last night. Told her I carried a lot of baggage from my past and planned to see a counselor."

Her actions took courage. "Good for you. What did she say?"

"Praise the Lord."

I laughed. If only the rest of our lives were this easy.

Carrington and I arrived early at the funeral home, allowing time to scrutinize each person who walked in. We recognized some who attended, and three strangers were Will's old school friends. I mentally jotted down the description of each person and viewed the guest book so I could line up names later. I believed if someone else hovered over the crimes, they'd be here gloating over what had occurred.

The family and Lyndie entered together with the Westfields' pastor. Skip and who I assumed was his wife spoke to Felicia. Two men and one woman from Border Patrol, agents from the long night of the hostage situation, took their seats. Sheriff Macmire arrived with another deputy and two men in suits. They took seats midway, and two additional deputies stood in the back. Corbin's high cheekbones and piercing eyes gave him a formidable look. He took in the small crowd, and while he wanted Carrington's and my assessment, he'd not give his. An older gentleman approached Lyndie, kissed her cheek, and sat with her. Probably her dad.

Patti Moore had chosen to stay away. A few members of the media joined the crowd respectfully. My curiosity piqued at the dozen or so people who filed in at the end. Felicia's former coworkers? I expected more, but under the circumstances, the lack of attendance seemed logical for those who questioned the Kendrixes' morality.

I studied Zora, whose face held a blank stare. Occasionally she smiled at whoever spoke to her. She'd affected Carrington strongly, and coincidental conversations weren't a part of my belief system. God always had a purpose, even those in disguise as painful. Zora wore the same cologne as Carrington's deceased grandmother, and I suppose Zora had said something to make Carrington think. A matter she didn't want to consider or deal with.

I glanced at Carrington. Her attention settled on Zora too. I took her hand. Although she wanted us to move ahead slowly, she allowed me to wrap my caring around her hand.

Before we left for the graveside services, I snapped a pic of the guest book. I'm sure the BP investigator and Corbin grabbed their shots too.

Only those people we knew surrounded the casket. Carrington and I took a folding chair in the back as the odd ones out. How soon before Corbin told us not to return, that we'd used up our time? At times, I worried that my determination might lead to our deaths.

FIFTY-SEVEN

CARRINGTON

Levi made a good point that talking to Jace could clear the way to find answers. But it must be soon. If Levi's and my involvement surfaced as helping Sheriff Macmire and Border Patrol determine if Timothy delved in criminal business, Felicia and her family would feel betrayed.

After the meal at the church, I asked Felicia if Levi and I could spend a little time with Jace. She refused, then later consented.

"I'm trying to lift the pressure from his shoulders," she said. "He's not talking to the pastor about his feelings, but he might with you and Levi since you were there when Will died."

Thirty minutes later, we closed the door to a spare bedroom at the Westfields' home. Perspiration dripped down the sides of Jace's face. He eased onto the antique iron-posted bed covered in a faded pink quilt. I joined him, keeping my distance while Levi took a chair at a small desk. He wanted me to begin the conversation, and he'd take over if necessary.

I offered condolences and complimented Jace on looking after his mother and sister.

"How much longer do you two plan to keep showing up?" Jace said. "It's sorta weird."

"Do you prefer we back off?"

"It's a reminder you were with Dad when it all happened." Jace swiped at the sweat.

"Because we were with your dad, Levi and I want to make sure when we back off, as you say, that your family's future is on the right road."

"Why? We're nothing to you but a job." His eyes flared with the anger he held inside. I understood bottled-up bitterness.

"When I deal with humanity and see wrongs, I can't walk away without knowing I did everything possible for a more optimistic outcome. Mistakes become lessons for me to learn from, and my goal is to help others. I like your mother. She's brave and working to be mentally healthy—"

Jace waved me away. "I know those things. How do I fit in your mission project?"

"You're angry, and the timing stinks since you just buried your dad," I said. "We can postpone our conversation."

"Just ask me what you came for. Yeah, I'm upset. Mad. Wishing Dad had made better choices. But go ahead."

"What I'm about to ask should bring closure to the raw past. Where were you the late afternoon of your grandfather's death?"

Jace's gaze darted everywhere but at me. "Where was I when my grandfather was killed?"

"Yes." While I ensured an impassive look covered my face, his response bothered me. By Jace repeating the question, he was stalling and thinking of an answer.

"I don't remember."

"The shooting happened on the Thursday after Labor Day," I said. "Around 5:30 p.m."

He pursed his lips and slowly shook his head. "A lot's been going on, and everything's a blur."

"I'd be the same way."

Jace swiped at his nose. "Sorry, I can't help. My time is better spent with my mom and sister."

I inhaled and exhaled, all the while peering into his face. He had to feel my study of him. although he focused his eyes to the left of me. "Were you with your dad?"

"I might have been."

"On the day of the tragedy, I believe the coach shortened football practice because your team had a game the next afternoon. If you went straight home, you got there around 4:30?"

"Yes, I remember now." Still no eye contact.

"I'm sure you were relieved to skip football practice. How did you spend the extra time?"

"Not sure."

"Did you see your dad?"

"Yeah. He was repairing the tractor."

"Did you offer to help?"

Jace paled. An involuntary eye twitch. "I don't think so. He had an errand to run at Grandpa's ranch."

"Did you ride along with him?"

"My mind's fuzzy with the funeral and all."

"Take your time, Jace. Spending a little time with your dad must have been a rare opportunity."

"Yes, ma'am." He inhaled as though breathing hurt. "I remember a little. Grandpa wanted help moving cattle. Dad and I planned to get the job done and drive into town for dinner—a guys' night out."

"A memory-builder evening with your dad. What happened at the ranch?"

"Grandpa was trying to move the cattle from a small fenced corral to a larger pasture. We got out of the truck to help. Grandpa started swearing at Dad. I'd never seen him so mad. I mean, he had his moments, and I didn't like him, but Grandpa was like a crazy man."

"You must have been shocked. What happened?"

Jace clenched his fists. His mother had done the same thing when under emotional stress. "Doesn't matter. They're both dead now."

"It's important to know why your dad shot your grandfather. You can tell me the truth. I have a good ear."

He worried his lips. "He said awful things to Dad."

"Other than swearing?"

"He called him a no-good, poor excuse of a man." Jace blinked. "I shouted at him, told him not to talk to my dad that way."

"Then what happened?"

"Grandpa called me some bad names. Sick stuff. Said I wasn't any better than Dad. Then Dad told him to shut up and leave me alone. We were leaving, and he could move the cattle himself. Grandpa turned to me and said the scars on Dad's back came from teaching him a lesson. He'd do it again, and then he'd put the same scars on my back. He stomped closer to us." Jace paused and trembled.

I placed my hand atop his. "Keep going, Jace. You're doing fine."

"Dad told me to get back in the truck. Said he'd take care of Grandpa and should have done it a long time ago. I didn't want to back off, but Dad insisted. All the time Grandpa shouted curses at Dad and me. Mom had told me Grandpa had mental issues and abused Dad when he was young, so the reason for the scars wasn't a surprise.

"When I got to the truck, Dad's rifle lay on the seat. I picked it up and walked toward them. I didn't know what I would do except I wouldn't let him hurt Dad. Grandpa knocked Dad down and pulled out a knife. He told Dad he should have killed him a long time ago. I pulled the trigger."

Jace met my gaze. "I killed Grandpa Kendrix. I thought he'd use the knife on Dad, and I couldn't let that happen."

I squeezed his hand. "I see. You shot your grandfather to protect your dad."

"Yes, ma'am. But . . ."

"But what?"

"After what he said, I might have shot him even if he hadn't pulled out his knife."

"I understand. You wanted to protect the man you loved, your father."

"Yes, ma'am. Everyone thinks my dad lost his mind. But he was protecting me from being charged with murder."

"Your dad told Levi and me how much he loved all of you and how proud he was of you."

Jace pulled his hand from mine.

"What did your dad say?"

"He got up off the ground and took the rifle from me. We looked at Grandpa. Blood poured out of his chest, and his eyes were wide open. He looked . . . just as mad. Dad told me not to worry, and he thanked me for saving his life. I asked what I should do. He told me to do nothing. Grandpa had enemies, and any of them could have shot him. I asked if the bullet could be traced, and he told me no. I know he lied about that, but I was scared. He took some brush and swept over our boot prints. At the truck he took an old rag and wiped off my fingerprints from the rifle. Then we drove home. Dad made me promise not to tell anyone. Except now I broke my word."

"You never told your mom?"

"No, ma'am. I heard Dad call Boyd and tell him that Grandpa's body had been found. Nothing else. After the funeral, Dad told Boyd that the sheriff's department wasn't doing their job. And he had something to tell Uncle Boyd in person. I didn't hear the rest of the conversation. A week later, Dad and Uncle Boyd took the hostages. Mom told me the rest, about Dad saying Uncle Boyd had been tricked into helping him. I knew better. I wanted to come to the hostage site and talk to Dad, confess my part. But he killed himself." Jace buried his face in his hands. "Dad killed himself to protect me. What am I supposed to do?"

"You can begin by telling your mother the truth."

He nodded. "She's pretty messed up. Blames herself."

"Is what you've told me why you've taken on your dad's responsibilities?"

He stared at me through young eyes brimming with suffering and shame. "If I hadn't shot my grandfather, Dad might be alive today. I'd even thought about being a Border Patrol agent like Granddad Westfield. Looks like I messed that up."

I put my arm around his trembling shoulders. "How might your dad have defended himself when your grandfather came after him with a knife?"

Jace leaned back. "I never thought about it. The truth is, I didn't own up to what I'd done. Grandpa was right. I'm a coward. I let a good man sacrifice his life for a coward of a son."

"There's nothing I can say to make you feel any better. No magic formula. I will tell you one important thing—you are a courageous young man to stand up to your grandpa and protect your dad. Most young people would have run."

"How long will I have to spend in prison?"

"My guess is none." I glanced at Levi.

"I agree with Carrington," Levi said. "Looks like self-defense."

"I feel sick most of the time. It's awful. Guess I deserve it."

"Trained professionals can help you get rid of those symptoms."

"I thought about that for Mom and Emma, but not me. It's like I deserve to feel guilty, horrible." He lifted his head. "I've got to tell Sheriff Macmire. Should have when we came back from the camping thing. Just afraid."

"Do you want your mother with you?"

"Yeah. I want to get it over with."

I glanced at Levi. Tears glistened in his eyes. Mine too. The reason for us to have befriended this family sat in the form of a hurting seventeen-year-old boy. Levi would claim God planned our encounter to help this family deal with the truth.

I honestly didn't know. Like Jace, I felt sick.

FIFTY-EIGHT

Howard, Zora, and Emma sat in white rockers on the front porch of the Westfields' cottage-style home while Levi and I joined Felicia and Jace inside the air-conditioned home. Jace asked his mother to join him on the sofa. He shared what had happened the afternoon his grandpa was shot and his desire to confess to Sheriff Macmire. Felicia sobbed silently and held her son. They cried together.

Neither Levi nor I could watch, and we slipped into the kitchen, smelling the delivered comfort food from those who cared about the family. The smells failed to live up to their description.

I hurt for the load Jace had been carrying. Will had made more than one poor decision in his role as head of the household. For that matter, would I cover up for a loved one who'd done the unthinkable? Stunned, I admitted I'd do anything to protect a child.

"Are you praying for Jace?" I whispered. If a God really loved and cared for us, the young man needed peace.

Levi nodded. "He's been living with far too much guilt. I better understand Will's role in what went down."

"My thoughts exactly." I looked at my bandaged, worn, and tired hero. "I have resources to assist the family's healing. I mentioned to Felicia a psychological autopsy. Are you familiar with the process?"

"Yes. I've read the results of those affected by a tragedy who find the strength to work through their grief by talking with professionals. There they work through what might have been done differently."

"Another thought is a critical incident debriefing for the BP agents and law enforcement involved since the beginning of the hostage situation. It's a means of getting them together to discuss how they are doing. It's not a 'stuff it' to make others think we're all fine, but a means of helping each other cope with the tragedy so no one develops acute stress or post-traumatic stress disorder." I glanced at the bright blue door to the home. "While Felicia and Jace are gone, I'll make a list."

"Are we going to attempt to talk to Emma?" Levi said.

"If her mother doesn't object."

He nodded and I stepped into the living area, where I asked Felicia if I could speak to her alone. I followed her back into the kitchen. After making my request, I watched her drawn features relax as though she'd anticipated a difficult question.

"You have my permission," Felicia said. "But only if you tell me everything she says."

Had Felicia already suspected Jace's story and now feared for Emma? "For your daughter to trust me, I can't repeat what she tells me without her consent."

"You mean like if she was talking to a counselor, the conversation would fall under patient confidentiality?"

"Yes. I'll ask Emma if sharing our conversation with you is okay, but I must honor her decision."

"Why wouldn't she want me to know?" Felicia's voice rose higher. "I'm her mother. We don't have secrets." She gasped. "I hid Will's abuse. Jace held back what he'd done. We didn't want Emma to hear her dad's story until she was older."

"I see your reasoning. But what if Timothy abused and threatened her if she told anyone?" Emotionally battering Felicia wasn't my normal method of proving a point unless absolutely necessary. Except she needed to grasp the worst-case scenario. If Emma hid a horrible secret, better it be brought out in the open now where a counselor and her family could deal with the trauma.

"If I'd found out Timothy hurt either of my children, I'd have killed him myself."

I offered a compassionate nod. "The very reason I need to talk to your daughter."

Her shoulders stiffened, a resolve I'd seen in the past. "You're right. We need to know if he touched her. Counseling won't work if she can't be honest. I just hope she's willing to talk to me too."

"Let's not jump to conclusions or worry about something that might not have happened. If Emma has been a victim or overheard a conversation, she needs to voice her concerns."

"Do you mind if it's just you and Emma? She's never been one to open up to men."

"No problem. I wouldn't want to discuss sensitive emotional matters in front of a man I barely knew either. I hope to win her trust."

"Do what you can, Carrington. I'm ready for all the Kendrix stench to be aired and over."

Jace entered the kitchen. "Mom, are you ready to talk to Sheriff Macmire?"

Felicia agreed and grabbed her purse and keys.

I met with Emma in the privacy of the same bedroom where Levi and I had talked to Jace. Her shivering body and belligerent stare showed me the discussion might not go well.

"How are you?" I said.

She shrugged. "My dad's dead. My brother's hiding a secret, probably a horrible one. My grandma has dementia. Granddad's quiet. My mom's a mess. And you ask me how I'm doing? That's lame."

"You're right. My apologies. My dad and mom were killed in a car accident when I was younger than you. Someone asked me the same stupid question."

"What did you say?"

"Nothing. Just cried. Which makes my insensitive remark even worse because I've been there."

"Okay, so what do you want?"

"Where are your thoughts, the things that keep you awake at night?"

Emma clenched her jaw and waved around the room. "I want to be anywhere but here. My dad killed my grandpa, shot my uncle, and committed suicide. The news said my dad had been beaten as a boy. Where am I supposed to be?"

"I wish I could take you away from all the pain."

Emma blinked. "Can you? Not with Granddad, Gram, and her poor crazy mind, but someplace sunny and happy?" She stared beyond me, not seeing. "Impossible. I know. What did you say to Jace? He looked awful when he left."

"Like you, he hurts. He needs to get a few things off his chest."

"Why did this happen to our family?"

"I don't know. But one day you will be able to work through your sorrow by thinking back to the wonderful times spent with your dad. There's a treasure house of good memories there. I suggest writing those down to read whenever you feel sad."

"The pastor suggested the same thing." Emma stopped talking, and I waited . . . as difficult as the task was. "Is that what you did when you were a little girl?"

I wanted to pull Emma into my arms. "What are you feeling right now?"

"Empty. Can't cry or scream or sleep. Like I'm frozen and no way to get warm."

"I remember those awful feelings."

"Do you really? I want to be with Dad."

An alarm sounded in my brain. "Are you thinking about hurting yourself?"

She stared beyond me. "Sometimes. I just miss him, and I'll never see him again."

"If you've thought about self-harm, how would you do it?"

Emma shook her head. "Pills, I guess. I want to stop hurting."

"Is there anyone or anything that would keep you on this planet?" When she said nothing, I added, "Because they would suffer the way you're suffering right now."

"I love Mom and Jace. And Grandma and Granddad."

"Good. They love you too."

"The news said Dad hurt people. They're wrong. My dad wouldn't hurt anybody." She swiped at a tear. "Uncle Boyd will be okay, right?"

"He's on his way to a full recovery."

Her features tightened.

"What is it?" I said.

"I won't miss Timothy."

Emma used his first name, a game changer. "You didn't have a good relationship with him?"

"He killed my dog."

The man had evil blood flowing through his veins. "How awful. And you're sure it was him?"

She nodded. "He admitted it. I thought she'd run away. Dad searched for her until he gave up. Grandpa called me. Said I wasn't taking good care of her, so he poisoned her."

"Oh no, Emma. I'm so sorry. When did he hurt your pet?"

She shrugged. "A year ago on October 31. He called it a Halloween joke."

"How did your parents react?"

"I never told them."

"Emma, did your grandfather Kendrix touch or hurt you?"

"No. But he said he'd tell Dad I'd killed my dog."

"Your mother needs to hear what happened."

"She's not doing very well." Emma choked back a sob. "I don't want to lose her, too."

"Your mother is stronger than you think. Telling her the truth is part of healing—for you and for her. The truth will make her so much stronger, and all the pieces will start to fit so your family can deal with the past and move forward."

"At least Jace is like a rock. He's doing better than Mom and me."

"He sounds like a good big brother."

"Yes. He told me we'd all be okay."

I smiled. "Do you and Jace talk?"

"I talk. He listens."

I braved forward. "Did you tell him about your dog?"

Emma crossed her arms over her chest.

"You can tell me."

"I got upset in Laredo about everything and told him what Timothy did. But not Mom."

"When your mom returns with Jace, can you tell her what you've told me?"

"She might get upset."

"Highly unlikely. She already knows Timothy had faults. I told her I'd share our conversation if you agreed, but I prefer you do it. I have a legal obligation to inform her about your thoughts about hurting yourself. Emma, I need to make her aware of how you feel."

"I hate feeling so depressed, but then I don't want to worry Mom."

"She wants to help you feel better. After I talk to her, I can still be there with you while you tell her the other things. But you would do the talking."

Emma slowly nodded. "All of it?"

"Every word and all the things that are hurting you on the inside."

She sniffed. "Okay. It'll be hard. Maybe she and Jace are having a counseling-type conversation, and I won't upset her too much. What if I ask Granddad to listen in instead of you?"

I smiled. "I'm sure he'd be honored to support you."

"He's the closest thing I have to a dad now."

"I'm texting your mom about your fear of self-harm."

"Is there hope for me?" Emma said.

I wrapped my arm around her small shoulders. "There is always hope."

FIFTY-NINE

LEVI

I was itchy to be doing anything but sitting on the Westfields' front porch with Howard and Zora while Carrington talked to Emma. Taking notes on my phone proved harder than dictation software with my one arm wrapped like a burrito. Yep, my attitude plunged below zero. These people weren't family or really cared if I helped or not. I mean . . . in the past, I'd jumped in to aid victims no matter the danger. The action moved fast, and I operated on adrenaline. The situation here was different. Psychological. Secrets were a harder wall to knock down than people motivated by selfishness and greed. If the Westfields suspected Timothy had been working with the cartel, I'd need a crowbar to pry it loose.

Originally, I intended to write a story that slanted toward helping families walk through multiple tragedies. The result wouldn't focus on exploiting the Kendrixes' hurt and pain but on educating others and offering community support. I'd released snippets to keep my name in the game, but I wanted a follow-up. Video interviews with victims tended to slow the healing process, but those in the community often had valuable advice.

"How's the arm?" Howard said in the rocker beside me. It squeaked like it kept time with my thoughts.

I forced a smile. "Better. Slowing my pace to heal is not easy for me."

He snorted. "Wait till you're my age and everyone wants to put you out to pasture."

I looked at the fit man beside me. I should be in such good shape when I'm in my late sixties. "Not sure I'd want to tangle with you on a both-arms-working day."

"I bet your parents are proud of you."

I shifted in my chair. "We're estranged. Our religious beliefs aren't the same."

"I'm sorry to hear that. I'll be praying for reconciliation."

"Thanks. Appreciate it," I said, thankful for good, kind people.

"They live in Houston?"

"Yes. Meyerland area."

"Felicia is my weak point. Always has been."

Zora humphed. "She should have listened to us and never married Will."

Not sure I'd heard her speak before.

Zora leaned forward in her rocking chair on the other side of Howard. "You ran him off so many times, but he kept coming back like a stray dog. Like he belonged here."

I fought a grin. Couldn't help it. Sounded like her mind worked just fine.

Howard took her hand. "Honey, we did our best."

"If I'd let you fill his rear with buckshot, we wouldn't be dealing with a widow and orphans."

"Would you like a glass of iced tea?" Howard said.

"No." Zora went back to rocking. Nothing else was said.

―――

Time crept by until Carrington and Emma emerged from the house. Carrington's slight smile told me the session must have gone all right. Emma climbed onto Howard's lap and curled up like a toddler.

Not long afterward, Felicia and Jace pulled into the driveway from talking to Corbin. As they left her car, my sights flew to Jace. Stoic.

Then to Felicia, whose slumped expression still showed her reaction to her son's confession. Jace rounded the front of the car and took his mother into his arms. They held each other for several minutes, Jace nestling his mother's head against his chest and Felicia clinging to her son.

When they approached the porch, Carrington and I stood to leave. Not our place to be here any longer. Although I wanted to know if Corbin planned to file charges against Jace. I wanted to know it all . . . But I'd find out soon enough.

"You have a quiet evening," I said to Howard. "Call if you need Carrington or me."

"Wait a minute." Jace joined Howard, standing a good two inches taller than the older man. "Granddad, Carrington and Levi already know the story, and I'll tell you all of the details later. But—" Jace took a deep breath—"I shot Grandpa Kendrix when he came after Dad with a knife. Dad covered for me, and I don't think he told Uncle Boyd."

"I'm glad you did," Emma whispered. "He was mean."

What had Emma told Carrington?

Howard gasped, then hugged him. "Wait here, son. I'm walking these folks to their vehicle." At the Tahoe, Howard shook my hand and nodded at Carrington. "You two have bent over backward helping my family and law enforcement since Will took those people hostage. Thank you for all you've done. I've got it from here. Between me, the pastor, and the good Lord, our family will grow strong again."

"I've put together resources that I'll e-mail you," Carrington said. "All are means to help your precious family heal. Emma has experienced suicidal thoughts. She misses her dad, and Felicia knows."

"I've neglected Felicia as a father, but I won't let her or those kids be bullied again."

"You know where we are if you need to talk." I repeated my earlier words.

"A couple more things," Howard said. "There's no need for you or Levi to contact us or return." He peered at me. "I'd appreciate you not writing a story about the hostage situation that raises negative talk about Felicia and the kids. Please let it go. None of us need reminders."

"I could let you read it before sending it to a publisher."

Howard pressed his lips together. "My daughter and grandchildren are not a project. Let me take care of my family. I don't want to get a restraining order, but I must protect them."

SIXTY

CARRINGTON

The idea of Howard running Levi and me off with the threat of a restraining order burned like acid. I'd assumed we'd choose when our time in Victoria ended. The hours spent there had been an unusual venture to say the least—and we had probed in something that was none of our business. Until Levi and I were used as target practice and Corbin requested our help. Now it *was* our business.

I respected Howard for stepping up to bat for his family, but I couldn't believe he had just threatened us. Or was he simply looking out for his loved ones, not wanting his family exposed to raw media coverage?

Questions still plagued me. Like who'd shot arrows at us? And why? Would the attacker be finished once we kept our rears in Houston?

Levi pulled away from the Westfields' home on their quiet street, and my instincts zapped me like an electrical charge. "I'm not pleased," I said, when I wanted to use words that my grandmother wouldn't have approved of. "I want—no, I *demand*—an explanation why we were chased off Timothy Kendrix's ranch and by whom."

"What about Howard's request?"

"He's looking out for his family. Remember, Jace told us he's

261

retired Border Patrol, accustomed to protective duty. You and I know more about his family than others. We're basically strangers and walked into their lives through unfortunate circumstances."

Levi snorted. "More like we wiggled in like snakes."

"Is that what you think of us?"

"Teasing, Carrington. We got caught up in a hurting family, and someone didn't appreciate it. My bet's still on Patti Moore or Lyndie."

"What do you think will be Corbin's reaction to Howard running us off? Will he continue to investigate who came after us, or will he drop it?"

"My impression of Corbin is he doesn't drop anything. In the past when someone chased me or fired shots, I knew why and most of the time who. I'm having a hard time not pronouncing judgment on the Kendrixes, Westfields, Corbin, Skip, Patti, and Lyndie. But that's anger speaking."

"We don't have evidence."

"Motive would be an asset," Levi said. "Details and being privy to all the conversations between that group sound even better." He braked at a stop sign. "We told Howard we were heading home, and he demanded we don't return. His pride's been hurt. He didn't approve of Will, then consented to Felicia marrying him, and now she's left with a mess. We can analyze later, but my old pal curiosity is knocking on my door. How do you feel about a drive to Timothy's ranch? Or are we gluttons for punishment?"

My instincts exactly. "I'm ready. I'm not wearing my suit of armor, but I'd love to find proof of something illegal hidden on the property. But we'd need a team to search every inch."

He nodded as though convincing himself. "I'd like a couple of hours to take a further look."

I pointed to my purse. "I have my handgun with me."

"And a license to carry?"

"I'm a rules girl, most days. You?"

"Mine's in my glove box." Levi pulled through the intersection. "I have no intention of clearing a trip with Corbin. We're good, unless there's surveillance on the property."

I held up my hands. "We're breaking the law, but I'm not telling. The caretaker might be there. If he is, we can deal with his questions, and he might answer ours. If he pulls a bow and arrow, we have our archer."

"I'm not talking about vengeance. But justice."

"What about your faith, Levi? Have I dragged you down?"

"Forgiveness doesn't negate consequences."

"You should have been a lawyer." I tossed him a grin, wishing my attraction to him wasn't so strong.

"We might need one if we're arrested for trespassing."

Levi drove through an open gate onto Timothy's ranch. No vehicles in sight. Not even the hungry dog. I crossed my fingers that Corbin hadn't decided to add surveillance at Timothy's ranch. The surroundings looked quiet and peaceful as before. Levi parked close to the shed where the archer seemingly positioned himself during our past trip. No one awaited us there.

Lowering his window, Levi looked and listened. "I don't even hear the dog. Do you think we're in anybody's sights?"

"Presumptuous, aren't we?" I said. "He didn't send an invitation the last time."

"Piercingly so."

I moaned at his pun. We took our weapons and exited the Tahoe. Levi double-checked the shed. Still no sounds or anything that caught our attention.

My gaze settled on the house. "I'm not ready for breaking-and-entering charges."

"Unless Timothy had a hidden room, he wouldn't have kept money or evidence here. Too smart for that." Levi pointed to the barn. "Shall we see if man's best friend is waiting for us?"

"Since we haven't heard his friendly bark, the hired hand might have taken him somewhere on the property."

Levi stopped and slowly turned. "Where are the cattle?"

"Good question." I took in the flat pasture, yellow-brown from a hot summer. A few oaks. "Maybe the hired hand moved them to better pasture."

At the door of the largest barn, Levi drew his gun—we both preferred a Glock. "Are you sure about our next move? We can hit the road if you'd rather."

"No. I don't want to be here for too long, but let's take a look." The acid whirling in my stomach earlier hadn't receded.

He unlatched the barn door and slid it open.

The building stood empty. No animals or equipment, as though someone had loaded up dump trucks and cleaned everything out. Telltale smells of animals, hay, feed, and machinery oil permeated the air. We explored the stalls and tack room. Empty.

I had his back while he climbed the ladder to the hayloft. "Nothing here either. Not even a hay bale."

Together we stood in the center of the barn and stared around us. "Levi, if all the land and goods now belong to Boyd and he's in the hospital, who helped themselves?"

"Dunno. There's another barn by the corral."

I followed him outside. He latched the door, and we scanned the area like two rookie deputies not sure what investigative step to take next. The whole business took me out of my comfort zone. Glancing at my Glock, I shuddered at the thought of having to fire it at something that lived and breathed.

At the second barn, Levi repeated the same process as when we approached the larger barn. He lifted the latch while holding on to his Glock.

He slid the door open. Paused. "You're not going to believe this."

"What's in there?" I stepped forward.

A dozen or more Hispanic men sat bound and gagged.

SIXTY-ONE

LEVI

"We're here to help," I said in Spanish to the bound men. "Carrington, let's get those ropes off."

We continued to reassure the men of our good intentions, speaking to each other in Spanish so as not to alarm them. The stench of toileting caused a few of the men to apologize, while embarrassment seared their faces. They were suspicious of us and rightly so. We dragged in a water hose attached outside the barn to help hydrate them while waiting for Corbin and Skip to arrive. Most of the men turned the hose on their whole bodies. I'd also requested an ambulance since two of the men had received blows to their bodies, and one had a broken arm.

One of the men, a younger man, acted as their spokesman. They'd paid two guides to get them across the border. Once in Texas, they were told they hadn't paid the full price and now owed the cartel for safe passage. The guides announced they'd be selling drugs to pay off their debts. When a man refused, he was shot in the head. The others were brought here and told someone would be back to train them in how to move drugs. Those who rejected the idea looked down the barrel of a gun or their families in Mexico were killed. They'd been held in the barn without food or water for over three days.

My thoughts rolled back to the dead men found on the property. They might have paid the price for not cooperating with the guides. I assured the men that Carrington and I were not the cartel. I didn't mention the Border Patrol or county deputies were en route. Wasn't a smart move since there were more of them than there were of us, and although the men were dehydrated and weak, they were scared. If they took off before Corbin and Skip showed up, Carrington and I faced more than a rear-chewing.

"Do you know Timothy Kendrix?" I said. "Or heard the name?"

Apparently not or they were afraid to say so. Carrington found rags in the barn and rinsed them in the hose to wipe dried blood from the two injured men.

I talked to them while assisting her. "Was anyone here when you arrived?"

"Sí, señor," the spokesman said, who hosted a swollen black eye.

"Did you hear a name, or could you describe him?"

"No name. Older. Maybe fifties. Silver hair in a ponytail. Boss man, I think."

I thanked him. "Do you know why the cartel used the Kendrix ranch?"

No response.

Corbin and Skip pulled into the property with two ambulances right behind. I'd requested no lights or sirens, and they'd honored it. Now the area swarmed with Border Patrol agents and county deputies. Carrington and I stood outside the barn gulping in fresh air with law enforcement until Corbin and Skip interviewed the undocumented immigrants and the men were examined by paramedics.

"Don't even think about leaving," Corbin had said, and Skip backed him up.

The afternoon sun waved a torch of fiery heat, like the anticipated questioning from Corbin and Skip.

The undocumented men exited the barn and were asked to sit on the ground near the door. The BP agents passed around water bottles, bananas, and granola bars for the men before they were transported in ambulances and Border Patrol vehicles to a medical facility.

Skip called out for us to join him and Corbin in the barn. He kept the door open, which helped to dissipate the stench.

"Ready for a rear-chewing?" I whispered to Carrington.

"I think I've lost my negotiation skills," she said. "I'm furious with what we found and the condition of those men."

Corbin stood legs apart and crossed his arms in front of his chest. One angry county sheriff who probably wanted to throw us back to Houston. But I thought better of telling him so.

Corbin eyed us with a distinct scowl. "Why were you two here without telling me first?"

Before I managed to form a response, Carrington took a step forward. "I wanted another look at Timothy's ranch. Someone shot Levi and me. I don't take that kind of treatment lightly." She took another step closer. "Arrest me. I don't give a flip. I'm furious about what we found. Those men would have died in this barn." She glared at Corbin. "Why haven't you tracked down the jerk with a compound bow? Explain that?"

Feisty Carrington might cause us to spend the night in jail.

Corbin studied her like she might have morphed into a red wasp. "I could go door to door and ask if the people living there have a bow and arrow. How about I lock you two up until I find out who shot you? I thought we had a deal." His face reddened. "Your respect for law enforcement needs an adjustment."

She drew in a deep breath and stepped back.

Skip picked up the conversation. "The BP is running thin on agents. Undocumented immigrants and their guides sneak by in the dark or know where our surveillance teams are positioned."

"Then you should be thanking us," Carrington said.

Corbin turned his attention to me. "What's your reason for trespassing?"

"The same. Add to that Howard Westfield informed us we were no longer needed and mentioned a restraining order. This seemed like our last chance."

Corbin wiped the sweat from his forehead. "Why doesn't he want you near his family?"

"He's concerned I'll write a derogatory story about them."

Corbin frowned. Sure would like to read his mind. "A couple of those men confirmed you'd asked questions. Anything you want to share?"

I offered in detail what happened from the moment we entered the barn.

Skip took over. "The description of the older man fits the hired hand. Problem is, those undocumented immigrants are too afraid for themselves and their families to ID him. I'll bring him in for questioning today under the pretense of finding those men while scouting the area. We also have three bodies and no one under arrest for their murders."

"Add the missing equipment, feed, and cattle," I said.

"We will." Corbin nodded at Carrington. "The hired hand had an alibi for the afternoon you were injured."

"His name?" she said.

"Won't hear it from me or Skip unless charges are filed."

I smothered a laugh.

"Am I under arrest?" Carrington said.

"You mean 'are we' since you had an accomplice?" Corbin was getting a lot of milage out of her outburst.

"Yes, sir."

Corbin shook his head at Carrington. "You and Levi have tried my patience until I want to lock you both in a cell and throw away the key. I suggest you both get back to Houston. Either Skip or I will call tonight or tomorrow once the hired hand is interviewed. What you two fail to see is *we* want answers to the murders, the human smuggling, and who's involved."

"Thank you," I said.

"Here's your final warning. One more bending of the law, and you two will enjoy the county's Hotel Victoria."

SIXTY-TWO

CARRINGTON

Levi and I stopped for dinner on the way home. Odd how adrenaline always made me incredibly hungry. And from the size of the steak vanishing on Levi's plate, he reacted the same way. We talked about everything but finding the men at Timothy's ranch. I needed silence to decompress, process, analyze, and all the other methods I used to work through trauma. And how did I stand up to Corbin and Skip when normally I'm the in-control woman who calms everyone else down?

"How do you do it?" I said, finishing up my last coconut shrimp.

He raised a brow. "What?"

"We've eaten our weight in food, laughed at a waiter's joke, checked in with what's happening with the Cowboys, and still, you understand how I couldn't handle one more comment about the problems that brought us together."

He popped half a roll into his mouth. "Sorta sensitive of me. Don't you think?"

My mind raced to where he traveled, and a smile twitched at my lips. "As I'm a drama queen, and you want to eat instead of hearing me rant?"

"I'm simply thankful we're not eating bread and water in jail."

I cringed. I should have left well enough alone. "Guess you made your point."

Levi burst out laughing. Startled, the urge to release the past several days of horrendous tension pushed me to join him. We laughed until tears rolled down my face. Reality slammed into my chest. I hadn't thought about my eyes all day. What a relief, but Levi still laughed like a kid on a sugar high.

"In the words of my grandmother," I said, "you're incorrigible."

"Would she have liked me?"

I tilted my head. "Hard to say. She had a weird sense of humor."

"Then she'd have loved me."

Five minutes from my home, my phone rang. I didn't recognize the number, but the area code was Victoria. "Someone from our favorite community is calling," I said and answered.

"Carrington, Corbin Macmire here. Is Levi with you?"

My gaze flew to Levi. "Yes. Were you trying to reach him?"

"Both of you. Can you put this on speaker?"

"Yes, sir."

"I told Skip I'd make this call. The Border Patrol arrested Walden Thurman for human smuggling of undocumented immigrants, a federal offense, and he's a suspect in three murder cases. The BP found three women held at his place. They were wives of three of the men you found. You questioned possible missing machinery and other items cleared out from the big barn. Cattle bearing the Kendrix brand were found on the Thurman property and an abundance of machinery. He claims he's responsible for the ranch and protecting Boyd's interests. Theft charges could get tossed out of court."

"Did any of the men held in the barn identify him?" I said.

"No. They're too scared. Considering what the cartel does to those who oppose them, I'm not surprised."

"Did Thurman name an accomplice?"

"You bet. Timothy Kendrix as the kingpin. Claimed that's all he knew."

"Did you find a compound bow?"

"Not yet. Thurman was working in his barn when Skip and I arrived. Machinery and cattle were obvious. A mean shepherd tried to take my leg off. I imagine Levi could ID the dog. I've requested a search warrant to check that out."

I sighed with a good degree of relief and thanked him.

Levi pulled into my driveway. "Looks like Walden Thurman and Timothy Kendrix are the missing pieces."

"Appears so." I looked at my front landscaping, my sanctuary, but my mind swept back to Corbin's words. "If evidence puts Thurman in line for a lengthy prison term or worse, he could opt for a plea bargain."

"Imagine how we'd celebrate if Thurman is an archer."

I snorted, not exactly a feminine trait. "That would be pushing our luck, but I'd pop open a bottle of champagne and treat you to the best dinner in town."

"Would I get a kiss?"

"Now you're really pushing your luck." I opened the car door and thanked him for putting up with my quirks.

"Can I say hey to Arthur?"

"Five minutes. That's all."

He grinned and followed me on the sidewalk to the front entrance. I stopped and stared at my front door before pressing in the code to enter. After a threat a few years ago, I developed a system to always alert me if someone had been inside my home. Alarms could be hacked, and my trust level in anything or anyone was rooted in ground zero.

"What has your attention?" Levi said.

"My front entrance isn't the way I left it." I pointed to potted topiaries on both sides of the door trimmed to resemble stacked balls. "Someone moved both pots, no doubt looking for a key." I bent to examine more closely. "See this clean outer ring on the concrete, then the dustier area beyond it?"

Levi joined me. "Do you keep a key under either of those?"

"Never." I stood and pulled my garage opener from my bag. "I feel better getting in the house my usual way."

The garage door lifted. My neat, organized garage looked like a tornado had whirled through. The last time someone broke in, I'd felt violated. My head pounded, and I trembled with paralyzing fear.

Oh no, what about Arthur?

SIXTY-THREE

I yanked open the door leading into the kitchen and remembered to breathe. Arthur greeted me with his can't-get-enough-of-my-mommy attention. I lifted him into my arms and held him close. "So glad you're okay, Arthur. Not sure what I'd do if you were hurt. Too bad you can't talk." I said to Levi, "Give me a minute. I need to check a few things."

"I have my gun," Levi said behind me.

I nodded my thanks and carried Arthur while we walked through the open kitchen to my office. Thurman sat in custody, and I thought the crimes were over. I cringed. Books were strewn on the floor. Desk drawers opened and emptied. Closet ransacked.

Breathe.

Dad always reminded me to breathe when I couldn't control the happenings around me. I took four deep breaths. The drumming in my chest slowed. "What was the person looking for?"

"Discovering that would take a while. Another question is how did the person get inside?" Levi said.

"So far I haven't seen a sign of forced entry, and any broken windows would have triggered my alarm."

"Have you been vandalized before?" Levi said.

"Once about three years ago. An unhappy man from a domestic

negotiation case. That's when I added a new alarm system and initiated my topiary-pot system." A lump threatened to rise in my throat. "I'll call Aaron at HPD." I connected to Aaron, letting him know what I'd found.

"Don't touch anything," Aaron said. "I'm dispatching officers ASAP, and I suggest waiting outside until they arrive. I know you have a licensed handgun, but someone could take it and use it on you."

My thoughts exactly. "I'm not alone. But we can stand outside. I have no idea if anything is missing, except my electronics are here."

"I'll be at your place in the next hour. I have questions about Levi Ehrlich's and your troubles in the Victoria area 'cause it sure looks like you brought them home with you."

Before gathering up Arthur and venturing outside, we walked through my living area to the other two bedrooms and two baths. An upholstered chair in my bedroom had been slashed. Drawers in both bedrooms and my bookcase filled with treasured books from my grandmother had been dumped in a mad attempt to find something.

"What is this about?" I said. "It's like one chaotic event leads to another, a mass of tangled threads."

"Carrington, let's put a little brain power to this. Why have you been targeted?" He paused. "Does someone think we've discovered incriminating evidence?"

Blood seemed to drain from my face, leaving me with a shiver. "But we don't know anything. Unless you do?"

Levi shook his head. "That's my only thought. Corbin might give us insight."

Levi and I left my home and stood by his Tahoe, while police sirens blared in the distance. He called Corbin and relayed what we'd discovered.

Once the police arrived, two officers introduced themselves and asked questions before entering my home. Another waiting game. The only positive in this list came from finding answers to who and why.

Aaron arrived, and he failed to disguise his frustration. After checking in with the officers, he made his way to Levi, shook his hand, and turned to me.

"I recently grounded my fifteen-year-old daughter for a month. She refused to listen to me about the company she was keeping." Aaron wrinkled his nose. "Exactly how I feel about you sticking your nose in police business."

I listened. So did Levi.

"I've ordered a team to sweep your house. You and I will walk through it in a few minutes to detect stolen or destroyed items. On the way here, I talked to Sheriff Corbin Macmire in Victoria. He filled me in on what you've been doing in his neck of the woods, the arrests, and what he and Border Patrol have learned."

I inwardly moaned while I offered my best congenial self. Levi was on his own.

"Let me share what he said . . ." Aaron took the next several minutes highlighting the trouble we'd been in. "Did I miss anything?"

"Seems like you covered it."

He stood tall and captured my eyes. "Part of your snooping is my fault. Remind me to re-anchor you in protocol. I double-checked on Nick Henderson, and he's still in jail. So doubtful your break-in is tied to that recent case. You've upset somebody, though."

"Apparently so."

Aaron nodded at Levi and leveled his gaze at him. "From the looks of you two, the other side is winning. With Carrington's and your methods of sniffing out facts, do you two have an idea who is behind the crimes other than Walden Thurman and Timothy Kendrix? Oh, and let's not forget our cartel friends."

Levi took the wide-stance approach. "Not with accuracy, sir. But I think the arrest and Thurman's confession handles the problem in Victoria."

"And you?" Aaron said to me.

"No idea."

Aaron studied me like I'd lied, and Levi must have felt the same.

"Here's where I am," Aaron said. "Thurman could have broken in right after you left this morning, went through your entire house and garage, then drove back to Victoria. Someone was looking for something that would keep them out of jail. While others might have reason to break in, seems strange you were conveniently gone today, and the damage done here took several minutes even with help. Does that make sense to either of you?"

"It's not impossible," I said, and Levi agreed.

"But highly improbable," Aaron said. "The officers here have checked all the windows and doors. No signs of forced entry. How the perp managed to get inside is unknown. So my report on the breaking and entering will state crime is under investigation, pending a report from those conducting the sweep."

Evening shadows ushered in nightfall, and weariness for the long hours ahead weighed on my mind and body.

The team assigned to dust for fingerprints arrived, and I wanted to cry. Wanted—didn't give in. Instead I thanked Aaron for taking care of the investigation. He requested the officers obtain statements from the neighbors and check security cameras in the area while the team did their job. Soon after, he drove back to the station.

I gave Levi my attention. "Why don't you go home? The team will take two hours or less, and I'm concerned you might find your condo in the same shape."

"I asked a buddy to take a look, and my place is clean. Carrington, I'm not leaving. You could crawl into my SUV and sleep."

"Not necessary." Stephanie Radison's voice sounded behind me. I hadn't seen her walk across the yards separating us. "I heard the 'crawl into my SUV and sleep' comment. Dear, I have a guest room. Please, rest there." She glanced at the police car and at my house. "I told the officer that I saw a van here most of the day with a construction crew emblem, but no phone number or website. I should have figured it out when three men entered the house, and they were there for several hours. I neither noted what they looked like or their license plate. I have no idea what's going on, and it's none of my business, but you look like you've been caught in a hurricane without an anchor."

What a dear lady. "I couldn't impose, and I should remain available for questions. Someone broke into my home. Surprisingly enough, I can't find what's been taken." I caught my rudeness. "Stephanie, I'd like you to meet my friend Levi Ehrlich. Levi, Stephanie Radison is my next-door neighbor."

"Both of you look horrible, and I do follow the news," Stephanie said. "You've had more than your share of troubles. Levi, my sofa is comfortable. You could sleep there."

"No, thank you, ma'am. Carrington needs the sleep. The officers will be done shortly."

"I'm staying right here," I said.

I could feel his argument surfacing. "I'll text or call if the officers have a question. Arthur and I just scheduled a playdate. Even if they finished in the next thirty minutes, the condition of your house, like finding your bed, will take most of the night."

I moaned like a child who demanded her way. Before I responded, Stephanie offered her approval of the idea. "Even in the dim street-lights, dear neighbor, you look like a . . . zombie."

I laughed. "All right. I'll sleep with my phone. Levi, promise me you'll call with any questions or updates."

"Promise. I'm going to let the officers inside know the plan."

Stephanie hooked her arm in mine. "Relinquish Arthur to Levi and let me escort you to my guest room."

Between Stephanie and Levi, my independence was waning. The whispers in my spirit told me more danger lay ahead, and I had no idea from whom.

SIXTY-FOUR

I never thought a guest bedroom could be so inviting as Stephanie's, decorated in my favorite blue with accents of yellow and green. Oh, the plants—real ones—philodendron, peace lily, and a huge spider plant that had "baby" shoots. Grandma would have been in "hog heaven" as she used to say.

Stephanie suggested I shower and offered me pajamas and a robe. I agreed and thanked her through watery eyes. In the morning, I'd walk home in my dear neighbor's clothing and hope I had the energy to put my house back in order.

She stood in the doorway of the guest room. "Would you like a cup of chamomile tea to calm you down?"

I'd always associated chamomile tea with my grandmother. She swore it cured everything. When blindness and cancer took over her body, I took up drinking coffee and nixed the tea. But I needed to appease this dear lady. "Thank you for your hospitality. I've imposed upon you enough."

"Nonsense. You go ahead and shower, and I'll bring you a cup."

I smiled. "You are amazing. Incredible. And so very kind."

"I had a good teacher. My husband had the gift of hospitality. Learned so much from just watching him look after others."

"How long have you been alone?"

"He passed four years ago. Once I could have given you the days and hours, but I'm doing better."

"Do you mind if I ask what happened?"

"Heart attack. He was playing golf with friends. They did their best, driving him to the hospital, but he died before they got there."

"I'm sorry. Many tragedies are impossible to understand."

Stephanie whispered her agreement. "I've heard people say when they get to heaven, they'll have a list of whys for God. I think I'll be so relieved to be there with my husband and all my loved ones who've gone on before me that the whys won't matter."

Would I ever find myself accepting Stephanie's philosophy? "I admire your faith and insight."

"I need to put more into practice. It's hard to visit his sister. Most times she doesn't recognize me, and other times she reminisces of days gone by."

Zora crept across my mind. "In her lucid moments, does she make sense, even offer wisdom or truth?"

Stephanie leaned against the doorframe. "Oh yes. In her limited mind functions, I can honestly say she's never lied to me. She still plays flute with excellence and recites Longfellow to the word. Do you know someone who has dementia?"

I nodded. "A friend who normally says little. Except recently she offered a lot of information into a confusing situation."

"Hard to say, and I'm no expert."

My cell phone rang, startling me, but it was only nine thirty. Long day. The screen showed Skip's name. When I answered, Stephanie disappeared from the doorway.

"I have a bit of information," Skip said. "If and when the story gets out, you didn't hear it from me."

Curiosity held me spellbound. "I'm listening."

"Corbin traced two of the unidentified burner phone numbers on Timothy's cell records to Walden Thurman and Patti Moore. The question is why did she use a burner? What was she hiding? Looks like Timothy and Patti had several conversations over the past several months, and the calls were incoming and outgoing."

"Has Corbin talked to Patti?" I said.

"He asked her if she and Timothy were involved in human trafficking. She denied it." Skip huffed. "If she had her sights on running for public office again, why risk it? Corbin talked to Lyndie. She had every one of her incoming and outgoing conversations with Timothy documented with day and time. He bribed her with fifty thousand dollars to call off the wedding. She hung up on him, and he left a message. The next day, he deposited the money into her account. Another round of calls. This time he offered to show Lyndie how to launder the money. A third round happened when he threatened to destroy her business. Lyndie's a smart woman. She turned the documentation over to Corbin."

Who made the threatening calls to Levi and Felicia? "Thanks, Skip."

"No problem. Are you two still on board for chasing this down? My wife wants me to focus on my own job at Border Patrol and let Corbin and the Feds handle it. She's afraid of the cartel."

"I don't blame her." I told him about three men breaking into my house. "Do you believe Timothy called the shots in a human trafficking ring?"

"Someone else must be involved. Timothy's dead and Walden's in jail," Skip said.

"I need more, Skip."

He blew out a huff. "All right. Patti told Corbin she witnessed Timothy's murder, and she said Will didn't pull the trigger."

I knew who did, but he wouldn't hear it from me. "Did she give a name?"

"No. Walden claimed Timothy had more brain cells in his little finger than she had. He said Timothy would never have trusted her."

"Why was she on the ranch unless she planned to kill him herself?"

"Timothy supposedly owed Patti money, and she drove there to demand it. Before you say another word, how did she know where to look on all those acres?"

"She must have followed him."

SIXTY-FIVE

LEVI

Stephanie Radison's front door closed, and from Carrington's driveway I peered into the darkness. From the shadowy figure moving through the grass, I figured it was Carrington.

"I thought you were headed to bed?" I said.

She wore a long, flowered, chenille robe from what I could tell in the streetlight. "I was until Skip called."

My ears perked like a dog who heard the word *treat*. Then again, did I want to digest any more bad news? "Must be important to bring you out here dressed like—"

"Stephanie insisted I take a shower, and she supplied the pj's and robe." Carrington giggled. "I must be near hysteria to find the way I look funny."

I prepared myself while I longed to pull her into my arms. "Very nice of her."

Carrington relayed her conversation with Skip, which shoved more puzzle pieces into place.

"What are your thoughts?" she said.

"If Patti Moore worked behind the scenes, wouldn't she try hard to show her Ms. Congeniality side? She treated Lyndie like dirt."

Carrington crossed her arms over her chest. "You're right. Bothers me that I didn't think about that while desperately searching for answers."

"How about all you've been through?"

"I wasn't alone. I have a partner in crime. I believe Patti's connected in some way, but how exactly? I wouldn't be surprised if she has info she's keeping to herself. Timothy was shrewd. Look at how he fooled most of the community with his domestic abuse. If there's one thing I've learned in the negotiation business, it's no one manipulates successfully unless he's a master of lies."

"Does that make Patti a pawn?"

"I don't know. They were together for a while, but that could have been all show. Would Lyndie hide evidence implicating her mother?" Carrington stared at me, and I felt her penetrating eyes peer through me. "Blood is thick when it comes to family." She hesitated. "Delete that. You've experienced the opposite with your family."

"I can't stomach Patti, but I think Lyndie's the real deal."

"Levi, will there ever be a solution? Or are the players and the motives knotted into a mess that will forever remain tangled?"

"How will you feel if we don't search for answers?"

She seemed to think about her response. "Incredibly sad. A failure for not seeing through behavior. The cowardly side of me says to move on and give 100 percent to the next negotiation."

"I'm not convinced you could live with not knowing."

"You're right. What will you do?" she said.

"The same as you—see the investigation through to the end no matter how long it takes. You and I have to earn a living, but it doesn't eliminate the reality that someone tried to kill us. And they might try again."

"It's not over. Go ahead and say it."

"People driven by extreme behavior are rarely satisfied when their prey runs."

"You're right for the second time tonight," she whispered. "As though my thoughts are speaking back to me."

I smiled despite the circumstances stalking us. "We're a team, Carrington. We will find those answers."

"Third time you're right if you're counting. How soon do we make another trip to Victoria?"

"I suggest we give it a few days' rest. We need time to sort out what if anything is missing from your house and give you time to recover. Wednesday I have my interview with *National Geographic*."

"Okay," she said. "I have plenty to do. What time is your interview?"

"Ten o'clock. Why?"

"In the afternoon, we could phone a couple of people. You have a good connection with Boyd, and I think checking in with Lyndie makes sense."

"Then we can map out our secret drive for Thursday or Friday."

"I agree. Let's nail down those who might have helped Timothy and Walden with the illegal activities. So many personalities. So many motives. Who among them is the missing link?"

SIXTY-SIX

CARRINGTON

Attempting to put my house in order took Stephanie, Levi, and me all day Tuesday. Earlier in the day Levi had brought a friend whom he introduced as Caleb, a dark-haired mountain-man type who looked more like a bouncer than a photographer. Together they helped put the heavy items in place. Not a whole lot Levi could lift or move with one arm.

"Hey, crip. You're a bit useless," Caleb said.

"I'll remember that the next time you need my advice on how to word an e-mail."

Levi's comradery demonstrated another side of him. Yes, I'd fallen hard.

Stephanie worked like a trouper until I feared she'd overdone it. Except I was the one who stopped to rest more than the others. Caleb referred to me as a hashtag—#stop2rest.

Not one item was missing, and I searched every corner.

Finding broken treasures that had belonged to my grandmother and parents saddened me to the brink of tears. Stephanie caught a few of those moments and wrapped her arms around me. Without a word, she spoke caring into my brokenness.

"Will you be at Shabbat?" Caleb said to Levi.

"Can't promise. But I hope so."

He shouldn't miss Shabbat. "Levi, we can wait on our errand."

"Maybe." He smiled in a way that held me captive.

Caleb laughed and suggested we come together. "How long have you two been seeing each other?"

"We're not," Levi said. "Just friends."

Stephanie rolled her eyes. Was it that obvious? I shuddered inside. My thoughts about Levi and me together slammed into it's-not-fair-to-him . . . my eyes.

Wednesday morning, I worked alone to finish my house while Levi interviewed with *National Geographic*. I refused Stephanie's help and ordered her to rest.

At noon, a text sent me scrambling to pull my phone from my jeans pocket. My pulse sped with Levi's name on the screen.

I GOT THE JOB! We'll talk later.

Congrats! When will you be here?

Soon as I finish the paperwork for NG.

Now, as Levi and I sat at opposite ends of my sofa, he talked about his job offer. I treasured the sparkle in his brown eyes and the lilt in his voice.

"Congratulations. I bet they offered you a six-figure advance to sign their employment contract," I said.

"Let me say, I'm more than pleased." He grinned, and an irresistible dimple deepened in his cheek. "We need to celebrate, and we will."

"I'd like that."

Levi picked up a broken pipe on the coffee table. "I can fix this."

I swallowed the rising emotion. "It belonged to my dad. I remember him smoking it on the back porch."

"Consider it done." He laid it back on the table and pulled his phone from his jeans pocket, rather awkward with one arm. "Time to check on Boyd."

"Would you place it on speaker?" I said.

He touched the Speaker button and pressed in numbers. "Hey, Boyd, this is Levi Ehrlich. How are you feeling?"

"A ton better. Going home tomorrow—not really home, but Lyndie's place."

"She'll take good care of you."

"My gal's a keeper. We're moving up the wedding date. Hope you and Carrington will come. After all, I'd be dead if not for you and Skip."

"Congratulations on the big day." Levi looked at me, and I grinned. "We'll do our best to be there."

"One day, I want to repay you and Skip for what you did for me."

"Nothing on my end. Live to do good, Boyd. That's what matters."

"Are you here in Victoria?"

Levi laughed. "Carrington and I got into too much trouble. Sheriff Macmire prefers we keep our distance."

"I heard about it all. Walden Thurman didn't confess to firing arrows at you two. In fact, deputies have yet to find the bow."

"Do you know anyone who uses a compound bow and arrow?"

"Not with the accuracy you've experienced." Boyd paused. "Been wracking my brain trying to figure it all out."

"Carrington had a problem." Levi gave him the story about my break-in.

"With Will gone and the hostages freed, why is someone targeting you and Carrington?"

"That's the million-dollar question. I have another question," Levi said.

"Fire away. Poor choice of words."

Levi chuckled. "After Patti and Timothy stopped seeing each other publicly, did they continue to see each other in private?"

"I'd say no. Dad and Patti thrived on controlling people, and when their devious ways no longer worked, they were out for revenge. Which is what I think happened in Patti's campaign efforts. She and Lyndie haven't spoken since a problem here at the hospital. I don't trust Patti any farther than I can throw her. She is one conniving woman." He paused. "Felicia told me about Jace's confession. I had no idea. But if Patti got wind of it, she'd destroy Felicia and Lyndie out of spite."

"She won't hear or read anything from me."

"Thanks, Levi. For a long time, I suspected she'd shot Dad. The thought of it made me worry about Lyndie handling it. What really happened was worse."

"Glad Lyndie has you and her dad. One more question, then I'll leave you alone. Would Timothy have hidden money on his property?"

"If you told me he'd buried people on his land, I'd not blink an eye. Nothing surprises me at this point. Once I'm well, I'll be looking for more evidence to prove he and Walden Thurman were into human smuggling."

"Are you concerned about the cartel giving you a bad time?" Levi said.

"Any indication of it and I'll stop. Not sure how I feel about moving back to my ranch or Dad's with the memories."

Levi thanked Boyd for talking to him and ended the call.

"Sounds like Patti is capable of as much evil as Timothy," I said.

"Definitely a pair." His phone buzzed again. "Boyd's calling me back."

"Maybe he forgot something."

"I need to update you about my dad's will," Boyd said. "When Felicia learns about this, she'll be devastated. Neither Will nor I had any idea what it contained. We assumed the estate would be split between us and never questioned otherwise. Dad's attorney has been out of town, and since he had a copy, I assumed he'd get around to letting me know. This morning, he stopped in for the reading. Anyway, Dad left Will one dollar and the rest to me. I have no idea why, but that's not happening. I'll divide everything with Felicia right down the middle. I've asked Lyndie, Felicia, and Howard to come by here later so I can tell them."

Levi blew out a sigh. "I don't know what to say."

"Me either. My dad was a piece of work. Yes, he favored me and I hated it. Anyway, thanks for all you've done for this family."

"Do me a solid and don't tell them we've talked," Levi said.

"You got it."

Levi stared at his phone and shook his head. "What kind of archaic rock had Timothy crawled out from under? If we didn't already know who killed him, I'd say Will had motive for murder."

"The crimes are like a spider's web," I said. "Murder, money, abuse, human smuggling, and who knows what else?"

"Has to be the most dysfunctional family I've ever met. Except for maybe mine. Even with my family, I understood their decisions. Remind me why we got involved?"

"We have compassion for others."

"Right." He pointed to my phone. "Your turn to make a call."

I pressed in Lyndie's number at her boutique and activated Speaker. "Hi, Lyndie, this is Carrington Reed. Are you free to talk?"

"Yes. I'm in my office, and one of my clerks is waiting on customers. How can I help you?"

"I'm checking to see how you're doing." I chose not to talk about my break-in. She'd find out from Boyd.

Lyndie shared about Boyd's upcoming hospital release. "My girls can handle the store until I feel safe leaving him. What about you and Levi? Are you healing?"

"We're fine, taking it slow. Thanks for asking."

"I should tell you what happened. I mean, the sheriff has the information, and I plan to tell Boyd this evening." Lyndie took a deep breath. "My mother called me. She hasn't gotten over our argument at the hospital. She told me if Boyd and Felicia didn't pay what Timothy owed her, she'd ruin both of us. I told her that wasn't my decision to make and asked how much money. She quoted three hundred thousand dollars, and I hung up."

"That's horrible. I'm so sorry."

"I used stronger words than that. I'll send you and Levi a wedding invitation. We've moved up the date at my insistence. I don't care if it means I push him down the aisle in a wheelchair. I want to be his wife."

Levi squeezed my hand, and tears pooled in my eyes.

"You must love him very much," I said.

"I do. Not the dead, my mother, or anyone else can destroy that invisible bond."

The conversation ended, and I set my phone on the coffee table.

"This is tied to money," Levi said. "And it's not over."

SIXTY-SEVEN

LEVI

Before sunrise on Friday morning, halfway through my first cup of coffee, Sheriff Macmire called me.

"Good mornin', Corbin."

"I hope so." He chuckled. "Guess you aren't still snoozing."

"Early riser. If you're at my front door, I'll pour another cup of coffee."

"The other way around. What are the chances of you and Carrington meeting me at my office?"

Telling him about heading his direction bordered on . . . *mishegas.* I'd been called insane in the past, and at times it fit. "For you to make that request, something new must have your attention."

"Yep. Have you or Carrington received any more threats?"

"Nothing other than the break-in at her place. Why?"

"Lyndie Moore's store was torched last night."

I groaned. "Any suspects?" My mind flew to Patti.

"No. Camera footage shows a man in a hoodie who conveniently avoided the video."

"Why do you need Carrington and me?"

"You two were the last to speak to Will Kendrix. You were the first to reach Boyd. You two found the undocumented immigrants, talked to them. And you agreed to be an extra set of eyes and ears."

"Which means?"

"I think you're holding back evidence. I'd rather you two drive here voluntarily than my going the legal route."

"I assure you we're not intentionally hiding anything, but we will be there today. Do we need an attorney?"

"Levi, that's up to you. The evidence isn't stacking up to end these crime sprees, and if you and Carrington are willing, I'd appreciate eliminating any knowledge either of you have that's impeding justice, knowingly or otherwise."

Less than two hours later, Carrington and I were on Highway 59 to Victoria. We'd discussed why Corbin contacted me instead of her, and neither of us had a clue except I witnessed Will's last words, and I'm the journalist. Maybe he realized publishing a derogatory piece about the sheriff wasn't good for reelection.

"Everyone is motivated by something," Carrington said. "What are we hiding from him or Skip? Even what we've done on our own is public record or easily confirmed from the people we've talked to."

"He could be pressured to put the crimes at rest and thinks we can help him tie up loose ends." I glanced at her studying the road ahead. "You answer Corbin's questions as you think best. I intend to be honest."

She nodded. "No other way. Wonder who else he's interviewing?"

"If he's desperate for answers, he's reviewing all the evidence and talking to the people we've met. More like interrogating." My phone rang. The screen's display flagged a potential spam call, but I answered and pressed Speaker.

"Levi, why are you headed to Victoria?" The Hispanic voice that had previously threatened had returned.

"A scenic ride," I said.

"You've been warned to stay away from there."

"Why? Do you plan to torch my condo like you did Lyndie Moore's shop? Or bring out your compound bow?"

"I suggest turning around. Now. Victoria is not safe for you, now or ever."

"When you're ready to talk reason, I'll listen." I ended the call. Carrington held up her phone. "I recorded every word. Corbin can run it through the national database."

"Good. Keep your eyes open. I bet there's a tracker on my vehicle." I took the next exit and pulled over.

Ten minutes later, I located a tracker on the undercarriage of the driver's side. My first thoughts were to crush it, but Corbin might want it, so I decided to leave it in place. Carrington and I raced ahead to Victoria with crazed threats beating down hard.

SIXTY-EIGHT

CARRINGTON

Sheriff Macmire greeted Levi and me with a plastered-on smile and escorted us to his office, a small, cluttered room hosting a window overlooking the parking lot.

His body language spoke of stress and fatigue, while sympathy for his responsibilities touched me. I placed my negotiation skills at the forefront. "Corbin, do you want to talk over an early lunch? On me."

He lifted his white-brimmed hat and placed it on a stack of papers. "Buying my lunch is considered a bribe. I still appreciate it, though." He motioned for us to sit in two chairs across from his desk and closed the door.

Levi caught my attention, and I lifted my chin for him to begin.

"Your call took me by surprise," Levi said. "You asked me about more threats, and I got one on the way here."

"Same person?"

"Yes." Levi shared the conversation that I'd recorded. "And we found a tracker on my Tahoe."

Corbin leaned back in his chair and ran his fingers through his wiry red hair. "Best news I've heard in a few days. I'd like to hear the recording."

I laid my phone on his desk and pushed Play.

While the conversation repeated, Corbin rubbed his hands together. Repeatedly. When the recording finished, he thanked me. "I'll make sure we reverse engineer the voice change and match it to a source. But I have an idea who's behind it."

"Who?" I said.

"I don't want to reveal that information until I have proof."

I leaned forward. "How can we help?"

Corbin frowned. "Are you using negotiation tactics on me?"

"If I am, it's because I know what stress does to the mind and body. You hold an office that either everyone respects you or they are adamant about destroying you."

"So right. The pressure to make arrests grows by the hour." He toyed with a pen on his desk. "I have more than one reason for asking you here. The recording is a bonus."

Levi picked up the conversation. "As Carrington said, how can we help?"

"Has anything else been written about the Kendrixes' hostage situation?"

"Not since what I released at the crime scene and later after I was treated at the hospital. Three total. I haven't finished the longer piece, neither do I want to drag Felicia's family through the mud."

"How are you slanting it?"

"An article that shows how domestic abuse destroyed a family and then tie it to how a community took positive steps to help heal and prevent domestic violence."

The sheriff blew out a huff. "The community hasn't gotten on board yet."

"Neither is the article finished. I'd want photos of those in action." Levi shook his head. "My plans for the article aren't why we're in your office."

Corbin tapped the pen on the desk. "Last night, I received an e-mail from a bogus address. The person claimed that when you two made the second trip to Timothy Kendrix's ranch, you found where he'd hidden cash, money he'd made from human trafficking with Walden Thurman." He waved his hand. "If for one moment I believed the sender, you two would be persons of interest. A person who is coward enough to hide their identity is usually a liar. My question is, have you told me everything you saw on your two visits to that property?"

I thought back to the first time when we were attacked. Nothing came to mind, and I didn't want to offer an opinion without proof. The second time we'd found the men held hostage. Had I forgotten a detail? Heard, seen, or smelled anything of importance?

"I can't remember anything we've not already shared," I said. "I'll continue to think about those trips and whatever I remember, no matter how small, I'll contact you." I remembered Felicia mentioning a prescription for Boyd. "Have Boyd's medical records given you pause?"

"No. Nothing for me to be alarmed about."

"What about an antidepressant?"

Corbin pressed his lips together as though deliberating his response. "Small dose."

He gave Levi his attention, who took Corbin step by step through both ventures again.

"The only odd circumstances were the undocumented immigrants' conversations after we untied them. Carrington had left the barn to check on Skip's and your arrival, and I listened to them talk. They feared what we planned to do and if the men would return who'd locked them in the barn. One of them, a younger man I pointed out to you at the time, was apparently their spokesman. He told them to shut up because the guides often paid someone to report what was said and done. I studied those men and didn't see or hear anything to suspect any of them betraying the others."

"Those men are still in processing, and Border Patrol has questioned them more than once. Although they claim to know nothing." Corbin expelled a heavy breath. "The threats, fire, and e-mail are not cartel behavior. They have no patience. Zero tolerance. If you've gotten in their way, you're dead."

"I've encountered a few terrorists with the same philosophy," Levi said.

My experiences had been mild in that regard.

"Another question," Corbin said. "Were there other trips to the property that I'm not aware of?"

"No." Levi responded for both of us. "What I don't understand is why we're still alive. Do they think we have evidence to convict them or make them more money?"

"Carrington's house was broken into," Corbin said. "According to HPD Detective Aaron Peters's report, nothing was taken. They wore ball caps, jeans, and black T-shirts. The logo on their van was bogus. A neighbor man said two men were slight in nature, and one was large, muscular. Again, do you know what they were looking for?"

I heard his frustration. "I have no idea. Whoever did the search couldn't have found anything incriminating."

"Or you had it with you."

"What would that be? My phone? Feel free to mirror it."

"Mine too," Levi said.

"Thanks. That won't take long, and you'll have them back when we're finished here." Corbin picked up his phone and requested a person to stop by his office. Levi and I handed Corbin our devices. After an officer left with our phones and Levi's instructions to the tracker's location mounted under his Tahoe, Corbin picked up the conversation. "Have you heard from any of the Kendrix family or Lyndie Moore lately?"

I shared about yesterday's conversation with Lyndie and Patti's threat. Levi shared about his call with Boyd.

"If you asked for law enforcement to investigate anyone about the Kendrixes' crimes, threats, your assault, the break-in, fire, undocumented immigrants found on the Kendrix ranch, or the three dead men, who would that be?"

Neither Levi nor I offered a name. If we suspected anyone, we'd not be in the current dilemma. I didn't trust Patti Moore, but I doubted she was solely responsible.

"Patti Moore," Levi said.

"She has a list of enemies, and my office is turning her professional and personal lives inside out." Corbin stood. "One more thing. Did Will give one of you evidence that points to who is behind this?"

I shook my head and Levi audibly denied it.

"For the sake of the investigation and your safety, drive back to Houston and stay there. I'll let you know if anything surfaces with the tracker or the recording. Understand whoever is tracking you won't know you've returned to Houston. Be aware of everything you do."

Cowering to a hidden killer's demands went against my personal beliefs. I'd promised Will justice, and we weren't there. I wasn't giving up.

SIXTY-NINE

LEVI

"Do you think Corbin believed us?" I said to Carrington once we were inside the Tahoe.

She snapped her seat belt into place. "Think about it. You are a highly successful journalist. Your story has potential for a series or a documentary, even a movie. You have so much to gain by staying involved. Add your curiosity, faith, and commitment to truth." Carrington sighed. "Would you believe someone in your shoes?"

"I get it. You're the one who's more credible. No reason to hold back information. Doing so would damage your reputation as a negotiator."

"No, Levi, you're not listening. The one factor casting a shadow on our credibility is me. I negotiate bumps and bruises, which means I say whatever it takes to encourage a good outcome."

"Forget that excuse. We're a formidable team." Levi started the engine.

She shook her head and laughed. "Formidable?"

I chuckled. "Right. Where to?"

"As much as I'd like to explore all the Kendrixes' properties, I'm sure we'd be spotted, either by the good guys or the bad." She tossed me a mischievous grin. "I'd like to talk to Patti and even her ex-husband."

"You're sure?" Carrington never ceased to amaze me.

"Absolutely. We have our phones, and we can snap pics and record what jumps out at us."

"Literally?" I said.

"Let's hope not. I have the address of her accounting firm. She might have a more congenial attitude than the last time we were at the hospital. Like Timothy, she seems to split her personality right down the middle according to her agenda."

"All right. Her ex-husband's name is Nathan. He's a geologist, and I have his office address."

"As you've said, we're a good team," she said.

"Imagine how good we'd be in fifteen years."

She rolled her eyes. "You're pushing it."

We entered an office building housing Moore's Accounting Firm on the second floor. Through a set of double doors, we met a dark-haired receptionist who greeted us.

"We'd like to see Patti Moore," I said. "Is she available?"

"Do you have an appointment, sir?"

"No, but we're willing to wait."

"Are you an existing client or one seeking our services for the first time?"

"No. We've met Patti and wanted to say hello." I forced a friendly tone into my voice, imitating what I'd seen from Carrington.

The receptionist took our names and invited us to a seating area while she contacted Patti. We'd barely eased down onto the tufted chairs when the receptionist joined us.

"I'm so sorry. Ms. Moore is working on a critical project and isn't available. She sends her regrets." The young woman smiled—her dismissal.

Outside, Carrington and I had a good laugh over Patti's avoidance of us. I drove to the oil and gas company where Nathan Moore worked. He didn't have a critical project taking up his time.

The slightly balding man invited us into his conservative office, personable with photos of hunting trips, a petite woman, and Lyndie. He gestured for us to sit and offered us coffee or a Coke. We opted for the coffee.

"I've heard good things about you from my daughter and my longtime friend Howard Westfield," Nathan said. "Both claimed you've been very supportive of the family and took a few physical wounds in the process. Miss Reed, you risked your life to end a hostage negotiation. Mr. Ehrlich, appreciate what you did for Boyd. My thanks to both of you."

"We're sorry for your daughter's ordeal with Boyd's shooting and the torching of her boutique."

"Don't get me started on her nightmares. I'm glad Boyd's recovering. He's a good man. By the way, he was released from the hospital today and is staying at Lyndie's town house. I'll help with his care as much as I can." His gaze wandered from me to Carrington and back again. "You two aren't here to chitchat. What do you need?"

"Do you think the arson and hostage situation are related?" I said.

He eased back, and his shirt gaped at the belly. "Absolutely. Coincidences only work in fairy tales and poorly written fiction. I'm convinced Patti torched our daughter's shop to stop her from marrying Boyd."

"That's harsh," Carrington said.

Sounded that way to me too.

Nathan hesitated, as though thinking through what he wanted to say. "The person wearing a hoodie looked like Patti's build. I pointed out the likeness to the sheriff."

"But why would she resort to arson?" I said.

Nathan huffed. "Here's a bit of history. Patti despised Timothy for not owning up to his sizable campaign donation. She must have ticked him off for him to ruin her political career. From what I've seen of Timothy, he always had a reason for his actions. Patti is vindictive too. She's my only suspect in the fire, especially since she demanded Boyd pay her what Timothy supposedly owed. Patti called me, told me she couldn't run for office if Lyndie married Boyd."

"What about the previous debacle with the campaign-fund scandal?"

"She withdrew from the race before charges could be filed." Nathan's face hardened. "I hate the idea of Patti representing good people. Anyway she begged me to change Lyndie's mind. If I refused, Patti would ruin Lyndie's business and destroy me. I told her where to go. I told Sheriff Macmire the same thing."

"Is there anyone else you suspect of foul play?" I said.

Nathan paused. "My two cents' worth regarding the human trafficking and who knows what else? Timothy's partner or partners are desperate and afraid he had incriminating information that's been passed on."

Corbin and Nathan tracked the same way. "Thanks. We're trying to better understand the picture before heading back to Houston." I glanced at Carrington for her input. "Do you have questions?"

She smiled, and the soles of my feet tingled. "Sir, do you approve of Boyd marrying your daughter? And if that question is none of my business, my apologies."

Nathan moistened his lips. "I repeat, Boyd's a good man. He knows I welcome him as a son-in-law. Not Boyd's fault his father and Lyndie's mother kissed the same snake. I'm considering if I should send him and Lyndie away until arrests are made."

"He could recuperate," Carrington said. "Especially if no one knew Lyndie's and his location."

"Anyway," Nathan said, "from the looks of you two here in my office fishing for answers, I assume no arrests have been made as to who pulled the bow and targeted you."

"No, sir," Carrington said.

"Here's a tip. Victoria County hosts an archery tournament every June. Might find your man or woman listed online. Not smart for someone to use a distinct skill to try to kill."

Nathan Moore's sincerity crashed into my good-guy theory. Was he laying the groundwork for Patti's arrest? Or were his suspicions grounded in experience? Too many people had dipped their fingers into a cauldron of guilt.

SEVENTY

CARRINGTON

The moment we slid into the Tahoe, I pulled my phone from my shoulder bag. I bent my head over my phone while my fingers flew over the keyboard.

"What are you looking for with so much determination?" Levi said.

"Background on Nathan Moore."

Levi tapped the steering wheel. "He's too helpful. Too easy to send us scrambling after Patti. She deserves to be behind bars if she torched Lyndie's shop."

I pointed to my phone. "Nothing here on him. He probably just wanted to be helpful. Still, I'll not be crossing him off our list."

Levi drove onto the street. "Where to?"

I looked at the time. "Victoria County Archery Club. I want to be certain no one in their club is anyone we've met. I'd like to see a list of their members and competition winners. How grand if our archery expert made a miscalculation."

Levi's GPS directed us to the club grounds that hosted indoor and outdoor archery opportunities for young and not-so-young. A sport I'd thought about taking up, but not with failing eyesight. At an information desk, I asked a young man about where I'd find a list of adult tournament winners for the past five years.

He directed me to a wall of fame. Tournaments were held every year, and the list of winners went back two decades. None of the names repeated, and none were names we recognized. While we stared at the honor wall, I checked the website for a list of club members and officers. Zero.

"Dead end." Levi turned to me and jammed his uninjured hand into his jeans pocket. "Are we out of our league here? We suspect everyone, then we suspect no one."

I shared his same disillusion. "I've never backed away from a challenge, and the idea that someone has gotten away with a series of crimes makes me furious."

"Add my frustration to the mix. Let's head back to Houston and go over all of it again. I'll order us dinner. Does that work for you?"

"Yes. I have plenty of paper to make graphs and charts to form connection points. My method of looking at the whole picture." I paused. "You have Shabbat tonight."

"I'm okay. Worship begins at ten thirty in the morning, and I plan to attend."

"I don't want to keep you from a service or time with your friends."

"No problem." He grinned. "You could go with me tomorrow."

My emotions ran both ways—to experience a Messianic worship service interested me since it meant so much to Levi, but attending a service reminded me of my problem with God, and I wanted to run in the opposite direction.

"I've never been to a Messianic church. I grew up Methodist," I said.

"I promise you it will be like no church service you've ever attended. Aren't you curious?"

"I am, just not sure it's for me."

"One visit will answer your question."

I wasn't a coward. "All right. I'll meet you there. Text me the address." That way if I felt too uncomfortable, I could leave.

From my house, Levi ordered Italian. Neither of us had eaten all day, and we were starved. I thought I was the rare person who got so wrapped up in my work that eating hit the bottom of the priority list. Add another star beside Levi's name—we shared the same weird eating habits.

We listed the names of potential suspects, drew lines indicating who connected to whom, and studied those whose names were related in multiple ways. Problem was, all the people were connected to the others, and those relationships were the key to finding out who had the most to hide.

Levi and I were so far from our comfort zones. I couldn't give up the investigation. All indications seemed as though God wanted us to see this through to the end.

SEVENTY-ONE

I hadn't attended a church service for fifteen years, other than funerals. This morning I googled what I should wear. Looked like slacks and a jacket for me. I spent time looking at a typical service, orienting myself for the morning. Why had I agreed to attend his church? If not for Levi's treasured friendship, I'd have texted as a no-show.

I drove to the address for the Grace Messianic Synagogue and arrived fifteen minutes before the scheduled start time. Sitting in the designated visitor parking area, I thought about sleep or work or time with Arthur at home. Monday I had a doctor's appointment to remove the stitches in my side. On Thursday morning, I needed to have a follow-up with Dr. Leonard to discuss the findings of my eye condition. What a fun week ahead.

A knock on my window alerted me to Levi, smiling like I'd brought him ice cream. I grabbed my shoulder bag and stepped out of my truck.

"You look great," he said, dressed in a blue button-down shirt and dress slacks.

No wonder my senses reeled like a twister whenever I was around him. "Thanks. You clean up nice."

"I thought you might cancel."

"Came close."

Inside we sat in a pew midway up. To the right of the podium, three men played upbeat music on guitars and a piano. Four men and a woman joined them in song. Levi introduced me to a few people, and Caleb smothered me in a hug.

A loud noise startled me, and I turned to see a man blow a huge, curled instrument—a shofar. I expected the call to worship, and yet this Old Testament trumpet ushered me into an unexpected sacred setting. My breath quickened with . . . was it holy anticipation? Typical Jewish music, some sung in Hebrew, perked my ears. Many of the congregation clapped. Women with tambourines played and danced from the back of the church to the front. Some adults and children danced in traditional Jewish style. I held my breath and fought the urge to weep. Nothing about the worship unfolding around me was orchestrated.

I could feel the intensity of praising God.

Levi raised his hands and sang. According to what I'd read online, Messianic Jews celebrated the traditions of the Old Testament and the New Testament, honoring centuries-old festivals with a blending of the two. What followed elevated my spirit, as though I'd been transported into another world.

After the music, a man offered prayers for everyone and those specifically in need. The service continued with the offering. The congregation faced east, and the rabbi led us in responsive reading that spoke of a sovereign God and His power. The congregation also chanted in English and Hebrew about God and His characteristics— those things I'd learned as a child.

The rabbi opened an ornate cabinet and grasped a scroll for reading. I'd learned the first five books of the Bible were called the Torah and contained the laws God gave Moses. After each reading, a man or a woman from the congregation stood beside the rabbi and repeated a blessing. A fluttering in my spirit swelled at the beauty unveiling around me. Indescribable. Emotional. I thought God had distanced Himself from me, but I felt Him. His love filled the room.

The sermon showed how an Old Testament's prophecy of the Messiah became reality in the New Testament's witness of His arrival and teachings. The rabbi shared how we could honor those teachings today, and I appreciated the practical application. Even if God and I weren't on the best of terms, He touched me. I wanted what I saw and felt, but I feared what following God with the abandon I sensed here truly meant.

The service concluded with the rabbi replacing the scroll and prayers. Without my realizing it, the time in the synagogue had gone an hour and forty-seven minutes. My grandmother's church concluded in one hour, on the dot.

As we left the building, Levi continued to greet and bless those we met. "Shalom" repeated around me. At my truck he took my hand, and I didn't fight his touch. "Thanks for being a part of worship this morning."

I smiled into his brown eyes. "The service moved me, emotionally. I have lots to process . . . not process but . . . Your church made me feel like God might really care for me."

"He does, Carrington. Would you like lunch? We could discuss the morning and your questions."

After moistening my lips, I carefully formed my words. "Levi, I need to be alone today. I need hours to reflect on this morning and what it means."

"I get it. Wouldn't hurt for me to do a little thinking too. Call me later, if you're up to it."

"Okay. Appreciate all you've done for me. Thanks for today's invitation. I'd like to return." He started to walk away, but I called out to him. "Remember you told me God had to be experienced?" When he nodded, I forged ahead. "This morning I experienced God."

I really wanted to spend more time with Levi, but I needed downtime. My life and my habits led to a solitary existence. Levi stepped in with his God, and I wanted—no, craved—what he offered. The children's delight in participating in the service reminded me how I believed I'd never be a mother . . . or a wife. The diagnosis surrounding my eyes, the danger we experienced in Victoria, and my personal beliefs in God—the whole dilemma of life.

I arrived home with a kaleidoscope of considerations bannering across my mind. After showering Arthur with attention, eating a turkey sandwich, and taking my mound of vitamins, I propped pillows on the sofa for a comfortable afternoon. Leaning back, my thoughts zeroed in on God. I had been furious with Him for years and told myself I'd gotten along fine without Him. He'd allowed my body to betray me and ruined my past and my future. I didn't want my parents' and my grandmother's religion . . . I wanted a personal faith, like I'd experienced today. During the dancing, many of the adults showed the children the steps. It seemed natural, and those today appeared happy.

How did they deal with hardship when it knocked on their doors?

God, is there hope for me? How can You ever forgive me for causing the car accident killing my parents? How can I forgive myself?

SEVENTY-TWO

I didn't contact Levi on Saturday evening and avoided him on Sunday. I needed a break from the confusion and interruptions in my normal life. Everything had unraveled, and I didn't know if the unraveling meant a better me or something less. Allowing Levi into my life meant giving God full control. If my fragile feelings were the beginnings of love, I couldn't handle years of it. So I pulled out my Bible buried under a pile of memorabilia in my closet and turned to Psalm 139, Dad's favorite.

"You have searched me, Lord, and you know me . . ." I blinked back tears. Grandma had told me that one day I'd know how much God knew and loved me.

Sunday evening, I texted Levi. **I've read more of the Bible in the last two days than I have in years.**

Finding answers?

I think so.

I miss you and I'm praying.

Prayers sound good, and I miss you too.

Monday morning, I drove myself to a nine o'clock doctor's appointment to remove my stitches from the arrow. The wound had healed nicely, and the spot of optimism brightened my mood. Once home, I took Arthur for a walk. Such a beautiful, sun-filled day, and I planned to enjoy it.

My phone alerted me to a call, and I hoped it was Levi.

"Miss Reed, this is Jace."

My attitude took a dip south. "Hey. No school today?"

"Between classes. I'd like to talk to you. Is it possible we can talk after school, like around two forty-five?"

"Sure. What's going on?"

"Need a listening ear. It's about my mom."

"Okay. Phone call or Zoom?"

"Zoom works. Got the app on my phone. Could you set it up and send me the link? Don't tell anyone, please. Not even Mr. Ehrlich."

"I'll text you the link. Are you all right, Jace? Do I need to contact someone?"

"I'll explain after school. Just need to talk."

After his call, I considered telling Levi, but I'd given Jace my word, and I didn't care if Howard found out about it.

I scheduled the Zoom session, texted the link to Jace, and connected at two forty-five. From the setting behind him, he looked to be in a restaurant.

"Thanks for arranging this," he said. "I'm at a coffee shop near my school." He held up the teen-typical caramel-and-sea-salt latte handwritten across the side of the cup in the largest size with extra whip.

I pointed at his coffee drink. "Got one of those for me?"

He looked at it. "Next time you're in Victoria."

"Jace, I'm worried about you."

"Mom is the one who's not doing so well."

"Grief takes time, and the emotions don't follow a set pattern. You are going through a list of anger, pain, sorrow, at times denying your dad's gone, and possibly overcompensating by taking on your dad's role."

"The counselor says the same thing, but she . . ." He stopped and inhaled. "The pastor passed us off to this woman psychologist because of our issues."

"Did he use those words?"

"No. But I could tell we were more than he wanted to handle."

"What about the woman counselor bothers you?" I said.

"She's always looking at the time like we're a charity case. Last time she told Mom we had three more free sessions, and then we were done without payment."

I wanted to drive to the woman's office and give her a huge piece of my mind. Maybe later, when I cooled off, I'd call the psychologist. Right now, Jace needed a listening ear and tools to help him manage his grief. "I'll make recommendations to your mom. Not every counselor is a good fit, like a dentist or doctor."

Jace nodded. "I have teachers and coaches like you're talking about." He ran his fingers through his hair. "Worried about Mom and Emma."

Emma had mentioned suicide. I'd shared it with Felicia, but Jace didn't need the burden, and I wouldn't betray Emma. "Caring for your family is a sign of a mature young man, and I commend all you're doing. But you must take care of yourself too."

A girl joined him dressed in a Chat and Sip green T-shirt and matching hat. "Hey, Jace, talking to anyone I know?"

He grinned at the girl. "A friend of my mom's."

"Oh, I'll leave you alone. So sorry about what's been going on with your family."

"Appreciate it." The girl walked away, and he stared into his phone screen. "Miss Reed, I miss my dad."

"Can you talk to your granddad?"

"He's been weird with Mom and all. My dad used to say Granddad Westfield was smarter than a tree full of owls."

"I think he'd welcome you opening up to him." With my words, Jace swallowed hard, his lips quivering. I continued. "A man reaches out for help so he can learn to help others. Your granddad may need to talk too."

"He's spent some time with Nathan Moore. They've been friends since they were my age."

"Nathan isn't you. I encourage you to sit down with your granddad, tell him how you feel. I'm sure he'll listen and offer sound advice."

"He's home now. We're still staying there until Mom feels like going back to our house. Her boss rehired her, and she's relieved about being able to pay bills."

"Good, Jace. All positive steps forward."

"Okay. I'll go to the house and see if Granddad's home. Emma has band after school, and Mom doesn't get home from the bank until six."

"That should give you time together."

"If his pastor will take us back, he might be a better counselor than Miss Money-Hungry." He pressed his lips into a smile. "Thanks, Miss Reed. I feel better with a plan."

I felt better knowing I'd helped someone.

———

After the Zoom chat with Jace, I couldn't get my mind off Levi. If only I didn't have cancer or signs of blindness. Levi said he didn't care, but how could I put him in a nightmare relationship? Dare I ask God? Wasn't that selfish?

My attachment to Levi took precedence over good sense. I needed to hear his voice and convince myself that friends—more than friends—checked in on friends. He picked up on the second ring.

"Are you busy?" I said. "I can call later. It's not important."

"Of course it is. It's you."

He always knew how to make me feel better, and I wanted to do the same for him. "I wanted to hear your voice."

"Great, because I miss you."

"I think it's Arthur who has your attention."

"He's second on my list. I'd like to see you tomorrow."

I had something to look forward to. "We'll make it happen."

"Hey, we haven't celebrated my new job with *National Geographic*. How about Saturday night? Steak. Seafood. Whatever strikes us."

What had started out as a downer day ended up nicely.

SEVENTY-THREE

Tuesday morning, I woke with more optimism than I'd felt in days. Levi had accepted a position at *National Geographic*, and he claimed the salary offer made him sing. I'd heard him sing on Saturday, and he needed a few lessons. We planned to celebrate Saturday night.

I responded to an e-mail request for a negotiator to assist in a child-custody suit in which the parents wanted to avoid court and extra attorney fees. Upon acceptance, they'd advance me half the fee and send all the documents I needed for a meeting at their attorney's office next week.

The case sounded so much easier than the past several days of unrest and danger.

I cleared my calendar for my Thursday appointment with Dr. Leonard to ensure my eye melanoma hadn't metastasized. I then scheduled church with Dixie and her family on Sunday with an invitation to lunch afterward. Who knows? I might ask to attend Levi's church on Saturday. I read the Bible like a first grader who'd discovered the power of words.

Midmorning my doorbell rang. Arthur barked his alert while I answered the door.

I opened the door and startled at the man before me. "What a surprise. Good to see you." I looked out at his car. "Are you alone?"

"Just me." He nodded.

"Come on in, and I'll make us a cup of coffee."

He stepped inside and fluffed Arthur's head. "I see your neighbor lady is enjoying the day on her front porch."

"Yes, she's a sweet lady." I pointed to the kitchen. "We can chat in there while the coffee is brewing. Are you in town for long?"

"No need." He pulled a Glock from his back jeans waistband and jammed it into my face. "Not a word, Carrington."

"What's going on?"

"We're taking a little ride. We'll leave together friendly-like. One wrong move or shout, and I pull the trigger on Miss Stephanie."

SEVENTY-FOUR

LEVI

Carrington wasn't answering her phone, and I'd left a text and a phone message. Any more communication and I'd look like a stalker. But it wasn't like her to ignore a call . . . and we'd shared a great conversation last evening. She might be sleeping, especially since we'd gone nonstop for the past several days.

Carrington and I had established an open and honest relationship, and she shared her life with me just as I had shared mine with her. She'd attended my church and let me introduce her to my friends. We'd talked about spiritual things and her doubts about God. I'd done my best not to push her. Yet maybe I'd gone too far in wanting to know her better, and she needed distance.

My head ached from worry.

Had the ones who'd broken into her house returned?

Had she received bad news about her additional eye testing? A discouraging report could easily cause a shutdown.

My phone buzzed, and I recognized Felicia's number. Maybe she'd heard from Carrington.

"Levi, this is Felicia. Is Carrington with you? I've been trying to reach her, and she's not picking up." Her frantic tone bothered me. She'd made such progress, unless another tragedy had struck.

"No, I haven't talked to her. I'm sure she's just busy. What's up?"

"Jace is missing. Didn't come home last night, except his truck is at Mom and Dad's. That's not like him. He's become ultra responsible to the point of me asking him to back off. Dad can't find him either. I thought maybe she'd heard from him."

"Has something upset him?"

"Not any more than what we're all going through."

"Is he at school?"

"No. Neither did he call them about an absence." Felicia's tone rose higher.

"Have you talked to his friends?"

"No one has seen or talked to him. Emma has no idea either. Dad suggested I call you since Jace respected how you tried to help Will. Dad said I might need to report it to Sheriff Macmire." Felicia's words tumbled out so fast that I feared she headed for a panic attack.

"Take a deep breath, Felicia. When was the last time you heard from Jace?"

"Yesterday afternoon he called and said he'd be about an hour or so late getting home from school. He was meeting a friend for coffee, and we'd talk later."

"Is there a coffee shop he frequents?"

"Yes. It's near the high school called Chat and Sip. A friend of his works as a barista. I'll check there."

"Call me back once you talk to the coffee shop and if you hear from him."

I paced the floor while I waited for Felicia to phone me. Jace would soon be missing twenty-four hours. As a minor, Felicia should have reported it last night. Why hadn't she? Had her life become drenched in surviving moment by moment instead of fulfilling her responsibilities as a mother?

My phone lit up with Felicia's number.

"I talked to the barista," she said. "Jace stopped in after school like he said. He had an online video call with a woman he claimed was a friend of mine. The barista described the woman as having long chestnut-colored hair, in her late twenties or early thirties. She called the woman gorgeous. Sounded like Carrington to me."

She hadn't mentioned talking to Jace yesterday. "Did you happen to ask if the coffee shop had a security camera?"

Felicia drew in a ragged breath. "No. Never crossed my mind."

"Maybe he needed time alone to put his thoughts together. Have you checked your ranch?"

"Yes. He's not there."

"Have you checked with Boyd?"

"Neither he nor Lyndie have seen him."

"To be safe, talk to Sheriff Macmire. Jace might even be with him." She agreed with a sob. "I'll contact the coffee shop about a security camera. And as soon as I hear from Carrington, I'll ask her to reach out to you. I'm sure Jace is fine. He's a smart young man."

"And he's always respectful of my feelings."

"I'm sure his absence is a misunderstanding."

"I've lost Will, and I can't lose Jace, too." Felicia sobbed and ended the call.

My spine tingled into the danger zone. *Jace, what a stupid thing to do.* Concern and anger rose to the top.

***

After confirming the Chat and Sip coffee shop had a security camera, I drove to Carrington's house. I rang the doorbell and knocked. She didn't answer, but Arthur barked. I peeked into her garage window and saw her truck, which led me to believe she visited Mrs. Radison next door. The older woman sat on the front porch reading with a tabby cat curled up in her lap. A picturesque scene until I got close enough to see the book—Fyodor Dostoevsky's *Crime and Punishment.* A little eerie considering . . .

"Afternoon, Mrs. Radison." I pointed to her book. "A little light reading?"

She gave me a sweet smile. "Part of my late husband's collection. I've read *The Brothers Karamazov* for the third time. Really good."

"I liked it too. Although I haven't read it but once."

"His books give me pause to reflect on life. What can I do for you?"

"Looking for Carrington. Her truck's in the garage, but she's not answering her door." I gave her my best grin. "Unless she's trying to ignore me."

"Not with your charms. I haven't seen her since she left with a man a few hours ago." Stephanie gave me a dimpled grin. "Are you jealous?"

I returned her smile. "I might be. Did you recognize him?"

"No. Not anyone I'd seen here before. For that matter, I don't know for sure if he was young or old." She bit into her lower lip. "Older but fit."

"Do you remember the car?"

"A white Chevy. Not a truck or SUV, but I don't recall the year."

Nothing came to mind either. "Thanks. If you see her, will you tell her I stopped by?"

"I will." I saw the girl in her sea-green eyes. "You're in love with her."

I hesitated to respond. Carrington would not appreciate it.

"It's all right, Levi. We'll keep your secret between us."

I returned to my Tahoe, my mind spinning in overreaction mode. Carrington and I had been attacked and threatened. Those responsible were still running free in the streets.

My cell phone rang—Sheriff Corbin Macmire.

SEVENTY-FIVE

Corbin jumped right into the reason he called. "Levi, Felicia Kendrix just reported Jace is missing. Last seen yesterday afternoon at a coffee shop, supposedly on a video call with a woman matching Carrington's description."

I shared Felicia's conversation and my inability to reach Carrington. "I talked to her earlier today, and she said nothing about Jace."

"I'll run by the Chat and Sip. May take a while before I get back to you. Have a couple of interviews first." He cleared his throat. "Patti Moore is in custody, charged with arson. Her alibi didn't hold during the time of the crime."

My past conclusions that small towns were safer to live in than cities shattered. Timothy and Patti had cruelty running through their veins.

An hour passed while I worked on the logistics for an upcoming story in Kenya for *National Geographic*. No need to relocate. I'd fly wherever the company sent me. I longed to share the good news with family, and that meant Caleb. I pressed in his number.

"Hey, bro," he said. "Missed our coffee time."

"We'll catch up soon. My apologies."

"I know your job sends you running at a moment's notice. Carrington is one beautiful woman. Kind too."

"Thanks. I'm trying not to mess up with her."

Caleb chuckled. "Is that why you called? You need woman advice?"

I grinned into the phone. "No, I'm good. I have a job. *National Geographic* hired me."

"Congrats. I'm not surprised they snatched you up. Knowing you is like rubbing shoulders with the rich and famous."

"I wish. I'm just glad to be employed. I start two weeks from yesterday."

"Have they given you an assignment?"

"Yes. I started it earlier."

"I've been praying for the perfect job to land in your lap. Before I forget it, bring Carrington to Shabbat on Friday."

"I'll do my best. Don't want to rush things. Last Saturday's worship left a positive impact. She's into the Word, so prayers appreciated."

"On it. I snatched a glimpse of her during the sermon, and she was definitely wrestling."

After the call, I checked the time. Over an hour had passed with nothing from anyone who had my messages. I sounded pitiful, even to myself.

SEVENTY-SIX

CARRINGTON

I lay face down on the floorboard of the car, wishing he'd speed and get pulled over.

Twisting against the flex-cuffs binding my wrists behind my back, I choked back a wince where they dug into my flesh.

He'd planned my abduction to the smallest detail before arriving at my house, even bragged about knowing Stephanie's name and habits. He'd rented this car too. His demeanor changed the moment he pulled a Glock on me. I'd done as he requested for fear of him following through with a threat to Stephanie.

He'd driven to the rear of a deserted shopping center, where he placed a filthy rag in my mouth that smelled of motor oil and tasted worse, bound my wrists, and shoved me onto the rear floorboard.

He'd said nothing during the drive about why he'd forced me to go with him. Neither did he use his phone. No indication where we were headed or his plans for me.

Howard Westfield. The last person I suspected.

SEVENTY-SEVEN

LEVI

With the midafternoon sun beaming onto the parklike grounds outside my balcony, I thought how ironic the weather promised illuminating light while people I cared about were missing. I'd prayed until the words drained from me, and all I could whisper was, "Jesus, please keep Carrington and Jace safe."

No reason for them to be together . . . unless they were in trouble. Where were they? Held by the same person? Their disappearances had to be connected, but for what purpose? What had Carrington kept from me? What did Jace know that caused him to either run or be held by someone?

My phone rang with an unrecognizable number. These days, I answered every call.

"Señor Levi," a man said, not the voice who'd threatened me and others.

"Sí."

"My name is Agustín Cedilla from the hostage situation. We spoke at the hospital while my wife was treated for a gunshot wound and my son for his diabetes," he said in Spanish.

"I remember you."

"Sí. I might have information to help you."

My pulse raced. "I'm listening."

"I heard you and the señorita were attacked and later freed men from a barn on Señor Kendrix's ranch."

"Who told you these things?"

"One of the men you found in the barn. He said if you and the señorita hadn't helped them, they'd be dead or forced to sell drugs for the cartel."

Which man had talked to Agustín? "Do you know who's behind the crimes?"

"I have one name, Walden Thurman, and he takes orders from another boss man."

That eliminated Patti or Lyndie Moore at least on one front. "Why are you reaching out to me and putting you and your family in danger?"

"Because of you and the señorita, my wife and son are alive. I'd rather take a risk, to thank you. Saying nothing is wrong."

"Is your family healing, and are they in a safe place?"

"Sí, señor. We are using different names, so the cartel and Border Patrol can't find us. I don't trust anyone but you and the señorita."

"Be careful, amigo. Many of us, including Border Patrol, are working to arrest those who are making money through human trafficking. Your words are safe with me."

"We have family in another state, but what I heard and learned on my own before leaving is important. So many of us desperately want to be in your country, make it our country, a better place for our families. But others come for evil things. Our son needs a doctor's care, and I need a job to support my family. I paid a guide to cross the border—the same one who held the men in the barn. Like them, I was told I hadn't paid enough and must sell drugs. Some of us got away, and that's when we were taken captive. Because of what happened after we were held hostage, I got my family to safety. I won't sell drugs for the cartel even if it means going back to Mexico."

"Did anyone mention a woman boss?" I said.

"No. Only men."

"Gracias, Agustín. May God bless you, your wife, and son."

"Gracias for taking a bullet to help others. God bless you and the señorita."

Agustín appeared to have no illusions about what he and his family had encountered, but he had hope for their future.

A suspect's name crossed my mind, but I quickly discounted it. The man wore honesty like a badge. I needed someone to blame.

SEVENTY-EIGHT

CARRINGTON

Howard drove with no apparent destination. Unless he was wasting time, and that didn't fit his personality—or crimes. Finally, Howard parked, cut my flex-cuffs with a pocketknife, and accompanied me inside a gas station, where I used the restroom. He took every precaution and threatened me with the gun in his jacket pocket. Others would be killed if I made a run for it.

On the way back to his car, I asked him why.

"Why what? All of it or the circumstances now?"

"Are you the one who made the threats using a Hispanic accent?"

He repeated a murderous phrase in Spanish with the voice I remembered. "Do I need to translate?"

"I understand perfectly. Who was in charge—you, Walden Thurman, or Timothy?"

"Who do you think? Smart men don't end up in jail or dead."

"Timothy had money, but I think you're more ruthless."

"Ole Tim flaunted his money and made more enemies than friends. I know how to deal the cards."

"You're right. Had me fooled."

"Carrington, I'll put it another way. I witnessed Timothy lose his temper and his life, his downfall. I followed Patti Moore to see

325

what she was up to. She'd threatened to kill Tim, and her pulling the trigger would save me the trouble. Thing is, Jace beat us to it, and everything worked out from there. You and Levi signed your death warrants by being inside the house with Will and those hostages. You have a disgusting Good Samaritan trait, and Levi has a nose for story, characteristics that put you both on a hit list."

"We know nothing."

His face reddened from the neck up. "He gave you proof of Tim's and my business. I want it."

Find your skills. "Howard, Will neither said nor gave Levi and me anything. There's no need to follow through with this. Turn yourself in. You're retired Border Patrol, well-liked, and respected."

"Respect doesn't pay the bills. Tim had the same issues. We risked our lives for others and collected pennies. We deserved more, and trust me, we found a way to get it. This time next year, I'll be living high where no one can find me."

"What about Zora? You'd abandon her?"

"The poor thing can't even put her shoes on the right feet. Some days she knows me, and some days she thinks I'm her brother." He paused. "Zora was brilliant in her prime, beautiful too."

"She loves you. I've seen it in her eyes."

Howard dropped a few curses. "I'm not a negotiation case. This country owes me. I'm just collecting my share."

I'd met men like him before, angry at the hand dealt them. I swore never to play the bitterness game, but it still crept in. "You can make a decision to change."

"I'm no fool, Carrington. My life suits me. I'm not stupid. Will told you what he'd discovered about Tim, where the document or flash drive is, or you wouldn't be scouring both ranches."

"I have no idea what you're talking about. We looked for evidence to find Felicia and the kids. Later we looked for the hired hand and information for what was going on."

Howard snorted. "Right. Doesn't matter now, does it? If you had kept your nose out of my business, Jace wouldn't be in a mess."

My stomach soured. "Is Jace okay?"

"Depends on you and Levi."

Rage boiled from my toes to my head. "He's a teenage boy and your grandson."

"Too late. He's safe for now."

"Where is he? Felicia must be worried crazy."

"She's already crazy."

"Where are you taking me? To join Jace?"

"Nope. To see Levi. End the problem. Get back to making money." He looked around us. No one caught his attention, so he opened the door. "Get back on the floor." I kicked him, but he grabbed my arm and raised it behind my back. Deftly he retied the gag and slipped new flex-cuffs on my wrists. He swore and slammed the door.

Why hadn't I picked up on his treachery when I first met him?

Fear wrapped its icy fingers around me. I'd challenged danger in the past during the chill of a negotiation, like I'd done with Will. But death seemed distant, unimportant. Adrenaline flowed, increasing my pulse. A quote from my detective friend Aaron came to mind. "The worst scenario is someone with nothing to lose."

If I didn't have such low esteem for those who made deathbed conversions, I'd pray for rescue. In my next breath, I asked God to protect Levi and Jace. A strange warmness replaced the chill. God hadn't abandoned me. He rode with me in the back of Howard's car. The future wore a mask, but the One in charge held it in His hand. I knew it. Felt it. Believed it.

Odd what a person thought when their life expectancy neared zero.

SEVENTY-NINE

LEVI

Shortly after three thirty, my cell phone rang. Brimming with anticipation, my gaze flew to the screen in hopes it was Carrington.

Panic startled me. Dad? He wouldn't be calling unless something terrible had happened. I hurriedly pressed the answer button.

"Abba?"

"Yes, Levi. How are you?" He sounded normal, no hint of alarm or strain in his voice. "I see you were wounded trying to stop a man from killing innocent people."

Heat flooded my neck to my face. Dad had been following me on media? "I'm good. Healing. I appreciate your checking on me. How's Ima?"

"She's fine. I'd like to see you, talk to you. It's been too long."

I shuddered. "Yes, of course. When do you want to get together?"

"As soon as possible. Bad things have gone on long enough between us."

"Abba, I am feeling all *verklempt*. I will be there within the hour."

"Keep our talk between us, okay? This is hard for me."

"It will be hard for me too. We can tell others some other time. See you soon."

Abba thanked me, and I slipped my phone back into my pocket.

Thank You, God.

A saying from my dad made me smile. *"A mensch tracht un Got lacht."* Man plans and God laughs.

Shaking like a kid who needed to face his parents for misbehaving, I stepped from my Tahoe and walked to my parents' front door. Memories from my last visit pelted my confidence. But Dad had reached out to me. I rang the bell and stood on weak legs. Oh, for reconciliation with my family.

The door opened, and my dad filled the doorway. He looked pale. He must feel the same trepidation that I did.

"You are here." He stepped back for me to enter. His face devoid of emotion.

I kissed my fingers and touched them to the mezuzah. Immediately I met the smells and sights of home. Sweet thoughts hugged me, but not my abba.

Let it be for Your glory, God.

Dad closed the door and pointed to the living room, the familiar tan sofa, paintings of Israel, family photos minus me—

My gut curdled.

Howard sat on a living room chair with a gun pointed at Ima and Carrington, who were bound and gagged on the sofa. My nudging had been right, and I'd not pursued it.

"I'm sorry," Dad said. "The man gave me no choice."

EIGHTY

CARRINGTON

The moment Howard had turned on the audio for GPS instruction to a Meyerland address, I knew we were en route to Levi's parents.

Felicia believed her dad hung the moon. He talked all the Christian lingo and claimed the tragedy might bring his daughter and grandchildren back to church. Howard prayed with them at the hospital. He'd arranged for his pastor to join the family at the hospital and supported his pastor to officiate Will's funeral service. He approved of his pastor counseling to help them heal, but he'd betrayed his *own* daughter and grandchildren. No amount of money took priority over family.

What kind of monster lived inside Howard Westfield?

Had Will been a part of the smuggling? Or had he been stuck in the middle of a father and father-in-law up to their eyebrows in atrocious crimes?

With my mouth gagged and my throat dry as dust, I peered at Levi, silently seizing his attention.

You can talk Howard into releasing us. Push aside your emotions and focus only on a slow, calm conversation.

If I believed in telepathy, I'd project the words and mannerisms to help Levi through the moments ahead. If he showed any emotions,

Howard would destroy him. Levi was praying. I could feel his silent communication—enough for me to embrace the conversion I formerly assigned to cowards and the weak.

God, not for me but for Levi, his parents, and Howard to release us peacefully.

The cool calmness I normally experienced in a negotiation fought to escape me, but I held fast by holding on to an almighty God.

I couldn't negotiate with Howard. All I could do was watch.

And pray.

"Joseph, on the floor beside your wife, there's a flex-cuff. Use it on Levi's wrists behind his back. I need info, so leave out the gag." When Joseph finished, Howard laughed. "Good job. Levi, take a seat on the right side of Mama, and Joseph you have the chair on the left. One wrong move, and I'll blow a hole through your son and the women."

Howard plopped down into a chair opposite us as though we were discussing the weather. A quote of my grandmother's surfaced. *"Unless we are willing to have our hearts cut raw, we'll never know the true meaning of love."*

I'd loved her deeply and the emotions and regrets plagued me for not loving more intentionally. My parents, Grandma, and the fire of new love for Levi had molded me into a woman who cared deeply. My sweet sister-friend Dixie and her family were my family. New friends in Victoria and all over the country had grown me. Then why did I feel so alone?

God, will You save these precious people?

EIGHTY-ONE

LEVI

I glared at Howard—my anger flamed to fury level. If I knew what he wanted or what he thought I'd done, then I might understand his holding my family and Carrington captive.

"What's this about?" I said. "What has anyone here done to you?"

Howard snorted like a pig. "Thought you'd never ask. Since it ends right here, I'll give you what the authorities will discover."

Anything to stall him. *Pikuach nephesh* entered my thoughts, an obligation to save those in jeopardy. Carrington said out-of-control people talked fast and loudly. "Let's hear it."

Howard waved his Glock in my direction. "I broke into your car and found your Glock in your glove box. Makes eliminating you a piece of cake. It's simple. You and Carrington paid Mom and Dad a visit. An argument broke out. You pulled the trigger on the others, then turned it on yourself."

"You have it all figured out. Flawless."

"Thank you for the vote of confidence. Joseph here asked you not to tell anyone, and the one person you might consider is Carrington, and she was with me."

"I admit you're brilliant," I said. "You blindsided law enforcement, and I never suspected you. Who else have you killed?"

"Never stopped to count. Mostly illegals who refused to pay or run drugs for the cartel."

"Like the dead men found on Timothy's ranch?"

"Sure. We—now me—received a cut for our efforts. Tim and I agreed from the start that the end justifies the means."

"Why break into Carrington's house?" I said.

He bolted forward. "Do you two think I'm an idiot? Will told you what he'd discovered, what Tim and I had done for years. And I'm sure he showed you where to find the documentation or gave you a flash drive."

"He didn't say a thing. Why not search my place?"

"I've got to hack into the security cameras there first. Heading that way as soon as you tell me where to find what I need."

The more I learned about Howard, the more my blood pressure spiked. "You don't seem like the type to put up with Walden Thurman."

"A grunt. I was ready to eliminate him. He'd gotten a little too greedy, demanded more money after Tim was killed. I learned about his archery ability, and you know how I used that." Howard paused. "He breathes a word about me, and his family is dead meat."

"Why trust Patti? Corbin told me she's been arrested for arson."

"Patti is a—" His features darkened. "The one thing I did for Tim is made sure her rear is in jail for a long time."

"You set fire to Lyndie's shop?"

Howard laughed. "Called her. Told her I had a way for her to get the money from Boyd. She fell for it, and I hired an illegal to do the job."

Howard Westfield . . . the man with two lives. "Where's Jace?"

"He's alive if that's what you're asking. He's my collateral, but you two aren't cooperating. Guess his fate is up to you."

"He's your grandson."

"And he might live to serve me in other ways. That's up to you. If he lives, then he'll sell drugs for me to keep his mom and sister alive."

The idea of verbally going after Howard sped through my thoughts. How low did a man sink to barter with his family's lives? *God, help me control my temper.*

"Jace must have found out the truth."

"He did. Tuesday, after talking to Carrington, he paid me a visit. I didn't hear him come in, and I was on the phone. He overheard a few things detrimental to his health. I have him in a safe place until we're done here."

God, keep Jace safe and give me wisdom to end the crimes without another death.

"Timing, Levi. Everything has to do with timing." Howard laid the gun—my Glock—in his lap. "Will figured me out a few days before Tim died. He followed me to a place where Tim and I met on his property, then he confronted me about it later. Considered killing him then, but Felicia's neediness makes me tired. I offered to set him up for a good and profitable life by working for me. He refused. Threatened to go to Corbin, and he'd documented evidence. Luck smiled on me 'cause he had no guts."

Howard smirked. "Will told you and Carrington where he'd hidden the evidence before his suicide. You saw dollar signs to blackmail me, and one of you shoved the gun under his chin and squeezed. The illegals were too scared to speak. I know you and Carrington have the evidence."

"Whatever Will knew went to his grave, and he did commit suicide."

Howard smirked. "Right."

"If you think we're hiding evidence, wouldn't we be smart enough to make sure the right people found it in the event we were killed?"

Howard's face reddened.

Yep, he'd thought about that very thing, and he didn't appreciate the gamble. "You and Zora protested Will and Felicia marrying. Were you and Timothy working together then?"

"Even before that. Making more money than you can imagine. Felicia doesn't have my intellect. Zora questioned some of the things I was doing, but I kept her satisfied. Then dementia set in, and who would believe anything she said? When Felicia refused to give up marrying Will, I decided to use it for my benefit." He held up the Glock. "I'm tired of talking."

"Why did Timothy leave his property to Boyd?"

Howard shook his head. "'Cause Will wasn't his son. Dorie had him before they met. He adopted Will and paid to alter their marriage records."

More and more pieces fell into place, but would any of us live to tell it? Why hadn't I told Howard that the evidence sat in a safe-deposit box? Stupid. That would have bought us time, but Howard didn't have anyone to hold the others here at gunpoint.

I glanced at Dad. None of what happened had been his fault or Mother's or Carrington's. Just me and my insatiable curiosity to find truth.

An idea nudged me, but I needed Dad's help to carry it out. "Abba, I may never have another opportunity to tell you how I feel, but I'm sorry for our differences. I love and respect you as a father and a man of God. Thank you for all you've done for me." I silently prayed, asking God to give Dad and me like minds.

"Ima," I said, "you are the best mother anyone could ask for. Your love and wisdom helped me grow into a man." From the corner of my eye, I saw Howard's attention on Ima. I nodded at Dad, and he lifted his chin, just like when I was a kid, and we were ready to play a joke on Mom and Deborah. I thanked God that Howard had failed to bind Dad's hands.

I continued to divert Howard's attention, hoping he didn't grow tired of my death confessions. "Carrington, I'm sorry for dragging you through the mud and endangering your life. You are one special woman."

I blinked at Dad. He and I bolted toward Howard at the same time. Howard grabbed the Glock and aimed it at me. Dad slammed into him, knocking the weapon out of his hand. I kicked the gun out of reach.

Dad and Howard wrestled, both men fit for their age. Both fighting for their lives. Both rolling across the floor into furniture and drawing blood.

Dad lay flat, and Howard clamped his hands onto Dad's throat.

I kicked Howard, then used my good shoulder to shove him off

Dad's weakening body. Howard rolled onto his back, murderous threats shooting from his lips.

I clamped my foot on his neck.

He wrapped both hands around my calves. I struggled to keep my balance.

"I have the gun on you." Dad's voice bellowed. He jammed the barrel into Howard's temple. "Either let go of my son or I'll pull the trigger. Your choice."

Howard stretched out his arms, palms up on the floor.

"Smart move. You saved your life." Dad hurried into the kitchen and returned with a knife to free my hands. He handed me the Glock. "Use it if you have to while I cut the women loose."

My eyes never left Howard Westfield. Neither did my foot leave his neck. My faith required mercy and wisdom, and my parents hadn't raised a fool after all.

After Dad released Mom and Carrington, he called 911 while I gladly kept my stance until the police arrived.

Dad studied Howard. "You remind me of a saying I heard once. 'An eye for an eye, and a tooth for a tooth. Welcome to a blind and toothless world.'"

EIGHTY-TWO

CARRINGTON

The moment the police took control of the crime scene, Levi and his dad embraced. Tears and unspoken love dripped from my eyes too. I turned to Eva and scooted next to her on the sofa. She leaned against my shoulder, and I wrapped my arms around her. The shaken woman trembled and sobbed.

"It's over," I whispered, although reality seemed difficult for me to grasp too.

We watched father and son reunite, and I thanked God, actually thanked God for saving us and bringing Levi's family back together.

A smile spread over Joseph's face. "The police need to know what happened."

"You go first, Abba," Levi said.

Joseph told the officers the story from the time Howard forced himself into their home with a gun at my back. Levi picked up on his end and gave the officers Sheriff Corbin Macmire's phone number, relaying Howard Westfield's role in several open cases in Victoria.

Howard lawyered up and claimed the four of us had lied and set him up for a crime he hadn't committed. Who would ever believe our story when he and his family had been victimized?

338 | LETHAL STANDOFF

I couldn't hold back any longer. Taking a breath, I forced, really forced, composure into my voice. "Howard, tell us where Jace is."

"Why should I?" Howard spat out his words.

"Your family loves you. Jace, Felicia, and Emma are innocent of any wrongdoing. For everyone to heal, the beginning must start now. I know a good man lives inside you." I stood from the sofa and walked closer, but I didn't invade his personal space. "I'll speak on your behalf to the judge if you will tell us where to find Jace."

"You're lying. How can I believe you?"

I infused more calmness into my voice. "I promised Will I'd not give up until I found justice. My word is my integrity. I will speak favorably to the judge confirming you cooperated in exchange for telling us where to find Jace."

Howard jutted his jaw, debating. "All right. He's in the hayloft at Tim's barn."

"Thank you, Howard. I knew you'd do the right thing, and I'll keep my word."

Levi whipped his phone from his pocket. "I'm calling Corbin."

"You're an idiot," Howard said. "Jace won't say a word against me. He's afraid of me."

An onslaught of anger rose in my throat. Incredibly hard to put my rage aside. I managed with supernatural control, and I knew exactly the source.

Howard spat at me. "Jace had the audacity to think I wouldn't stop him from going to the police. I pulled a gun on that smart—"

"Your grandson?" I said.

Howard snorted like a feral animal. "Didn't shoot him. Punched him in the chest with it. Then he saw I was serious. My family is money and power. Watch me. I'll bail out of jail with a slap on the wrist."

At that moment, I believed Howard Westfield and Timothy Kendrix capable of the vilest of crimes. Yet my training had instilled in me more than satisfaction of an ended ordeal. I celebrated in the hope of restored lives.

Howard attempted to jerk free from the police officer's hold. "You gave your word to speak to the judge on my behalf. My wife's crazy. My daughter's weak, and my grandkids are a disappointment. I have connections if you fail me."

The police drove Howard to jail, and the four of us stood in Joseph and Eva's living room. The power of silence reigned as though we all internalized the reality of a near-death experience.

"What a horrible man." Eva spoke softly, as though stating the truth hurt. She moved to Joseph's side, and he pulled her against him. "You are a hero," she said.

"More than a hero," Levi said. "You were nearly killed."

Joseph stared at his son. "We all do what seems impossible for those we love."

Tears dripped from Levi's eyes. I hurried to his side and took his hand. "I thought I'd lost you." My words flowed from my growing love for him.

Levi kissed my forehead, and his smile sealed the unspoken caring we had for each other.

"The blame is all mine," I said to Levi's parents. "I gave Levi my consent to write a story about a hostage negotiation, and danger stalked us ever since."

"I know my son and his wild side," Joseph said. "I assure you none of his involvement was your fault."

"Thanks, Abba. I'm sorry for what happened to you and Ima."

Eva stepped forward and embraced Levi, the moment so tender I had to look away. Levi and his family would say we all were verklempt. Being overwhelmed fit.

"God must believe a stubborn old man needed a jolt of lightning to reconcile with his son." Joseph pressed his lips together. "I believe you're wrong and have betrayed our people with your belief that the Messiah has already come. The hurt and anger struggles inside me for how you've left the true faith, but my love for you has not changed and never will."

He nodded at me. "Young woman, I sense more than friendship between you and Levi. Keep him in line. He needs a gentle leash and a good woman to love him."

EIGHTY-THREE

Two hours later, Levi and I waited at my house to hear word about Jace. We took turns pacing, saying more in our body language than what we might say aloud. The minutes ticked by, reinforcing my dislike of not having answers. But I believed good news would come. How long had Jace gone without water in the hot hayloft? The temps had soared into the upper nineties, hot for September.

I broke the silence and sank onto my sofa. "I encouraged Jace to talk to his grandfather. He didn't bond with the counselor."

"Are you blaming yourself?"

I peered up at him. "It was the worst thing I could have done."

Levi sat beside me and took my cold hand. "You advised him to reach out to a man who you thought loved him. Not your fault, Carrington. I'm right here for you."

I laid my head on his shoulder, and he drew me closer. "Have we only known each other a lifetime?"

"Longer."

I couldn't argue with my feelings leaping far ahead of logic. "I'd love a kiss."

He brushed his lips across my forehead, my nose, each cheek, and to my lips, the touch deepening until we finally parted. Yet his touch continued to linger, caressing me in wordless devotion. The moment seemed sacred in a way only God could orchestrate.

"That is a promise kiss," he said. "More and more to come for as long as God allows."

"Even with my eye problem? The diagnosis scares me, and I'd never want you to face a tragedy."

"I don't care. We'll walk that path together, hand in hand."

I bit my lip to keep the tears from spilling over my cheeks. This sweet, sweet man. He deserved much more than a woman who could go blind. What about children? I'd resolved not to give birth with my eye melanoma. What if we agreed to have a child and that little one inherited the family disease? Would he resent me then? Right then I refused to dwell on an uncertain future when hope held me tightly.

"I think God has the future," I whispered.

"Always."

My cell phone sounded, causing both of us to jump. I snatched it from the coffee table and pressed Speaker. "Felicia?"

"Miss Carrington, this is Jace."

A shower of relief poured over me. "Are you okay?"

"Yes, ma'am. Other than dehydrated, I'm good. Sheriff Macmire and Mom want a doctor to check me out."

"Good idea. The sound of your voice is like . . . well, music. I'm sorry I suggested you talk to your granddad."

"If you hadn't, none of us would have learned the truth. Are you and Mr. Levi okay?"

"I'm here too," Levi said. "Like you and your family, we are survivors."

"I wanted to tell you what happened when I drove to see Granddad on Monday night. He didn't hear me come in at first, and I heard him on the phone talking about a shipment of illegals headed to my other grandpa's ranch. He expected his normal cut. When he hung up, I asked him if he was smuggling humans across the border for the cartel. Grandpa got real cocky and said yes." Jace took a breath. "Sorry, it's hard."

"Take your time," I said.

"Grandma walked into the kitchen, and he told her to take a nap, that we were going for a ride. She gave me a hug and left the room. Not like she could have done anything. Granddad reached into a tall cupboard and pulled a gun. He ordered me into his truck. At my other grandpa's, he made me climb the ladder to the hayloft. There he tied my hands and feet. Told me I had a choice—either sell drugs or he'd kill Mom and Emma. Told me to think about it, and he'd be back in a couple of days for my decision."

Normally, conversations didn't attack me like rocks during traumatic discussions, but I wanted to moan and groan with Jace's words. "All I can say is I'm sorry for all you've been through. Like you, I was surprised to learn your granddad's part in the crimes."

"No one is more surprised than me. Mom's crying, and Emma loved him. Please tell me how you found out. I owe you my life and my family's for not giving up on us. Both of you refused to back off."

I gave Jace an abbreviated story of Levi's and my experience with Howard.

"I asked Granddad why he'd broken so many laws. He said my other grandpa and him talked about how to make money so no one would find out. They decided to show the community opposing personalities and to let on like they despised each other. It worked."

"Jace," Levi said, "Patti's in jail on false charges. Please tell Sheriff Macmire about that conversation. You've shown a lot of courage. When you are asked to testify in court, can you speak out against both grandfathers?"

"Yes. Decided that when I was in the hayloft. Is this whole nightmare finally over?"

I glanced at Levi, who gave me a reassuring smile. "The truth has surfaced. Now you and your family can heal."

"That will take a long time."

"Jace, pain can be a beautiful thing if we allow it to work miracles in our lives."

EIGHTY-FOUR

LEVI

The days and weeks ahead whirled into October like the falling leaves. Today after Carrington and I attended my church, we treated Arthur to a nearby doggy park. I held her hand firmly in one hand and Arthur's leash with the other.

With Carrington's help, a psychological autopsy took place the day after Howard's arrest. Not just family and close friends attended, but the BP agents and county deputies who'd worked the cases over the past several weeks. We addressed the crippling situation and why things happened.

Felicia found a new counselor for her family, a Christian man who helped her family begin the recovery process. The counselor immediately involved them in critical incident debriefing. The process not only encouraged them to express their mental and physical anguish but also included discussions on how to face the future. The one criterion I appreciated came from the urging of no judgmental comments or criticisms from or against family members. Felicia also found a safe-deposit box at a bank in Houston listed in Will's name. Inside were dated documents that implicated Howard and Timothy in illegal activities.

Felicia welcomed parenting advice in group sessions, books, and online resources. Jace recognized his inner drive to take over as head of the household, and he was receiving counseling to assist him in understanding his position as a seventeen-year-old son. Emma needed extra counseling for suicidal thoughts and how to overcome those who bullied her at school. The counselor recommended homeschooling for Emma, but Jace preferred to meet the problems head-on.

Carrington broke through our silence as though reading my mind. "Felicia plans to work through the counseling, then move to a suburb near Columbus, Ohio. Her bank has a branch there, and it would be a fresh start for all of them."

"With the stigma that will always be associated with the family, I think relocation is a good idea. What about Boyd and Lyndie?"

Carrington shook her head. "They haven't decided. The community is supporting her rebuilding her shop, and they haven't changed their wedding date. Who knows what the future holds for them?"

"Do you think Patti is innocent?" I said.

"The jury will make that decision. She's a smart woman and has hired a prominent defense attorney from Houston. My guess is if she knows where Timothy and Howard laundered their money, she'll lay low until enough time has passed."

"And Zora?"

"Doctors suggest a memory-care facility, and Felicia is exploring those in Ohio." Carrington paused to watch Arthur chase a squirrel, but it was obvious that her thoughts were on Felicia and her family.

"I want the family healed, but as Jace said, it will take a long time."

"I remember the first time I met Howard, and he claimed he'd do anything to protect Felicia and his grandkids. What he meant was he'd kill to protect himself. To think, for over twenty-five years he and Timothy kept up their charade of despising each other while all along working with the cartel to smuggle undocumented immigrants, drugs, and who knows what else."

I thought of a Jewish quote. "'Rejoice not at thine enemy's fall— but don't rush to pick him up either.'"

"That's sobering, but great advice."

I glanced at the time. "I'm reminded we have another court

hearing on Friday." We stopped for Arthur to drink from a doggy fountain. "The following week, I have a story to cover in Kenya."

"I'll do my best to keep busy while you're gone. We have our hero capes to wear—and bear."

I planted a kiss on her soft lips. "That's because we're outliers and proud of it. We'd be miserable if we weren't the first ones to shout out an injustice and be prepared to act."

"Even if we're almost killed in the process."

"Amen."

EIGHTY-FIVE

CARRINGTON

I wish I owned an answer book to explain Timothy Kendrix's and Howard Westfield's sense of entitlement. But I believe the closest I'll ever find is the Bible. We live in a world of greed and selfishness. I'd come to know Jesus as my Savior, and I'd joined Levi's Messianic church. The observance of Jewish traditions and the arrival of the Messiah fit what I believed was how I should worship.

Levi's parents were welcoming, but his sister, Deborah, still refused to acknowledge him. But she hadn't been here when Howard threatened to kill all of us. She hadn't witnessed Joseph and Levi putting aside their differences to stop a deranged man.

By the grace of God, the eye melanoma had not metastasized. I'd agreed to a trial medicine that made me want to sing from the rooftops—and my voice, like Levi's, left a lot to be desired. My eye tumor responded to the medicine and had shrunk in size. Dr. Leonard assured me that if I wanted to give birth, the baby would be monitored for any signs of the family disease, and the problem would be treated before it became an issue.

Levi and I walked through a nature trail at Sam Houston Park. The coolness of spring and fresh buds shooting through the earth held a promise of new beginnings. Like me with my faith and my love for Levi. The freshness lingered in the air, and the sound of doves made me smile.

"Did you finish the edits on your story about the Kendrixes?" I said.

"Yes, until the editor at *Hope for Today's World* picks up her red pen."

"Do you have it on your phone? I'd like to hear a preview."

He chuckled. "Do you want to ruin a great day by me reading you an unedited article?'

"We're both a part of that story."

"We are. Without the experience, you and I wouldn't be together."

"My point." I gestured to a park bench. "We can sit here. I remember your original thoughts were to show others how to face multiple tragedies and enlist community support."

"You remembered." He paused to kiss my cheek. "Okay, one page."

I sent him a smile and found my way to the bench. Arthur could relax a few minutes.

Phone in hand, Levi eased down beside me. "I've titled it 'Restoring Humanity.'" He paused. "The title might change. I honored Howard's request to keep his family's name out of the article, although his reasons were selfish. Instead, I framed it to show how I learned much about myself and humanity by reaching out to others in times of need."

I touched his arm. "Honey, just read it."

He took a deep breath, and his hand trembled slightly. "Humanity has suffered much since the beginning of time. We can be a selfish, noncaring people until we experience how helping others restores us in a rightful relationship with God, our communities, and our nation. As a journalist, I seek truth and I am committed to showing that God's best plan is to bring His light to a lost world. While covering a tough story involving a tumbleweed of family tragedies, I learned we were created to tear down the walls of sin's devastation and help others to find hope, but we can't do an effective job until we are fully restored to God.

"I experienced a family's sad tale that involved domestic violence, verbal abuse, and the resulting physical and mental scars that manifested in explosive behavior. That unveiling of tragedy became my story to tell. I'd survived addictions and family issues beyond my control, and found healing. They could too.

"Pain is beautiful if we allow it to transform and restore us into the people God intended. The call to cover a story came late one night . . ."

I blinked back tears. "Levi, that's incredible. The insight into the Kendrixes' family drama shows us how we are 'better together with God.' It's beautiful."

Levi squeezed my hand. "Today is perfect."

"I agree. Made for us."

"Gotta question for you. What are you doing in June?"

I thought ahead to my calendar. "Nothing at this point. Why?"

"I was thinking of a destination wedding in Hawaii."

"Who's getting married?"

He turned me to face him. "I hope you and me." He pulled a small black velvet box from his jeans pocket and dropped to one knee. "Carrington Yana Reed, I love you. Would you do me the honor of marrying me and sharing my life?"

Never to be outdone, I dropped to my knee and faced my beloved Levi. "Levi Benjamin Ehrlich, I love you, and I'd marry you tomorrow."

He grinned and reached for my left hand. A glittering diamond caressed my finger. "We are a dangerous pair. Curiosity and compassion. Always in trouble."

I kissed him. "I can't think of a better way to spend my life."

A NOTE FROM THE AUTHOR

Dear reader,

Thank you for choosing *Lethal Standoff*, a story of danger and intrigue, faith and doubt, love and hate. Greed is a nasty sin.

Heroes and heroines are not born with badges that indicate their future. They begin as individuals who process life's experiences and choose to make a difference. Carrington and Levi are two people who chose to overcome their fears and challenges to benefit others. They stepped forward to help people turn their obstacles into victories.

Dear reader, we are all called to accept a divine purpose that God intended before time began. I pray you have accepted yours, as Carrington and Levi did.

Neither Carrington nor Levi expected the blessings of love amid the chaos. But that's the way God orchestrates our lives. I hope you've enjoyed the story and seen how you can help someone else walk through a difficult circumstance.

Hearing from readers and connecting with them fills me with joy. I hope you will take the time to let me call you friend from one of the many links at diannmills.com.

DiAnn

ACKNOWLEDGMENTS

Hallee Bridgeman—Thank you for sharing your knowledge of Messianic Judaism and your worship.

Heather Kreke—Love the brainstorming and your knowledge of diabetes, archery, and human nature.

Dr. Deborah Maxey—Thank you for sharing your psychological expertise and negotiation skills. Through your knowledge and experiences, you helped me make Carrington's and Levi's story credible and filled with emotive conflict.

Rabbi Michael Vowell—Thank you for answering my questions!

DISCUSSION QUESTIONS

1. Carrington claimed she preferred working alone and limited her friendships. Did you interpret her few friends as self-preservation, the result of life experiences, fear, or a combination?

2. Levi faced a life change when he accepted Jesus as the Messiah. Have you lost relationships with loved ones who have criticized your faith? How did you respond?

3. Carrington faced a possible end to her career because of potential blindness and death. She based her life's worth on her negotiation skills. This meant reading body language and emotion. How would you have counseled her?

4. Levi's family conducted a ceremonial burial for him when he chose Jesus. Put yourself in his shoes. How would you have felt?

5. Domestic abuse plays a role in the lives of the victims in this story. What is the best way to help someone who is a victim of domestic abuse?

6. A bully inflicts cruelty on others to build ego and false self-confidence. The problem oftentimes originates in the bully's youth. What would motivate a child to take on those traits? How can a bully be helped?

7. Levi would rather lose his job than write an article that omitted or skewed the truth. Have you ever been in a work environment where you were faced with the same challenge?

8. Levi sensed he was falling in love with Carrington, but she refused to burden him or anyone with her medical dilemma. How do you define love?

9. Carrington and Levi were proud of their title as outliers. How do you define an outlier? Is that a trait you want to add to your life?

10. This story showed many personalities thrust against love, greed, truth, justice, and power. Now that you've read the novel, how would you describe in one sentence what this story is about?

ABOUT THE AUTHOR

DiAnn Mills is a bestselling author who believes her readers should expect an adventure. She weaves memorable characters with unpredictable plots to create action-packed, suspense-filled novels. DiAnn believes every breath of life is someone's story, so why not capture those moments and create a thrilling adventure?

Her titles have appeared on the CBA and ECPA bestseller lists; won two Christy Awards; and been finalists for the Golden Scroll, Inspirational Reader's Choice, and Carol Award contests.

DiAnn is a founding board member of the American Christian Fiction Writers and a member of Advanced Writers and Speakers Association, Mystery Writers of America, Sisters in Crime, and International Thriller Writers. She is the director of the Blue Ridge Mountains Christian Writers Conference and Mountainside Retreats, where she continues her passion of helping other writers be successful. She speaks to various groups and teaches writing workshops around the country.

DiAnn has been termed a coffee snob and roasts her own coffee beans. She's an avid reader, loves to cook, and believes her grandchildren are the smartest kids in the universe. She and her husband live in sunny Houston, Texas.

DiAnn is very active online and would love to connect with readers through her website at diannmills.com.

CONNECT WITH DIANN ONLINE AT

diannmills.com

OR FOLLOW HER ON